THROUGH
Dust & Ashes

OREGON PROMISE SERIES

by Lynnette Bonner

Through Dust and Ashes – BOOK ONE

Beneath Brazen Skies – BOOK TWO (Coming soon.)

OTHER HISTORICAL BOOKS
by Lynnette Bonner

THE SHEPHERD'S HEART SERIES

Rocky Mountain Oasis – BOOK ONE
High Desert Haven – BOOK TWO
Fair Valley Refuge – BOOK THREE
Spring Meadow Sanctuary – BOOK FOUR

SONNETS OF THE SPICE ISLE SERIES

On the Wings of a Whisper – BOOK ONE

THE WYLDHAVEN SERIES

Not a Sparrow Falls – BOOK ONE
On Eagles' Wings – BOOK TWO
Beauty from Ashes – BOOK THREE
Consider the Lilies – BOOK FOUR
A Wyldhaven Christmas – BOOK FIVE
Songs in the Night – BOOK SIX
Honey from the Rock – BOOK SEVEN
Beside Still Waters – BOOK EIGHT

Find all other books by Lynnette Bonner at:
www.lynnettebonner.com

THROUGH
Dust & Ashes

OREGON PROMISE – BOOK 1

Lynnette BONNER
USA Today Bestselling Author

Pacific Lights

Through Dust and Ashes
Oregon Promise, Book 1

Published by Pacific Lights Publishing
Copyright © 2024 by Lynnette Bonner. All rights reserved.

Cover design by Lynnette Bonner of Indie Cover Design, images ©
   Depositphotos:149855280 – Tall Grass
   Depositphotos: 657661110 – Man's Face
   Depositphotos: 64546223 – Leather Rein
   Depositphotos: 495764086, 492075066, 386369830 - Grasses
   AdobeStock: 482613519 – Horses and Wagon
   MidJourney: Woman's Face and Man and Boys
   Line-Thin Watercolor Flowers copyright Pamyatka Shop via Creative Market

Scripture taken from the New King James Version®. Copyright © 1982 by Thomas Nelson.
Used by permission. All rights reserved.

Paperback ISBN: 978-1-942982-31-9

Job 42: 5–6

My ears had heard of you but now my eyes have seen you.
Therefore I despise myself and repent in dust and ashes.

Chapter One

Late February, 1853

"Mister, please. I'm not asking for much. Just a place to sleep under your wagon." Mercy Adler plucked at the lace of her high collar and tossed a glance over her shoulder to search the dusty street. She truly was taking a chance out in the open like this. She kept one arm carefully wrapped around her ribs. The pain wasn't as sharp if she held herself just so.

Avram poked his curly mop from behind the water barrel at the corner of the mercantile. His brown eyes were wide with fear. She flapped a hand for him to return to his hiding spot, and was relieved when he obeyed. While she stood here talking to this stranger, the last thing she needed was for Herst to stumble onto Main Street and see her son. Their son. For he would surely use Avram against her.

Again.

And yet, if she took his son from him, he would come after her.

Her heart tumbled in fear. She swallowed. Searched the road in the other direction.

She couldn't worry about Herst's retribution right now. First, they must escape. Then, they could concern themselves with surviving the aftermath.

A haze of heat danced above the surface of the street. Down the way, Old Man Dawson's hound flopped into the dirt and rolled onto its back to writhe through the dust. But other than the dog and the somber blond man before her, all seemed quiet.

Relief eased through her.

The murder in Herst's eyes last night had been the last straw.

It was one thing to put up with his fits of rage when they had only been directed at her. But now there was Av to consider. He was a boy—rambunctious, as all happy boys should be. But his exuberance too often set Herst on edge. And Herst on edge constituted a flame hovering near dry tinder.

She and Av were too often in the path of the inferno.

Especially now that Av was old enough to try to come to her rescue. Her fingernails bit into her palm. Yes, the last straw had finally nudged her over the edge. No more inaction, or they would both die.

With the goal of escape in mind, she had waited until Herst left this morning. He'd said he was going to look for work, but she'd heard that before and knew it was a lie. As soon as he'd departed, she had swiftly packed a few essentials into haversacks. One for her and one for Av. After that, she'd headed to the mercantile.

It was the least likely location where Herst might be since he didn't have any money, and since he owed Old Griff, who would want to collect. It was also the place where anyone traveling through Chamblissburg would stop. And standing in the dim corner near the tall shelf of sewing notions, she could assess passersby without drawing too much attention.

After an hour of measured study—fearful that she was taking too long and Herst would come looking for her—she'd approached the man who seemed the most affable.

However, the one she'd chosen was now practically ignoring her.

He had barely paused loading his supplies into his wagon as he'd barked, "No" a moment ago.

Desperate, she strode to the front corner of the buckboard, where he tied the last corner of his tarp and touched his arm.

The man froze and pegged the place where her fingers rested with a hard look.

She snatched her hand back to her side and wrapped it once more about her ribs, wishing that one touch hadn't revealed so much about his physical strength. Because the rocky glint in those steely blue eyes had her questioning her judgment of character. Yet . . . these wagons heading to Independence were her only immediate chance of escape, and this man had seemed the—

What? What had he seemed?

Of the two men in this particular group of travelers, he'd seemed the friendliest, perhaps. She'd liked the way he'd treated his wife—a beautiful brunette woman, just the opposite of him in coloring—with gentle respect. And as he'd laid a length of rope into their basket, he'd asked her if there was ought else that she thought she might require between here and Independence. The brunette had smiled and said she felt they'd thought of everything, and they didn't want the wagon to be too heavy for the horses. Then, at the counter, he'd purchased a dime's worth of penny candy and told the woman to hide it away in a jar for "Joel" to have a treat now and then . . . Those slim hints of his character were the things that had made her approach him for help to get to Independence. Herst, after all, would never deign to waste money buying candy for a boy.

The safety of Independence seemed far off. Yet . . . to escape Herst, she must find a way to get there. Once she made it to Independence, surely she could hire on with one of the wagon trains that she kept reading about in the papers. Someone would have need of a cook or a governess to look after their children, wouldn't they? And she would lose herself in the wilds of Oregon country and never have to see Herst again.

Please, God. She swallowed.

She'd retreated to a respectful distance, and thankfully, the blond man had at least paused now. He stared at her with a frown of assessment, hands resting on the tarp atop his load.

She took another step back from the ire in the man's gaze, but willed herself to be brave. For Avram. "Please? I have my own oil cloth to sleep on. I'll walk the whole way. I only need the shelter of your wagon come nights." The party had one covered wagon and this farm wagon, so she presumed he'd planned to sleep in the covered wagon with his family.

Her hope soared when the man hung his head between his arms for a moment as though he were pondering her request. And then he straightened. Faced her. Folded his arms and gave her a sweeping assessment. "And what of food?"

Mercy's heart jostled between hope that he might agree to take her and terror over her lack of planning. Her only thought after last night's beating had been escape.

"I've food, yes, sir." It was a lie, but if he only agreed to take her, she would go into the mercantile, buy enough to fill a pack, and have Griff put it on Herst's account. It was the least he owed them.

She would carry whatever necessary to help Avram escape from his father. To keep herself alive so that she could raise him with love and care.

She trembled with anticipation as she fiddled with her collar and searched the stranger's face.

Please, please, please, dear God in heaven, if ever there was a time that I needed You to turn Your face back to me and prove that You actually do care, it would be today.

Not that her pleadings had ever garnered her any special favors from the Almighty. She'd pleaded with Him on the night Herst had first attacked her as she walked home from the schoolhouse boxed supper—an evening of fun and dancing to raise funds for a new porch. Earlier that evening, vibrant and full of life, she had danced. Oh, how she'd danced with abandon. And she'd felt joy in her very core. Afterward, Carl Johansen had offered to walk her home. He'd been the perfect gentleman and parted from her at the fork that would take her the remaining short distance to Father's cabin. The lights of the house glowed golden and inviting as she walked between the tall grasses up the path. And then, in the span of a few nightmarish moments, all had changed.

She banished the memories of that night, locking them deep inside.

Carl Johansen had never come to call again after that long-ago night. But the memory of walking home with him as an innocent girl would always be the place she pointed to as the last moment of happiness she'd experienced.

Now, despite her poor history with the Almighty, she continued to plead with Him as she waited for the stranger's response. Not that she really believed He was listening.

She pulled in a breath that was too deep. Sharp pain stabbed through her, but she conscientiously kept the agony from her features, knowing from experience that any display of weakness would leave her open to more abuse.

"You married?" The words were sharp and sudden.

Mercy swallowed. Did she lie? Or tell the truth? If she said yes, he wouldn't feel comfortable taking her with him. If she said no, the same would be true because it would be unseemly for a single woman to travel in such proximity to a family of strangers. And it might make his wife uneasy.

"I think your hesitation tells me all I need to know, ma'am. I'm sorry." He shook his head. "I'm not in the habit of helping women leave their families. You have a good day now." He turned from her and strode to the other side of the wagon.

Despair weighted her shoulders. It seemed her record of unanswered prayers remained unbroken.

She notched her chin up. He wasn't the only wagon traveling through. She could try someone else. "Thank you just the same."

She may as well have spoken the words into the wind because the man wasn't paying her a bit of attention.

Tears came unbidden. She blinked hard to hold them at bay. She couldn't fall apart. Not here. Not ever. Avram needed her to be strong.

Her gaze collided with that of the other man that she'd seen with the blond one and his wife. He stood in the road next to the covered wagon just ahead and had apparently been listening to their conversation.

This second man was dark, foreboding, and, if possible, even broader and stronger than the first. His shoulders stretched the material of his white shirt to near capacity. His hands were propped on the waistband of his tawny buckskin trousers. Even from this distance, she could see that despite his dark hair and golden-brown skin, his eyes were a piercing blue. His frank scrutiny sent a shiver through her.

She focused on the ground. What was she going to do now?

None of the other men who had passed through the mercantile had seemed even half as approachable as the one who had just rejected her. And most of them had pulled out with their wagons already.

Clearly the dark man she could still feel watching her wasn't approachable. His scowl made her knees knock. She at least knew Herst well enough that she could escape his foul moods sometimes. The changing emotions on his face sometimes gave her enough advance warning. But with this dark man with the blue eyes . . . She had a feeling he could strike faster than a rattler. He looked lithe . . . and deadly. One to stay away from.

Maybe she and Av should just start walking? No. She hadn't done enough planning for that.

In hopelessness, she pressed one hand to her forehead. Pain knifed through her ribs, nearly taking her to her knees right there in the street.

She must think what to do now. She certainly wouldn't go to Father this time. He would only tell her duty prescribed that she remain with Herst as his helpmate.

Abandoned.

Misunderstood.

Unwanted.

Unloved.

Each emotion pounded into her with unshakable certainty.

She was all those things, indeed. But she had a son who needed her, and she must come up with a plan.

If only she could stop trembling.

Standing on the street next to his wagon, Micah Morran gripped the back of his neck. He should turn and walk away. Georgia wouldn't like him helping. But just the sight of the woman's discolored face filled him with a roil of nausea. The sight took him right back to the little cabin where he'd spent his boyhood in the foothills of Virginia. He could smell the acidic scent of the cedar-log walls. Hear the crackle of the fire in the creek-stone fireplace.

He could hear Ma's muffled sniffles through her bedroom door. See as clearly as if it were happening right now, her stepping from behind it with the side of her face all blue and purple tinged with ochre.

His gut churned.

"What is it, Pa?" Joel's gaze slid from him to the woman who remained forlorn and alone in the middle of the street near Gideon's wagon.

Micah rested one hand on his son's head. "Just a lady who's asking for some help, son. Hop up in the wagon now."

Joel moved to do as told, but not before he said, "If she needs help, we should help her, shouldn't we, Pa?"

Micah shuttered away the scene before him, trying to concentrate on the darkness behind his eyelids, clawing and scrabbling in a search for dispassion. She was none of his concern. He had his own family to worry about.

A wife barely holding herself together. A son suffering the same grief as the rest of them.

But it was no use. How might his life have been different if someone had helped Ma when she so desperately needed it?

His brother-in-law, Gideon Riley, tugged off his hat and swiped a trickle of sweat onto one shoulder. From his expression, he felt about as torn as Micah did. Resettling his hat, Gid hesitated on the final knot in his tarp rope. He glanced back, and Micah lifted one hand to let Gid know he was thinking.

It might be evident from one look at this battered woman that she needed their help. But that kind of help would only bring trouble. None of them needed any more difficulty. This trip was about escaping hardship. Looking for a better life.

Well, if there was such a thing as a better life. Mostly he hoped leaving Virginia behind would also leave some of his pain. But he couldn't dwell on that.

Gideon folded his arms, looking dark and foreboding—how they all felt these days, Micah supposed. Probably trying to decide how to get this woman to move along.

And Gid was right. They really ought to say no.

Guilt rushed in to proclaim him callous. He could almost see his mother's eyes looking back at him through this woman's. What kind of man was he if he couldn't even bring himself to help someone he understood so deeply?

He bit back a grunt.

Why had she approached Gid anyhow? She must be *some* desperate to be asking a total stranger for help.

But then, one look at the split skin on that swollen lump that had practically closed her left eye was likely all the evidence he needed of her desperation. The whole left side of her face was badly bruised. She was standing awkwardly, too. Like she might be in an all-fired amount of pain.

She pressed her hand to her forehead, dejection clearly written in her posture. The movement made her gasp and wince. After that, she remained nearly perfectly still, one arm clutching her ribs as though to hold them in place.

He wasn't stupid. If they helped her, they were either helping her escape her husband or some other male relative, and he wasn't sure which scenario made him want to throttle the man who'd done this to her more.

Gid must have been thinking along the same lines as him because he jutted his chin at her eye. "Who did that to you?"

Seemingly startled, she lowered her gaze to the street, but not before Micah saw a flare of fear in her eyes. Her head remained bowed for only the briefest of moments, yet when she raised it, her features had been schooled. "This?" She waved a hand and pulled a face. "I'm a bit clumsy. Would you believe I was going to the barn to milk the cow yesterday, and I tripped in the dark and fell right into the corral fence?"

Lips thinned, Gid glanced over at him.

Micah shook his head. He would not.

Gid returned his scrutiny to her, and she must have noted his disbelief, for she focused on her twisted-together fingers. "Very embarrassing."

She might be desperate, but she was also a liar. Could he condone a lie in a situation like this? Maybe. Maybe shame over how she'd been treated had her trying to protect the man who'd done it—though the man deserved none of her protection.

Still . . . she wasn't their responsibility. There would be other wagons coming through. Steeling his heart, Micah shook his head at Gideon.

Chapter Two

Gideon Riley felt about as low as the dust on his boots. "Take a few days to prepare. Pack some food and extra clothes. Another party will be coming through any day now, I'm sure."

"Sir, please—" She reached toward him.

"Mama?" A little boy who couldn't be more than four dashed from the alley between the mercantile and the saloon next door.

Her hand fell mid-air. She spun to spread her arms to the boy.

The kid crashed into her legs, and she belted out a sharp cry that Gideon could tell had been a reflex from pure agony. Despite that, in the next moment, she fell on her knees, gathering the boy to her like a hen winging in a chick in the face of an oncoming storm. "Shush, Avram love. Shush. Mama is here."

Gideon clenched his teeth. Hooked his thumbs into his belt loops. Met Micah's glance for just long enough to see his brother-in-law resettle his hat with consternation tightening his features. His face had gone so pale, it seemed a near match to his wagon tarp.

Micah's mother had been killed by his pa when he was but thirteen. This situation must be igniting memories.

One of the arms the kid threw around his mother's neck held a bruise from a man-sized hand. Gideon could see each place where fingers had been wrapped from wrist to elbow.

He swallowed, prickles stinging the backs of his eyes. He dragged the toe of his boot through the dust of the street.

His sister, Georgia, appeared suddenly beside him. Her attention lowered to the pair still hugging in the street.

Gid watched her carefully. Would the sight of the boy bring on her melancholy? She'd been doing better the last few weeks.

Thankfully, the only sign of raw emotion was a deep swallow. "Who are they?"

"I don't know, but she's asking to join us."

Georgia gaped at him. "Gid." She kept her volume low. "Do we have enough supplies to take on two more people?" The flicker of a frown that she leveled on the boy revealed there *was* more to her resistance than mere worry over supplies.

He shrugged a shoulder.

Georgia clasped her hands. "I think we've had enough heartache. Let's hold our concerns to taking care of ourselves for a little while, please?"

She was right. This wasn't his concern. They were simply passing through and had stopped to resupply.

"My arm hurts." The little boy whimpered.

"I know, love. I know." The woman raised the tiny arm and pressed a gentle kiss against the bruise. "I'm so very sorry."

The sight made Gid's gut twist with what might have been. How could he be so cruel as to refuse to help?

In many ways, the woman on the ground reminded him of Georgia. They had the same brown curls twisted into a messy knot at the back of their necks, the same tawny complexion—if he could rightly judge what lay beneath the woman's bruises—and the same delicate build. What would he want someone to do if Georgia ever found herself in a similar situation? Not that Micah would ever allow anyone to mistreat his wife, but it was the principle of the matter.

Gid glanced at his sister. "She says she has supplies enough for both of them."

Unless she'd been lying about that too.

Georgia continued to look down at mother and son. She swallowed, and her eyes, though soft with understanding, filled with certainty. She stepped closer and turned her head toward him so the woman wouldn't hear. "Someone like that can only bring trouble on us all, Gid. That's the last thing we need." The broken cadence of her whispered words tore open soul-wounds that he'd thought might finally be starting to heal. Guess not yet.

Micah called from where he still stood near their wagon, and Georgia bustled off.

Even though she had only stated what he'd already been telling himself, Gideon's fists tightened. It didn't mean he had to like leaving this woman and boy to fend for themselves. But what else was he supposed to do? They didn't have enough supplies, and that was the truth of it. Besides, the open trail was no place for a mother with a child so young. Especially not injured as they both were.

Micah was already pressing them hard because he'd thought Georgia would be fine with taking the steamer up the Missouri River to Independence, but she had flatly refused for fear of it sinking with Joel on board. She hadn't quite been herself since the tragedy.

Now they were far behind schedule.

The government was giving land to settlers who arrived in the Oregon Territory and tended the land for four years, but they had to arrive before December first of this year. That meant they needed to connect with a wagon train heading out this spring, or they would lose their chance for free land. Micah could get six hundred and forty acres—a whole square mile—because he was married. Gid would get half that. But they planned to settle on plots next to each other and start a small spread. Then maybe they'd be able to buy adjacent land at some point in the future to expand.

They'd taken off a day later than planned because they'd needed to buy wagons instead of simply hiring one to take them to the steamer.

Then, they'd needed to purchase and pack extra food and supplies for the overland journey.

Micah hadn't been too happy with Georgia, and Gideon couldn't blame him. But Micah was also coddling her since she'd been unpredictable in temperament lately.

No matter the reason, the last thing they needed was another shaft thrown into the wheels of their trip.

He must stand firm.

The woman nudged her son to step back. Still on her knees, she lifted her gaze to him, hope shining from her one good eye. "Might you change your mind now that you've seen my son?"

Of course, she couldn't know that her son made him all the more determined to stand by his decision.

He broke eye contact, unable to meet her searching look when he denied her again. He studied the dusty tip of his boot instead. "No, ma'am. Don't reckon I can do that. I'm right sor—"

"Mercy!" Down the street, a large man lumbered from between two buildings. He stumbled forward, obviously drunk, based on the way he canted to one side. His hair, long and unkempt, dangled over one shoulder where a suspender hung loose—the other rode over the paunch of a dirty shirt. "Mercy. I'm 'ungry!" Dust puffed up each time the man's boots flopped against the roadbed.

He seemed to be bellowing the words to the town in general. He hadn't yet seen them standing here near the wagon. But there was no doubt in Gideon's mind that the person the man yelled for was the woman with the boy. And if he hadn't already been certain, he would have been made so when she snatched up her son and scurried to the far side of his buckboard.

She cowered low, shushing her son, who had started to whimper.

The oncomer seemed about Gid's own age.

So, not her father, then.

The bottom dropped out of Gideon's resolve. What was the right thing to do here? Helping a woman leave her husband wasn't biblical.

On the other hand, leaving her to the likes of the wavering man still searching the town with bleary eyes would be a death sentence. And that certainly wasn't biblical.

He also had his duty to his sister's fragile state to consider.

Gideon felt his every muscle tense as he moved to the other side of the wagon to stand next to mother and son.

Micah appeared beside him, watching the drunk over the top of the canvas-tarped bed. So, he'd changed his mind then?

Frustration churned through Gideon. Why, under all of heaven, had they stopped in this no-bit town?

Something stirred in his spirit. Something that begged for his awareness, but he tamped it down.

"Mercy! Where y'at?" The man stood on the boardwalk just down from the mercantile now. He scrubbed his fingers through a shock of unruly hair, almost losing his balance.

Micah gave Gideon a look. He nodded toward the tarp covering the bed of his wagon. "Get her and the boy out of sight."

Gideon felt tight. Every muscle coiled, ready to spring. "Georgia—"

"She'll be fine."

Gideon wished he could be as sure.

The little boy turned to study him, his brown eyes large and full of worry.

Gideon blew a breath of frustration and gave Micah a nod. It was time to move. Gideon nudged the pair toward the back of the wagon.

"Sir, please!" Near panic laced the woman's whisper. Her wide caramel-brown eyes pleaded with him.

He hesitated. She must not have heard Micah's words and thought they were forcing her out into the open. What else was she to believe after the way they'd been responding to her requests?

"We're not ousting you," Micah said quietly as he stepped from behind the wagon.

Gideon watched as Micah approached the man and spoke to slow his progress. "Looking for someone, sir?"

The drunk hesitated, swaying as he tried to focus on Micah.

Micah had bought them a few moments.

Gid flipped back the corner of the tarp. He lowered the tailgate, and yanked the large trunk that contained Ma's tea service from within. Georgia had insisted they not leave it behind. He'd thought it frivolous at the time, but he was thankful for it now. He put the trunk on the ground and quickly hoisted the little boy into the spot, then motioned for the woman to follow.

She scrambled to climb onto the tailgate, and he heard her release a muffled whimper as she crawled forward into the small dark gap after her son. Her legs had to bend in order for her to fit into the cramped space, but she wrapped her arms around her knees and gave him a nod of thanks.

"Outta my way, shtranger!" the drunk barked at Micah.

Gideon latched the tailgate into place and pulled the tarp over just as the drunk clomped around the heads of his team.

Gid set to tying down the tarp. It would be some hot under there, and he didn't envy the woman and boy at the moment. He only hoped the boy would keep silent and not give them all away. He had no desire to be drawn into a confrontation with this man, drunk or not.

As though just noticing him, the drunk lurched to a stop and swayed with one foot on the step down from the boardwalk while he eyed him.

Micah moseyed past, heading toward his own wagon now. Grateful that he'd stepped in to help him do the right thing despite Georgia's hesitation, Gid would have given him a nod, but the drunk continued to study him with a frown.

"Howdy." Gid touched the brim of his hat. He hefted the china trunk and hauled it to the front of the wagon, where he hoisted it onto the bench and began to strap it down.

His heart hammered. Was the man drunk enough that such an abnormality would go unnoticed?

The drunk swiped at his watery eyes and scanned the breadth and width of the street. He almost fell as he spun in a circle but managed to catch himself with one hand on the side of the wagon bed. "You sheen a woman an' a boy?" He held out an unsteady palm above his knees.

Careful.

"Saw a woman and kid a bit ago. Might have been them. But I don't see them now."

The man cursed under his breath and commenced another tottering spin as he searched the street again. "Blash'ed woman," he muttered. "She'll get wha'sh comin' to her when I fin' her."

The muscles of Gideon's jaw pulsed. He concentrated on tightening the straps that held the trunk in place.

Ahead, Georgia stood by the other wagon. With her skirts fisted in her hands, she watched him with a bit of a wide-eyed look. Gideon saw her say something sharp to Micah as he rejoined her. Micah gripped her shoulders and turned her to face him. He said a few words that Gid couldn't make out. Georgia seemed to calm after that, even if she did fold her arms and return her scrutiny toward his wagon.

Done with the last strap, Gid stood and made a to-do of stretching out his back. "You ready to light a shuck, sis? I'm done, and we can go anytime." *Please, Father, don't let this cause Georgia more distress.*

Georgia's eyes narrowed, and her lips thinned a little, but after a quick glance at the inebriated man by his wagon, she strode to where Micah waited and let him help her up to the bench. As she climbed to the seat, she disappeared behind the canvas draped over the arched stays fastened to Micah's wagon bed. But her call drifted back, "We're ready too."

Relief swept through him. At least her spirits seemed to be holding for now.

The drawstring that could be used to cinch the canvas and give them a semblance of privacy come evenings had been left loose at the back of their wagon. And Joel, with his mop of dark hair, already balanced on the cargo, with his skinny seven-year-old legs dangling over their tailgate. His dog, Mattox, named after the creek near their Virginia home because of his glistening blue-black fur, panted from where he lay in the shade beneath the wagon.

"Get up," Micah called. Gideon heard the snap of the reins when they connected with the rumps of his team. The wagon lurched forward. Mattox let the wagon roll past him, then leaped up and kept pace beside it, tongue lolling. With his wavy black fur, long snout, and fierce golden eyes, the curl of his bright pink tongue, which made him appear to be smiling, looked out of place. The dog might seem sweet-tempered, but Gid knew that dog would fight to the death to protect his boy.

Gid chirked to his team and pulled in behind the forward wagon. He leaned his elbows casually against his knees, not giving the drunk another glance.

From the wagon bed behind him, the boy whimpered, and Gid felt a jolt of battle-readiness, but the woman must have calmed him because he didn't make another sound, and no one yelled for Gid to stop.

He'd gone and done it now. Stealing a man's wife, no matter how ill he treated her, was a fighting matter. Would the man put two and two together? If so, he would come after them.

Tonight, he and Micah would need to talk about setting up a watch.

He angled a glance at the sky. He sure hoped Micah understood what he'd gotten them into!

Chapter Three

Micah urged the team up a low hill outside of Chamblissburg, doing his best to simply sit and listen to Georgia's concerns without retort.

Her complaints rang true on many counts.

"You know that woman's husband, or whoever did that to her, will come after us."

Yes. He knew.

"And we've had enough grief recently, haven't we, Micah? Don't you think the good Lord would have understood us passing by just this once?"

He clamped his jaw tight on that last comment, knowing she didn't understand the first thing she said. How many times had good citizens passed Ma by before his father had finally killed her?

"She said she had food and supplies, but you and Gid rushed her into that wagon so fast, she had no time to gather anything."

Micah nodded in reply to that. "I realize. But we aren't so hard up that we can't handle two extra mouths to feed. Neither of them looks like they'll consume much."

Georgia huffed and flicked irritably at invisible dust on her skirts. "Says the man who won't have to do all the cooking."

"Maybe she'll be a help."

"Do you even still love me, Micah?"

Shock washed through him as he shot her a look. "Of course I do. What would make you ask that?"

She fiddled with her skirt, refusing to meet his gaze. "It's just that . . . You went rather quickly to her aid. And . . ."

He grasped the reins with one hand and her fingers with the other. "The only thing I saw back there was a woman like my ma. If people had stepped in to help Ma, then maybe . . ." He shrugged. "Maybe I'd still have her with me. Maybe I wouldn't have had to run from home at thirteen and make my own way in the world at such a young age. I couldn't stand the thought of that boy going through all the things I went through. But that doesn't lessen my love for you. Never forget that."

Georgia sighed and laid her free hand over their clasped ones. "I know. Really, I do. I've just not felt like myself since . . ." She waved a hand to dismiss the subject of their shared pain.

Micah swallowed. Yes. He knew that, too.

They may be grieving the loss of their daughter, but he also lamented the loss of his vibrant, humorous, fun-filled, kind, and caring wife. It was as though that version of her lay buried back in Virginia, and this woman beside him was a stranger.

He'd spoken true when he said he loved her. But he couldn't deny that the future stretched before them, long, and bleak, and blue.

The confined space beneath the tarp held in the heat like an oven with the temperature rising. Av lay still, wide-eyed. He was sucking his thumb, a habit she'd been trying to break him of, but she couldn't bring herself to chastise him for it.

Every jostle of the wagon felt like another punch to her ribs, and it was all she could do to prevent a cry of agony with each bump. She was practically sucking her own thumb, with her knuckle jammed into her mouth the way it was.

They had made their escape. Now, she must figure out a way to leave this party, or she would bring Herst's wrath down on them of a certainty.

At that thought, her eyes flew wide, and a whimper did escape. Their bags!

The man driving this wagon gave a sharp whistle, likely directed at the other members of his party, and then the jostling eased and stopped. She was thankful for the relief from the pain, but her dread mounted with each heartbeat.

She had left their belongings in the alley with Av. And when he'd run out, she'd been so concerned about his arm that she'd momentarily forgotten about them. Then Herst had shown up, and they'd climbed beneath the tarp so quickly . . .

Her teeth sank into her knuckle. Her eyes fell closed.

The haversacks were still in the alley.

They had nothing. Absolutely nothing.

Light flared. She flinched and then gasped at the startling pain the movement caused.

"Sorry about that." The man's tone rang with resignation. "It's mighty hot today, and we didn't want to leave you back here any longer than necessary. Come here, son. You want a drink?"

Av scrambled to the end of the wagon, and Mercy heard the man lift him to the grass, but she couldn't seem to bring herself to move.

Tears trickled into her hair, and the ache in her heart was almost strong enough to rival that in her ribs. She didn't gasp or sob. It was as though her body knew both would be too painful. But neither could she seem to stop the tears.

The relief of even momentarily being out of Herst's reach . . . The terror that their freedom would be all too short-lived and he would appear out of thin air, harm these people, and haul her back home . . . The horrible realization that they had not one thing to their name except the clothes on their backs . . . The shame of having asked for help from these total strangers . . . All of it piled on her like one heavy buffalo robe after another.

Stifling.

Smothering.

Suffocating.

Strangulating.

"Wait right here, okay?" The deep voice must still be speaking to Av.

She realized she didn't even know any of these people's names. She had to find the gumption to sit up and get off the wagon. But she couldn't seem to push through the pain again.

The wagon dipped, and something blocked the warmth and light of the sun. "Ma'am? Can you sit up?" Concern clipped the edges of each word.

This was a different voice. The other man. The dark man who'd watched her back in town.

"I can help you to the wagon bench."

She winced before she could stop herself. The jostling had been agony while she'd been lying here. She would rather walk and yet couldn't seem to face that prospect either. Still, he was being so kind, even though he hadn't wanted to bring her along in the first place.

She squinted one eye.

He hovered over her, all shadow with the sun high above him. He waggled something in his hand. "Water?"

Taking a fortifying breath, she tried to sit up. A slash of pain elicited an embarrassingly loud gasp.

Feeling humiliated to her core, she concentrated on rubbing the worn patch near her knee. At least she was sitting now. Not moving, but at least sitting.

"Ma'am . . ." The man sighed. "We need to have my wife look at your ribs. I'm afraid to move you much farther without an assessment."

His wife . . .

Mercy squinted to get a better look at the man leaning over her. It was the dark man with the piercing eyes. And they bored into hers now. His lips were pinched into a tight line. But it wasn't anger she saw. Rather, simple concern. Perhaps the first look of understanding she'd seen on anyone's face since her whole ordeal began.

An expression that brought her near to tears for the relief of it.

In the mercantile, when she'd seen the three of them, she'd thought the blond man and the dark-haired woman were married. But then, by the wagons, she'd gotten the reverse impression. It seemed the latter was correct.

The man nudged the canteen a little closer. "She's coming now." He nodded toward the brunette striding toward them from the other wagon with a dark-haired boy by her side.

A boy.

A shiver of fear swept through Mercy. If Herst caught up to them . . . As much as she didn't want Av hurt, she wouldn't see Herst's wrath visited on any other child, either. She shook her head, unable to contemplate that further.

If the woman was this man's wife, then what was her relationship to the blond man? They'd certainly seemed like family. Sister maybe? Her concerns mounted with each thought. In one fell swoop, Herst could obliterate an entire family.

But not only that . . . She'd chosen to approach the blond man because she'd thought him happily married.

She pressed one hand to the most painful part of her ribs and, ignoring the offered water, cautiously scooted toward the end of the wagon.

The blond man squatted by Av, helping him to drink from a canteen.

The other boy jogged over with a huge smile on his face. "Hello," he said to Av. "My name's Joel. What's your name?"

"We should leave you." Mercy blurted the words before she thought better of them. Though they were true for the travelers' safety, they were more true now because she didn't want to give the wrong impression. Didn't want the blond man to think . . . Well, didn't want him to think about her at all.

Back in town, she'd been stupidly desperate. But giving the wrong impression in a situation like this could be just as deadly as if she'd stayed home.

The dark-haired man held out the now-open bota. "At least let us help you get to the next town."

Mercy eased the canteen into her hand, careful not to make any sudden moves. The moment the water coursed over her tongue and slid down her throat, she realized how strongly thirst had hold of her. She felt like a piece of desert land soaking up the first rain of spring. After several long draughts, she angled the bag back toward him, again without moving her arm too much.

He accepted it and stoppered the end of the bag. "My wife is a fair hand at nursing."

Mercy despaired. "I left our bags in the alley back in town."

The woman folded her arms and didn't look any too pleased to have her here. But then, she'd recognized her animosity back on the street, too, so it came as no surprise.

The dark man leaped off the end of the wagon, and landed in the grass by his wife with a soft thud. "All the more reason to let us help you get to Blacksburg. At least there you'll be . . ." He looked down, his throat working. "Away from your other situation."

His wife shifted and tilted her head. "I guess we better introduce ourselves. I'm Georgia Morran." She gestured to the dark-haired man. "This is my husband, Micah. And our son, Joel. Joel is seven." She swiped a hand at the blond man who still stood beside Av. "That lug is my brother, Gideon Riley."

Everything in Mercy cried out at giving them her name. Yet, what could it hurt? They already knew her situation much more intimately than she would have liked. And it would only take a few well-placed questions in the next few towns for them to learn the truth. Bad news traveled faster 'round these parts than a sleigh on greased skids. And she'd had plenty of bad news to propel her into the parlors of every home within a fifty-mile radius.

She realized they were all staring at her and cleared her throat. "I'm Mercy Adler. That's my son, Avram. He's four. Five next month."

To her surprise, Georgia stretched out her arm and motioned for Mercy to join her. "Well, we can't have you in so much pain that it's torture to travel, so come on down and let me help you get those ribs wrapped. I've some cotton set aside for just such a need."

She angled her husband a glance, and he must have understood her unspoken message. He and his wife shared a lingering look and his lips lifted with gratefulness before he turned and ambled toward their wagon and started rummaging through a trunk in the back.

"Come, come." Georgia rolled her hand for her to hurry. "We still need to put in several more miles today before we make camp." The gentle smile she bestowed on Mercy stood in sharp contrast to her brusque words.

Mercy wrapped one arm around her ribs and forced herself to scoot the rest of the way to the end of the wagon. Every inch shot her through with agony. She barely managed to keep from crying out. Once she reached the tailgate, the ground seemed an unattainable distance.

"Wait one moment, ma'am." She heard the rustle of Gideon's boots rapidly approaching and then the sound of him tugging something from the wagon.

A second later, he appeared by her side. "Here, this should help." He placed a crate below her.

Concentrating on her gratitude would overwhelm her, so she focused instead on gingerly lowering her feet to the step. And then the task was done. Blessed grass lay beneath her boots.

Georgia surprised her again by giving her a sympathetic smile. "Let's take a look at you, shall we? Gid will watch . . . Avram, did you say his name was?"

Mercy nodded.

"Such ... a handsome boy." For some reason, her voice broke as she said the words. But then she cleared her throat and hurried on. "Gid will watch him while we get you fixed up. Don't worry. He's had plenty of practice with Joel." She smiled as she gave a tilt of her head toward the lanky lad who still chattered quietly to Av.

Some of Mercy's tension eased. Georgia may not have wanted to help them, but at least she wasn't being mean-spirited about it now.

"Thank you." She closed her eyes and pressed her lips tight, unable to say more without falling apart.

Gideon watched Georgia lead Mercy behind a tree on the other side of their wagon. That poor woman looked like she was barely able to move.

He folded his arms, fists bunched into tight knots. What he'd like to do would be to march back to that town and teach her lout of a husband what it meant to be a gentleman.

He felt eyes on him and glanced down to see Avram studying him seriously with his little hands tangled together in front of him. Joel had darted to the other wagon and was animatedly prattling to his pa.

Gideon eased his stance and squatted to his haunches.

Avram took a step back, eyes widening. He inched toward the wagon, and from the way he assessed the space beneath the bed, Gideon had no doubt that the boy was laying plans for how to escape if necessary.

Heart panging, Gideon showed the boy his palms. "I bet you might be hungry?" He rose unhurriedly and stepped toward the buckboard, reaching beneath the tarp to extract an apple from the crate of fruit he'd bought at the mercantile back in town. He held the fruit toward the kid, careful not to make any sudden moves.

Avram continued to study him with his brown eyes narrowed in assessment.

Gideon slowly sank to a squat once more. He held the apple out again and angled it to catch the light.

The boy's focus lowered to the apple briefly before rising. Then, without taking his eyes off Gideon's, he inched a step forward and reached out as far as he could to take the apple.

Gideon remained careful not to move through the whole process.

As soon as Avram had the fruit within his grasp, he beat a hasty retreat to the end of the wagon.

Gid hung his head. No kid ought to be that skittish.

He could hear the boy crunching on the fruit and felt pleased to at least have given him that paltry pleasure.

After only a moment, his curly mop appeared from around the end of the wagon, and then his wide brown eyes. He swiped apple juice from his lips with the back of one hand. Then he lifted the partially eaten fruit to draw Gideon's attention to it. "Thank you." His words were soft, almost inaudible above the gentle breeze rustling the branches of the trees around them.

Gideon gave him a nod. "Sure, kid."

With that, the boy retreated to his hideaway once more.

Gid glanced up at Micah, who stood with his hand on Joel's shoulder.

A world of pain filled Micah's eyes as he shook his head. "Makes a man contemplate things he ought not."

Gideon knew just exactly what he meant.

He stood and set to unstrapping the crate with their mother's tea service. He would need to return it to the back of the wagon so that the woman and her son could ride on the bench beside him. He hoped Georgia would be able to help her with her pain. He didn't imagine riding on a jostling wagon bench in her condition would be too comfortable. However, they needed to make good time if they were going to get to Independence before the last of the wagon trains headed west this year, so they didn't have time to allow her to walk.

Avram continued to maintain a safe distance as Gid worked. He had the tea service back in the wagon and the tarp tied down before Georgia returned with Mercy by her side.

Even past the swelling and bruising on her face, he could see that her eyes were redder and puffier than they'd been a few minutes ago. But she made no comment. Only hurried to her son's side and exclaimed over the apple he was still working on.

Georgia stopped between Gideon and Micah with her hands folded in front of her. She released a breath. Shook her head. "She didn't make a sound. Not one sound. I didn't even know she was crying until I looked up and saw the tears streaking her cheeks."

Gid folded his arms and kicked the toe of one boot into a clump of grass at their feet. "How bad was it?"

Georgia's shoulders sagged. "Bad." She turned pain-filled eyes on him. "She's black and blue from her waist to her shoulders. I'm sure some of her ribs are broken. I wrapped them as tightly as I could."

His fists tightened, and he worked his lips over his teeth. "Is she going to be able to ride?"

Georgia spread her hands. "I can't imagine that walking would be any more comfortable for her at this point. But I'm going to get one of our down pillows. At least with that at her back, it might prevent some of the pain she's bound to suffer."

With that, she hoisted her skirts to skim the grass and bustled toward their wagon with Micah on her heels.

Gideon made sure the horses drank some water while he waited for her to return. And then, with the pillow in his hands, he approached mother and son, who remained on the grass where he'd last seen them.

He hefted the pillow. "We ought to get moving again. My sister hopes this will minimize your discomfort. We're trying to maintain a good clip. We must get to Independence on time to join a wagon train this year."

Her eyes widened at that. "You all are planning to head west?"

Gideon nodded. "Micah has talked of nothing but the promise of Oregon for months now. Georgia was, of course, going with him, and, well, she's my only remaining relative. So I'm along for the ride." He gave her a wry smile.

Mercy looked uncertain about something. She tucked a long dark strand of hair behind one ear, plucked a blade of grass, and set to methodically ripping it. A frown puckered her brow.

Beside her, Avram sucked on the apple core.

After a long moment, Mercy raised her eyes to his. "We really ought to leave you. Herst is . . ." She waved a hand. "Not a man to be trifled with." She tucked her lower lip between her teeth for a moment before she continued. "I would not want to bring trouble on you all. You've been more than kind."

Gideon's guilt mounted. He had not been more than kind. He had planned to leave her behind. If it hadn't been for her husband showing up just when he had and Micah's intervention, he might have driven away and not given her much more thought.

He would not do that to her now. Especially not when she didn't have a single item to her name.

He tilted his head. "Like Micah said, let us at least help you get to the next town. We've plenty of food, and I wouldn't feel right about leaving you here in the middle of nowhere."

She lowered her attention to the piece of grass she continued to shred. Indecision furrowed her brow.

Gid propped one hand on his hip. What was he going to do if she refused?

It was Micah who rescued him. He must have been halfway listening to their conversation as he helped Georgia up to her seat because he strode this way now. He paused beside them, propped his hands on his hips, and surveyed the rugged country all around them. "Besides having no supplies, you might be able to walk a good distance, but I'm betting Avram's little legs will give out not too far down the road. And you're in no state to carry him. Much less protect him if, say, a mountain lion shows up."

Gid wanted to cheer Micah's words. Instead, he held his breath. Would she let herself be convinced?

Her brow scrunched even tighter. Good, let her consider the truth Micah had spoken. She would be putting her son in danger if they went off alone. She tossed aside the stem of grass and kept her attention to her clasped hands.

Gideon looked at Av. "What do you say, kid? Do you want to drive the wagon?"

Avram's brow puckered to match his mother's. He shook his head, sending his mop of curls swishing, and stepped closer to Mercy.

Gideon raised his hands. "That's all right. You can watch me today, and then maybe you'll want to give it a try tomorrow."

Mercy darted him a look before returning her gaze to her fingers. He hadn't missed the irritation tightening the skin at the corners of her eyes. She didn't like him making promises to her son about the future.

Noted.

"Gid, we need to get going." Micah clapped Joel on the shoulder and instructed him to get into the wagon.

Offering one hand to help the woman up to the bench, Gid replied, "We're right behind you."

He hoped.

The woman was now staring off toward the horizon that undulated in the heat waves of the warm spring day. Would she give in? He waited silently.

Micah and Georgia's wagon clattered and squeaked as Micah called to the horses and directed them onto the road. Georgia peered around the canvas with a worried frown, but Gid ignored her.

He nudged his hand closer to Mercy. "Please let us help you?"

Thankfully, she only hesitated another moment before accepting his assistance. "Just to the next town, then."

Relief coursed through him. As carefully as he could, he helped her to the seat and then handed the boy up to her. He did his best not to jostle the wagon too much when he climbed aboard from the other side. Even so, he saw her clamp her lips tight.

With Av settled between them, he snapped the reins and glanced at her as the team stepped out. "Did Georgia give you anything for the pain?"

She shook her head. "She offered. But I'll be fine. I want to be clear-headed." She settled a gentle hand against her son's back in a way that made Gid realize her thoughts had only been for her boy.

He returned his attention to the road, trying not to let his mind wander into the past with its regrets and might-have-beens.

Chapter Four

Herst Adler woke next to a cold hearth in the dim light of dusk. He wrinkled his nose and smacked his tongue against the bitter taste in his mouth.

He squinted at the fireplace. Why was it not lit? The coals didn't even hold any warmth, which meant it hadn't been lit for hours.

His jaw jutted to one side.

Mercy and her neglect. He would definitely have a word with her about that.

He sat straighter. Frowned while rubbing a cramp in his neck.

Why was the house so quiet?

The need for the privy pressed at him. He rose. Dizziness crashed over him, and he broadened his stance to catch his balance. When he opened the door, a cool breeze raised gooseflesh. It might be March with the hot days of summer looming on the horizon, but evenings this time of year could still be cool in these parts.

He folded his arms against the chill as he stumbled down the path to the necessary. The tension in his brow spread across his scalp and threatened to return the cramp in his neck.

The chickens were certainly putting up a big fuss from the pen. His eyes narrowed. They only did that if danger lurked nearby or if they were hungry.

That woman! Where was she off to with chores waiting for her here at home?

He banged through the privy door, wincing at the stench that greeted him. And then banged back out again as soon as he had relieved himself.

Pulling his suspenders up and adjusting them at his shoulders, he surveyed the yard. "Mercy!?"

Nothing. Only the continued cackling of the chickens. He stomped over to the coop, scooped up a double measure of feed, and slung it through the fencing. The chickens converged on the grain with excited cackles and clucks.

Herst threw the scoop back into the grain bin. "Avram?" He plunked his hands on his hips.

The tickle of a memory nudged his mind. He'd gone out drinking this morning. He remembered leaving the house. Arriving at the saloon and ordering his first drink. His second. His third. After that, his memory grew a little fuzzy.

But both Mercy and Av had been here when he'd left today. And Mercy's face had been swollen and bruised.

He scowled. He could dredge up no memory of the evening before.

She must have done something to make him upset. She knew how he got when he was drinking. Why didn't she just obey like a good wife should? Then she wouldn't need correction.

Still, he couldn't help but feel remorse over what he must have done.

He glanced toward town, concern clenching his gut. Had he injured her more today? Maybe she'd needed doctoring and taken Av with her?

He grunted.

Sighed.

He supposed it fell to him to go looking for her. But one of these days, she would push him too far. He would keep the boy. But the woman, well, she might just be dispensable.

He banished the guilt that nudged him at that thought. It was her own fault.

That woman had been nothing but trouble since the first night her beauty had seduced him.

She was first an enchantress. And now a disobedient annoyance.

Surely, there were other women who would be less trouble. Anyone could make his meals and warm his bed, after all.

Speaking of meals. He was hungry. And with her off, who knew where, he wouldn't get to eat anytime soon.

He sucked at his teeth. Yes. It may be time.

With a sigh, he headed for the barn to saddle his mount.

The fire crackled, gold and ocher in the blue haze of dusk. Smoke crafted a circuitous column against the new stars of the evening sky. Behind Mercy, the horses munched grass contentedly, the rhythmic tugging and chomping somehow soothing in the quiet. The only other sounds were the gentle burble of the creek not too far away and the clank of forks against tin plates.

She tried to ignore the ache of hunger in her stomach.

Earlier, when they'd stopped for the night, they had pulled the two wagons near three large evergreen trees that grew in a curved row. The trees formed one side of an oblong and the two wagons the other.

While the men set to gather and chop wood and haul water from the nearby creek, Mercy did her best to help Georgia with meal preparations. But Georgia seemed in a hurry, and with pain shooting through Mercy from every angle and Georgia's constant rush, she felt slow and unwelcome.

Once the meal of rabbit stew had been served, Mercy helped Av get a tin plate and held it for him while he ate since there was no table, and she didn't want him ending up with stew all over himself. By the time he finished, Joel and Micah had wandered off into the trees, and Georgia was already gathering dishes.

Mercy felt conspicuous about asking for a few minutes and taking more from the pot. So she merely thanked Georgia as she handed her the plate and sank down by Av's side.

It was probably better this way. These people wouldn't begrudge her son a meal, but feeding a full-grown adult was another matter altogether. She'd gone days before without eating and could do so again. As soon as they got to Blacksburg, the Morrans and Mr. Riley could be on their way, and she would find a job.

The sound of Gideon scraping more stew from the pot drew her attention. She thought Georgia had already taken all the plates, but Gideon must have hung on to his, wanting a second helping. She had halfway expected him to pester her with questions all day as she rode by him on the wagon bench. But thankfully, he seemed to be a quiet man who'd left her to her peace.

Now, as she watched him add two biscuits to the side of his plate, she ignored the rumble in her stomach and spoke quietly to Avram. "It's nearly time for sleep, son. Let's find a place to take care of our ablutions."

"How about I take the boy into the woods, and you sit here and eat some dinner?"

Startled to hear his voice so near, Mercy looked up to see Gideon holding the plate toward her. The savory scent of the stew wafted to her and made her stomach rumble loudly. She settled one palm over it, embarrassed.

Gideon waggled the plate gently, still holding it toward her. "My sister is a bit of a taskmaster and forgets to consider people's feelings in her drive to get things done." He tilted his head. "It's a weakness, and she knows it. However, she has—" He cleared his throat. Lowered his voice. "Not long before we undertook this trip, she and Micah lost their daughter." He jutted his chin toward Av. "About your son's age. She's not been quite the same since."

His gray eyes were soft when he squatted to his haunches and held the plate nearer.

Mercy gratefully accepted it. "I'm very sorry for your loss."

Gid nodded somberly. "If you could . . . maybe not mention it. We are all trying to give her the space she needs."

"Of course." Mercy felt guilty about her frustration with the woman.

"Thanks." Gideon transferred his gaze to Av. "What do you say we take a trip into the brush? Just a few paces. And downwind." He winked.

Av lifted her a questioning look.

She gave him a nod. "It will be all right. I'll be right here when you return."

Without a word, Av hopped down from the rock where he'd been seated and followed Gideon into the brush. Gideon spoke soft reassuring words as he hacked some branches out of their way with a hatchet.

And as Mercy savored the first bite of the delicious stew, she frowned, pondering her change in circumstances.

Could it be that God had answered her cries for help this time?

Herst grumbled as he tucked into the plate of cold chili from the saloon in town. His day spent wandering the streets, asking if anyone had seen Mercy or Av, had proved futile. Finally, the mercantile owner mentioned that he had seen them in his store earlier. However, the man hadn't seen where they'd gone after. And then he'd had the audacity to ask Herst to pay his tab. Not wanting to be seen as a no-account, Herst had grudgingly slapped his remaining few dollars onto the counter, promising to pay the rest of his bill soon.

Of course, he hadn't been working for a few weeks now. But Old Griff didn't need to know that.

Now, he sat in the saloon without even enough money for another drink and still no idea where Mercy had taken his son.

Someone sank onto the seat across the table from him. He snapped his head up, ready to tell them to shove off, but it was his cousin. He grunted a greeting instead.

Henry gave him a dip of his chin. "I hear you're looking for Mercy and your boy."

Herst swept his tongue around the perimeter of his mouth, irritation mounting. The last thing he wanted was Henry gloating over him. "I am."

"Saw them." Henry drummed his thumbs against the table.

Herst straightened. "Where at?"

"Mercy spoke to a wagoneer. Not for certain . . . But, looked like his party stopped at the mercantile to resupply." Henry motioned with one hand. "I went into the livery to fetch my horse, and you were speaking to the man when I came out. I didn't see Mercy or the boy, and I figured you'd sent them on home."

Herst narrowed his eyes. If he'd spoken to a wagoneer, he had no recollection of it. But if Henry had seen Mercy speaking to a man and then she'd been nowhere in sight only a few moments later . . . "I reckon I ought to talk to this man. He still around?"

A bit of humor filled Henry's eyes. "You don't remember, do you?" He didn't give Herst time to answer. "Couldn't hear y'all's conversation, but I saw the man shake his head, and then he got up on the wagon bench and drove off with his party." An irritating smirk nudged his lips. "When's the last time you saw her?"

Herst scratched at the back of his head. "I came here first thing this morning. When I got home a couple hours later, she was gone." He frowned, fighting to conjure memories of the empty hours. "I came back to town looking for her, I guess." That must have been when Henry had seen him. "You think she could have hitched a ride with this fella?"

Henry lifted one shoulder. "Don't see as how it could have been anybody else. Wasn't enough time for her to work her wiles on any other fella."

Herst flopped against the slats of his chair and stared vacantly at the wall across the room. His anger mounted with each breath.

She actually thought she could leave him? Not only that but take his boy too?

He closed his eyes, tapped his fingers against the table, and concentrated on breathing slowly through his nose.

When he opened his eyes, Henry was eyeing him slyly.

Herst wanted to put his fist through the man's face, but one thing held him in check. "You still a crack shot with that Sharps of yours?"

With a sly grin, Henry folded his arms and leaned back in his chair. "You know I am." His brows raised. "I always did admire that back ten acres on your property."

Herst grunted his irritation. If he took this road, there would be no coming back from it. Yet how could he even hesitate? The woman had taken his son from him! "Five acres."

Henry shook his head. He leveled Herst with a look and leaned a little farther across the table. "The price is ten acres." He held up a blunt finger. "Think carefully before you deny me again. You're quibbling over a few acres you don't use, cousin." He tapped his chest. "I can make your problems disappear and bring your boy back home. I never did like that uppity gal of yours."

Quick anger shot through Herst, and he straightened. His scrutiny sharpened on Henry, but then he eased back against his chair. Henry had never liked her because she had refused his advances.

Herst simply hadn't allowed her to do the same to him. His lips lifted at the edges.

But now, the shock of what they were considering began to settle in.

Perhaps there was another way . . .

He could fetch them back home and punish her by making her regret that she'd even thought about leaving him. Though . . . that seemed like a lot of hard work.

He could let her go. He shook his head. Maybe he would have if she had left alone—but every man needed a son.

He pondered his cousin's placid expression. Ever since they were boys, Henry had possessed a singular talent with the long rifle. Herst had once witnessed him bringing down a rabbit at one hundred paces.

He swung his jaw to one side. "You would do that for only ten acres?"

Henry chortled. "So now it's 'only' ten acres, is it?" He shrugged. "I've done such jobs for less."

A thrill of recompense shot through Herst. Such justice would undoubtedly teach her! What had she been thinking to go off and leave him the way she had? What kind of a woman did that to a man who had provided a roof over her head and given her a son?

He narrowed his eyes at his cousin. "You injure my boy, and it'll be the last thing you do."

Shifting in his chair, Henry frowned, seemingly hurt that he'd even thought to mention it. "I wouldn't risk your boy. You know that. He's blood."

Herst scrubbed one hand over his jaw. He would like nothing more than to send Henry to fetch Avram alone. But his cousin might need his help. The boy had taken a dislike to his cousin for some reason. Likely something that Mercy had put into his head. He didn't want Avram to make a fuss and somehow get hurt in the process.

So, Henry would put his skills to work. And then they could ride closer and fetch the boy. Herst slapped his hand against the table. "Those wagoneers are going to rue the day that they deigned to help Mercy try to escape. We leave in an hour."

Henry arched a brow. "You're coming with me?"

"Of course, I'm coming with you. We're going to fetch my boy."

The wagons would be slow and need to stick to the road. He'd be willing to bet they would catch up to them by tomorrow evening.

The next day, Gideon rose with the sun and hitched the team. Mercy and her boy climbed onto the bench beside him and sat in silence.

For several long hours, the road stretched, empty and dusty, until it disappeared into the horizon. And the sun arched across the sky unimpeded by even one cloud, creating a merciless oven of heat. They stopped at noon to water the horses and down some grub, and Gideon fetched a yard of cloth that Georgia had used as extra packing in the tea trunk.

He handed it to Mercy as they climbed onto the wagon bench again. "Here, this will help keep some sun off you and the boy."

In the places not discolored by bruises, her face was already a near match to a watermelon.

"Thank you." She spread the cloth above their heads and continued to ride in silence.

Hours later, with the sun falling low in the sky, Gideon's hands ached from the tension of holding the reins all day. And his backside wasn't in much better shape. There was nothing comfortable about the jostling seat of an unsprung farm wagon. And even though he considered himself a quiet man, the lack of conversation grated on him. Not because of the silence itself but because of the revelations residing in it.

Mercy and her boy were not just quiet. They were somber. He'd never known a boy who could sit mutely for such a long period. And Mercy sat so still and stiff with one arm wrapped around her ribs, just so. It made his gut ache, and red blur the edges of his vision.

He wanted to ask so many questions but chose instead to allow them their solitude. Perhaps, in time, they would come to see that they could trust him.

In time? What was he doing contemplating things like that? She'd made it clear she would leave them at the next town, which they should arrive at in the next couple of days. Except he found himself hoping...

Hoping what? That he could talk her into continuing on with them?

With Verona in the grave these short two months, his heart was definitely still hers and hers alone, so it wasn't a romantic notion that had him wanting to help this woman—not that he would allow himself to act on feelings for a married woman even if he was having them. What was it then?

Perhaps simple Christian charity.

He cut off the thought with a shake of his head. He had no right to even contemplate the state of his Christian charity when only yesterday, he'd been ready to leave this mother and her son in the dust of a street.

He sighed. If Verona were here, she would know just the right words to convince the woman to stay with them. His eyes stung, and he blinked hard.

As usual, he didn't have the right words—even if Mercy's circumstances raised the protector in him. So when the time came, he would drop her off as she wished and pray that God would send her another protector to keep her safe from the man who had betrayed his vows to her. And who had betrayed the blessing God had bestowed on him in the form of that boy.

The image of Verona and little Jessica buried together in one casket flashed into his mind. His gut roiled. His jaw ached.

Georgia hadn't wanted Jessica buried alone. And even though Gideon knew that both Verona and little Jess had entered heaven the moment their spirits quit clinging to this mortal world, burying them together had somehow given him some comfort, too. He had put them into the pine box himself, with Verona's arms cradling the girl.

Perhaps it was that recent memory contrasted with the sight of Av's little arm all bruised and purple that lit such rage inside him. What he wouldn't do to have Verona and Jess here once more, yet here he found a man whose son still lived and despite that had treated him so ill!

Gideon tucked the reins between his knees and slugged back several gulps from his canteen. He needed to cool off, or he would be saddling a mount and returning to that no-bit town to give an abuser the treatment he deserved.

Lord forgive him for such thoughts.

Mercy accepted the canteen and took a drink, then helped her son do the same. Gid was accepting it back from her when he noticed Micah pulling his covered wagon off the road and onto a flat spot beneath a willow just coming into this year's leaves. Surprise washed through him. The sun still hung a good way above the horizon.

Gid followed his lead, pulling the team to a stop in the shade behind him. Perhaps Joel needed a stop?

However, the moment Micah hopped down, he helped Georgia descend from the seat beside him, and she practically ran to the back of their covered wagon and clambered inside.

At his questioning look, Micah lifted one shoulder. "She's not having such a good day today."

Gid forked his fingers through his hair and resettled his hat, wishing he could do something to lift his sister's grief. But they were all wallowing in that sea of sorrow up to their necks. None of them seemed to have extra strength to lend.

He jumped from the wagon and helped Mercy to the ground, then hefted Av down beside her.

Striding a few steps from his wagon, Micah propped his hands on his hips and stared off toward the rolling hills. His own eyes were red-rimmed. He blinked several times. "Sorry to stop early. I don't think she could have sat for much longer, and this seemed a likely place for the night."

"We could keep going while she rests on your pallet." Gid hoped that might get them a little farther down the road.

Micah shook his head, shoulders slumping. "She doesn't rest well with the worry of a crate or box toppling onto her. Sorry."

Gid brushed away his brother-in-law's concerns. "No need to apologize." Even though he said the words, he worried whether they would reach Independence on time at this rate. And he knew Micah shared his concern. They couldn't stop early every night, or they wouldn't be able to catch a wagon train west this year. If they didn't arrive in Oregon by December first . . . Well, he would just have to leave that in the Lord's hands.

If only Georgia could shore herself up, they would be all right. The necessities of life with the wagon train would be good for her. Give her something to focus on other than the crippling anguish.

"I could do tonight's cooking if you like?" Mercy's soft voice drew their attention.

Adjusting his hat, Micah swept a glance over the discolored side of her face. "We appreciate the offer, but I'm not sure you're in any shape to be cooking, ma'am. I heard a flock of turkeys. I'll take my shotgun and see if I can fetch one since we have some time. Gid, maybe you could get a fire going? I'll get some water when I return." His feet almost dragged as he shuffled toward the wagon to get his gun.

Mercy shifted her feet. "I could get some biscuits baking if you have a Dutch oven."

Gid nodded, appreciating her desire to help.

Though she'd made the offer, now she looked toward the wagon but didn't move. She seemed a little lost as to what to do. She likely didn't feel comfortable snooping through Georgia's things to look for the proper supplies. And the oven would be too heavy for her to lift in her condition.

"I'll help you find what you need," Gid offered, leading the way.

As they pulled flour, leavening, sugar, lard, and salt from the box, the sounds of Georgia's muffled sobs were nearly his undoing.

Mercy gave him a sympathetic look as he hefted the heavy Dutch oven from within the box.

Av stopped by her side and tugged on her skirt. "Joel an' me go play in the field?" He swung an arm toward the prairie across the road from where they'd stopped.

"I invited him to come with me," Joel offered with a gap-toothed smile.

Gingerly settling the bowl of ingredients against one hip, Mercy looked at Mattox. Gid could see her assessing the large black dog that lingered next to Joel's side. Her attention shifted to Micah, who had fetched his double-barrel from beneath the seat of the wagon and was heading toward the sound of turkeys gobbling in the distance.

He waved a hand to brush away her concern as he strode by. "He won't hurt your son."

She still seemed uncertain, and maybe with just cause since the dog stood almost as tall as Av, but Mercy nevertheless ruffled her son's hair. "Sure, love. Just don't go far, okay?"

The hesitation in her voice had Gid reassuring her. "The dog is big, but he'll protect those boys with everything in him."

Without another word, she pulled a few more things from within the box.

"Son, you stay where Uncle Gid can see you," Micah called to Joel as he paused just this side of the woods on the other side of the clearing where they'd stopped.

Joel led Av across the road with a wave. "Yes, sir." The dog trotted happily beside the boys.

Gideon watched the boys for a moment, thankful that Joel seemed fully recovered from the sickness that had taken his sister and aunt. They'd nearly lost him, too, and Gideon thanked God every day that Georgia hadn't needed to suffer the loss of both her children.

For though no one knew it, his Verona had gone to heaven, taking not only herself from him but his unborn child as well. His guilt compounded every time he remembered the little one. For he missed Verona as if the very breath had been stolen from him, yet the sorrow for the babe often came as an afterthought—more like the memory of pain than actual pain itself. What kind of a man—father—did that make him? Realization of how far he fell short rolled over him in wave after wave.

He hung his head.

Would that he could go back in time, for grief was an everyday companion he'd sooner not know so intimately.

First, he would get a fire going, but then he needed to vent some frustration.

Chapter Five

Mercy settled near the fire Gideon had built, waiting for enough coals to form so that she could fill the lid of the Dutch oven. The biscuits were always better when they were cooked from both the top and the bottom. They would also be better if there were enough coals to rake some to the side so they could cool a mite. She liked her biscuits golden brown instead of black on the bottom.

As Gid pounded the cast iron support stake near enough to the fire for the swing arm to reach the hottest part of the flames, they heard the sharp report of a single shot.

Only one shot must mean he'd succeeded, right? Her mouth watered at the thought of fresh roasted turkey. She'd not tasted any meat other than chicken since she'd married Herst.

Even in the shade, it was hot with the late-afternoon sun beating down at an angle. But a soft breeze caught in the branches of the willow, and she relished a moment of watching the fronds dance in the current.

Gid slumped onto the log across the way with his body hunched morosely over his knees. After several long minutes, he rose sharply and stomped off.

"I'll chop some wood," he declared as he clomped to the back of his wagon. He yanked the axe from its place just inside the tailgate and then marched into the forest.

It wasn't long before Mercy heard the fevered hammering of his blade against wood. He was chopping so furiously that she wondered how he had time to raise the axe and get it back down again in such rapid succession.

He had sat beside her so quietly all day. She'd been thankful for his silence. Yet, perhaps he was also suffering over the loss of his niece in a way she hadn't realized.

The fire had a good number of coals now, so she set about mixing the batch of biscuits. Stabs of pain sliced through her, but she was determined to repay these folk for their kindness, so she pushed through the agony.

She felt eyes on her and looked up to find Micah walking toward her from the wood with a turkey dangling upside down by his side. He laid the turkey on the end of the log that Gid had just vacated, tipped her a nod, and then went to the back of the covered wagon. He took down a large bucket and the big cast iron pot before he ambled to the creek she could hear but not see.

When he returned, he put the bucket to one side and hung the pot on the end of the swing arm. He pushed the pot of water over the hottest part of the flames.

Mercy slathered lard in the bottom of the Dutch oven and then spooned the biscuit dough in with practiced ease, forming round balls side by side. She would let them rest until the turkey was nearly done cooking.

As soon as the water began to steam, Micah pulled the pot from the fire and plunged the whole turkey in. The bird's back end protruded into the air.

Humor lit the eyes that he angled to her. "Guess we need a bigger pot."

Mercy chuckled. "I'd hate to have to haul around any pot bigger than that."

He nodded. "True enough. My arm liked to have broke just getting this water here from the creek."

Mercy smiled, knowing the words were naught but jest. He'd hardly seemed to be working at all when he'd hoisted that heavy pot onto the arm.

Micah pulled the soaked turkey out and plunged the other end into the steaming water. After a moment, he removed the whole thing and set to plucking the feathers into a pile at his feet.

Mercy checked on the boys, and by the time she returned, Micah had the bird plucked and butchered, and pieces skewered on a spit over the flames. Fat sizzled as it dripped from the meat into the fire.

Tonight, those blue eyes so at odds with his golden-brown skin seemed less intense. He held a blade in one hand, and the pile of shavings at his feet revealed that he'd been taking some frustration out on the piece of wood in his other hand.

Mercy used the fire tongs to scoop some coals to one side and placed the Dutch oven over them. Then she scooped more coals onto the lid.

They could still hear Gideon's rhythmic axe, though the beats of the percussion had slowed some. Surely they didn't need so much wood for only one night.

Micah pointed the sharpened end of his stick toward the sound. "He tell you we lost our daughter?" His words were so soft as to almost be a whisper, and from the quick look he darted toward his own wagon, Mercy had a feeling he hoped to keep his wife from overhearing this conversation.

"Yes. I'm very sorry for your loss." She looked away from the pain in his eyes to where Joel and Av had both squatted to their haunches to study something in the grass.

From the corner of her eye, she saw him nod. "Thank you. Gid lost his wife that same day."

Mercy's shock yanked her gaze back to his. "That, he did not tell me."

Micah went back to whittling shavings from the stick in his hand. "Figured as much."

Sinking back onto the rock that she'd chosen as her seat, she let her focus drift to the edge of the forest. The sounds of Gideon's axe had fallen silent now. "Why does God allow such evil and such pain to exist in this world, do you think? Are we simply not worth His time?" When Micah darted her a questioning look, she busied herself with smoothing at some wrinkles in her skirt. "Sorry. I shouldn't have said that."

He whittled off a few more curls of wood, jaw set in a hard, grim line.

She was a fool with loose lips. What was she thinking? Expressing such heretical thoughts to a virtual stranger. He was probably regretting the fact that he'd urged her to stay with their party!

"Heard a traveling preacher say one time that God made some people to love and others to bear the brunt of His vengeance."

Mercy stilled. Lifted her focus to him. She felt an immediate connection to his sentiment but was too horrified to say so. Had she been created solely for God to afflict and torment?

Micah shook his head. "At the time, I thought I disagreed, but now . . ." For a long moment, his concentration blurred against the back of his wagon.

Mercy could still hear the soft sounds of Georgia's crying. "Should I go to her, do you think?"

Micah shook his head. "Best to leave her be. She's not much for company when she gets like this." He turned the meat a quarter turn above the crackling fire, then dropped his attention to the stick in his hands and put his knife to work once more.

They both fell quiet then. Mercy took a lingering walk, never leaving the sight of the fire, but she couldn't shake their conversation, and as dusk began to fall, she realized that she had a deeper appreciation for what made her feel connected to this family after such a short time of knowing them.

The understanding of shared pain formed a powerful bond.

It also explained what made Gideon a man of such few words. Why Micah seemed so severe when she'd first laid eyes on him. And why Georgia was so reluctant to have her along.

She almost wished that she could believe God loved all equally. She would ask Him to relieve their pain. But as things stood, she couldn't bring herself to believe it would do any good.

Her conscience panged her. After all, hadn't God answered her prayer back in town and helped them escape?

She frowned, pondering. Maybe He had. Or maybe it had only been a coincidence that she happened to ask the right family for help.

Micah whittled until only a stub of the original stick remained in his grip. Then he tossed that into the fire and carefully gathered all the shavings into a canvas bag. He also carved some moss from the log he sat on, as well as a couple of beads of pitch. He methodically rolled the pitch into cocoons of moss and then thrust them into the canvas bag with the chips.

As Mercy turned the meat, and rotated the coals atop the Dutch oven, she felt appreciation for Micah's planning. There might come a day when they needed a fire, but there was only damp wood. But with Micah's preparations, they wouldn't need to worry.

She stilled, struck by a thought that brought a frown. Why was she contemplating a future with these people? They hadn't even wanted to help her to start with, and it was clear that they had their own grief to deal with and had no capacity to help her figure out her own—much less a new path for her and Av. She would be leaving their party as soon as they reached the next town. And it was best she remember that.

Herst reined to a stop and reached for his canteen, only to find it empty. "Blazes! It's hot out here! I need to find some water."

Henry jutted his chin toward a ribbon of green that cut through the brown of the prairie on either side of the road. "Trees yonder."

Greenery likely meant water. Herst nudged his horse in that direction. "Let's hole up for a few hours and let the worst of this heat fade. We can ride on after dusk."

They trotted their mounts into the shade of some low oaks that grew along the banks of a shallow creek that barely trickled. Henry used his hatchet to hack out a small pool and then, while they waited for the dirt to settle, they unsaddled their mounts and turned them loose to graze in the succulent grass nearby.

Herst sank onto a root and leaned back against the trunk of the tree, crossing his ankles. He plucked a stem of grass and tucked the end between his lips. His head pounded, and he would give just about anything to have a drink of the stronger variety. But with the last of his money spent at the mercantile, thanks to Mercy, he wouldn't be able to buy one even if there was one available.

His hands started to shake, and he folded his arms to tuck them out of sight. Henry was already stretched out on his bedroll with his hat over his face. A long, slow snore filled the glen.

Herst huffed. Snatched up his canteen and stomped to the now clear water. He carefully immersed his canteen so as not to stir up any more sediment, drank his fill, and then filled the canteen again.

If Henry was going to sleep, he might as well too. Just a few hours. And then he would catch up to Mercy—and he would instruct Henry to make it quick.

He smirked.

Mercy for Mercy.

One moment, she would be a happy mother and husband-abandoner. And the next, she would be snuffed from existence.

He thought of Av, and his brow slumped. He might be ready to part with his wife, but no boy ought to witness his mother's death. Perhaps they should wait until well after dark. Then Av would be asleep. It would also allow them to get closer for a better shot. The boy would fall asleep early, but the adults would likely sit around the fire for a while. That would be the perfect time.

Even though the party did not know Mercy well, there were bound to be a few moments of chaos in which he could grab his son. He simply

needed to position himself to swoop in at the right moment. The
darkness would also help to conceal his identity as he made his escape.

He nodded. He liked a good plan.

With one last check of the horses' hobbles, he unfurled his own
bedroll and flopped down next to Henry.

By this time tomorrow, he would be back home with his son.

An hour later, the savory scent of the roasted meat had Mercy's
stomach rumbling in anticipation. She hoped the biscuits would not
be too hard, for she'd put them on too soon. They had long since
finished baking, and she'd simply been keeping them warm in the
Dutch oven. But since Micah had butchered the turkey into smaller
pieces, the meat had cooked faster than she expected. So hopefully
they wouldn't be too bad.

Now her anticipation for the meal practically had her salivating.
She and Av had probably eaten more over the last two days than they
had each week back home. Tonight, she would eat lightly because she
hoped to experience a full night of sleep and didn't want to be overly full.

Back home, she always slept fitfully. She never knew when Herst
might arrive from a late night of imbibing and fly into a rage. It had
only taken one time of being awakened from a sound sleep as Herst
hauled her from the bed by her ankles to make her a light sleeper.

Last night the pain had woken her more times than she could
recall. But today, with her ribs still wrapped tightly in Georgia's cloths,
she'd been amazed at how much better she'd felt. If she could just get
a good night of rest, maybe that would also aid in her healing.

Mama had passed when Mercy was only eleven. But she
remembered Mama saying a warm meal and a good night of sleep
could fix almost anything.

With Micah pulling the bird from the spit, Mercy strode across the
road and called the boys to return with her. It did her heart so good

to see Av laugh as he and Joel decided to race to see who could get to "Uncle Gid's" wagon first.

Despite the years he had on Avram, Joel seemed small for his age, and the race was a close one. In the end, Joel was kind, and they declared a tie.

Mercy smiled as the boys sank down happily beside each other on a log near the fire.

Gideon had been gone for so long that she'd started to worry about him. But now, he emerged from the forest with an armful of wood that he set close by. His eyes were red-rimmed, but Micah didn't ask if he was all right. There seemed to be a mutual understanding that none of them were.

Gid sank down beside his nephew, propped his elbows on his knees, and scrubbed a hand through his unruly blond hair, head hanging wearily.

Mercy's heart went out to the man. Now that she knew how deeply he grieved, she wondered how she hadn't seen it sooner. His expression and posture, after all, mirrored the exact emotions that she'd been feeling for most of the past four years.

Mercy took up a plate from the stack that she'd discovered in the corner of the supply box and added two biscuits. She handed it to Micah.

He nodded his thanks. And started forking meat from one leg of the bird.

She waited until he had enough meat sliced to fill the other plates, then gave the first to Gideon and a lesser measure to each of the boys. Her own, she placed on the large rock that Micah had rolled near and then took up the last plate. After adding a generous portion of meat and a biscuit, she strode to the back of the covered wagon.

"Georgia?" she called softly. "I've some dinner for you."

Silence stretched for so long that she assumed Georgia must have fallen asleep. She was just turning away when the sound of shuffling drew her back.

Georgia's face was blotchy and puffy when she pushed aside the canvas.

Mercy held the plate aloft, biting her tongue against the fissure of agony that punched through her side.

Georgia hesitated for a moment but then finally reached to accept the offering. "Thank you."

"My pleasure." Mercy pressed her hands against the apron she'd donned, thankful to have her arms once more at her sides, but suddenly feeling awkward for having put the apron on without asking. However, Georgia retreated into the wagon without so much as another word.

Mercy returned to the fire, ate her fill, and then set about cleaning up as Micah sat the boys down to tell them a tall tale about a man with a wooden leg that he used as a hammer.

She scooped the last of the biscuits and some meat onto her plate for the dog, and from the lick she received to the back of her hand as he waited patiently for her to place the offering before him, she felt she may have made a fast friend.

By the time she returned from washing the dishes in the creek, the dog had flopped down in the grass near the fire and closed its eyes. The boys were giggling with glee at Micah's stories.

She almost hated to call Av away from the intimate family scene, but weariness had caught up to her. "Av, it's time we retire."

He looked up and blinked as though he were coming back to reality from a distant land. He'd momentarily forgotten the burdens of his young life, it seemed.

She hated that she'd been the one to bring him back from the freedom of Micah's silly stories.

Micah settled a hand on Joel's head. "Time you turned in, too, son."

"Aw, Pa. Just one more story?"

Micah motioned toward the wagon. "Not tonight. Go on with you. I'll join you in a few minutes."

Joel sighed and dragged his feet toward the wagon.

It seemed to make Av feel better to see that Joel didn't want to retire any more than he did. He stepped close and wrapped his arms around Mercy's legs, smothering a big yawn in her skirts.

An emotion she couldn't quite define softened Micah's eyes. He nodded to Av. "His laugh does my heart good." He made a sound in the back of his throat and lowered his gaze to the ground as though the words had caught him off guard.

"Thank you for your stories." She settled a hand on Av's curls. "It does my heart good also."

Micah fiddled with the bark of the log on which he sat. Nodded.

Gideon still seemed to be struggling. He didn't acknowledge their conversation but stared into the fire, clearly with his mind in a distant place.

Mercy had been surprised to note the night before that he hadn't gone into the covered wagon with his sister's family. Instead, he had slept underneath the stars near the fire.

It was then that she had realized that she and Av had taken his shelter. She intended to amend that tonight. She rubbed Av's back as she looked at the man. "I've spread the cloth you gave me to sleep on last night beneath those trees. Av and I will sleep there tonight so you can have your wagon back. It's a lovely night." She gestured to the stars glimmering above. "I don't think we'll need the covering."

Mattox leapt up. His hackles rose, and he took several steps away from the fire, his attention fixed on something in the darkness. He growled low in the back of his throat.

Prickles spidered across Mercy's neck.

She snatched Av up, slamming her teeth against the agony that pierced through her at the sudden movement, and stepped into the dark shadows away from the fire.

When she looked back, both Gideon and Micah were nowhere to be seen. They must have scattered into the darkness as well.

Mercy held her breath. With her back pressed to the bark of a tree in the darkness and Av still cradled on her hip, she watched the dog.

His attention remained fixed on some point across the road. He sank lower and crept forward a couple of steps.

Mercy studied the area where he looked but couldn't see anything but shades of gray, lighter where the grass grew and darker where trees stretched high to block the light of the lowest stars.

Mattox sank onto his belly. For a moment, he still studied the field across the road, but eventually, he propped his head on his paws and seemed to lose interest.

Mercy released a breath of relief, but a tingle of worry still lingered in the back of her mind.

Across the fire, she heard the shuffling of feet, and both men returned to the circle of light and sank into their respective seats.

Fear held her back from doing the same. If it was Herst out there in the darkness, it would be best if he didn't see her here with these people.

Mercy resisted a whimper and pressed one hand against her ribs as she put Av back on the ground. She took his hand so he wouldn't step into the light.

"What was it, Mama?" he asked softly.

"I don't know, love. Perhaps only a coon or possum." She tugged him toward their pallet, staying well back in the shadows. "For now, we need to get some rest. Morning will come early."

She released him then, for she didn't want him to feel the trembling that overtook her without warning. She felt an urgency to get to the next town so this family would no longer be in danger.

Still well back in the darkness, she was skirting the fire behind Av when Gideon said, "I can sleep under the trees just as well as you." Though she knew he'd spoken the words to her, he didn't turn to face her. He seemed to be studying the ground between his knees.

She nudged Av to keep moving. "We're already set up over here for tonight. Tomorrow we can revisit the discussion. Good night for now." With that, she hurried to follow her son into the darkness, willing down the terror she felt at doing so.

The only thing that allowed her to keep moving was the knowledge that the dog had been studying the field in the opposite direction of her pallet.

And if Herst was out there, she prayed the dog would warn her before her husband snuck up on her in the dark.

Chapter Six

Herst and Henry lay on their bellies in the blackness at the crest of a low hill. They had slept longer than Herst had intended through the day, and now that they'd come upon the fire, no one seemed to be in sight except a huge black dog.

They'd been walking their horses down the trail, with dusk falling fast all around them, when they'd heard the low sound of conversation over the next ridge. They'd quickly dismounted, ground-hitched their horses, and crept to the crest of the hill. But now Herst looked at Henry, who studied the camp below with his field glass.

Hang, but it was hard to see anything in this dark side of half-light. "Anything?"

Henry made a chopping motion with his hand. "Quiet."

Herst pressed his lips together, not liking his cousin's uppishness. But when the dog lowered into a crouch and darted a few steps toward them, he had to agree that maybe speaking hadn't been the wisest move. He held his silence and remained still.

It seemed forever before the dog lost interest enough to drop its head to its paws. But they were rewarded for their patience when two men stepped out of the night and sank onto seats near the fire.

Herst looked at Henry for confirmation that these were the men he'd seen in town. Of course, he'd apparently seen them too. If only his memory of that morning wasn't buried beneath the sludge of inebriation.

Henry nodded and pressed a finger to his lips as he continued to search the camp through his field glass.

Herst narrowed his eyes. He didn't know how Henry could make anything out through that old glass anyhow. It distorted things so much that it was near impossible to sort out one detail from another. But Henry prided himself in his ownership of the piece. It had been their grandfather's when he'd been a captain for the Royal Navy.

Herst's patience was wearing thin. His head pounded, and his hands trembled with the need for a drink. He just wanted to get this over with and get back home. He still had half a jug of homebrew chilling in the creek behind the house.

One of the men spoke, but his words were so low they couldn't make them out from this distance, and the other man didn't respond.

Henry eventually lowered the field glass and shook his head. He leaned close and pressed his lips to Herst's ear. "Don't see that woman of yours." He eased back with a questioning look. What did Herst want to do now?

Herst held his silence as he contemplated. Could they have been wrong? Perhaps Mercy wasn't here? The only place she could be was . . . inside the covered wagon! He lifted his head. That had to be it!

He leered. She had somehow tricked these men into giving up their warm beds for her and Av? Fools.

He pointed for Henry to pay attention to the wagon and motioned that they should wait. Much as he wanted a drink, he wanted his son more.

That, and to make Mercy pay for her impudence.

Micah Morran felt weary to his very core. He stared into the snapping flames and wondered if life would ever be good again.

Had it really only been nine weeks ago that he had twirled Jessica through the air when she'd run to greet him as he'd arrived home that evening?

He'd felt so full of hope and excitement for the future. Finally, leaving behind the drudgery of life in Virginia. The wagon had been secured, and he and Georgia sat at the dining table to plan all the things they would need to purchase and pack for the trip west.

Georgia, as meticulous as ever, created sections on their list for everything from "Medicines" to "Treats for the Children."

"So they'll have something to enjoy in difficult moments on the trail," she'd said.

When he'd remembered they would need horse liniment, she'd insisted that he create a new section on the list titled "Animal Husbandry." He laughed and teased her about her stickling nature. To which she light-heartedly responded that he would be ever so thankful for her detailed planning before this trip was through. He tugged her closer and told her he was already thankful for more than just her detailed planning.

They'd been sharing an intimate moment at the table when Joel had come out of his room, glassy-eyed with fever. Little Jess had never come out of her room at all.

Micah gave himself a shake and brought himself back to the present. Right now, he would love nothing more than to drown his grief with the bottle of spirits packed in Georgia's medicine box, but she would frown on that.

Instead, He took up a stick and prodded the fire to spread it so that it would die down. "Guess we'd better turn in."

Gideon dipped his chin and pressed his hands to his knees to stand.

From the morose look on his face, Micah figured he, too, had been languishing in a quagmire of memories that were better forgotten. They were quite the group, weren't they? Each with their own pain silently tucked away. Even the new woman and her little boy.

They had both gained their feet when a rustling at the back of his wagon drew his attention. Georgia's hand came into sight as she swept the canvas to one side.

Looked like she wanted to come down for some reason. That made his heart lurch with hope. Micah hurried around the fire and started toward her.

One of his biggest concerns since the loss of Jess was whether Georgia would be able to handle life without her. Would he ever get his wife back? He could only hope that, eventually, she'd be able to laugh again.

He'd crossed partway to her when she scooped a long strand of her dark hair behind her ear and grabbed the top of the tailgate to aid with balance as she descended. In her other hand, she held the plate that Mercy had taken to her earlier.

"Georgia, wait. I'll help you," he offered.

She stilled, her slender body a dark outline against the lighter canvas now draped behind her.

Mattox growled deep in his throat and crouched low with his attention directed toward the field across the road.

Fear jolted through Micah like a lightning bolt! "Georgia! Get back in—"

Georgia slumped and tumbled toward the ground even as the sharp report of a shot shattered the night.

With a cry of anguish, Micah stretched to catch her.

And just like that, his question was answered. Life never would be good again.

Gideon felt every horror imaginable surge through him all at once.

Mattox gave a feral bark that was mostly growl and took off like he'd just been blasted from a cannon.

Everything slowed then, and Gid saw each detail with a clarity he hadn't known possible.

Georgia mid-air with her hair splaying around her as she toppled from the wagon.

Micah, arms outstretched as he groaned and lunged forward to catch her.

The two of them falling to a heap at the back of the wagon. Georgia clutched to Micah's chest.

Joel in the mouth of the wagon, staring down at his father and mother, jaw slack.

Reality slammed home, and Gid fell to a crouch as horror sapped all his strength.

Micah grimaced, and the tendons in his neck bulged as he screamed at the heavens. In the next moment, he seemed to pull himself together. He clenched his jaw and turned his focus back to his wife. He brushed her hair away from her face. "Georgia! Sweet Georgia. Oh, God, please, no!" Micah tenderly adjusted her in his arms so he could assess her injury.

A fist seized Gid's heart when her hair fell back farther, and he glimpsed the rapidly spreading crimson stain on her white blouse.

Georgia's eyes stared blankly at the sky overhead.

Gid rocked, fist pressed to his lips.

And then Micah was laying her carefully on the ground. He settled her head as gently as he might have if she'd been sleeping. He was already pulling his pistol as he stood. He thrust a finger at Joel. "Get back in that wagon." When the boy hesitated, still staring in shock at his mother, Micah yelled. "Get back in the wagon, Joel. Now!"

Joel blinked and eased behind the canvas, wide eyes disappearing into the darkness.

"Get between the bacon barrels, and don't move." That command was spoken softly, and then Micah disappeared into the darkness at a sprint.

Everything in Gid hurt. He wanted to flop onto the ground and kick and scream. Might have if his feet didn't feel so firmly rooted to the soil where he'd crouched. What curse had they brought upon themselves to keep incurring such tragedies?

With a start, Gideon realized he'd left Micah to fight on his own. He snatched his Colt and followed his brother-in-law. He ate the ground with long strides, only certain of one thing in that moment . . .

Justice would be rapid.

Who would shoot a woman in cold blood like that?

The long grass of the prairie tugged at his boots as he thundered up the rise. The scent of dust filled his nostrils. His breath pounded loudly in his ears.

And then the answer stabbed straight into his heart.

He had done this.

He and Micah and their desire to help that woman.

That had to be it, right? Mistaken identity? Even he had recognized how much Mercy resembled his sister.

Ahead, Mattox flew into a fury of yapping and growling.

A man cursed loudly, and Mattox yelped, but then he attacked again. The sound of the dog's teeth snapping together cut loudly through the darkness, audible even above his frenzied snarling.

This time, instead of a curse, the man whimpered, "Herst, help me. Dear God, help me!"

Gid heard no response.

Herst! Mercy's husband! He was right!

"Mattox, down!" Micah's command ushered in prompt silence.

Panting from exertion, Gideon topped the hill to find Micah standing next to the panting dog and a man who cowered on the ground with his arms around his head. Moonlight glinted off slick moisture that lay thick on one side of the man's face. Dark splotches on his arms also glistened in places. Beyond the man, a long-barreled rifle lay on the ground.

Micah leveled his pistol. "You'll answer my questions, or so help me, I'll let my dog finish you."

Gideon darted his brother-in-law a look. He'd never heard such hatred vibrate in Micah's voice.

Micah's hand trembled, and for one moment, Gid thought he might shoot the man where he lay.

Still whimpering, the man raised bloodied palms. "All right, all right. I'll tell you anything."

Micah stepped closer and bent with his pistol pointedly pressed to the man's forehead. "Who are you?"

The man winced, keeping Micah in view with only one eye. His face was so lacerated on one side that Gideon could see bone in the moonlight. He would be surprised if he didn't lose that eye. And blood pulsed from a gash on his throat. Gideon couldn't tell if he kept the injured eye closed or if it had been injured beyond use. Too much torn flesh disguised the extent of his injuries in the moonlight.

"Henry. Henry Adler." He trembled.

Adler. The name made Gid swallow the bile that rose in the back of his throat.

"You alone?" Micah grated.

Henry hesitated, then nodded. "Yes."

Micah thumped the point of his pistol into the man's forehead with a loud crack. "Liar. Where's Herst?"

As Henry wailed in pain, Gid's chin shot up. His eyes widened, and he immediately turned to sprint back toward the camp.

He'd left Mercy and the children alone!

Chapter Seven

All Mercy's fears had come upon her.

Herst had caught up to these fine people, bringing his fires of destruction with him.

She had squatted on their pallet, watching in horror as Micah caught and cradled Georgia's lifeless body for mere moments, and then both men had sprinted from the encampment.

She dragged Av closer to her side and kept her arm around him, waiting for her nightmare to step into the light. Terrified that he would have hold of her before she could see him.

Then he stepped out of the inky night. Taking up a long branch from the pile of wood by the firepit, he thrust it into the still-red coals until it caught flame. He threw two more logs onto the coals, and a blaze flared with traitorous light.

Mercy sank into the shadows and willed herself to breathe quietly as she cowered with Av against the trunk of the nearest tree, praying Herst wouldn't come in this direction.

When he turned toward the wagon, she felt relief, but then she remembered poor young Joel, cowering inside.

She eased Avram from her, pressed his back against the trunk of the tall pine, and put her finger to her lips. She motioned for him to remain still as she crouched, ready to move if she had to.

Avram rocked silently, terror trembling through him, but she couldn't comfort him without drawing Herst's attention to him. All she could do was rub his small, heaving chest with the hope that it would soothe him.

When Herst reached Georgia's body, he crouched and raised the firebrand to see her face.

Mercy heard his soft curse the moment he realized Georgia wasn't her.

He pivoted on the balls of his feet and tilted his head to study their encampment.

She held her breath. *Just go.*

But he did not go. He remained—searching for her, she knew without a doubt. This whole thing was her fault!

Despair threatened to choke her.

If she tried to run, she would never escape him, especially not in her current condition. He was a large man, but she knew from experience that he moved with surprising agility and swiftness. Today, she hadn't had enough warning.

She was still trying to decide what to do when Joel hurled himself from the back of the wagon. "Leave my ma alone!" He landed on Herst's back, biting and gouging and kicking. He knocked Herst's hat from his head and grabbed two handfuls of his hair, yanking hard.

"No, Joel!" Mercy leaped forward even as Herst reached back with one beefy hand, grabbed Joel by his hair, and flung him toward the fire!

For one heart-stopping moment, Joel seemed to be suspended in the air, arms and legs sprawled, eyes wide with horror.

Mercy felt as though each of her feet were mired in mud. Each step met with resistance. Each breath carved painful channels through her lungs.

Too slow.

The fire glowed orange against Joel's skin as he began a downward arc.

Never enough.

Joel's mouth opened, and a whimper escaped.

Her fault.

No time!

Arm outstretched, she dove.

Her hand mercifully connected with Joel's shoulder. She pushed him hard toward the grassy spot between the log and the rock where she'd sat earlier. He landed with a thud.

She cried out her relief.

Then sand and shale gouged into her palms. Something hammered into the space just beneath her ribs, and all the air left her. Agony shocked her into stillness. Struggling to breathe, she felt heat enveloping her ankle! She forced herself to roll further from the fire and sit up. Her skirt was on fire! She beat at it with her hands, thankful when it extinguished to a mere charred hole with black edges.

She lay back in the grass, willing herself not to pass out. Even the tiniest inhale felt like she was swallowing shards of glass.

And then Herst leaned over her and planted his boot on her chest.

She cried out, hating the satisfied smirk that curved his lips.

Herst drew his pistol and pointed it at her head.

So, this was it then.

In the distance, Mattox's barking quieted. Everything seemed unnaturally silent, as though the disturbed nature collectively held its breath.

Hatred narrowed his beady eyes to mere slits. He leaned forward, adding more of his weight onto her as he propped both arms against his knee.

She rolled her lips in and sealed them tight. Breathed through her nose. Managed to clamp off an outcry this time.

He didn't like it. He sucked his teeth. "Did you think you could escape me, Mercy, darlin'?" One corner of his lip ticked up like a snarling wolf.

She wouldn't answer him, and she didn't want her last view on this earth to be his leering face. She looked to the swath of stars above instead.

Midnight blue stretched in a smooth dome pierced through with pricks of light. She focused on the brightest one.

When Herst added even more of his weight to her, she lost the rest of the breath in her lungs in one long, slow, unquenchable whimper.

Her one regret was that she hadn't managed to save Avram from his father.

God, please. Help him get away.

There she went praying hopeless prayers again. She immediately felt guilt at the thought and fought through the haze of pain clouding her mind to voice an apology. "I'm s-sorry. Forgive me."

Herst grunted. "Not likely."

She didn't bother to correct his misperception. She hadn't been talking to him.

"Where's my boy?" Herst gritted.

Mercy shook her head. That was one thing he would never be able to torture from her.

He cocked his pistol, the sound loud in the stillness of the night. "I ain't gonna ask you again, woman."

"Good . . . because . . . I wouldn't . . . tell you." She had to fight for each breath now, and spots floated in and out of her vision.

"Well, don't worry." He straightened suddenly and spat to one side.

The loss of his weight was almost more painful than the addition of it had been, but this time, her cry was because she knew she'd run out of time.

"I'll find him."

She caught a glimpse of him leveling his pistol toward her head before she squeezed her eyes shut. *Please don't let Avram see.*

The shot blasted through the night. Followed closely by two more. *Bang! Bang-bang!*

Mercy winced tighter and tighter with each report, then realized that she'd felt nothing. She uncoiled herself and looked up.

Herst stumbled back a step, mouth agape. His pistol fell, landing in the grass with a soft thud. He braced himself with a sideways step and reached to touch his chest.

Mercy's eyes widened. For in the light of the fire, she could clearly see a gaping wound over the left pocket of his shirt.

And then he fell backward like a toppled tree.

"Oh, dear God." Shock and horror collided. She scrambled backward on all fours. Stabs of pain pulsed through her chest. With a cry, she collapsed to her side, curling into a ball that she never hoped to move from again.

"Mercy!" Gid called. Footsteps slapped the ground.

She didn't move. Didn't even want to breathe.

She heard him kick Herst's gun away. And it was a few moments before he fell to his knees by her side. "Are you okay?"

"Is he dead?" she whispered.

"Yes. I just checked."

"Please get Avram. Check Joel."

From the corner of her eye, she saw him lift his head. "Joel already has him. They're both fine. Right here by the fire. You're all safe."

Safe.

She could hardly comprehend the word.

Yet it eased through her, loosing coiled muscles and tight fists.

At least until she remembered Georgia.

She forced herself to push through the agony and turn her head. She looked toward the covered wagon where Georgia still lay on the ground. She wanted to say how sorry she was, but the words seemed flat and unhelpful.

Micah dragged back into the camp with Mattox by his side.

"Where's Henry?" Gideon looked toward the field across the road.

Micah shook his head as he fell listlessly to his knees by Georgia's side. "He bled out. Didn't make it." He used one finger to gently brush a strand of Georgia's hair away from her face.

Mercy looked down, unable to handle the wretchedness and guilt she felt at the way his shoulders sagged.

"Pa?" Joel's voice trembled.

Micah waved him over. "Come here, son."

Joel ran until he crashed into Micah's chest. He buried his face in his father's neck and sobbed long and loud.

Micah's big hand rubbed up and down against his back, but he never took his eyes off the lifeless body of his wife.

Mercy blinked, trying to clear away the black spots that were dancing in her vision again. The pain radiating from the side of her chest where Herst had practically stood on her nearly blinded her.

"Mama?" Av's soft little hand touched her cheek, but she couldn't find the breath to answer him just yet.

Gideon felt empty. Lifeless. Hopeless.

The sight of Joel sobbing on his father's shoulder made him want to collapse. Instead, he stood and yanked a canvas tarp from the back of his wagon.

The law would have to be fetched come morning, but until then, they needed to preserve Henry and Herst's bodies and the scenes as best they could. If they hoped to prove their innocence in this, he also needed to secure Henry's rifle so the law could have it as evidence. At least, he assumed that was the weapon that had taken the life of his sister.

Herst didn't seem to have a gun that could have made that shot from that distance.

They might not know more until morning because he couldn't search for a gun without potentially bungling the evidence. But he'd noted the rifle near Henry earlier.

He strode away from the distressing scene near the wagon with the tarp clasped in one hand.

At the top of the hill, he found Henry, expired from his injuries, just as Micah had said. He stretched the tarp flat on the downhill side of the man and then rolled his body repeatedly until he was firmly encased in the tarp. He slung the rifle over his shoulder and then set about dragging the body back down the hill where it would be nearer to the firepit.

Fear of the flames would keep all but the most desperate critters at bay.

By the time he returned to the camp, sweating from exertion, for Henry wasn't a small man by any means, no one seemed to have moved except Joel, who now sat on his father's lap. Georgia remained distressingly uncovered, almost appearing to be asleep if it weren't for the ugly, dried, black stain on her shirt.

Mercy remained in a curled ball on her side, and Avram, seated on the end of the nearby log, rocked in distress, with his eyes seemingly tethered to his father's body.

Gid frowned. It troubled him to think that the boy might have seen him kill his father. He dragged the tarped roll next to Herst and freed one end enough to also drape it over him.

He should go and see if Micah would let him deal with Georgia, but he couldn't bring himself to face that yet. He'd been with his sister from the time they'd shared a womb. It seemed unfathomable that she was gone. He had no one now.

He approached Avram.

The boy's dark curls tousled in a breeze as he sat hunched into his shoulders with his little hands pressed between his knees. He rocked faster the closer Gideon drew.

He stopped several paces away. "I'm sorry about your pa, Av." He wasn't sorry. He shouldn't have said it. But he wanted to relieve some of the kid's distress.

Av snapped his gaze to him. His rocking eased slightly. He pointed one short finger toward his mother.

Gideon's heart lurched, and he wrenched his focus to Mercy. Only then did he realize how deathly still she lay. He bolted forward, his mind going to the way that Herst had stood over her with his boot planted on her chest.

He fell to his knees by her side. "Mercy?" The material at the shoulder of her blouse felt cool beneath the pads of his fingers when he touched her. "Mercy? You all right?"

The only response he got was a strangled moan.

Without another thought, he rolled her onto her back.

One of her arms flopped to the side, and she made a strangulated sound at the back of her throat, but other than that, she didn't move. Her eyes were closed, and even in the dim light of the fire, he could see that her lips were an unnatural blue. "Micah! I need you over here right now!"

Micah was always the one who knew how to treat the animals' ailments back home. Would he know what to do now?

Micah nudged Joel off his lap, but he wasn't moving fast enough.

Gid pressed his cheek close to her nose. "Micah, she's scarcely breathing!"

Micah leapt up and jogged to him. He dropped to his knees, nudging Gideon aside as he felt the pulse in her neck, then lowered one ear to her chest and listened for a moment. He snapped his head up and studied the rise and fall of her chest.

At first, Gid thought she had stopped breathing altogether, but then he noticed very slight movement, but only on her left side.

Micah dove for the pile of turkey feathers by the fire. "Get me the bottle of spirits from Georgia's medicine box."

Gid hurried to do as instructed. He stepped around Georgia, biting off a cry of grief as he did so, and found the box at the back of the wagon in easy reach when he lowered the tailgate. The corked bottle of whiskey chilled his sweating palm.

By the time he returned to the fire, Micah had stripped away all of the feather except the thick, hollow quill. With one quick thrust of his knife, he sliced an angled cut that left the quill sharply pointed on one end. He chopped the other end off flat and then blew through the quill.

Gid heard air whistle.

Micah gave a nod of satisfaction and scrambled back to Mercy's side.

He felt the ribs on her right side, seeming to be counting up from the bottom of her ribcage. Then, with his knife, he sliced her blouse and ripped the material aside. Beneath her shirt lay the tightly wrapped bandages that Georgia had bound her broken ribs with. Had that only been yesterday?

Gid wanted to bellow at the sky.

Micah cut away that binding too, and then snatched the bottle of spirits and doused the feather, his hands, and her side liberally.

Mercy rolled her head from side to side and pathetically tried to push Micah away.

"Gid, I need you to hold her arms. Now!"

Gid edged closer to do as he was told on the opposite side of her from Micah. "It's all right, Mercy. We're here to help you." He eased her arms above her head and held them there as gently as he could.

Micah seemed to have found the spot he was looking for. He shoved the sharpened point of the feather straight into her chest.

"Micah!" Gid gasped.

A short, sharp sound, like steam escaping a locomotive, burst through the quill.

"What are you doing!" He reached to snatch the shaft of the feather out of her.

But Micah pushed his hand away, and Mercy gasped, drawing in a huge breath and then writhing in pain. She coughed. Wheezed a moan. Coughed again.

After a few panted breaths, she opened her eyes. They widened as they settled on the knife Gid only now saw that Micah had clamped between his lips. She struggled to sit, and Gid scooted closer to help her. She gaped at the blood seeping into her blouse and then shot a glance, wide and full of fear, to Micah, who now gripped the hilt of his knife.

She raised trembling palms, "Please . . . forgive me . . . For . . . my son."

Terror warbled her words.

Micah shook his head and gritted, "I'm not trying to kill you. Here." He eased her gently back to the ground. "You must lay still for a few minutes. If you have a punctured lung, air will continue to come from this tube. Let's hope that doesn't happen because you're not likely to survive such an injury."

Gideon planted his fists against his thighs and hauled in a lungful of air that he held for several beats and then released through pursed lips. His brother-in-law was as sapheaded as they came. Gid moved until he could capture Mercy's attention. "You're not going to die."

But Mercy didn't seem to hear him. If possible, her face went even more pale.

Gid scowled at Micah, who was now removing his coat.

But Micah didn't pay him any mind. He leaned over Mercy, wadding the leather into a pillow beneath her head. "Sometimes, however, air can get into your chest from a bruising blow. In that case, we'll just need to wait for a few hours before cauterizing this wound. Just lay still until I tell you otherwise, understand?"

Mercy's eyes were nearly as large as the moon climbing into the dome of the sky, but her lips weren't so blue anymore.

Gideon laced his hands at the back of his neck. He couldn't imagine all that this woman had been through and now the best-case scenario was that they would have to cauterize the hole Micah had just stabbed in her chest? It made him feel sick just to think of it.

With a defeated droop of his shoulders, Micah glanced toward Georgia. "Gid, I need your help."

His throat felt as though it was strangled by a strong fist, so he only nodded. They couldn't just leave her lying there like that.

Micah gave Mercy another order not to move and then strode toward his wife and son.

Joel hadn't left his mother's side for the past several minutes, and after they fetched a blanket from inside the wagon, it took some coaxing to get him to let go of Georgia's hand.

Micah laid the quilt out beside her, and then he lifted Georgia's shoulders while Gid lifted her feet. He sobbed as they positioned her on the blanket. He couldn't help himself. He ground his molars until he regained control.

Micah didn't make a sound as he gently wrapped her, tucking the blanket tight, and then they carried her closer to the light of the fire.

Micah scrubbed his palms against his trousers, as though to rub the feel of her dead weight from his hands, and then he purposefully added two large logs to the fire. They would need to keep the blaze going now to keep critters at bay.

They brought the canvas Mercy had planned to sleep on closer to the fire and helped Mercy onto it. Micah removed the tailgates from both wagons and the top rails from his own wagon bed. Gideon helped him—holding boards as he cut them, bracing joints as they were nailed together. Once the coffin was done, they set it to one side. None of them were ready for their last glimpse of Georgia yet.

After that, Micah checked Mattox over, declared that he looked fine, and then they sat for hours simply staring into the flames. Gid couldn't seem to process any of it. So much loss. So much heartache. So much burden sitting on him and threatening to crush the life from him. Joel and Avram eventually fell asleep. Once in a while, Mercy shifted as though trying to find a more comfortable spot.

Finally, when the first bloom of daylight blushed the horizon, Micah took the lid hook from where it lay atop the cleaned Dutch oven and thrust the cast iron handle right into the coals.

Gid swallowed.

After that was done, Micah returned to Mercy's side. Gid trailed after him, feeling helpless to do anything other than follow his lead.

"You been hearing any air hissing out of that?" Micah asked as he knelt by Mercy on the canvas.

She blinked tiredly and gave a little shake of her head. "I don't think so."

Gid noted the glistening tracks of tears that trailed back into her hair. How long had she been lying here crying? He hadn't known a woman could cry so quietly. His fists clenched. Why was life so unfair?

"Good. That's real good." Micah leaned down and placed his ear close to the tube, holding up a hand for silence. After a few moments, he rose upright. "I think you're right. That's good news." He leaned over Mercy and looked her right in the eyes. "So here's what's going to happen. First, I'm going to give you several swigs of whiskey. Then, I'm going to have to pull that quill back out of your chest. And then we'll need to cauterize the wound quickly. Understand?"

Mercy swallowed hard but nodded.

"Right. Let's sit you up." He nodded for Gideon to help him on the other side of her.

Gid fell to his knees and eased an arm behind her back. Together, they helped her into a sitting position. He expected her to cry out, but she didn't make a sound other than a small, sharp hiss.

"Here." Micah thrust the bottle of spirits into Gid's hand and motioned that he should help her drink.

Gid urged her to take several sputtering swallows as he watched Micah stalk toward the fire. He removed a thick leather glove from his back pocket and donned it, but instead of reaching for the glowing metal handle as Gid expected him to, he sank down on the log and propped his elbows on his knees.

He must have felt Gid's frown because he looked over. "We'll give the alcohol some time to work."

Gid kept pressing the bottle to her lips until she raised one hand and pushed it away. Still, Micah waited. After several minutes, her head lolled to one side.

Micah gave a short, curt nod, stood, and yanked the glowing red handle from the fire. "Let's be quick. Lift her shirt."

Gid carefully lifted the hem of her blouse over the quill and pushed aside the tattered shreds of the binding that were left after Micah's knife had done its earlier work. Her whole side was mottled blues and purples and golds. He remembered Georgia's description of it, but he hadn't felt the deep impact then that he felt now.

Feeling sick, Gid looked up. He could see a muscle working in and out on Micah's jaw as he took in the bruising, but he only said, "Lay her flat and hold her steady."

Gid followed orders.

Micah stood by her side, and with his free hand, he yanked the turkey feather from her chest and then immediately pressed the glowing handle to the wound.

Flesh sizzled.

Mercy gasped and gave one futile jerk, but then the task was done.

"Fine job. You did fine." Micah collapsed wearily against his ankles. His gaze drifted back to the quilt that encased Georgia as he motioned that Gid should take over now. "Get a rag and soak it in cold water, then wring it out. Put it on the burn to help cool it. We'll put egg whites on it after about an hour. In a couple of days, we can put a mixture of honey and lard on it."

Gid tugged his bandana from around his neck and followed instructions. With the cool cloth resting on Mercy's skin and her somewhere between wakefulness and sleep, Gid watched in sorrow as Micah shuffled right back to Georgia and sank down beside her, drawing Joel onto his lap in the firelight that was losing its brightness to the creeping dawn.

Chapter Eight

Mercy woke to the sound of voices. She frowned at the bright sunlight filtering through the canvas stretched tight over the arched stays above. Where was she?

Something shuffled by her side.

Cautiously, she turned her head.

Avram stood looking down at her with large, solemn brown eyes. His little hands were clutched tightly before him.

Mercy reached a hand to soothe the tension from his brow. "Hi, love." She hoped her smile didn't seem too forced because her whole body vibrated with agonizing waves. She eased in an inhale and then released it on a long slow push between pursed lips. She soothed Av's forehead again. "You look so serious."

He relaxed a little, seemingly happy to have her speaking to him. Leaning close, he pressed the gentlest of kisses against her cheek. "You bettew?"

Waves of agony sluiced through her when she nodded. She tried a whisper instead. "I'll be just fine. Have you had breakfast?"

The boy's brow slumped. He dipped his chin. "That man maked oatmeal."

Humor tilted the corners of her mouth. She wasn't sure if he meant Gideon or Micah, but she knew the frown had its genesis in the fact that Av hated oatmeal.

"I bet you're still hungry then?" She stroked his hair, trying to ignore the waves of agony in her side.

He nodded. "But we gots a wabbit fow lunch."

"That's nice."

Now that she was a little more awake, she searched their surroundings and realized that they must be inside the Morrans' covered wagon. Av stood in the narrow aisle that led to the tailgate. This soft tick that she found herself on was at the front of the wagon bed, just behind and parallel to the driver's bench. On either side of the aisle, crate after crate was stacked one atop another and strapped to the stays all the way to the top of the canvas.

It was a good setup that kept the crates from falling and also kept the wagon balanced.

It seemed that she'd not only taken Gid's bed under his wagon, but now Micah's and Joel's inside theirs.

She looked back at Av. "Where's Joel?"

His shoulders bobbed. "We not feel like playing today."

With one finger, she swept a curl off his forehead. "I understand, love. I'm sorry about Pa."

His brow slumped, and anger filled his dark eyes. He folded tiny arms over his chest. Other than that, he made no response.

She wished she could know what was going through that little head of his. But she would leave it be for now. "Where is everyone?"

He relaxed a little at that question. "Joel's pa is sitting by his ma. Uncle Gid told me to stay in hewe with you. He went to get the shewiff."

"I see." Weariness sapped her strength.

Of course, that was logical since he would need to learn of what happened here and maybe even collect the bodies of Herst and his cousin. But . . .

Had they sent for the sheriff for more than just that reason? Would she be carted off for her part in this? If he had ridden back to Chamblissburg . . . Sheriff Cooper, who had grown up with Herst, had never seemed to like her. She hadn't the energy to contemplate what he might do.

She ought to rise but couldn't find the strength to even move, much less stand. She tried to pull in a deep breath, but a sharp spasm made her pause. Gingerly she felt the spot on her side that seemed to be the origin of the excruciation. A cloth was tied around her ribs. A shudder slipped through her when she recalled sitting up the evening before to find Micah leaning over her with his knife. She frowned. They must have added this tight binding around her at some point, but she had no memory of it. Had she passed out? She must have because she also had no recollection of being transferred to this bed.

She could feel the throb of each pulse in her temples like a hammer tapping away at her. If only the agony would cease.

Her eyes felt heavy. So heavy.

Her mouth dry. She worked her tongue over her cracked lips.

"We gots watew." She heard Av grunting softly as he struggled to lift something from the floor. He rose into view a moment later with a bota held carefully in both little hands. He pushed it toward her. "I can't open it."

With her eyes closed against the throbbing that crested over her in waves, Mercy worked to tug the stopper from the end of the bag. Once the agonizing task was accomplished, she held the bag so that Av could drink and then drank thirstily herself.

Av took another deep draw, and when he stepped back and wiped his mouth with the back of his hand, she stoppered the bag once again. And that was all the energy she had. She handed the bota back to Av and heard him settle it on the floor.

"Mama's going to sleep a little longer. Stay in the wagon, okay?"

She heard him sigh, but the bliss of sleep had already sucked her under.

"But my ma telled me to stay in hewe!" Av's cry woke Mercy from a sound sleep. She jolted upright, every instinct screaming for her to come to his protection.

She was halfway to a sitting position when she realized it was only Gideon trying to coax Av from the wagon.

So he was back with the sheriff, then?

Gid's lips pressed into a grim line. "Sorry about that. He's been in here all day, and I thought he might need the necessary."

The mention of it brought her own need into sharp focus. "Yes, maybe we both could step away for a few minutes." She swung her legs over the edge of the bed and was embarrassed to see that her feet were bare, and her blouse torn.

Gid looked down. "Uh, your boots are here, just outside the wagon." He disappeared for a moment and then reappeared to thrust her boots and stockings through the opening. After setting them down, he pointed. "Micah left you a shirt there."

She turned to see a white blouse folded neatly on a crate near the bed.

"Thank you." She felt as though she'd wandered into a stranger's life. Who had cared for her enough to remove her boots so that she would sleep better? She'd never had a thoughtful man like that in her life. "Av, it's okay for you to go with Gid now. I'll be right out, okay?"

Gid looked torn. "Wait for me, and I'll help you down after you get your shoes on. Are you sure you should be moving?" He hoisted a now-compliant Av to the ground as he spoke.

For a man who may have called the sheriff to have her arrested, he acted rather friendly.

"I'll be fine." She said the words, but when Gid and Av disappeared from the opening, she couldn't bring herself to move. She looked at her boots. They seemed an insurmountable distance below her.

Finally, she painstakingly lowered her feet to the floor and padded the length of the wagon. After a long moment of looking at the boots again, she grabbed the edge of one of the crates and bent her knees to lower herself. That allowed her to keep her back stiff. Even so, spots danced before her eyes.

How was she ever going to get the boots on her feet? The only way would simply be to shore up her gumption and bear it.

It took her several agonizing minutes, but with the task done, she now faced the even more daunting task of getting out of the wagon.

She approached the opening and cautiously poked her head out to assess the best way to descend with the least movement possible.

Gid was pacing nearby and hurried to her the moment he saw her.

Caution raised a moment of panic. Where was Av? There. Relief flooded her. He sat near the firepit. The same firepit she had saved Joel from falling into.

Dread swept in to expunge her relief. So just as she'd worried, they hadn't moved on from the place of the tragedy. She'd wondered how long she might have slept. What would happen to Av if she was carted off to jail?

"Wait one moment," Gid said. He tugged two crates from within, creating a set of steps to help her descend. He then reached out one hand to take hers.

She couldn't bring herself to take his hand. "Are you having me arrested?"

His gaze snapped to hers. "What? No. What do you mean?"

She studied him. Nothing but sincerity shone in his blue eyes. She relaxed, if only marginally.

Relieved not to have to battle through another round of agony, she accepted his help, and when she returned from the brush, she sank down on the log next to Av. Gid was there, seated next to them on the rock.

Thankfully, none of the bodies were in sight, but neither were Joel or Micah. A familiar buckboard sat nearby, however. She swallowed.

So they had sent for Sheriff Cooper, after all. Even if Gid hadn't demanded her arrest, she would likely be in for a rough time.

Gideon concentrated on a pair of boots that he was oiling.

"How long have I been sleeping?" she asked.

He looked up. "All night and most of the day. I was starting to worry."

Her brow furrowed. "I'll be fine. I'm surprised we haven't moved on?"

He returned his focus to the boots. Dipped his cloth back in the boot oil before he said, "We weren't certain if you would want to continue with us now that . . ." He shrugged and tipped his head back in the direction of town. "We thought you might want to go home. And we all needed some time to grieve for . . ." He swallowed hard. "Georgia."

She rolled her lips in and pressed them together. She had zero desire to return to Chamblissburg. Herst's land had been under threat of repossession by the bank for months due to his lack of payment. She'd been doing whatever side jobs she could and giving that to the bank to keep them from being dispossessed.

However, she had no desire to go back to that town of people who had known what she faced on a daily basis and never once stood up for her.

She had nothing to go back to.

No family other than Pa, and he would remind her daily what a failure she was for causing her husband's death.

No possessions.

Of course, Gideon and Micah likely wouldn't want to travel on with her as a constant reminder of what she'd cost them. Would they even let her accompany them to the next town? Neither of them had really wanted her to join their caravan in the first place. And now, with Georgia gone, she wouldn't blame them for refusing to allow her to continue.

But perhaps they would be kind enough to take her to the next town with them as they'd previously discussed. There, she could try to find work.

Even before she'd learned that Gideon and Micah were heading west, she'd planned to escape there. Now, even though Herst's death gave her more choices, she found that she couldn't quite let that dream go.

She would just have to find a way to get to Independence on her own. And then she would stick to her plan and hire on with a wagon train and take Av west.

West to the promise of a brighter future.

Hopefully they could now leave all the troubles of their past behind them.

Micah and Joel strode into view with another man.

Mercy stiffened. Sheriff Cooper.

His lips pressed into a thin line when he saw her, but he did touch the brim of his hat. "Mrs. Adler, I hope you can see now what tragedy has been wrought by your disobedience to your husband."

Mercy's jaw fell slack. She'd known the man was callous. After all, he hadn't locked Herst up on any of the multiple occasions when she'd gone to him after Herst had nearly beaten her to death. But she hadn't pegged him as a man who thought all the beatings were her own fault.

Gid leaped to his feet before she could even blink. He took a step toward the sheriff, but Micah, his face impassive, stretched out a hand to stop him.

Gid seemed to rethink what he'd been about to say and instead offered stiffly, "Will you be needing anything more from us, Sheriff?"

The man resettled his hat and shook his head. "No. I reckon you can ride on. It's pretty clear that Herst and Henry came hunting trouble."

A muscle bunched in Gid's cheek. "They came hunting my sister, you mean."

"No." The sheriff shook his head. "They came hunting her—" one blunt finger stabbed in her direction "—and your sister just happened to be in the wrong place."

Mercy swallowed. His tone left no doubt that he felt the world would be a better place if Herst and Henry had succeeded. Despair sloped her shoulders. Maybe it would be. Oh, the regret she would always carry for costing these good men the woman they loved.

Gideon's fists balled tight, and he paced away from the lawman.

Micah hooked his thumbs into his belt loops and hung his head. "Seems to me, Sheriff, that if you'd done your job on any number of occasions, Herst here would have been locked up. Maybe Henry too." He spoke the words so calmly that at first he seemed a bit indifferent, but the hard, cold glare that he settled on the sheriff was anything but.

Mattox stood from where he'd been lying near the wagon and lowered his big black head, eyes fixed on the sheriff. A low growl rumbled from deep in the recesses of his thick chest.

Micah continued to hold the sheriff's eyes.

And this time, Mercy could see that a flame of anger threatened to become an all-out blaze. Her stomach quavered. Micah topped the sheriff by a good six inches and probably outweighed him by fifty pounds, but she'd once seen Cooper draw on an outlaw and knew he was fast.

"Micah," she cautioned, rising to take a step forward.

With a blink, Micah retreated a pace from Sheriff Cooper.

Mercy released a breath.

At a snap from Micah's fingers, Mattox sank to his haunches but never took his golden gaze from the sheriff.

Fixing his attention on the dirt before him, Micah spoke softly. The flames in his demeanor had died. In their place, all that remained was icy despair. "I reckon we'll be moving out, then. Soon as we bury my wife."

"Th-that would be f-fine." The lawman cautioned a glance at Mattox, backing away slowly at first and then pivoting sharply on one heel and practically dashing toward his wagon.

With her hands clasped in her lap, Mercy watched Sheriff Cooper beat his hasty retreat. She massaged one thumb over the other.

One chapter in her life was closing. What would the new chapter hold?

At least now she didn't have the worry of Herst catching up with her. Lord forgive her for the sheer relief that realization brought.

They were now blessedly alone, she and Av. But they would be fine. Because nothing could be worse than what they'd already survived.

Now she only had to figure out what skills she could use to make a living and provide for her son.

Chapter Nine

Gideon stood next to Micah with his hat pressed over his heart. The gaping hole that he'd helped Micah dig lay before them, a dark maw waiting to swallow the sweetest and best of sisters. They'd picked a pretty spot surrounded by wildflowers on a knoll high above the creek.

Micah had spent a good portion of the afternoon washing Georgia and dressing her in her best gown. Now he held the Good Book in his hands, and Georgia lay in the coffin inside the hole.

They hadn't covered her yet, and Gideon studied her, hardly able to believe this was the last time he would see his "baby" sister as he used to tease her she was—even though she'd been born a mere fifteen minutes after him. She would often retort by calling him "old man."

Though the memory brought a smile to his lips, it also raised a sob from deep inside him. He gulped it down before he could embarrass himself.

In her hands, she held the bouquet of wildflowers that he had helped Joel pick. He had no idea the names of any of the flowers, but there were purples, pinks, oranges, and yellows, and he had a feeling Georgia would have approved of the colors against the plain dark blue of her good dress. Mercy had seen the bunch when they'd returned from the fields, and with a few adjustments—moving one flower here and another there—she'd deftly shaped the bouquet into a beautiful oval of melded colors that Georgia now held clasped in her hands.

Cold, lifeless hands. Would Micah ever get on with it? This was too painful. Gid glanced over at his brother-in-law. He'd offered to speak, but Micah had insisted he should be the one to do so. It seemed Micah was struggling with the task.

Despite wanting to escape this painful ceremony, Gid didn't actually mind the wait. For as soon as Micah said a few words, it would be time to cover her with the lid of the crude coffin and then the mound of dirt. He could hardly fathom leaving her here in the dust of the earth all alone.

He wanted to cry out with the torture of it.

None of them were ready to face that reality. He certainly wasn't. His heart ached. It had already been aching something fierce for the past two months since they'd lost Jess and Verona and his unborn little one. He'd thought his heart at full capacity for pain, but apparently not.

This ache was compounded by the guilt.

If only he'd listened to Georgia's caution and hadn't helped Mercy . . .

But the moment that thought entered his mind, he wondered what kind of man that made him? Remorse swept over him. He never ought to regret helping someone. But if he hadn't helped her, Georgia would still be here.

And the cycle went round and round in an unrelenting whirlpool of anguish.

Mercy stood at the side of the hole with Av and Joel by her sides. Her hands rested on each of their shoulders. He imagined that it couldn't be any too comfortable for her to be standing there so long, but she hadn't moved or even shifted.

He was a cad for wishing that he hadn't helped her, and that was the truth of it.

Yet he couldn't help the surge of anger that overcame him. "Why did you marry that bas—" He checked himself with a glance at the boys.

Micah tossed him a surprised look even as Mercy lifted wide eyes to him.

He lowered his focus to his hat. Crimped the crown. Dusted the brim. "Never mind. Sorry."

Still, Micah didn't speak.

Silence stretched.

From the corner of his eye, he saw Mercy lift her chin. "He ravished me."

What? Gid's shocked gaze darted to hers.

Her eyes snapped with indignation and anger. Her chin jutted higher.

She had married a man who ravished her?

Shoulders thrown back, she met him look for look. "I was coming home from a social. A boy walked me to the base of the path that led to our door and said his farewells. Before I could reach home, Herst . . . Well, he . . ." She waved the explanation away.

Gideon felt his brow slump. He didn't understand. How could she have married someone like that?

Apparently, Micah didn't understand either because he asked, "And still you married him?"

Mercy swallowed. "I crawled home and told my father. He . . . strapped me because he said my wayward ways had shamed our family."

Gid exchanged a look with Micah, seeing the same horror he felt reflected in his brother-in-law's eyes.

Mercy continued. "After that . . ." Her eyes lowered to Avram, who stood beside her studying his little hands. "Well, Father marched me to Herst's house a few weeks later at the point of a gun. The minister was there, waiting, and though I protested, he pronounced us husband and wife without my consent." A glimmer of challenge sparked in her eye. Her chin rose another notch higher as though she were challenging him to judge her in such a manner again. "I went to the sheriff. Yes, that very sheriff who just drove away with Herst's and Henry's bodies in the back of his wagon. He told me the ceremony was legal, and there was nothing I could do about it."

Gid's guilt over his anger compounded and then compounded again. He swallowed. "I'm sorry. I spoke out of despair. Your situation is . . . incomprehensible."

Mercy lowered her lashes and pressed her lips together. "I'm very sorry to have dragged my misery upon you."

Micah's expression turned soft as he studied the face of his wife. "If Georgia had been herself, she would have insisted that we help you that day. It was her own grief filtering the way she saw you. You were a reminder of all that we'd recently lost." His gaze slid to Avram, before darting back to Georgia's body.

Gid settled a hand on his brother-in-law's shoulder. "You're right. It was unlike her to refuse help to anyone. Why I recall a hobo that she brought home one time when we were kids. Said she'd found him wandering down the back side of the orchard and figured he might be hungry." Gid couldn't help a chuckle. "Ma was horrified. But the old guy was harmless and right appreciative of Georgia's generosity."

Micah's lips slanted into the semblance of a smile. But his eyes were red and glistening. He nodded. "Yeah. She was like that. Even on this trip . . ." He gestured to the wagon in the distance. "She insisted that I bring an extra crate of rice and another of jerky so that we could help anyone who might have need."

"Even though our circumstances were . . . difficult," Mercy added, "she was gentle and sympathetic as she helped me the other day. I think that we would have been friends—at least, I hoped that we would."

Her voice grew soft on those last words, and Gideon felt a renewed determination not to hold her responsible for her lout of a husband's actions.

Micah cleared his throat. "I've been standing here trying to figure out what to say. She was too good for me, and well I knew it. But when I had a dream to see what lay in Oregon, she supported me immediately even though it meant leaving all that she'd ever known behind." His voice broke. "I'll always . . . regret . . . asking that of her."

Gid blinked as he realized he wasn't sure if Micah would want to continue on to Oregon. Would this tragedy make him want to give up his dream? Yet, they'd sold everything they owned back home. What else were they going to do?

Whatever decision he made, Gid supposed that he would stick with him. They were all each other had now. And he wouldn't want to lose touch, especially not with Joel. The boy looked so much like his mother that it made Gid's heart ache to look at him.

Micah had been holding the Good Book in his hands for so long that Gideon wondered if he would ever read from it, but he drew it nearer now and flopped it open to the place where his finger had been saving a passage.

His voice was rough when he began to speak. "Georgia would have wanted me to read from the Good Book. And these verses from Proverbs, chapter thirty-one . . . Well, they speak for themselves, I guess." He worked his lips in and out, trying to compose himself. After a long moment, he pulled in a deep breath and continued . . . "A wife of noble character who can find? She is worth far more than rubies."

As Micah read, Gideon's thoughts turned to memories. The red ribbons Georgia wore in her hair on their first day of school. The mangy kitten she rescued from their neighbor's barn and nursed back to health. The way she tended both their ma and their pa in their hours of passing. The joy that filled her eyes the day she'd proudly presented Joel to him.

He shook the memories away and forced himself to listen to Micah.

"Charm is deceptive, and beauty is fleeting; but a woman who fears the Lord is to be praised. Honor her for all that her hands have done, and let her works bring her praise at the city gate."

When he'd finished reading and closed the Bible, silence hung heavy for a moment. Then Micah concluded. "Georgia, honey, I honor you . . . We honor you for all that you did in this life. I love you."

"I love you too, Mama." Joel's voice was barely audible above the rush of the wind.

Gideon felt too choked up to say anything at all.

Finally, Joel spoke up. "Pa?"

"Yes, son?"

"We don't got no city gate."

Humor penetrated enough of Gideon's grief to bring a smile.

Micah dropped a hand on Joel's shoulder. "I know, son. But we will. Somewhere out in Oregon. We'll build one ourselves if we have to."

Gid swiped one hand around the back of his neck. He supposed that answered his question well enough.

Looked like they were still headed to Oregon.

He transferred his regard to Mercy. One of her hands remained on each of the boys' shoulders.

What would she do now that she needn't worry about fleeing her husband?

Micah asked him to say a prayer, which he did, keeping it short because he didn't feel like anything he had to say was quite right in this situation. And then they nailed the lid onto the coffin and lowered dear Georgia into the ground. It just about killed him to throw the first shovelful of dirt.

Dust to dust.

It was a sobering reality that drove spikes of agony through his heart.

When Micah insisted that Mercy could use his wagon again that night, she tried to refuse. She didn't want to take anything more from him. But he pressed without relenting until she gave in.

She and Av slept on the soft feather tick.

Av slept soundly. However, she tossed fitfully because of her pain and woke with the first rays of dawn, feeling almost more tired than she had when she went to sleep. By the time both men arrived at the fire, she had painstakingly worked her way through making a meal of oatmeal and hard-boiled eggs. They all ate in silence, and when the wagons were packed and ready to roll, neither man protested when she requested to walk.

She knew it would cause them further delay, but she couldn't face hours of jostling on the seat beside Gideon. The walking wasn't much better. If she went too fast and breathed too hard, the shooting agony almost took her to her knees. If she slowed, the day would only stretch longer, and she hated that she was delaying their journey.

By noon, when Micah again offered the use of the bed, she humbled herself enough to agree, but only if they continued to drive while she slept. Micah agreed with what she felt must be relief on his face. She had slept the day away and most of the night, too, for Micah had once again refused to allow her to sleep anywhere else.

Today, she had forced herself to walk the whole day through even though she'd felt a sheen of sweat dampening her forehead all the way. Maybe the exertion would allow her to sleep better tonight.

And after today, she would give herself a few days to rest. For they hoped to reach Blacksburg today and even though she had no money, she and Av could rest for a few days.

What of food?

Her brow crimped. She hadn't thought that far, she supposed.

And how would she work and still keep an eye on Av?

She settled a hand over the ache in her belly.

And then they topped out on a rise, and there lay Blacksburg stretched out before them.

She felt an immediate wave of loneliness. She and Av were truly on their own now.

The men pulled the wagons to a stop before an affluent-looking brick mercantile. Gideon swung down and, as Mercy approached, lifted Av from where he'd been riding on the seat beside him this afternoon.

At lunch, the men had stated that they planned only to see if the mercantile carried any fresh flour, since the one back in Chamblissburg had been out. Then they wanted to drive on and camp a few miles outside of town.

Mercy took Av's hand as Micah strode up with Joel and Mattox by his side. "I'll see about the flour," he said to Gideon. "Ma'am." He hesitated for a moment, feet shuffling. "Joel, ah, he tells me that you saved his life. I just wanted you to know . . ." He coughed then swallowed. "Well, I just wanted you to know how much I appreciate it." He tipped his hat in a gesture of farewell and then strode on past to ascend the steps up to the boardwalk. He snapped his fingers and then pointed down, and Mattox sat obediently by the door.

Joel seemed torn between following his father and staying with her and Gideon. But after a moment of hesitation, he gave Avram a big hug and blurted, "Goodbye, Mrs. Adler," as he dashed after his father.

"Goodbye." Mercy felt a strange loss—like a part of her had been severed—and she couldn't account for it. Undoubtedly, she would forever be connected to this family, but it was them who had suffered a loss, not her.

Pushing the disconcerting thoughts away, she turned her gaze to the bustling street. A busy town, it seemed, with plenty of folk, one of whom might be willing to give her work that she could do with a little boy underfoot.

The street seemed to waver in her vision and she blinked hard to refocus.

Repairing curtains, perhaps, for that hotel? Or tending the garden of that boardinghouse?

Gideon cleared his throat.

When she looked back at him, he was holding out a poke. "I want you to have this." He jingled it. "Just a few dollars to get you started."

Her eyes shot wide, and she stepped back, shaking her head. "Thank you, that's very generous of you. But you owe me nothing, and I would like to make my way on my own."

Gid remained still, his expression soft. "It's no hardship to me."

She tightened her clasp on Av's hand and retreated another step. "We'll be fine. Thank you, just the same."

Gid blew a breath of frustration and sank to his haunches in front of Avram. He held the bag out to him. "Here, kid. You use this to help your ma get a new start, understand?"

The audacity!

Mercy snatched the leather pouch before Avram could accept it. She immediately regretted the rapid movement. It took everything in her not to gasp at the bolt of fire that ripped through her side and the wave of dizziness that almost knocked her off her feet.

Thankfully, Gideon didn't seem to notice.

When she felt that she could once more move, she held the bag back to him. "He'll do no such thing."

Gideon held his hands up, palms out. An annoying sparkle of amusement danced in his gray-blue eyes. "Far be it from me to take back a gift that has already been accepted."

She pinched her lips. "I did not accept it. I was keeping my son from accepting it." She stepped forward and thrust it closer.

Gid ignored her offering. Instead, he tilted his head and propped his hands on his hips. "Please take it. I'll feel a lot better about leaving you here if I know you'll have a safe place to sleep until you can get your feet under you."

Giving up, she dropped her hand holding the bag back to her side in defeat. "You're too kind after all that—"

He held up a palm to silence her. "None of this was your fault. Like Micah said, if that sheriff had done his job on any number of occasions, you wouldn't have needed to flee for your life." When she snapped her focus back to him, he arched a brow. "Well? Am I right?"

Her shoulders slumped. "I did go to him on many occasions, yes. At least at first. I guess I gave up at some point."

Gid continued. "If your father had been a support. Or even if your husband, if he can even be called that, hadn't made the choices that he did. Both Micah and I know that you didn't intend to bring harm."

She studied the brown leather of the bag in her hand. "But I knew it was a possibility."

"All of us did. The moment we caught that first glimpse of you. But we chose to help you, and—" He swallowed. "—it was the right thing to do, no matter that the price was so dear."

She searched his face, hardly able to believe he'd said that. And yet, his face shone with a sincerity that she found hard to deny. "You are a good and kind man, Gideon Riley, and I wish you all the best on your travels to Oregon."

He lowered his attention to the toe of his boot that prodded at the dust of the street. "So you'll stay here then? In Blacksburg?"

As she swept the street with another searching look, her brows knitted. "At least until I get enough saved to travel to Oregon."

His gaze sharpened on her. "You still want to go to Oregon?"

She looked down at her son. "I first planned to go there because I felt it would be easier to . . . escape from Herst. But I find that I've thought about it for so long that I'm reluctant to give up the dream. It was . . . a promise of sorts that kept hope alive."

"What if Micah and I hired you?"

She drew in a measured breath and searched his face.

He looked surprised to have blurted the words. He shrugged. "I mean. You know, Micah and I are no hand at cooking, and Joel still needs a woman's soft touch, I'll wager."

Mercy's heart pounded with the hope of it. "Truly? You would do that?"

He shrugged. "We would have to hire someone in Independence anyhow. We'd be ahead of things if we arrived with our help already hired."

She shook her head. "I don't know. I don't have any supplies or even a change of clothes for either me or Av."

He motioned to the bag in her hands. "Seems the good Lord already took care of that. In fact, you can consider that payment for the cooking you've already done these past few days if you're of a mind to."

A weary smile caught her unaware. She turned to look at the bustling street again. She wouldn't have to worry about finding a job that would allow her to work with Av around. It would be an answer to so many of her concerns. Such a perfect answer, in fact, that she wondered what the trap might be.

And yet, she couldn't bring herself to turn him down. She lifted the bag. "The cooking I already did should be in payment for you and Micah's doctoring. So . . . Only if you consider this an advance on my future wages."

He dipped his chin. "Fine. We can consider it that."

"All right then, please give me thirty minutes to purchase a few supplies?"

He nodded. Pointed. "We'll take lunch at that boardinghouse there. How about I bring Avram with me to get a bite to eat while you shop?"

"Thank you. I appreciate that."

As they walked away, he called, "I'll order something for you. Just come on over when you finish here."

Mercy nodded but despaired as she considered the steps leading up to the mercantile. Exhaustion sapped her strength like an iron blanket weighing her down. Would she even be able to reach the top step? She put a hand on the rail but couldn't find the gumption to lift her foot. Just raising her hand to the rail had shards of agony shooting through her like shrapnel.

Micah appeared at the top of the stairs. His attention sharpened on her for one moment before he handed Joel the sack of flour and pointed in the direction Gideon had gone. "Go to Uncle Gid. Tell him I'll be along shortly."

Joel's two arms barely reached around the bag, but he didn't seem to have any trouble carrying the weight.

She couldn't even seem to turn her head to see how far away Gideon was now.

Micah descended and stopped by her side. He propped his hands at his belt and searched her face. "What's wrong?"

She frowned. "I don't—" The whole town suddenly seemed to be spinning with her at its axis. She clutched for the rail to maintain her balance, but the warmth of Micah's hand already enveloped her fingers. He turned her. "Sit down." He held her hand until she eased onto one of the steps.

Feeling the heat of her humiliation in her cheeks, she gave her head a little shake. "I'm sorry. I don't know what—"

"You've been overdoing it, that's what. I should have noticed, but—" He brushed away further words, his jaw firming. "Here, put your head on your knees." His gentle hand rested, broad and strong, against the back of her head as he nudged her to follow instructions—large enough that his touch should have elicited a quaver of fear that never came.

With her face buried in her skirts, she heard him crouch before her. He sighed, and when she peeked up at him, he had propped his forearms across his thighs and was scanning the street, jaw hard, brow slumped.

He angled his eyes toward her, then turned his face to study her more fully. "You're as pale as dairy skimmings. What was Gid thinking, leaving you alone like that?"

Thankfully, she felt a little better now that she was seated. She had a sudden urge to come to Gideon's defense. "I felt fine when he was here." That was true—mostly. "I was only hit with a wave of dizziness after he walked away. He hired me." She nipped her lower lip, wondering how Micah would take the news.

She would have thought it impossible, but Micah's brow slumped further. "He what?"

Something in her felt a little irritated at the abhorrence in those words. Even though she was slumped forward with her arms wrapped around her knees, her chin nudged higher. "He wants me to work for you on the way to Oregon. Cooking. Watching the boys. That sort of thing."

Micah pushed back his hat, scooped his fingers through his curls, and then resettled it again. "Perfect."

Her eyes narrowed. He hated the idea. Of course, he hated it. He'd probably been relieved at the thought of leaving her here.

"What is that supposed to mean?" She mashed her lips together. One of these days, she would learn to think before she spoke.

He rose with a weary huff. Looked down at her. "It means I should have thought of it. I'm going to pick you up now. You need food and rest."

She glanced up the stairs toward the mercantile. "But I have to—" Her words were cut off by a sharp little squeak when he scooped her into his arms. "What are you doing?" Pain shot through her side, and she squirmed. But she did note that he'd placed her with her injury to the outside so it wouldn't receive any excessive pressure.

Adjusting his grip and holding her gently against his chest, he glanced down at her, one brow nudging upward. "Didn't you hear what I said?"

She had heard him, but she hadn't expected him to—well, she wasn't sure why she hadn't expected him to do exactly what he'd said he was going to do. "I'm perfectly capable of walking on my own two feet."

He scrutinized her face, already striding across the street. "Right. That was perfectly clear from the way you were swaying back there. I didn't want you getting a case of the vapors."

Mercy felt her indignation rise. "I've never fainted. Not once."

Seeming to ignore her, he continued toward the boardinghouse. "We'll get a room. You can eat and rest, and I promise I'll give you time to do your shopping come morning."

What could she say to that? He'd just countered the only reason she might have come up with for him to put her down. So she simply endured the humiliation of being carried like an invalid. And perhaps it was a blessing to be supported by the strength of his arms. She wouldn't want this to be the first time she fainted. She would choose instead to be thankful not to need to exert any effort.

She tried not to notice the sheer power of him—or the way the sunlight caught in the stubble of his jaw. Failing at both, she turned her study to his eyes. This close, she could see that the blue probably seemed so intense because they were shot through with shards of cobalt and turquoise and edged with a nearly black rim. With those dark curls and the angular plains of his face, he was a handsome man, no two ways about it.

With a jolt of surprise, she realized he had stopped. They were inside the inn—and he was looking down at her with consternation tightening his brow.

She tore her focus to the tips of her boots poking out above her skirt.

Micah cleared his throat and settled her gently on the floor, one hand splaying against her back to steady her. "They are just there." He reached past her to point into the dining room, where Joel and Avram sat across from Gideon at a table against the far wall. The two chairs nearest the side wall remained empty.

She felt relieved to see it. If she could just make it that far, she could prop her shoulder against the wall, and with the chair at her back and the table at her front, she would be supported on three sides.

"Can you make it?" His voice rumbled in her ear.

"Of course." She injected all the confidence she could muster into the word, but drat if the floor didn't practically dip out from beneath her boots with her first step. She stumbled to catch her balance.

"Whoa there." The firm warmth of Micah's hand settled against her elbow. He didn't let go until she sat in the chair closest to the corner.

Gideon divided a concerned glance between them. "What happened?"

Micah strode around the table and yanked out the chair across from hers. "We pushed her too hard. She didn't even have the strength to make it up the stairs to the mercantile." He plopped into his seat. "We need to get rooms here for the night."

Gideon searched her face with concern. "Yes. I ordered us all vegetable soup to start. Our other choices are pot roast or fried chicken. We can all tell her our wishes when she returns with the soup."

Even though Mercy's stomach rumbled at the thought, her side felt afire, and her eyelids seemed weighted with lead.

Maybe she could just rest her head against the wall until the soup arrived . . .

Chapter Ten

M icah hooked his hat on the spindle of his chair and spread his napkin in his lap. And by the time he looked up, Mercy had tilted her head against the wall and appeared to be sound asleep.

He frowned, chastising himself for moving on too quickly after her serious injuries. They should have stayed put and let her sleep and lay about for a couple of weeks. If only they didn't have that looming deadline. His stomach tightened into a hard knot. With Georgia's passing, he would only get half the land. He hated to even lament that because Georgia had meant more to him than any piece of land ever could, but running cattle required a lot of acreage. Would only a square mile between him and Gideon be enough?

He blew out a breath. If they didn't make it to Oregon in time, he supposed he wouldn't have to worry about it. And now, with Mercy needing rest, they faced yet another delay. He was a cad for being frustrated.

Why did he always have to be so driven? Unsettled? Discontent? If he wasn't, then maybe Georgia—

He raked his fingers through his hair to brush away that thought.

He wished Mercy hadn't fallen asleep. She needed some sustenance. But obviously, her body thought she needed rest more.

The serving girl arrived at their table with a tray filled with steaming bowls.

Micah was already scooting his chair back. As she began to place the bowls on the table, he asked, "You wouldn't happen to have two rooms available, would you?"

She smiled. "We do. I can show you above as soon as you all finish eating."

Micah laid down his napkin. "I'm afraid I need to get her into a bed right now."

Gid flashed him a look. By the way his lips quirked, Micah knew he'd said something wrong. But he didn't make the connection until the girl's brows rose and her cheeks turned almost as pink as summer strawberries. She darted a look from the sleeping Mercy to him and back again as she set down the bowls of soup.

"Don't be daft." He felt heat sweep across the back of his neck. "She's sick. Needs rest. That's all."

"I'm sorry." The girl sniffled.

He wasn't sure what had brought her tears. And was she apologizing for being daft or for the fact that Mercy was sick?

Gid gave him a pointed look, and he realized that his words had sounded more like a growl than an explanation. He also shouldn't have called her daft.

Still, there was no need for the serving girl to go caterwauling.

He daggered his brother-in-law a glower. Gideon showed his palms, then gave a little shake of his head as he tucked into his soup. If anyone understood, it was Gid. Neither of them were the type to leave love behind so quickly.

"I'm sorry." He looked at the girl. "I spoke unkindly. It was not my intention to insult you."

She rubbed a finger at a fleck of nothing on her tray. "Please pay me no mind. I accept your apology."

"Is now a good time for you to show me to a room?"

"Yes." She blinked hard a couple of times. "Right this way." She snugged the tray beneath her arm and started down the aisle.

It took him a second to gather Mercy back into his arms. This time, she wasn't stiff and resistant.

The moment he hefted her, she curled against his chest and settled her head beneath his chin with a soft sigh of contentment.

Micah swallowed his bitterness. It shouldn't be her here in his arms.

As he approached the serving girl, who had paused near the foot of a staircase to wait for him, a man bellowed from the table beside him. "Wench, you mush be the shlowesht molly in thish whole town. I shaid to fetsh me 'nother ale!"

Micah leveled a glare on the man. "She's busy. And you ought to check your assumptions, sir."

The man blew an inebriated breath and waved a limp hand. "Get yer wife on outta here, shtranger."

Wanting to do nothing more than shove his boot into the middle of the man's chest, Micah spun on his heel and stomped toward the girl, who remained at the foot of the stairs.

She brushed away more tears.

Micah felt even worse for having used the word daft. "Ignore him. And I'm doubly sorry for snapping at you and adding my problems to yours." He adjusted Mercy in his arms, realizing at that moment how much heat radiated into his chest from her body.

The girl dabbed at her cheeks and offered him a watery smile. "All is forgiven, but my it has been a night. Right this way, and I'll show you to a room." She led the way up to a landing and opened a door before she handed him two skeleton keys. "This is room four, and five there is also yours. Need anything else?"

Micah scanned the interior of a room that was practically no bigger than his wagon. Two narrow beds were pressed up against each side wall, and there was barely any room to navigate between them. Other than the made-up beds and a wash basin by the door, the room was bare. But it was warm.

"This will be fine. Thank you." He angled Mercy into the room, careful not to bang her head or ankles on the doorframe. By the time he got her laid out on the bed, the serving girl had disappeared. Micah checked the wound he'd cauterized and was thankful to see there were no red streaks shooting from it. He tied the bandage into place once more, then laid his hand against her forehead.

Just as he'd suspected. Burning up. Concern tightened his brow as he sank onto the bed across from her to tug off her small boots.

Blazes, if he didn't wish he could simply lay down right here and wail away all the hours back to the moment his kids had taken sick. Set his world to rights. Talk to Georgia one more time. Restore her happiness and good cheer. Hug Jess tight and hear her spritely laughter.

But of course, he couldn't do any of that. Nor did he have any more skills to help Mercy recover. He'd done his best. She was in God's hands now.

His chest felt tight, like it was caught in one of the tobacco presses back at the factory. His fingers fumbled with the laces of Mercy's boots, and then he was sobbing. He released her foot even though he hadn't gotten her boot off yet, and buried his face in his hands.

His chest heaved, and he could barely seem to pull in a breath before it shot out of him on a gasp, or a groan, or a guttural cry.

This loss of control terrified him almost more than the actual losses he'd suffered. He had to pull it together. Had to be strong.

But all he could find the strength to do was sob.

Thankfully, Mercy continued to sleep through it all.

Gideon felt concern tighten his brow and shifted in his seat. The boys had long since finished their meals and were now getting antsy. But Micah hadn't returned from upstairs.

What could be keeping him?

Gid banished the image that came to mind of Micah carrying Mercy up the stairs. Had it been more serious than he'd thought?

She'd been fine only a little while ago when he'd walked away from her, so it couldn't be too serious, could it? But what was delaying Micah?

He couldn't keep the boys here much longer. He'd already had to stop them from flicking wadded-up pieces of bread at each other.

He squinted at the plate of pot roast that he'd ordered for Micah. By now, it was undoubtedly cold.

"Bang! Bang!"

Avram "shot" Joel with a finger pistol, his loud shout making the lady at the next table jump and then glower in their direction.

Joel—apparently a wild turkey, based on the strangulated gobbling that Gid would have to admit sounded quite authentic to a dying turkey—flopped back in his chair, arms flinging dramatically out to his sides. And then promptly burst into tears. "I don't want to play at dying."

Avram lowered his gaze to his lap. "Me neither."

That did it.

Gideon dropped their payment on the table before he took up four of the bread rolls and split them open. The vegetables would have to stay, but he scooped one-quarter of the meat into each roll and folded them closed again. These, he layered into one of the linen napkins on the table, adding the potato beside them, then folded the four corners up to create a handle of sorts.

"Come on, boys. Let's go find our rooms."

The boys slumped out of their chairs and trailed after him without enthusiasm.

He wondered how he was going to figure out which rooms were theirs, but when they reached the top of the stairs, Micah was emerging from one.

"Pa, I miss Ma!" Joel ran and flung himself against Micah.

Micah awkwardly tried to ease the door shut behind himself and hug Joel at the same time.

Gideon didn't miss the redness of his eyes or the way they were slightly swollen. So that was why he hadn't reappeared downstairs.

His brother-in-law may be a man of few words, but it appeared he felt emotions as deeply as the rest of them, after all.

Micah scooped Joel into his arms and cupped the back of his head. "I know, son. I miss her too."

Joel sobbed against his shoulder.

Gid fought his own emotions. He held out the napkin. "Brought some of yours up."

Micah accepted the offering with a nod of thanks. He pointed to the next door down. "Our room is here. Av, why don't you plan to sleep in our room tonight?"

Avram's brows immediately crashed low over the bridge of his nose. He shook his head, tears of his own making his eyes shine in the hallway lantern light. "I want Ma."

Micah squatted to his level, still cuddling Joel against his shoulder. "Your ma isn't feeling well. She needs her rest."

"I be good."

"I know, but—" Micah shot Gid a look as though seeking his help.

Gid stepped forward and rested a hand on Av's mop of curls. "For now, how about you and Joel come into our room, and you can sketch on Joel's slate? While you do that, I'll pop over to the mercantile and buy us a book. We can read for a bit tonight."

Avram's furrowed brow eased only a little. Gideon could see the battle being waged. He liked drawing and stories but also wanted to be with his mother.

"After I read to you, we can go over and see how your ma is doing."

That seemed to convince him. He gave a short nod.

Gid exchanged a look with Micah as he rose and slipped the key into the lock of their room. Hopefully, by the time he finished reading to the boys, the kid would be fast asleep.

Mercy woke with sunlight streaming through her window. She blinked at the painful rays, working her lips and tongue to wet her mouth.

A cup sat on the little table beside her bed, and she found it nearly full of cold water. She downed the whole cup in one long draught, relishing the cool liquid slipping over her parched tongue.

On the floor near her bed, a bowl with a rag in it caught her eye as she reached to set the cup back on the table. She had vague recollections of a cool cloth being laid on her forehead in the night, of a deep rumble and gentle but firm hands brushing her hair away from her damp face.

Her gaze flew to the other bed. Empty.

She frowned, fighting to remember what had happened the evening before. The last thing she remembered was resting her head against the wall downstairs.

Embarrassment shot through her. Had she fallen asleep at the table? How had she gotten here? A vague picture formed of curling herself against a sun-warmed wall that carried the scent of sage and leather.

Her frown returned in full force. Now that she was out from under the blankets, she recognized the slight chill of a fever. One hand pressed to her forehead. She must have been hallucinating, but what a strange thing to conjure.

Had it been Gideon? That sun-warmed wall that she had snuggled against?

She shook away the image, unsure why it filled her with disquiet. He would never hurt her. After years of knowing Herst, she would be willing to bet her very last penny that was true. So why was it that the thought of being held in his arms filled her with unease?

Micah, on the other hand . . . The image of him with his knife clenched in his mouth as he leaned over her flashed into her mind. He'd seemed so fierce, and even now, she shivered with the fear she'd felt in that moment. Of course, she knew now that he'd been saving her life. Still, in comparison to Gideon, he definitely wasn't as . . . Safe? Harmless? Nonthreatening? And yet, when he'd carried her across the street, she'd felt . . . Well, the best word to describe it was attraction. An emotion that horrified her now. After all her years with Herst, how could she allow herself to feel attraction to a dangerous man?

It didn't matter how she'd gotten here, she supposed.

For now, she must find Avram!

Her boots were paired neatly on the floor by the little table. She reached for them, but a wave of dizziness made her clutch for the table instead. She knocked the cup, and it clattered to the floor, bouncing and clanging like a toppled bell.

Before she could even find the clear-headedness to go after it, a knock sounded at her door. "Mercy? You all right?"

Gideon. It must have been him who brought her up last night.

A glance at herself revealed that she remained fully clothed. So she called, "Come in. Yes. I'm fine."

He poked his head around the edge of the door.

Humiliation tilted her head to one side as she pointed to the tin cup that had bounced almost all the way to the door.

He stepped inside and scooped up the cup. "You could just ring the bell. You don't have to go throwing cups at the door."

Lips pinched into a thin line, she rolled her eyes at him. But she did note that he wasn't joking about the bell. One rested on the table beside her. "When did that get there?"

Gid refilled the cup from the pitcher by the door and crossed to set it on the table once more. "Micah had me buy it when I went over to the mercantile last night. I told him you could just as easily bang on the wall that separates our rooms, but he insisted you needed the bell. Not that you used it." He hung his head and roughed a hand over the back of his head, watching her through his eyebrows. "At least, I don't think you did. I slept the night through like a man unconscious. Micah has Avram, by the way, down in the dining room."

Micah.

She remembered the deep, rumbling voice and the cool cloths.

"Did you bring me up here last night?"

Gid shook his head. "Micah."

Mercy pondered that revelation. Maybe he wasn't as dangerous as he seemed? And if that was the case, how was it that after the curse of living with Herst for these past many years, she'd fallen in with two men who were so kind despite all she'd cost them?

She motioned to her boots. "I was just going to see if I could find Av."

Gid retreated to the door. "How about I go get him and bring him to you? I'm under strict instructions that you are not to leave this room." The smile he tossed over his shoulder told her he valued his life too much to disobey the order. "Stay put. I'll be back inside ten minutes."

Mercy sank against the pillows, thankful not to have to go anywhere.

Chapter Eleven

It took five days before she could rise without severe pain and dizziness. Through it all, both Micah and Gideon cared for her. They brought her food and a bucket for bathing. They took care of Avram, and she missed him terribly.

Now, on the fifth morning, knowing that both men were chomping at the bit to continue on their way, she headed into the mercantile. She was able to take the stairs with no lightheadedness and only a ghost of her former levels of pain remaining in her side.

She still had the money Gid had given her. She would portion the money carefully to buy Av some clothes, but she didn't need anything for herself. For though her blouse had been torn at the shoulder and bloodied, most of the stain had come out when she'd scrubbed it, and she'd repaired the shoulder only yesterday after she'd asked the girl at the front desk for a needle and thread. The job certainly hadn't made the shirt look brand new, but it would suffice until she earned some more pay for either a store-bought one or some material to sew one. She had washed Georgia's blouse and would return it to Micah as soon as she found the right moment.

Near the front door, she took up a basket and filled it with jerky, apples, and two sets of boy's clothes—one the next size up—and an extra pair of boots for Av. He was growing so fast now that she would be thankful to have those things in a few weeks.

She passed an aisle filled with tiny red, purple, blue, and gold glass bottles. "Toilet Water for Ladies" was delicately written on a slate propped at one side of the shelf. Below that, smaller lettering read, "five cents per ounce." Before she thought better of it, Mercy lifted a blue bottle, wiggled out the cork, and inhaled the aroma. Lavender. Delicate and lovely, but not something she needed. She returned the bottle to the shelf. The contents of a red bottle smelled of roses and a gold one of something pungent that she couldn't quite identify but that made her wrinkle her nose as she put it back. Lastly, she picked up one of the purple bottles. That scent swirled out to tantalize her, making her close her eyes, draw the bottle closer, and test the fragrance a second time. Lilac. Her favorite. She quickly stoppered it and put it back on the shelf. But she didn't move. She simply stood there looking at it.

She had paused, intending only to indulge her senses for a moment. She should walk away. But she hadn't owned a perfume since just after Ma had passed. And since she planned to buy only these few things for Av, she had plenty of money. She read the sign once again. Five cents. She ought to leave it. Instead, she took it up and dropped it in her basket. Tamping down her guilt at spending money on such a frivolity, she hurried toward the shopkeeper.

As she set the basket on the front counter and counted out her coins, she felt as if she'd been given a king's ransom.

Once she returned to the boardinghouse, she packed up her and Av's things and then stepped out to meet the men and the boys at the livery as they'd discussed over breakfast.

A sigh slipped free. Things seemed to be going so well.

She couldn't help but feel like the Almighty might be setting her up for another great fall.

Gideon was weary and wagon-bench sore. From dawn to dusk, they traveled, for Micah pushed them hard, intent on reaching Independence on time.

Days turned into weeks, and weeks turned into months as they slowly made their way toward Independence. No one said anything about the fact that they could likely buy passage aboard a steamer now that Georgia wasn't here. They simply continued on as they were. Maybe because they both would have had to part with a good deal of the goods they'd packed into their wagons. Maybe because neither of them could bear to leave behind anything Georgia had deemed necessary for "survival in the Wild West."

They'd been putting in twenty miles a day, and now they were only five days out from Independence.

The animals were weary, plodding slower each day.

Micah grew more churlish and sullen with each passing hour.

From all their reading and the settlers that they'd bumped into along the way, they'd learned that no wagon master worth his salt would leave Independence past the middle of May. For it could take as many as six months to reach the Oregon Territory, and if the wagon train didn't arrive on time, winter could wreak all manner of havoc on the travelers, not to mention their animals.

And, their livestock, one old-timer had told them, ought to be oxen, not horses. "Slower, I'll grant you. But they can travel for miles longer each day, hauling those heavy loads. And . . ." He held a finger aloft. "Mind that you only take the absolute essentials with you. My boy, he went through three years ago now. Got our first letter just t'other day." He beamed. "He told of a time when they come to the base of some mountain they needed to cross and how they found all sorts of paraphernalia abandoned beside the trail. Even a pianoforte, if'n you can believe it." The old man shook his head. "The way he described them mountains . . . Whooeee, they must be sockdolager! Anyhow, yes, sir, you offload any non-essentials, and ya take along blankets and sewing thread and cloth. The way he tells it, the Indians are right happy to trade for things such as that. Said it saved 'em from what they feared might be an attack a time or two. Sugar too. They like thet there sugar."

Gideon thought of the huge chest full of china in the back of his wagon. But when he glanced at Micah, he was already shaking his head with a stern look, as though he knew exactly his thoughts and was telling him not to even consider it. Gideon let it drop. They could talk about it later.

They'd left the old-timer waving a farewell several days back.

Micah had driven them even harder after that. Determined not to miss the deadline.

Gideon worried that all the decent wagon masters would have left weeks ago, but he didn't say anything to his brother-in-law because he figured Micah had enough weighing on his mind already.

Micah had handled his hiring of Mercy surprisingly well, considering how deeply he grieved for Georgia. Though Gideon didn't think he'd made her any too welcome, neither had he been unkind to her, and that was a blessing. The other evening, Mercy had even arrived at the fire after dinner with Georgia's blouse in her hands. She'd tried to return it to Micah, but he'd curtly refused, telling her to keep it, though only a moment later, he'd risen and stalked away from the fire.

Gid felt like the lowest kind of man. He should have noticed that she had returned to wearing the same blouse that she'd had on when she first joined them—repaired, but still visibly torn.

The sight of the shirt must have filled Micah with melancholy, for later, Gid had found him chopping down a much-too-large snag for firewood. His axe pulverized the wood with all the ferocity of a man trying to crush his past into oblivion. Gid hadn't dared approach for fear of flying debris, but when Micah noticed him there, he'd stilled, rested on the axe handle, and gulped air. Once. Twice. Then again. He raised a hand to indicate he was fine, and Gid had moved on, leaving him to his grief.

Most mornings, Gid still woke with an ache in his heart big enough to fill the whole state of Missouri, and he figured he and Micah had a pretty good understanding of one another. Mercy, too, for that matter.

They rarely spoke more than a few words, but Mercy fixed a hot meal twice a day without fail or complaint.

The rolling hills of Virginia and Kentucky gave way to the flatter plains that stretched for endless miles in every direction. Gid had never been able to see so far to the horizon. The vast emptiness made a man feel small.

The day had been long. Mercy's whole body screamed for rest and relief from the agony, but still, there was dinner to prepare. She was much recovered comparatively. However, each evening, when she lay down her head, she struggled to sleep while fighting the pain in her ribs.

This made dreary days drearier.

The vastness of the prairie that stretched in every direction initially made her uncomfortable and leery. With not a landmark in any direction, she worried about Avram and Joel. If they wandered too far from the wagons, they might not have the bearings to find their way back through the grasses that grew well above their heads. But as day had stretched into day without incident, she had begun to find comfort in the prairie, too. It represented a new beginning for her. For Avram.

A brighter future.

Tonight, as the men saw to brushing down the horses and picketing them near the shallow stream, and the boys sank down near the fire, solemn and weary, Mercy searched the supplies for something easy.

Bacon and biscuits were what she had made the evening before and what again lay ready to hand. She could make soup if only there were some potatoes and milk, maybe an onion. But she found none of these. There were beans aplenty, but they took so long to cook, and one glance at the boys proved they wouldn't remain awake that long.

She withdrew two pounds of bacon and the makings for the bread, thankful for the flour purchased in Blacksburg.

She studied the boys as she laid strips of meat into the hot pan. They had moments when they seemed able to forget the recent tragedy—moments when they played, smiled, and raced to see who was fastest, if only for a short span.

This was not one of those moments.

Tonight especially, Joel's little face fell in hard lines and moisture glistened in his eyes.

Mercy returned her attention to her task, allowing her guilt to fill her fully. His loss lay firmly at her feet, and well she knew it.

With the bacon chattering in the pan, she immersed her hands into the dough, roughly kneading fat and flour, salt and soda. Punishing herself with the searing shards that shot through her with each movement.

Micah returned first and sank onto the log beside his son. Hands clasped, elbows planted against knees, he studied the grass between his boots. But after a moment, he lifted his head. His eyes glittered hard and steely when they fell on her.

She ignored him, refusing tears that wanted to weaken her knees like withered grass. Jaw tense, she kneaded, cut, and layered the dough into the Dutch oven.

She turned the bacon, and near the last piece, grease popped onto her fingers. With a hiss, she yanked back her hand, which caused another gasp because of the pain the sharp movement birthed.

Micah rose. "Careful," he said. "We don't need more delay because you relapse."

She tried not to let the words sting but failed. It seemed that he cared about her only so much as to keep her from further delaying their trip.

Despite the cutting words, he gently took the fork from her and turned the last strips of the meat. That done, he looked at her again. "You okay?"

No. I'm not.

She sealed her lips to prevent the words and gave him a nod instead. "Only weary."

"As are we all."

"Yes."

Gideon returned then, with the hem of his shirt turned up to form a pouch and showing damp spots. "I found a patch of sponge mushrooms. Thought we could fry them up in some of the bacon grease."

Mercy's stomach rumbled just at the mention of the delicacy. "That sounds lovely."

"I don't like mushrooms!" Joel groused.

None of the adults made a reply, realizing there was more to his low temper than his dislike of the food.

Mercy's heart felt heavier still when Joel leaped up, folded his arms, and then plunked down with his back to them, scrunching himself into a ball next to the log he'd been sitting on.

It wasn't long before the mushrooms had reduced, leaving behind a lovely sauce. When she pulled the biscuits from the coals, they were a perfect golden brown, and she set to plating portions for the boys.

She didn't put any mushrooms on Joel's plate, but he didn't bother to look when she held a plate out to him.

"I don't want any!" He shot up one arm and sent the plate flying, then jumped up and dashed toward the back of Micah's wagon.

"Joel Alexander Morran!" Micah's voice cut sharply through the dusk as he set his own plate on the rock beside him and started to stand.

Mercy raised a palm. "Please. Don't punish him. 'Tis only natural that he take some of the brunt of his grief out on me."

Micah stalked past her. "It's never alright to take his displeasure out on another, especially not a woman."

Remembering Herst's fits of rage whenever Avram had challenged him, she cast Gideon a concerned look. However, he seemed content to tuck into his food and let father and son hash out their disagreement.

Lifting her skirt to skim the grass, Mercy hurried in Micah's wake. However, when she rounded the back of the wagon, it wasn't to find Micah vindictively castigating a cowering boy, but instead, she found Joel sobbing against Micah's chest and lovingly wrapped in his arms.

Micah met her gaze above the boy's head, eyes soft and filled with so much pain that her guilt reared its head and filled her with self-contempt.

He must have seen some emotion flicker across her face, for he shook his head and asked, "Give us a moment?" His voice grated like one forcing words past a tight throat.

"Of course." Mercy returned to the fire and sank down to wearily consume her food. She ate out of necessity, not hunger, for she had learned several weeks before that not eating would weaken her for the next day's trek.

Avram finished his meal and placed his plate in the wash pot, as was the norm. Then he went and flopped down onto the canvas that Mercy had already laid out nearby. She finished her bite and started to call that she would help him with his evening wash and brushing his teeth, but saw that he was already asleep. She let it go. She would help him with the tasks in the morning.

Gideon rose and said he would fetch more wood for the morning's fire, then strode into the darkness with his ax.

A few minutes later, with her plate now empty, she eyed Joel's toppled plate and Micah's, which remained where he had set it when he'd gone after his son. She was just wearily wondering if she could also plan to do the dishes come morning when she heard a noise and turned to see Micah and Joel approaching.

The moment her gaze connected with Joel's, he started to run—directly toward her. He crashed into her and wrapped his arms around her tight.

Her heart was so touched that she barely noticed the ache his jarring raised in her ribs. Blinking back tears, she settled her arms around him, knowing she didn't deserve his contrition.

"I'm sorry." The boy's words were muffled beneath the tightness of her arms.

She cupped one hand around the back of his head. "Hush, Joel. It's fine. We're all beyond exhausted. And grief comes in waves that sometimes tug us under."

He stepped back, used his palms to scrub tears from his face, sniffed, and then, after a nod, started back toward his and Micah's wagon.

Mercy darted a look toward his plate. "Joel, wait. Your—"

"Joel will go to his pallet without dinner tonight," Micah interrupted.

"Oh. But—"

"He'll be fine." The blue of his eyes intensified on her in the light from the fire. "I, too, have an apology to make."

"Micah, no. Please don't—"

"Some of his attitude is a result of what he's seen in me, and for that, I'm sorry. You deserve better."

Mercy frowned and turned to watch the flicker of the flames consuming the wood. "You all deserved better, as well."

To her surprise, Micah's hand settled on her shoulder. He gave a squeeze but didn't comment further. He went to his plate and tucked in to his meal, and Mercy let the matter drop.

Too weary to wait for him to finish, she decided the dishes could soak overnight and hurried through her ablutions before lying next to Avram.

When she woke the next morning, she found that the dishes had been washed and dried and returned to their place in the storage box on the side of the wagon. And when she layered an extra helping of porridge into Joel's bowl and added an extra spoonful of honey, she received a shy smile from the boy and a bob of his head.

Finally, they arrived!

Gideon had never felt happier to see a place than when he reined his team to follow Micah's wagon down one of the main streets. They now needed a temporary place to encamp.

Independence felt like a cattle yard milling with a distressed herd. Chaos roiled everywhere he looked as he followed Micah's wagon down Main Street, sitting beside Avram and Mercy, who'd long since healed enough to ride beside him on the wagon bench.

Here, two men brawled. Around them, a crowd of cheering onlookers appeared to have money on the fight, based on the man with the slate who seemed to be keeping a tally of who landed each punch.

There, two more had their arms slung across each other's shoulders as they drunkenly danced in the street.

Hawkers roamed the boardwalks, calling out the benefits of their wares.

Bawdy women yoo-hooed from the upper-story windows of several different buildings. Mercy turned red and pointed for Avram to pay attention to several boys who raced by on unshod ponies.

Gideon shook his head. He had to wonder what they were getting themselves into. If this town at the edge of civilization was so unruly, what would it be like when they reached the Wild West?

He followed Micah's wagon all the way to the other end of town, where they pulled into the shade beneath a large maple at the edge of a field that was more dirt than grass. As he reined to a stop, his mind went once more to the crate filled with china in the back of his buckboard.

Micah hadn't said a word since they'd exchanged that look, and Gid figured that what he didn't know wouldn't hurt him. The man wasn't even going to realize that he'd traded off the china until perhaps they needed the trade goods out on the trail. He hated to get rid of

Mother's tea set, especially considering that it had meant so much to Georgia, but the practical side of him said to be smart and plan for the future.

Micah might be a silent soul, but he had always been more sentimental—likely what had made Georgia fall in love with him.

Now, Gid leaped from the wagon bench and reached up to help Mercy and Av down. "I need you to do something for me." He kept his voice low and one eye on Micah, who was checking something in the back of his wagon.

Mercy's brow furrowed with curiosity. "Yes? Av, come here, son." She motioned her boy closer but kept her questioning inspection on him.

"I need you to stay with Micah and give me a bit of warning if he decides to come into the mercantile."

Her frown deepened as she bent to straighten Avram's jacket and brush his hair with her fingers. "What are you up to?"

"I'm not up to anything, Ma!" Avram spread his hands.

Gideon smiled as Mercy tweaked her son's nose. "I know you aren't up to anything, love. It's your uncle Gideon that I'm questioning."

It still gave Gid's heart a bit of a start when she referred to him as Av's uncle, but with Joel always calling him "Uncle Gid," it had been natural for Avram to start doing the same, and things had cascaded from there.

Gideon met her, raised brow for raised brow. "Listen, it's for his own good. He's still tender emotionally, and I need to offload some things that he's not going to want to part with."

Mercy's face softened. "Don't you think it would be better just to talk to him?"

He shook his head. "He's got enough on his mind. Besides, he's so busy already, trying to find us a wagon train, he won't have time for such paltry concerns."

She thinned her lips and tilted him a look to let him know she thought he was making a mistake. He'd received that exact look from Verona more times than he could remember. The problem was, he was having a harder and harder time picturing it. Sure, he could remember that she'd given him such looks, but when he tried to recall the exact replica of her features, it was Mercy's visage that floated into his mind instead.

He frowned and lowered his focus to the rope he needed to untie at the corner of the wagon. It wasn't right that he should so quickly be struggling to envision his sweet Verona's face. Only a few months since she'd taken leave of him. It felt like a betrayal on his part.

Mercy's footsteps started away. "All right. I'll stick with him this afternoon." She sauntered off, holding out her hand to her son, who skipped up beside her and slipped his chubby fingers into her own.

Gideon rolled his shoulders to release some tension, relieved that she hadn't questioned him further.

What he was not relieved about was the task placed before him. Not only was he a betrayer of his deceased wife, but of his departed sister also.

He grunted and set about untying the crate of china.

Mercy stood near Micah's wagon, waiting for him to finish. She closed her eyes and tipped her face to the warmth of the sun, relishing the softness of Avram's little hand tucked into her own.

Safety.

Awe filled her at the feeling she was still coming to terms with.

When she opened her eyes and looked up, it was to find Micah watching her with a bit of a shimmer in his eyes.

He jolted and looked away across the field the moment their gazes connected. "Sorry. You just . . . look so much like her."

"Is my presence a distress to you?" She wished she hadn't blurted the question the moment it popped from her lips.

He prodded the toe of one boot at a clump of grass. "I'll not lie and say that you aren't a reminder of what I've lost. But I . . ." He lifted one shoulder. "I don't hold you responsible for her death."

"And yet if I hadn't sought shelter with your party . . ." Mercy swallowed and studied a single blade of green grass that had somehow survived the crush of wagon wheels that had pulverized this field. This was a conversation that had ever been on her mind, and yet they'd somehow never quite gotten around to it.

"If you hadn't been violated and then betrayed by your own father, not to mention your townsfolk and the law who stood by and let—" He waved a hand, jaw jutting to one side in irritation. "I don't pretend to understand all that you've been through. Would I change the past if I could? Of course, I would." He blinked hard and then made a sound of self-contempt, apparently frustrated with his nearness to tears. "But we can't. So let's not harp on it."

She felt helpless to alleviate his suffering. But . . . She took in the bustle of activity all around them. Two distinct clusters of wagons had formed on either side of the sparsely grassed field. Two separate wagon trains heading west?

Micah and Gideon would likely join up with one. But if she and Av joined the other . . . Of course, Gid had said they wanted to hire her. But now that they were all here in Independence, surely another woman would need the work as much as she did. The sooner she separated herself from them, the sooner the daily painful reminder of all she'd cost them would be removed from them. She would like to give them that if she could.

Her heart thumped rapidly at the thought of trying to find a safe party for her and Av to travel with. But she would be careful, and all would be fine. It was a risk but something to consider, at any rate. She would make inquiries. These men had been good to her, and she didn't want to cause them further anguish.

She followed Micah through the streets of Independence, keeping an eye on the boys, who were fascinated by every little detail of the town after weeks on end of seeing nothing but waving grass and billowing dust.

After Joel's one incident of anger toward her that night on the trail, and the resulting hug of apology, he'd seemed to release a little more of his grief each day. She wasn't sure Micah liked seeing his son run to her with a bouquet of wildflowers that he'd picked, or the way Joel often settled next to her as they sat around the fire of an evening, but if displeasure reared a head, Micah's love for his son stood stronger. He'd held his tongue and uttered not a word of displeasure about it—at least not that she'd heard.

Mercy pulled her thoughts back to the present.

Mattox trotted obediently at Micah's heel, his head nearly the height of Micah's belt, his black fur ruffling in the breeze. Even though Micah's footsteps were hurried and heavy, the dog seemed to be sauntering by his side. The worn leather saddlebags over Micah's shoulder swayed and thumped his back.

Realizing they'd fallen behind, Mercy nudged the boys to hurry and keep up.

Micah glanced back and slowed his pace, if only slightly.

One industrious boy rode up and down the street on a contraption with two wheels and a leather seat. Mercy had read of such contrivances in the papers but had never seen one in person. She inched up her skirts to climb a set of steps, trying to remember what she'd heard them called.

The boy rolled up to them and came to a stop with his feet propped on either side of the front wheel. Mercy could see, now that he was stopped, that the wheels were a metal rim with leather sewn tight all around them. His hands gripped a wooden bar that was attached to the front wheel by two wooden stakes.

"Hiya!" It was obvious from the way the word rolled off his tongue that he wasn't from these parts.

Mercy smiled at his greeting. "Good afternoon." They couldn't stop, or Micah would leave them behind.

"Wid yer tikes 'ere like tae ride?" He pushed the apparatus along on the street beside them as they hurried down the boardwalk, trying to keep up with Micah's lithe tread.

Av looked up at her hopefully, and Mercy felt like the meanest of mothers as she shook her head. "I'm sorry," she said quietly.

She had no idea how much the boy was charging, but whatever it was, it would be more than she could afford. She hadn't quite spent everything Gideon had given her to purchase those few items back in Blacksburg. But the last two months on the trail had proven to her that they would need more. Every penny that remained would need to be parceled out to necessities. Especially if she was going to join a wagon train on her own.

Thankfully, in addition to the one blouse, Micah had offered some of Georgia's clothes a few weeks back. Her own blouse had been okay for the trail, but wouldn't do for meeting new people. However, the thing she'd been most thankful for after his gift was that she no longer had to put damp clothes on after she washed them.

Micah stopped and spun back to face the boy. "How much?"

Mercy squeaked when she nearly bowled into him. The sharp movement revived some of the lingering pain in her ribs. She settled one hand against the spot and stepped to one side, lowering her gaze to the boardwalk. She hadn't even known he'd been paying attention.

Mattox sank to his haunches. His attentive golden stare fixed curiously on the boy and his contraption. A low growl escaped, but at Micah's snapped fingers, the dog seemed to relax.

The boy didn't miss a beat, even if he did eye Mattox with a good deal of caution after that. "Ainlie a penny, suh. An' baith yere wee jimmies'll git themselves a spin."

Micah assessed the two wheels and the bar that connected them. "What is that?"

The boy grinned proudly. He rubbed a hand affectionately across the seat. "This 'ere is what's cried a swift walker."

Micah looked from the walker to Joel and Av and back. "Don't think the young one's legs are long enough."

The boy swept a broad gesture to Joel. "That's okay. Whilst yere older laddie rides, I'll git yere younger laddie strapped intae some lifts."

Micah cast Mercy a look, and it was the first time she'd seen him show even a hint of humor since Georgia's passing.

"Industrious," he said under his breath.

Mercy smiled. "Indeed."

"Is it okay with you if Av has a ride?"

Mercy frowned, darting a glance between Micah, the contraption, and Av's hopeful expression. "I don't—"

"I'll pay." Micah hurried to finish.

"Then yes. It's fine with me. So long as you're certain."

"Braw!" The boy thrust the walker at Joel. "On ya git, laddie."

As Joel swung his leg over the seat, the boy hung onto the front steering bar and thrust his palm out to Micah. "Juist a penny, suh."

Mercy nipped back a grin. It didn't look like he planned to let Joel move an inch until he had his penny firmly in hand.

Micah dug into his pocket and produced the required copper coin.

Quick as a wink, the money disappeared deep into the boy's pocket. "Thank ye. Now, lad . . ." He turned to Joel. "Let th' wheels dae maist o' th' wirk, aye? Ye push aff with first one shank and then th' ither until ya git 'er rollin' right along. Then ye lift yer feet an' enjoy th' breeze in yer britches, aye?" Leaving Joel to his own devices, the boy then turned to Av. "Now ye, wee jimmie . . ." He patted the edge of the boardwalk. "Sit yerself doon, right 'ere."

Micah touched Mercy's elbow, drawing her attention. "I'm just stepping into the expansion offices." He pointed down the boardwalk.

Mercy saw the carved wooden sign above the door he'd pointed to. "Official Society for the Organization and Encouragement of Westward Expansion," the sign read.

She tucked her shawl more tightly around her shoulders. "We'll be down as soon as we finish."

Through Dust & Ashes

"Son?" Micah waited until Joel, who was still trying to get the hang of balancing on the two wheels, paused to give him his attention. "You listen to Mrs. Adler."

"Yes, Pa," Joel called.

Micah strode off.

Mercy turned her attention to the boy who was helping Av strap tall blocks of wood to the bottom of his shoes.

The boy glanced at Micah's retreating back as he threaded a strap through a buckle. "Nae yer 'usband, then?"

Mercy shook her head. "No." Heaven's no. "Just a friend."

She twisted her lips to one side. Could she call him that? Gid, yes. She would call him a friend. But Micah . . . He'd been suffering in silence for months now. She hardly knew what to call him since they'd rarely spoken. Today was really the first conversation they'd had in weeks. She glanced after him and watched until he disappeared into the office. Even though he'd said he didn't hold her responsible, she couldn't help but wonder if he'd been honest.

And she couldn't blame him if he hadn't, could she?

She returned her attention to the boy, who was now helping Avram to his feet. Av giggled at the feel of walking much higher off the ground than he was used to.

"'At's it, fella. Yer a natural."

"What's your name?" Mercy asked the boy.

He looked surprised. "Cannae recall th' las' time a body asked." He spread both arms and then swept them in toward his torso as he gave her a courtly bow. "The name's Declan Boyle, mam. At yer service."

Mercy resisted a chuckle. "I'm Mrs. Adler, Declan. And this here is Avram, and that . . ." She motioned to Joel, who was just returning and swinging off the speed walker. ". . . is Joel. It's a pleasure to meet you."

"That was so much fun!" Joel gushed. "Thank you so much!"

Mercy wanted to press Declan for more details about why he was here selling rides on the streets of Independence, where he was from, and if his parents were near, but he was already helping Avram onto the seat, so she withheld her curiosity.

Instead, she leaned a shoulder into the pillar by the edge of the walk and enjoyed Avram's squeals of laughter.

It was a good sound. A good sound, indeed.

Chapter Twelve

M icah pointed for Mattox to stay beside the door, then slammed into the expansion office with a frown firmly slumping his brow. He wished that woman didn't remind him so much of Georgia. She was even wearing Georgia's clothes because, of course, it hadn't made sense for him to selfishly keep them with Georgia no longer here to need them. Uncharitable man that he was, it had been a good many weeks before he'd been able to bring himself to open the trunk in the wagon and pull out some of Georgia's things.

Just the reminder of her scent permeating the air when he opened the lid thrust a shaft of grief through his heart.

Mercy had resisted when he'd offered them, and that made him feel even more of a cad. What kind of man was he if he couldn't share things that weren't being used and were, in fact, no longer needed—even if parting with them did practically take the breath right out of him?

The clothes had been somewhat large on her, for where Georgia had been a healthy weight, Mercy was naught but skin and bones. But at least she now had clean things to wear.

She was a quiet woman, keeping her distance. She made their meals with calm proficiency and zero complaints.

Strong.

Any woman who could do all that she had begun to do only a day after he'd punctured and then cauterized her side was mighty strong. He still felt terrible about the way that she'd nearly collapsed back in Blacksburg. But he'd simply been trying to breathe beneath the drowning waves of grief. He'd have to remember that she was the kind to push herself until she could push herself no more.

If only Georgia had possessed that same indomitable spirit. Maybe they wouldn't have stopped early that night. Maybe Mercy's husband and his cousin wouldn't have caught up with them, or Georgia wouldn't have been alone in the wagon and thus mistaken for Mercy. Maybe the two women would have been seen together, and Mercy would have been recognized rightly.

He gritted his teeth, hating that he'd even considered the thought. He wouldn't have wanted Mercy killed any more than Georgia.

He tried to tell himself it was true, but he knew in his heart that it wasn't. He would have rather had her taken than his dear Georgia.

Before they'd lost Jess, he never would have expected Georgia to fold in on herself as she had. She'd gone from vibrant and joyous to solemn and surly—a husk of her former self.

So Mercy's quiet faithfulness to her duties and the fact that he'd never once heard her complain compounded his contrition.

She'd taken Joel under her wing and included him in any moments of entertainment that she set in motion for Avram.

Both boys had been in a funk of boredom after days of travel through barren flatlands the first time he'd noticed it. She'd given them toy pistols made from broken-off tree branches and sent them ahead of the wagons to "hunt us some dinner."

The boys ran ahead and returned later, laughing and shouting about how they'd actually seen a rabbit and would have bagged it, too, if she'd dared to give them real guns.

It was the first time that Micah realized life would indeed continue without Georgia. Joel's laughter drove it home—like a stake to his heart.

But he wouldn't begrudge the lad any happiness. He still cried himself to sleep most nights. So any joy he found during the daylight hours, Micah wanted to nourish—even if it meant compounding his own grief.

Micah grunted at the fresh pain of it.

He would rather not have the constant reminder of her presence accompanying them all the way to the west, but he couldn't help but admit to himself that she had likely made Joel's loss more bearable. She'd certainly made life around camp easier for them all, what with all the washing and cooking she'd done and the quiet way she'd taken it upon herself to entertain and care for the boys.

He sighed now as he flopped his saddlebags onto the counter in the expansion office. At least they'd made it in time to join one of the wagon trains.

The man who looked up from the other side of the desk had round spectacles that emphasized the roundness of his face, a long drooping mustache that brought to mind a squirrel tail, and a huge smoke-billowing pipe. He spoke with the latter tucked into the corner of his mouth. "Howdy, mister. What can I do fer ya?"

"Looking to buy passage aboard a wagon train for two wagons and five passengers. Two of them are just boys if that matters. Name's Micah Morran."

The man behind the counter chewed thoughtfully on the end of his pipe. "What kind o' wagons you got?"

Micah frowned. "Good sturdy farm wagons. We drove here because my wife feared the journey aboard the Missouri steamer."

With a sigh and a near roll of his eyes, the man puffed a few times on his pipe before he offered. "Farm wagons won't make it. You'll have to see a wainwright. If he thinks he can salvage them, you might be all right."

Micah felt the beginning of a headache pinching at the base of his skull. "I didn't think we had time for that?"

The look the man gave him brought to mind his boyhood schoolmaster. "You ain't got time *not* to get yer equipment right, mister.

You want light wagons. But they have to be made with hardwood, which ain't light at'all. Not only should you caulk the beds to make 'em watertight, but you also gotta strap 'em with extra iron. If you cain't put right the ones you got, you might have to buy new 'nes. You got oilcloth?"

Micah shook his head. "Canvas. And we planned to buy a tent." Two tents now that Mercy and her boy would be joining them.

Round face wagged his head. "Mister, I strongly suggest that you plan to winter over here in Independence. You ain't ready for the trail. Last caravans are pulling out tomorrow, and you ain't got time to finish preparations. But we'll learn ya all that ya need, and you'll be right happy on the trip that you took time to provision proper." He snatched up a pamphlet from his desk and slapped it on the counter in front of Micah.

Heart falling, Micah studied the page. At the top, the list was titled. "Necessary Supplies for Survival." Below that, a caption read, "Prepare to Live."

His first instinct was to demand to speak to the captain of one of the trains pulling out, but then he got to reading the list.

- Water-ready hardwood wagon. Light of weight. Able to carry 2000 pounds. (Recommend loading no more than 1600 pounds.)
- Oilcloth of double weight for a covering.
- Tent, military or wall style. Tent poles of iron. With pegs at least a foot in length. (Prairie winds been known to carry whole families away.)

Micah pressed his lips together. That had to be a stretch of the truth. He kept reading anyway.

- Tools: Ax, Hatchet, set of augurs, set of chisels, drawing knife, handsaw, short crosscut saw, wrought iron nails, spade, and at least one hundred feet of one-inch rope.

- Extra caulk.
- Extra wheel and tire.
- Axel grease.
- Five gallons of soaking oil.

The list continued on into foodstuffs then, but Micah's gut already churned. He'd read books and articles and gotten advice from several men he admired. He'd thought he was prepared for the trip.

He wasn't.

He had most of the tools but not the oilcloth, and his wagon wasn't watertight, nor could it hold even half the required weight, he felt certain. And Gideon's wagon wasn't even in as good a shape as his.

Yet, if they didn't leave right away, they'd never make it to Oregon in time to get their allotment of land. The grant offered by the government expired this year. Did he risk the journey without all the right equipment for the possibility of getting good land?

Joel's face came to mind, and right next to it was little Avram's.

Defeat washed over him.

He couldn't risk the boys' lives for a potential piece of land. Even after they got to Oregon and received their allotment, they had to reside on and cultivate the land for four years before it would be signed over to them. And who knew what might happen in the next four years? Anything could come up that might prevent them from making good on their end of the contract.

Disheartened, he hefted his saddlebags and returned to the boardwalk. When Mattox leaped up, he bent to pet the dog's head, needing the comforting familiarity of his soft fur and the warm lap of his tongue.

How much more could a man take?

Lord, I'm asking—

The prayer slipped free before he thought better of it. An old habit.

No. I'm not asking anything because You don't—

He sealed his lips and forcibly wrenched his thoughts from the habit of prayer. He was not asking anything.

When Jess and Joel fell so sick, he'd spent hours on his knees, asking God to heal them. When Georgia hadn't been able to come to terms with her grief, he'd done plenty of praying. When he'd held Georgia, trying not to look at the bloom of blood on her shirt, he'd cried out to be heard even though he wasn't sure God even cared by that point. But God had remained uncaring and had only given him sorrow as an answer. He was done asking anything of God.

"That was so much fun!" Joel strode toward him, walking beside Mercy and Av, who laughed with him. The sound of their merriment grated. Their ecstatic footsteps pattered on the boardwalk, and Mattox bounded ahead to greet them with a happy bounce.

Mercy hesitated the moment she caught sight of him. "What is it?"

He brushed past her. He didn't owe her any explanation. "Where's Gideon?" He paced to the edge of the boardwalk, taking in the chaos of the milling street. He couldn't have his son living here for half a year.

"Uh . . ."

He spun on one heel to find her plucking at the collar of her blouse—Georgia's blouse—and looking uncertain.

"Did you hear me? Where's Gideon."

She didn't seem to want to meet his gaze. "What did you find out?" She thumbed a gesture over her shoulder to the office he'd just escaped.

Was she trying to put him off? His mind flashed to the look Gid had given him when that old-timer mentioned not bringing extras on the trip. His heart beat a rapid tattoo in his chest.

He stepped toward her. "Where is—"

She cowered against the support pillar at the edge of the boardwalk with her arms curled to protect her head.

Micah froze. Had such a mindless fool ever walked the trails of this earth? He lowered his attention to the boards between them and stepped back deliberately. "I'm sorry. I should never have . . . I would never hurt you. You know that. Right?"

She eased and straightened her sleeves, then smoothed her hands over the front of her skirt. She remained silent, eyes downcast.

She didn't know that. How could she? After all, her own father, the man who should have flown to her defense after her attack, had betrayed her. He swallowed. If only Jess were still here so *he* could be *her* defender.

But she wasn't. The only woman here was this one whose beauty and strength called to him, and yet the very sight of her dredged up so much sorrow. She had cost him dearly.

He clamped his teeth. No. Not her. She'd only been looking for an escape. Fighting to be a defender for her son.

His mind knew that. Just like Ma.

Micah swept one hand around the back of his neck. He studied her. She watched a wagon trundle down the street. Both the boys were looking at him, a bit slack-jawed.

Here was a chance for him to set a little bit right in this world gone so terribly wrong.

"Mercy?" He waited until she peeked back up at him. "I'm sorry. I should have thought better of stepping toward you. But it's very important that I know where Gideon is at this precise moment."

She swallowed. "He asked me not to tell you." Her voice sounded hollow. Tense.

"That's what I was afraid of." He folded the list and thrust it into his back pocket. "Is he selling Georgia's tea service?"

Mercy pursed her lips. Then pressed them together.

"I'll take that as a yes." He pivoted on his heel and hefted Avram, who would be the slowest of them all. "Come on, kid. We've got to stop Uncle Gid from making a big mistake." He looked at Mercy. "Which mercantile?"

Her eyes widened. "I—I don't know. But I only saw one." She motioned down the street. "Not long after we left the wagons. He's probably there."

His pulse thundered in his ears. "We need to hurry." He assessed her with a sweeping glance. "Can you keep up?"

"Yes. I'll be right behind you. Here, Joel, give me your hand." She notched up her chin and arched her brows as though telling him to get moving.

Micah gave a curt nod. Snapped his fingers at the dog. "Mattox, on guard." With that, he started off at a jog, leaving Mercy, Joel, and Mattox trailing behind.

Gideon didn't know it, but all his savings were in that crate. It had been Georgia's idea. She reasoned that if any bandits came upon them, they might smash some teacups but likely wouldn't dig all the way through the straw to the bottom of the crate.

He burst into the mercantile just as Gid was hefting the large crate of china onto the counter.

"Stop!"

Gid jolted and spun toward him.

The red-haired shop mistress leaped back and thrust her hands into the air, eyes shooting wide. She hardly looked old enough to be behind the counter.

Micah forced himself to take a breath and set Avram on the floor as Mercy and Joel tumbled in behind him. He motioned for the shopkeeper to put her hands down. "I'm not here to rob you. I just need something out of that crate before my lunkhead of a brother-in-law sells that to you." He glowered at Gid as he pried off the lid and began taking pieces from inside. Teacups, saucers, and plates all scattered bits of straw across the counter.

The shopkeeper lifted one of the delicate cups. "Oh my. These are beautiful."

Micah swallowed. How Georgia had loved the blue and gold pattern with the pink flowers. It had a woman's name . . . Something that eluded him now. He couldn't think on that, or he would end up a blubbering mess right here at the front of the mercantile.

He pulled out a cup and envisioned her standing in the morning light of their window back home, sipping coffee as she took in the sunrise. He pulled out a small plate and saw her leaning over the table in the soft light of the dinner lantern with that gentle smile of hers and tendrils of her dark hair tantalizing him as she handed him a piece of pie.

He shook the memories away and continued to unload the crate, one blazing piece of delicate dinnerware after another. Eventually, nothing but straw remained in the crate. That, and the false bottom he was looking for. He thrust his arm inside and felt along the bottom edges until he found the hole. He slipped a finger inside and tugged, lifting the bottom out of the crate. Under that lay a flat leather bag and the single layer of twenty-dollar gold pieces they'd laid in the bottom. Two hundred and fifty-six of them in the four-foot-square crate.

With relief coursing through him, he took out each of the coins and thrust them into the bag. His heart hammered with irritation at how close he'd come to losing his life's savings.

He was still scooping out coins when Gid stepped up beside him. "I'm sorry. I didn't know."

Micah glowered at him. "You didn't ask though, did you?"

Gid swallowed. "I thought it was the china you didn't want to part with. And that old-timer said we would need trade goods."

Micah finally dropped the last of the coins in the sack. He hefted it out and cinched the ties. "Well, looks like we aren't going to need trade goods this year." Hard as he tried, he couldn't disguise the defeat in the words.

Gid tilted him a surprised look. "We're not?"

Micah shook his head. "We're not prepared. The man at the expansion office gave me a list. The last of the trains leave tomorrow, and there's no way we'll be ready on time."

Gideon propped his hands on his hips and looked out toward the street. His shoulders drooped slightly. "No land for us, huh?"

Micah felt the weight of all their shattered hopes. "No."

"Well, okay then. We'll just have to live in the wagon for a few months longer than we planned. We'll save up money and buy our land fair and square."

Micah regarded the tumultuous activity on the street out front. It was more than just the expense of land. They'd meticulously planned how much food they would need for the six-month journey. Living here in Independence meant that the six-month supply in their wagon would need to be replaced. They would also need a place to live. As it stood now, they were about four beds short of what they needed to winter over here in Independence. All of these were expenses he hadn't planned for. Didn't need. Especially not if he now had to have money to buy land and build a home on the other end of this journey—to say nothing of the expenses of getting a ranch started.

"I can do you one better than that," the shopkeeper piped up from behind the counter. Her red hair had come loose from her bun in several places, and she had the straightest, whitest teeth he'd ever seen. "My father is looking to hire some men to help him build several wagons through the winter. He hopes to sell them next spring. He was a wainwright before he inherited this store, but his hands aren't as young as they used to be. Crafting a good wagon takes skill and strong hands. He'll train you if you are interested."

Gideon beamed. "Well, there you have it, see? I guess the good Lord hasn't forgotten us after all."

The woman behind the counter gasped. "He most certainly hasn't! Why would you even think that?"

Micah exchanged a thin-lipped look with Gid.

Hiding a smile, Mercy looked down at the fringe of the shawl she was running through her fingers.

Micah wished he, too, could find humor in the girl's shocked exclamation. He roughed a hand through his hair and resettled his hat before taking up his bag of money. "Can we have a day to think about it?"

She nodded. "Of course." If Micah wasn't mistaken, the woman gave Gideon a surreptitious glance. "Just let me know by tomorrow evening. There will be room and board with the job."

Micah swept a hand toward Mercy. "We'd need an extra room for our . . . friend."

The woman's eyes widened with a little curiosity. "Oh, I'd have a job for you, too, if you want it. Helping me here behind the counter. Independence has truly been booming lately, and I can't keep up. Can you do sums?"

Mercy frowned. Nodded. "Yes, but . . . the boys." She flicked a glance off of Micah, and he didn't miss the way she nipped at one side of her lower lip before continuing. "Boy. I have a son, you see."

"There's a school."

Mercy's eyes widened.

As did Joel's. "A school, Pa! Could I go?"

At the same time, Mercy said, "I'm not certain Av is old enough to attend."

Micah sighed. It seemed they had a lot they needed to discuss. "We'll let you know," he said, then started toward the door. "Gid, as soon as you are done here, meet me back at the wagons so we can talk."

With that, he tromped out the door and snapped his fingers for Mattox to keep up. The dog scrambled up from where he'd been lying beside the door, and his claws clacked noisily on the boardwalk as he trotted behind.

Parson Adam Houston paced before the wooden altar at the front of his Independence sanctuary.

With one finger holding his place in the book of Micah in the Bible clasped behind his back, he glanced toward the ceiling. "You do remember what happened to me the last time you sent me to proselytize in a saloon?" He moved his jaw back and forth, almost able to summon the anguish he'd experienced for weeks after being beaten from the premises.

The heavens rang with silence, but he didn't feel released from the impression he'd gotten only a moment ago as he'd been kneeling in prayer. At first, he'd thought the name whispered into his thoughts had to do with the book of the Bible. Only after going to the book and reading the whole thing did he realize that wasn't why he'd heard that name.

But the message would not leave him—the yearning for the salvation of a soul. A yearning birthed in the very heart of heaven and then transferred into his heart through some miracle of grace.

Adam sighed and returned his Bible to the shelf in the pulpit. He propped his hands on the sides and hung his head. Forced a breath. Then another.

Finally, he straightened and took a breath.

Where You lead me, I will follow.

He was to go to the Indy Belle Saloon and wait for a man.

A man named Micah.

Mercy hung back and waited for Gid to finalize the sale of the china. She and the boys wandered over to admire a section of carved wooden toys. There were bears, wolves, buffalo, and a floppy-eared dog. There was even a carving of a bear riding a speed walker.

Mercy grinned. She had to wonder if the clever artist might not be a precocious young lad with a speed walker of his own.

As far as she could tell, while eavesdropping from across the room, the shopkeeper gave Gid a fair price. She was a beautiful woman with so many curls piled atop her head that Mercy had to wonder how she managed to carry that head of gorgeous red hair all day without getting a severe crick in her neck. From her observations, the woman did plenty of batting her eyelashes and blushing through the process.

When Gideon had thanked her and taken up his payment, he turned and called that he was ready. The boys dashed ahead to his side, with Mercy trailing.

When she looked over at the shopkeeper, the woman pressed four fingers to her lips and made eyes at Gideon's retreating back in a womanly show of admiration and camaraderie.

Mercy smiled and waved her farewell. She had a feeling she could easily be friends with the woman, given the chance, but after her years of being shut away with nothing but Herst's animosity, she wasn't sure she knew how to make a friend anymore.

She'd never really thought of Gid as handsome. However, now that she thought about it, she supposed he certainly was. His shoulders were broad and strong as he led the way down the boardwalk and paused at the street. Sunbeams emphasized the outline of his trim physique. She stopped beside him and looked up. There were also those blond curls that needed a trim. And his blue eyes that sparkled with humor as he bent to point the boys' attention to a portly man attempting to ride young Declan Boyle's speed walker. Eyes that could turn deeply serious as they did now when he turned to look at her. They seemed even more startlingly blue beneath the sun-browned slump of his brow.

"What are you looking at?" He swiped a hand at his face self-consciously and resettled his hat.

Mercy blinked and turned her focus to where Declan attempted to help the portly man untangle himself from the wheel of his contraption. "Just noticed how that pretty shopkeeper was fawning all over herself in your presence." She felt her lips slant as she looked back up at him.

He snorted. "You're imagining things."

Mercy arched a brow. "Am I?"

He tossed a frown back toward the store, then rested a hand on Joel's shoulder. "Come on, boy. We need to get back to the wagons, so your pa can carve a lump of chaw from my shoulder."

Joel tilted his head in confusion. "But Pa don't use chaw."

Gideon made a reply that she didn't quite catch because a wagon lumbered by, and his chuckle drowned out the rest.

As she followed them across the street, her thoughts turned to other things. From what Micah had said, he and Gideon wouldn't be able to join one of the wagon trains tomorrow. But that didn't mean that she couldn't perhaps find a position of service at the last minute. She ignored the fist that closed around her heart at the thought.

Maybe when they got back, she would see if Avram could stay at the wagons with the men while she meandered over to speak with some of the families on those wagon trains. If she could secure a job, she would be one less burden for Micah and Gideon to think about as they planned.

Chapter Thirteen

The men were already deep in discussions by the time she reached the fire with Av, who had been distracted by a large team of draft horses pulling a wagon loaded with a large plow. Micah was saying something about new wagons, and Gideon alternated a frown of frustration between their own two and a pamphlet in his hands.

"Ours won't work?"

She bent to pat Mattox's head when he trotted up to her with his tongue lolling in happiness even though they'd only just parted a few moments earlier. Though her focus was on the dog, her preoccupation remained on the men's conversation.

"Not according to the fellow at the expansion office," Micah responded.

Such weariness flooded his voice that she couldn't help but wish there was a way for her to lift some of his burden. After all, she was part of the reason so much weighed on him at this moment. She was at least responsible for most of the grief.

He seemed to be carrying the weight of the world on his shoulders as he continued. "He says we need to have a wainwright look at them. But from his descriptions, it seems ours might be a mite large. And without question, not sturdy enough."

Gid handed the pamphlet back to Micah. "Maybe that's a good reason for us to take the job at the mercantile."

Mercy smiled. Of course, his comment could have nothing to do with the pretty woman who ran the store.

Apparently contented with the amount of cosseting he'd received, Mattox wandered over to Micah's wagon and flopped down in the shade beneath it.

The conversation lulled as both men stared morosely into the fire. Mercy hated to interrupt, but now seemed as good a time as any. She couldn't lift any of this burden except to maybe remove herself from their party.

"Would you two mind if Avram stayed here to play with Joel while I... run an errand?" She motioned to where the two boys were already engrossed in a game of marbles that they'd carved into the sand.

The blue eyes of both men landed on her, but somehow Micah's seemed so much fiercer.

Mercy found sudden fascination with the fringe of her shawl as she waited for them to reply.

Gideon was the first to speak. "Sure, we don't mind—"

"Where are you going?" Micah cut him off.

She looked up to find two blue flames burning into her as he rose to his feet. Even though he stood across the firepit, she clutched her shawl and took a step back. She thought of the way he'd leaned toward her earlier. Tasted the metallic prickle of familiar fear on the back of her tongue. She couldn't help but wonder if poor Georgia had ever experienced anything sharper than his barbed tongue. And yet, not once had Herst retreated or apologized when she'd flinched or cowered.

Still, he was so intense lately.

"Micah." Gideon's soft voice penetrated the golden glow of the afternoon light.

Micah glanced over at him and then eased into his heels. He plunked his hands on his hips. "Sorry. I didn't mean to snap. I'd rather you didn't wander the city on your own, however. I'd be happy to escort you."

Mercy straightened her shoulders. She wanted to retort that he had no right to tell her where she could and could not go. But that would be foolish, especially considering her history—and that had happened in sleepy Chamblissburg. Her scrutiny drifted to the chaos of Main Street. This certainly wasn't Chamblissburg. And the last thing she wanted was to attract the attention of another ne'er-do-well.

Men would doubtless leave her alone if this scowling hulk of a man accompanied her!

She bit off a smirk, even as she rubbed away the chills that came on at the thought of some man's unwanted attention.

Those first days after Herst's attack, she'd wished to die, so great had been her humiliation and fear. At least now she had one thing going for her. She knew she could survive almost anything. And Micah didn't need to expend energy mollycoddling her.

She tilted her head toward the first of the two wagon trains parked across the field. "You'll likely be able to see me the whole way. I only planned to see if anyone had need of a cook or—"

"Truly?" It was the incredulity in his voice that stopped her more than his interruption.

What was that edge in his tone all about? "Yes."

"I thought you were going to work for us?"

She worked up her courage to speak. "I only thought that my presence might be a . . . distress." She rolled in her lips and sealed them tight.

He snatched off his hat, roughed his fingers through his wild curls, and then resettled it. His shoulders seemed to slump even more, though she would have been hard-pressed to detect any movement. "You don't know any of those people."

So he wasn't denying that her presence was indeed a distress.

He waved a hand. "The only ones who likely need a cook would be single, lonely men. Think before you make such an undertaking, if only for the sake of your son."

Anger, hot and sure, shot through her. "It seems I've survived the last few months with two such men who are both single and lonely. I don't see why I couldn't . . ." Horror washed through her at what she'd just said. She closed her eyes. She spun to present him with her back. Hung her head in shame. "I'm sorry. That was an awful thing to say, especially considering . . ." She couldn't bring herself to finish the sentence. "Please forgive me."

Micah stalked past her and headed toward town. "Do what you want," he growled. He didn't look back even once.

She watched until he disappeared through the swinging doors of the Indy Belle Saloon.

Mercy swallowed. Yet one more reason to wonder if he'd treated Georgia as ill as Herst had treated her. It would no doubt be best to make herself scarce when he returned tonight.

Gideon rose wearily and came to stand beside her. "He's not been himself . . . lately. He only means to look after you."

Mercy pressed her lips together, not sure that she believed him.

Gideon motioned toward the wagon trains. "You'd really want to hire on and leave us?" A note of hurt lingered in his tone.

She turned to look at him. Laid her hand on his arm. "It's not that I don't appreciate all you and Micah have done for me. You'll never know how grateful I am for your help and how regretful I am for my part in your loss. But it's precisely that loss that compels me to leave you. I don't think he can heal with me continuously near."

Gid nodded and covered her hand, giving it a gentle squeeze before stepping back. He nudged his chin toward the wagon train on the right side of the field. "Go on and ask. I'll stay here with the boys. But do try to stay where I can see you, huh? And don't be taken in by the first offer?"

She took up two fistfuls of her skirts and started across the grass, tossing over her shoulder, "Thanks, Gid. I'll not be long."

Behind her, she heard Gideon speak to the boys. "All right, boys, what are we playing here?" The sound of him sinking onto the dirt beside them and the happy chatter of their replies drifted into the distance as she eyed the wagons ahead.

Micah stormed into the saloon but paused just inside the door. He eyed the counter and swallowed. He hadn't touched a drop in years and wasn't sure what had propelled him through the doors.

He spun to look back in the direction from which he'd come.

Mercy remained by the fire, with Gideon at her side now. Gid said something, and Mercy laid her hand on his arm. Then Gid covered her hand with his own.

Micah's molars banged together. He didn't begrudge Gid any happiness. Lord knew they both had suffered their fair share of loss. But he couldn't help but hope that Gid would pick anyone but that woman. No matter what he'd said to her earlier, the last thing their family needed was the constant reminder of the nightmare that had come about because of her presence.

"You believe in God, sir?"

Micah twisted toward the voice. He was surprised to see that the deep baritone belonged to a man about his own age. He sat at a nearby table with a glass of clear liquid before him. His cap hung on the newel of his chair, and the sleeves of his shirt had been rolled up to reveal strong forearms that showed he was no stranger to hard work. A miner or logger, maybe? Profession wasn't easily nailed down in a town such as this.

Either way, it was a strange question for someone to ask in a saloon.

Micah looked back toward the counter with the green and clear bottles on the shelf behind it. He met his own gaze in the warped gray patina of the dirty mirror. His shoulders were slumped. His expression weary. Not surprising, considering the burdens he'd been carrying for months now.

He roughed his fingers through his hair and looked back at the man who had asked the question. "I don't think that's the right question." The man's brows lifted. "Oh? What is the right one, then?" Micah sighed. "I believe there is a God . . ." He shrugged. "But He rejoices in my destruction, it seems." Micah corralled his tongue behind his teeth. Why was he blurting such things to a total stranger?

"Allow me to counter your assessment." The man nudged a chair at his table with the push of one boot.

Micah frowned at the action. The last thing he wanted was to sink into the chair at a table with a stranger. Especially one who wanted to talk to him about God.

No. Not true. The last thing he wanted to do was give in to the call of the bottle. He had a son to think of, and he was the only family his son had. Well, other than his uncle Gideon. And . . . He shook away the image of Mercy that came to mind. He refused to consider that woman family when she had been the cause of Georgia's death.

"If you'll excuse me." He hightailed a retreat to the boardwalk. But after he reached it, he wasn't sure where to go.

A glance at the fire revealed Mercy trekking across the field toward one of the wagon trains while Gideon sank down next to the boys.

His stomach bucked. Why did it bother him to see her going off on her own when merely the sight of her brought him daily sorrow? Maybe it was his earlier realization that he ought to be her protector. And the fact that when he really thought through all that happened, he knew Mercy wasn't at fault. Herst and Henry clearly were at fault, but they had received swift retribution. He could go back further and blame Mercy's father. Or he could blame himself for not being more cautious. He wasn't sure what he could have done differently, but if he'd only known . . . He scrubbed a hand through his too-long hair. The problem was, no satisfaction came with the knowledge that Herst and Henry were both dead. They hadn't suffered nearly enough for their evil.

Anger, sorrow, horror, and misery coiled in his chest like a cobra ready to strike. Like a boa constrictor, choking the life from him. Like a rattler that had already sunk its fangs and now watched for him to die. Behind him, the saloon's batwing doors squeaked and then knocked closed again. Footsteps came to a stop beside him. The stranger held a jacket draped over one shoulder and his cap in one hand. He tapped it against his leg. "Whether you believe God loves you or not, He loved you enough to send me here to talk to you today. Your name's Micah, right?"

Micah spun toward the man, unable to stop a sharp huff of unamused laughter. What kind of charlatan was this?

"Who are you?" His brow pinched in puzzlement. He'd only given his name to one person in town. "You a friend of the man with the round spectacles and bushy mustache down at the expansion office? Because if he's the one who gave you my name, I don't think he's God."

The man tucked his hat beneath one arm and thrust out his hand. "Name's Adam Houston."

Micah shook his hand more out of reflex than out of a desire to be polite. "Micah, as you already know. Micah Morran."

Adam shook his head. "I didn't know it, but God did. I'm the minister here. At least until my replacement arrives. Then I'm heading west as a missionary to a tribe called the Snohomish in the far north of the Oregon Territory."

Micah didn't want to talk further with this man, and yet he found himself saying, "Seems to me the tribes have been getting along just fine all these years without our influence. We should leave them be." He pressed his lips together before he could blurt anything more that the man might take as an insult. "Sorry. I just think they're fine. If we left them to themselves instead of trying to force our way of life on them, we might all get along better."

Adam lowered his head, looking sad. "Wanting to share the gospel of salvation is never about a way of life. Does the Lord Jesus change our hearts? He certainly does. But it's not because He feels one culture is better than another. He created all cultures and longs for a relationship with all men."

"Heard a lot of men say so. Including a lot of charlatans." He watched the man attentively to see what his reaction to that accusation would be.

"I understand that it's got to be quite a surprise to have me know your name before an introduction. But I'm no charlatan."

Right.

"Because all good ministers drink rotgut in a saloon?" Micah jerked his head to indicate the drink the man had abandoned, hating the bitterness in his words. He just couldn't seem to find geniality within himself these days.

"It was water. And I was waiting for you." The man must have read the disbelief in the look Micah shot him because he smiled in a way that revealed that he recognized his story was far-fetched. "Will you allow me to buy you a meal?"

Micah shook his head. "Can't. Sorry." He wasn't sorry. The last thing he wanted was a lecture from the likes of this shyster. He jutted his chin toward Gid and the boys by way of excuse. "I've got a family who'll want to eat soon."

"So that's why you stormed into the saloon? To buy your family a meal?" Sarcasm hung thick in the minister's words.

He probably deserved that barb. Still . . .

Hot anger surged. Who was this man to gallop into his life in such a manner? "Mister, you've got no idea what I've been through in the past six months, so I'll thank you not to sit in judgment."

Adam tilted his head in contrition. "Forgive me." He showed his palms. "Zero judgment here, friend. I have a story to tell you, and then if you want to walk away, I won't say another word. So please, I'm asking for fifteen minutes." He pointed toward an establishment across the road with a sign that read *Felicity's Fixings*. "Can I please buy you a cup of coffee? I'll even order a batch of her fried chicken and potatoes, and you can take that down to your family, and trust me, you'll be the hero of the hour when you arrive with that meal in hand."

His smile was the kind that drew men in, and he had likely taken a lot of men unawares. Micah wouldn't be one of them. Still . . . if he was buying dinner . . . maybe he could take advantage of that. Micah wasn't ready to return to their camp yet, anyhow. A hot roil of boiling anger still threatened to erupt each time he spoke.

He shrugged. "Don't see why I can't give you ten minutes."

Adam started across the street with a nod of acquiescence. "Ten minutes . . . I'll have to talk fast." He grinned.

"I'm sure you're good at that."

The man only chuckled, seemingly unoffended.

Micah was suddenly in no mood to pander to the man's strangeness. He already regretted his agreement as they pushed through the doorway into the dim interior of the building across the street.

"Parson Houston!" A woman, middle-aged, judging by the faded look of her thin brown hair, balanced several plates in each hand as she bustled past heading toward a busy table in the corner. "I'll be right with you."

Her beaming smile reminded Micah of his grandmother.

The parson gave her a nod and then leaned closer to Micah. "That's Felicity. Wonderful woman and an even better cook."

Micah scrutinized the man. He wondered again at the strength of him. Most ministers that he'd known had been portly men, often overly fond of their drink.

Yet another tally mark in favor of shyster.

Though they remained standing near the door, the minister looked over at him. "Since you've put me on a timeline of ten minutes, I'll jump right into my story, shall I?"

Micah shrugged. He was just here for the food.

The minister gave him a nod. His face lost some of its cheer then, however, and Micah watched him closely.

"I grew up as the son of a minister. My father was a hard man. Harsh really. So harsh that now, looking back, I have to wonder if he knew my Lord at all. However, I have no complaint against him because his harshness was what eventually pushed me to the foot of the cross."

Micah shook his head. What did that even mean? Pushed to the foot of the cross? Maybe the man was crazy. Did he belong in an asylum? That still didn't explain how he'd known his name.

"I began drinking at a young age. I think I was eleven the first time I snuck some of the communion wine from Pa's cellar." He smiled self-deprecatingly. "I woke with a raging pain in my head and soon had another in my backside when my father discovered what I'd done."

"This way, gentlemen." The woman named Felicity breezed past them in a blur and swiped a table with a rag before motioning for them to sit. "Coffee? I'm Felicity, by the way," she said to Micah. But she didn't give him time to respond before looking back to Adam for an answer to her question about the coffee.

"Yes, for me," Adam said, lifting a questioning brow at Micah as they sank into their seats.

Micah nodded. "Sure. Thank you. Name's Micah."

"Nice to meet you, Micah." She practically trotted toward what Micah presumed must be the kitchen at the back of the place.

The minister didn't miss a beat as he continued. "Pa's whupping didn't stop me. I continued to drink. I couldn't reconcile the God of Love that Pa preached about with the Father of Fury that he was. But then, ah ... then ..."

As tears filled the minister's eyes, Micah frowned, uncomfortable.

"I met my dear Eden. I'm telling you, Micah, if ever there was love at first sight, it was me with Eden. She and her family moved to town the year I turned eighteen. I was in the front row, all pained because of a humdinger of an evening I'd indulged in the night before. We sang the last notes of the final hymn, and I stood, anxious to be the first one out of that building. And there she sat, toward the back on the right, beside her parents."

He leaned back and to one side slightly as Felicity reappeared with a coffee pot and two tin mugs.

"I had such a twist all inside my chest. Couldn't breathe. Couldn't think. I just stopped right there in the aisle. Thanks, Ms. Felicity. Say, give us the family-size fried chicken and potatoes, would you? In fact, make it two."

"Coming right up." She bustled away again.

"Time's ticking." Micah felt low, even as he snapped the words, but he honestly didn't have time to waste listening to stories of this swindler's woman troubles. He sipped the coffee and was surprised to find that it was the best he'd had since leaving Virginia.

"I'm telling you, Micah, I suddenly wanted to become a better man. And so I did. I gave up drink. Got myself cleaned up. Even started doing better at respecting what my father said instead of what he did. I courted that girl, and we got married." He sighed with a faraway look in his eyes. "Those early years were the good ones. But something always felt like it was missing. And I never could shake the hankering for a drink, if you know what I mean." His gaze leveled on Micah and honed in.

Micah refused to squirm in his seat. He also refused to acknowledge just how closely this man's story resembled his own. Only he hadn't been in church when he'd first laid eyes on Georgia. He'd been coming out of the tobacco warehouse where he worked, and she'd been waiting for Gid, who had only recently started there too.

Micah couldn't figure how this man knew so much about him. He had indeed given up drink to attract Georgia. She'd insisted, or he wouldn't have even thought about it. But how had this man known? That was what bothered him and kept him in his seat. He was invested now and wanted to see what kind of chicanery this was.

"Eden fell with child. And we were blissfully happy. I decided this life of service to God wasn't so bad. It was easy. I never woke with crippling headaches. Eden made me happy. All was well." He paused and sipped his coffee. His lips thinned grimly. "Until it wasn't. Eden is small. Childbirth did not go well for her. We laughed with excitement when the first pain took her. But by the time she was able to birth, two days later, our . . . son was no longer among the living." The minister flicked at his eyes with his thumb.

"We lost our daughter," Micah blurted. His jaw ached but not as much as his heart. It was a selfish thing to do in the face of the man's obvious suffering, shifting focus to himself. "Sorry, I don't mean to brush over what you and your wife went through. I just—" He hadn't planned to say that either. What power did this man have to make him talk when he didn't want to? Focus lowered, he twisted his cup on the table.

Adam set his coffee aside and leaned forward as though it were of the utmost importance that Micah hear his next words. "Around noon today, when I was at the church in prayer, the Lord strongly impressed on me that I was to wait for a man named Micah at the saloon. And I was to give you a message."

Micah felt a chill sweep down his back despite his continued skepticism.

"God sees your tears, Micah Morran. And He cares. And He has a promise for you. If you do things His way, your sorrow will be turned into joy. The Lord wants you to know, 'Most assuredly, I say to you, whatever you ask the Father in My name He will give you. Until now you have asked nothing in My name. Ask, and you will receive, that your joy may be full.'"

Feeling the hair on the back of his neck stand on end, Micah sank against the slats of his chair, willing himself to stay dry-eyed. He had spoken to no one, those thoughts about the futility of asking God for anything. How had this man known? Awe filled him, and yet . . .

Anger hardened his jaw. "Did you ask God for a miracle? In those two days when your child was dying? Did you pray for God to give your baby life?"

Adam didn't even hesitate, as Micah had thought he would. He nodded. "I most certainly did."

"So?" Micah shrugged. "God obviously didn't answer your prayer. How does that align with Him caring for us so much? Or maybe He only cares for some and not others."

"God's word can't be taken piecemeal, Micah. God specifically told me to share those verses with you. They are out of the gospel of John, by the way, the sixteenth chapter. However, there is a place in James that talks about why God doesn't answer our prayers sometimes. And that's because we ask with wrong motives. You see, I begged God to save my wife and child not so that it would give God glory, but simply because I was selfishly banking on her—them—being my joy, but at the end of those verses from John, it says, 'that your joy may be full.' The Lord knew that my joy would never be full so long as I was counting on Eden or my son to give it to me. He had better plans, both for my son—who I firmly believe went straight to heaven and never had to experience the temptations of this sin-sick world—and for me. True joy, full and lasting joy, comes only from Him." He paused. Micah felt his searching scrutiny deep in his bones. "You lost more than a child, didn't you, Micah?"

Micah's teeth pressed together so tightly that his jaw ached. He looked into the depths of his coffee cup. Once again, he didn't intend to speak, but suddenly, the whole story was pouring from him. How they had been filled with excitement to head west. How the sickness struck, and he lost his daughter, and Gideon lost his wife. How Georgia collapsed in on herself. How they stopped to resupply in Chamblissburg, and how they rescued Mercy, even though Georgia hadn't wanted to get involved. And lastly, how Mercy's husband caught up to them and mistook Georgia for Mercy and how his cousin shot her. "My Georgia," he waved a hand. "She was the one who believed in God. She was the one who made me get to services each Sunday. But there at the end . . ." He shook his head. "I just . . . She wasn't the kind woman I'd known. She became hard. And I worry, parson . . . I worry that maybe she lost her way." He hadn't meant to spill that either. He clenched his jaw and looked away, fiddling with his cup again.

"If there's anyone who understands the frailties of our flesh, Micah, it is the God of heaven who, Himself, came down, was born as a babe, and grew up on this earth in a human vessel. He understands grief. He understands sorrow. In fact, the Word says he was acquainted with grief. Grief is so powerful that it can break us for a time. But the Lord remembers that we are dust."

Felicity arrived with two platters piled high with pieces of chicken and another platter laden with baked potatoes, split open and mounded with butter and soured cream. A fourth platter held a pyramid of steaming golden corncobs, and more butter slid from the top down the sides.

The savory scent of the chicken made Micah's stomach grumble, and he realized that he hadn't eaten anything since the day-old biscuit and hard-boiled eggs he'd devoured when they'd broken camp at dawn.

Adam stood and took up a platter of chicken and the potatoes. "I believe my ten minutes are concluded. Please allow me to help you carry this to your family."

Micah rose, casting an uncertain glance toward Felicity, who seemed to be taking an order at a table across the room. He didn't figure she'd fancy them absconding with her platters.

Adam gave a pointed jut of his chin to the two plates that remained on the table. "Come on. We don't want all this delicious food growing cold. I'll bring the platters back when I return to pay. Felicity knows I'm good for it."

As Micah hefted the food, Adam called across the room.

"I'll be back shortly, Felicity."

She waved a distracted hand as she bustled toward the kitchen once more. It was only when they were almost to their wagons that Micah realized he hadn't heard the end of the minister's story, and for some crazy reason, he really wanted to hear it. Was his wife here with him? He'd said, 'Eden *is* small.' Not was. That meant she'd lived, right?

As they stopped near the fire and set the platters of food on a large flat rock, he glanced over at the man. "Please stay and join us."

The minister beamed. "Thank you for the hospitality."

The man did not mention his wife. Micah remained curious, but he let the matter drop. "Let me introduce you." He held a hand toward Gid and the boys.

Chapter Fourteen

Mercy asked after a job at the first two wagons and received kind and apologetic refusals. The woman at the second wagon was as talkative as a magpie. Mercy despaired of ever escaping the conversation, but finally was able to politely extricate herself and continue on her way.

As she approached the third wagon, a man with a missing front tooth leered at her. "Howdy." The scrape of his scrutiny from her head to her toes shot Mercy through with horror. Why hadn't she listened to Micah?

She spun on one heel and raced back toward Micah's and Gideon's wagons with her heart beating in her throat. Her ears strained to hear every noise behind her.

Was that the rustle of footsteps? Or only the wind in the grass?

She tossed a look over her shoulder.

Thankfully, though he still watched her, the man remained where he sat by his fire.

And then she reached Micah's wagon. She stepped between it and Gideon's and pressed her back to the side, tipping her head against a stay to catch her breath.

On the other side of Gideon's wagon, she could hear the happy sound of the boys' voices and a gentler, deeper response from Gideon.

But she wasn't ready to face them yet. She was still trembling like a newborn filly trying to gain her legs.

Breathe. Just breathe. It was nothing.

She drew a long, slow breath through her nose and pushed it out through pursed lips.

Micah's voice drifted across the wagon now. "This here's Adam." So he'd returned from the saloon, had he? And brought a friend? What else had he brought, she wondered bitterly.

It hadn't escaped her thoughts that while they'd been on the trail, the men hadn't had access to drink. But now . . . She shook away that worry. She had enough of a fist clamping off her airway as it was.

"Pleasure to meet you," Gideon responded.

"Fried chicken!" Joel exclaimed.

A strange man's voice responded with a chuckle—presumably the "Adam" Micah had just mentioned.

She frowned. Shook out the tingling in her hands. Drew another long breath. Tried to banish the terror that had overtaken her the moment she'd seen the hunger in that man's eyes. But just picturing it made her tremble anew.

She focused on the stillness around her. *You're fine. He didn't follow you. Breathe.*

Grass rustled and a boot crunched against dry stalks.

Mercy screeched and spun to face the sound, even as she crouched with her arm up, ready to protect herself.

Micah froze at the end of the wagon. He lifted his palms, brow slumping. "Mercy, it's just me."

Her breath whooshed from her, taking so much strength that she had to prop her hands on her knees.

Micah strode nearer. "Did someone touch you?" His words grated like wagon wheels over a stony road.

Mercy flapped a hand. "I'm fine. You startled me, is all."

She forced herself to stand. That put her very close to him, but never had she been more thankful for the presence of a man. She pressed a palm against the thumping she could feel in her chest. "Micah, thank you for being safe."

He examined her face as though not quite sure whether she had all her senses. And then inspected the field in the direction from which she'd just come. "You're not telling me something. What is it?"

Mercy felt her shoulders droop. "It was just the way a man looked at me. That was all. He didn't do anything but offer a greeting."

His gaze sharpened on her again. His lips bunched into a tight press like he wanted to say something but was withholding his opinion. He retreated a couple of steps. "I'm sorry I startled you." He motioned to the box on the side of his wagon next to her. "I was coming to fetch the plates and cups. I—we—brought back dinner, so you won't need to cook tonight."

Mercy allowed herself one more short inhale. "We?"

Micah eased close again, raised the lid of the box, and reached for the basket of tableware. "Met a minister."

Her brows rose. "A minister? In the saloon?"

He dipped his chin. "Seems a nice enough fellow." He hefted out the basket and closed the lid, and then searched her face once more. His voice softened. "You sure you're all right?"

She felt like a fool. She wondered if she would ever be able to feel like a normal woman again—one unafraid and carefree.

Realizing Micah still waited for her answer, she brushed away his concern with a swish of one hand. "I just needed a moment. I'm fine. Honest."

He looked toward the wagon trains and scrubbed at his jaw with his thumbnail. "Did you find a job?"

A sound halfway between a huff and a laugh escaped before she could stop it. "No." She didn't elaborate that she'd come skittering back here after only the third wagon.

His inspection darted to her and then settled back on the wagons in the distance. "You going to ask more folk later?"

Mercy concentrated on her folded hands. "I think I've decided to stay here in Independence for a few months."

From the corner of her eye, she saw him give a short nod. "Good." He swept out an arm. "After you."

Feeling miserable and defeated, Mercy led the way. She'd wanted to spare him her presence, but it seemed she was too broken to do so.

It only made her feel marginally better when both Joel and Avram rushed to her with happy greetings.

Gideon frowned to see Mercy back so soon and with such tension in the line of her shoulders. He narrowed a look on Micah. Had his beef-headed brother-in-law set her on edge again somehow?

Micah placed the basket of tableware on one of the flat rocks a distance from the fire. When he met Gid's scrutiny, he wagged his head as if to say they could talk about it later. Then he had the audacity to turn his back and sweep a gesture from the minister to Mercy. "This here is Mercy Adler. Mercy, this is the minister, Adam Houston."

Gid's eyes narrowed further when the minister lit up like a lantern and stretched out one hand. "Pleased to meet you, ma'am."

"Likewise." Mercy settled a hand on Av's shoulder. "This is my son, Avram. And this handsome fellow here . . ." She ruffled Joel's hair. "Is Joel, Micah's son."

"Yes. We met just now. The boys and I were just discussing whether I could beat them at a game of marbles." The minister laughed.

"Well, maybe after dinner, you can give it an attempt." Mercy set Avram from her and lifted the lid of the basket. She pulled out the stack of tin plates and handed Gid the first one.

He accepted it but searched her face. Something *had* happened. "You all right?"

"Yes." Mercy spun away too quickly. "Here, boys." She held out the plates, and Joel and Avram each took one. "Mind that Mattox doesn't steal your chicken now. And no sneaking him bones."

She smiled at the dog, whose nose practically pirouetted through the air as he inhaled the scent of the chicken. A long pink tongue swept out to slurp his chops.

Micah snapped his fingers and pointed for the dog to return to his place beneath the wagon.

Hanging his head, Mattox slunk back to his spot.

Mercy handed the last two plates to Micah and the minister, and both men promptly held the plates back toward her.

"Wouldn't want to take yours, ma'am," the minister said.

Micah nudged the man's plate toward him. "She can have this one."

Gideon scowled at the plate in his hands. He was a selfish lout. He rose and thrust his plate into Mercy's hands before she could accept Micah's. "It's just fried chicken. I can eat that with my fingers. Don't need a plate. Let's eat." He clapped his hat to his chest and bowed his head, hoping they would get on with the praying. It gave him some satisfaction when both the minister and Micah retreated a few steps from Mercy, both still with their plates in hand.

Micah motioned for Joel to remove his cap and then said, "Adam, I guess you ought to say grace. And we thank you again for your generosity. Ought we to fetch your wife to join us?"

Gid felt his curiosity rise when the minister hung his head. "I—no. She's not with me." A sharp pain filled his gaze before he blinked it away and smiled. "But I'm happy to say the prayer." Adam's voice rang with deep sincerity as he blessed not only the food but also their family.

Gid kept his hat clapped to his chest. In addition to his curiosity about what had happened with Mercy, he couldn't help but wonder what had transpired between Micah and this man. One minute, Micah stomped into the saloon, and the next, he'd returned with platters of food and this minister by his side.

Once everyone filled their plates and he had nabbed two pieces of chicken, one for each hand, it pleased him when Mercy sank onto the rock next to his.

Across the fire, Micah continued to scowl hard enough to scare the food on his plate into submission.

Gid grinned, not quite sure why Micah's displeasure gave him so much pleasure. He glanced over at Mercy, who was picking at her food more than eating it. "You get a job?"

She shook her head. "No. I was just telling Micah that I've decided to stay on here until next year."

The night just kept getting better and better.

Gideon filled his mouth with chicken, pondering that thought. Why was he so happy to have Mercy staying on? His heart still suffered with missing Verona, and he couldn't see himself moving on any time soon. But over the past few months, he'd also come to care deeply for this woman by his side as a friend.

He glanced at the boys, who were both happily chattering to the minister. The minister's deep laugh made Gideon want to smile. Even Micah's expression seemed to have softened some.

Gideon tossed the bones from his first piece of chicken into the fire and tucked into the second one.

He nudged Mercy with his elbow. "I'm glad. Right glad."

If Mercy's smile made him go a little soft inside, well, it was only because he considered her a friend. That was all.

The next morning, Mercy walked down the dusty street with the boys, Micah, and Gideon, to the mercantile where the woman had offered them jobs the day before. She'd never gotten the woman's name, she realized.

Poor Mattox had been tied to the wagon and instructed to stay. He barked in protest, but when Micah snapped his fingers, the dog flopped down with a sigh and rested his chin upon his paws.

She'd snuck a few scraps of leftover chicken meat into his mush by way of apology. He'd wagged his tail approvingly and had been happily chomping from his bowl as they walked away.

She turned to Gideon. "Did you learn her name yesterday?"

He frowned. "Whose name?"

A grin tilted her lips, and she studied him for his reaction. "The pretty redheaded woman at the mercantile."

He looked away, but not before she caught the uptick at the corner of his mouth. "I didn't ask her name, no."

Micah tromped up the steps to the boardwalk without adding to the conversation. He seemed to have been in a bit of a funk since last night. Silent and moody. Well—she allowed herself a smile—*more* silent and moody. In fact, she didn't think she'd heard him say one word since the minister left the fire last night.

He was right that the minister seemed a nice man. She couldn't deny that she had been a little surprised by that because of her experience with the one back home. She had halfway expected him to try to proselytize them at some point. But the man hadn't appeared to have an agenda. He had remembered his promise to the boys and played a round of marbles with them after the meal. And on the whole, he had been most congenial.

The bell above the mercantile door jangled as Micah pushed it open. He stood to one side and waited until they all swept past him before stepping in and closing the door behind them.

The pretty redhead looked up from behind the counter. "You're back!"

Yet another surprise.

Mercy had halfway expected the woman not to remember them. At the very least, she'd expected that maybe the jobs would already be taken. She supposed they would find that out soon enough.

If the job remained available and truly did come with room and board, the first thing she planned to do this evening was indulge in a long soak in a tub. So long as she could talk one of the men into watching Avram for a bit.

She was also concerned about Avram and the school situation. At barely five, surely he was too young to be sent off to school every day.

But neither could he entertain himself for hours while she worked. It was a concern that she didn't yet have an answer for.

Micah and Gideon swept off their hats. Micah stepped forward with his clapped to his chest. "Yes, ma'am. We're here to see if those jobs you spoke about are still available?"

The redhead's eyes sparkled, and Mercy didn't miss the way her attention darted past Micah to settle on Gideon. "They sure are! And is Pa ever going to be happy to have you."

Micah's boots shuffled against the floor. "We do want to be clear that we have no experience as wainwrights. But I think you'll find that we are both quick to learn and hard workers."

The twinkle in the girl's eyes spread to lift her lips. "Don't worry. My pa is an excellent instructor, but he'll be pleased to have men of such intelligence working for him." She offered a bold wink that left Micah stammering that he hadn't meant to overstate their capabilities.

An uncharitable twinge tightened Mercy's stomach.

"My name is Willow Chancellor."

Micah gave her a nod. "I'm Micah Morran. This is my brother-in-law, Gideon Riley."

"Oh." Willow's gaze dimmed even as it darted to Gideon, and Mercy realized the word "brother-in-law" had made her hesitate. "So . . . you're . . . married?" Red tinged her cheeks. Her focus dipped to the counter between them, and she brushed at a crumb.

Mercy wanted to roll her eyes. This girl was confusion itself.

Hanging his head and propping his hands on his hips, Micah seemed determined to simply wait out this exchange. He swung his attention toward her, humor grooving lines at the corners of his eyes.

Mercy grinned, relieved to see Micah finding amusement in the situation. More than that, she felt as though she'd won a ticket to a show. And it didn't hurt to know that the girl's fascination still remained on Gideon, despite her bold wink at Micah. Mercy's grin fell away. Why should it bother her if the girl wanted to flirt with Micah? She certainly wanted no claim on him. He made her feel safe and protected. That was all. She mustn't misconstrue those feelings of gratefulness as interest.

But, because she liked the girl, she didn't want to see her with someone as severe as Micah could sometimes be. Yes. That must be it. Her grin returned, and she leveled it on Gideon, waiting to see what his response would be.

Gideon glowered at her good-naturedly. He shifted his feet and replied, "I was married. She passed."

Compassion immediately flooded Willow's eyes as she sought his again. "Oh, I'm so sorry to hear that. My ma passed on when I was just a girl, so it's just been Pa and me for a lot of years now, but I don't think the pain of losing someone is something you ever forget."

Gideon swallowed. "No, ma'am."

"Miss. It's Miss. Or Willow. Willow Chancellor. As I said."

Gid swept the brim of his hat through his fingers. "The jobs?"

"Of course!" Willow pivoted and hurried toward the back. "I'll return momentarily."

As she rushed away, Mercy couldn't withhold a chuckle, but at Gid's sharp look, she did manage to withhold her words, if not the arched brow she angled his way.

Gid thrust his hat at her. "Stop that." He whispered fiercely. "She can't be a day over fifteen."

Though humor still danced in Micah's eyes, he shook his head at her behind Gid's back, so Mercy folded her hands and forced herself to lay off the teasing.

Chapter Fifteen

Micah couldn't figure Mercy out. Just last night, he'd seen her in intimate conversations with Gid on two separate occasions, yet here she stood teasing him about another woman.

He switched his focus to his brother-in-law. Based on his expression, he didn't seem to mind her teasing too much.

Micah swallowed a grunt. Maybe he was off the mark in his thinking that they were developing feelings for each other.

He gave his head a little shake. It didn't matter to him what either of them did. They were both full-grown adults and could do as they liked. He had more important things to concentrate on right now.

An image of the minister's sincere expression from the evening before popped into his mind—along with the warm shiver that swept down his spine at the memory of the words he'd spoken that felt like they were for Micah alone, but he pushed the thoughts and feelings away. He didn't have time for such . . . wishfulness right now. Even if it did sound mighty appealing that the Almighty had sent a message just for him. He had his family to get settled and duties to attend to.

Like learning how to be a wainwright.

He'd never done any job other than working at the tobacco factory. He'd started at fifteen—the first year they'd deemed him old enough to work. But in the ten years that he'd been at the factory, he'd worked hard and risen through the ranks to become the supervisor of the drying department. It had involved requisitioning new crops, overseeing the workers who hauled the tobacco drying racks into the ovens, making sure the ovens were never heated too hot, and properly turning the product for even drying. Then, after all that was complete, they had to crate the dried leaves and transport them to the assembly department, where everything from pipe tobacco to cigarettes were assembled. The cigarette machine was such a modern contraption that the company had only acquired it a few months before his departure.

He only hoped that he would be able to assimilate to wagon-making as quickly as he had to his position at the factory.

The redheaded girl returned with a man in tow. "Gentlemen, this is my father, Wayne Chancellor. Papa, this is the Misters Riley and Morran and . . ." Her voice trailed away, and her face heated as she realized that she'd never completed the introductions earlier.

"Mercy Adler," Mercy supplied with a slight curtsy.

"And these are our boys, Joel and Avram." Micah stepped forward and extended his hand to the man. "Pleased to meet you, sir."

The man had a healthy head of brown hair touched with silver near the temples. "Oh, you've no idea just how happy I am to make your acquaintance, fellows. No idea!" His face spread into a broad, welcoming grin, and his grip was firm.

Micah had a sudden understanding of where the sprite behind the counter came by her perpetually sunny disposition.

"Mr. Riley. Y'all are a godsend, and that's certain." The man pumped Gid's hand vigorously.

"And you, Ms. Adler. Willow will be so pleased to have your help here in the store. I'm afraid I rather took on a bit more than I expected when I decided to try to run both the store and a wagon-making business. But things are looking up. Yes, sir. Looking up already." He turned on his heel and rolled a hand in a follow-me gesture. "Gentlemen, right this way. We can get right to work, and Willow will show Ms. Adler to her duties here in the store."

Mercy's mouth opened and shut as she divided a glance between the boys who were standing off to one side and Mr. Chancellor's back.

"Father . . ." Willow said.

Mr. Chancellor turned around.

Micah felt like he should be the one to explain. "Ah, Mr. Chancellor. I'm afraid we can't start today. Tomorrow, yes. But we have some things to settle. We just arrived in town yesterday afternoon, and we have the boys to consider, you see." He nudged his hat in the boys' direction. "And . . . your daughter said something about room and board?"

The man leaned down to prop his hands on his knees as he eyed the boys. "Of course. Forgive me. Willow says I'm forever rushing headlong into things without thinking. How would you boys like to share a stick of penny candy while we show your parents the rooms upstairs?"

Joel's eyes widened with surprise and anticipation, and he turned a pleading look on Micah.

He nodded. "Fine by me." Recently, the boy had been deprived of such joys, and it raised Mr. Chancellor in his estimation to have him be so thoughtful.

"Please, Ma?" Avram asked.

"Of course." Mercy nudged him to join Joel, who had followed Mr. Chancellor to the candy jar on the counter.

In his hurry to catch up, Avram tripped over his own feet, and Micah caught him with a flat hand to his chest just before he sprawled across the floor. "Slow down, there, tyke. That candy doesn't have legs. It's not going anywhere."

Avram regained his balance and looked up with wide brown eyes. "S-sorry." He pressed his small chubby hands together and didn't move.

Micah felt consternation tighten his brow. Genuine fear shone from the boy's eyes.

He squatted down so he was more on the kid's level. "Did you hurt your hands?"

Av shook his head and splayed them for Micah to see. He seemed fine.

"All right, well, nothing to be sorry for. When I was your age, my feet were often bigger than I expected as well."

He offered the boy a smile, hoping to alleviate his fear, but only received the same wary scrutiny in return.

Realizing this was a war best won in small victories, he swept his hat to where Joel waited by the candy jar. "Go on. Joel's waiting for you to help him decide on a flavor."

He watched the boy go, wondering why this was the first time he'd noticed the way the kid feared him. But looking back, he realized it was true. Av mostly avoided him.

When he regained his feet, it was to find Mercy with her lips rolled together and pressed tight. She gave him the barest of nods, but gratefulness filled her expression.

He hated to think what these two had been through. He wished he didn't have an inkling of what they'd suffered. But, in fact, he understood it all too well. No one deserved family that had tried to have them killed.

He was glad that she hadn't found a job with those wagon trains. He wanted to help her and the boy find a good position that would see them supported and cared for.

Ask of Me.

The thought was almost audible. So much so that he darted a look behind himself. Of course, no one was there, but hang it if he didn't feel as though he'd just been struck by lightning. Every hair on his body seemed to be standing on end. When he turned back around, Gideon and Mercy were both frowning at him as though trying to figure out what he'd been looking for.

Chagrined, he squeezed the muscles at the base of his neck. He wasn't about to admit to hearing voices. Especially not the voice of God. Gid would laugh him out of the room. What was it God wanted with him all of a sudden? He had nothing to offer. A whole lot of nothing, in fact. Just a broken heart and a chest full of pain.

Realizing Gid and Mercy were still watching him, he swept his hat in Avram's direction, "Good kid."

Mercy nodded, her gaze drifting to her son, patiently waiting for Mr. Chancellor, who was behind the counter halving the red stick of candy the boys had chosen. "He is that."

"I can show you all to your rooms now if you wish?"

The tiny redhead appeared next to Micah. The top of her head barely reached his shoulder. He stepped to one side, and she started off through the shelves and barrels of goods. Micah motioned for Mercy to precede him and then fell into line behind her with Gideon on their trail.

He smoothed his hands over his arms, brushing at the tingling sensation that remained.

"Joel, watch Avram," he called as they reached the foot of the stairs. "We'll be right back. You boys stay inside and out of mischief."

"Yes, sir." Joel nodded, then immediately returned his attention to Mr. Chancellor, who seemed to be regaling them with a story of some sort.

When they reached the landing, Miss Chancellor paused in the hallway. Three doors led off the dark narrow passageway. Two on one side and one on the other. She swept a hand to the single door. "This is the larger of the rooms. It has three beds." She nudged the door open and swept inside.

They all followed.

Micah stepped to one side of the door and paused to survey the room. It was spacious, with two windows that let in plenty of light. There were two quilt-covered beds that were longer, though narrow. And one smaller one pushed into a corner.

"Other than the beds, which you can plainly see, there is a wash basin here behind the door. You'll get fresh bed linens once a week and clean towels every third day." She extended a motion to a set of hooks where three sheets of toweling dangled.

"The bureau there might be small for three, but if you need another, we'll see what we can do."

"We'll make do." As Micah scanned the room, his reflection snagged on Mercy standing just inside the doorway beside Miss Chancellor. She was only an inch or two taller than the little redheaded girl. He'd known she was underweight, but why was it he'd never realized just how short she was? He cut a glance to the hem of the skirt she wore. Sure enough, the material dragged a good inch along the ground.

He folded his arms.

Georgia's clothes were not only too large on her because of her weight but also because of her height. He ought to have noticed that. But even now, he could barely look at those clothes without wanting to claw his chest open to pulverize the pain.

"Mr. Morran?"

He snapped his attention to the doorway and realized the three of them were clustered there, staring back at him.

A bit of a sparkle lit Miss Chancellor's blue eyes. "Want to join us across the hall?"

Feeling discomfited to have been caught gathering wool, he rubbed at his jaw with his thumbnail. "Of course."

In the hallway, Miss Chancellor pushed open the first of the two doorways across the way. "This is the water closet. Pa rigged up this pulley so you can lower the slops out the window. And hot water will be provided for each of you once a week on Saturdays."

Micah eyed the small, galvanized bathing tub dubiously. His knees would be up around his ears in that thing, but at least there was a separate room for bathing. That would make everything easier.

"There is an outhouse out back." She pointed out the window. "I'll also bring a fresh bucket and fresh water up each morning. And this . . ." She glided out of the bathroom and pushed open the other door. "Is the smaller of the bedrooms."

This room was similar to the one across the hall, minus the space that had been taken up by the bathing room. There was only one window and one double-wide bed. Everything else seemed the same right down to the carvings on the front of the bureau.

Mercy stepped near the bed and pressed one hand to the mattress. She didn't speak, but from the look on her face, he had a feeling she would be grateful to sleep on a real bed tonight. They all would, he supposed.

Miss Chancellor paused in the doorway and folded her hands. "Will these rooms suffice?"

Micah checked with Gid and Mercy with a quick look before he nodded. "Seems fine to us. What about the board?" He hated to keep pushing but figured it would be better to get everything out in the open right from the get-go.

Miss Chancellor didn't seem bothered by his question. "Two meals, breakfast and dinner, will be paid for over at Felicity's Fixings. You'll be on your own for the noon hour and on Sundays."

Mercy and Gideon nodded their agreement to that plan, so Micah did too. "That sounds fair. If you'll allow us today to settle in, we'll be ready to start work first thing tomorrow."

"Of course." Miss Chancellor turned and led the way back down the stairs. "I'm sorry about Pa. He's always so ardent that he forgets others don't often rush ahead as he does."

Gid spoke from the back of the line. "Is there someplace we can park our wagons where they will be out of the elements?"

"Oh, yes." Miss Chancellor reached the floor of the mercantile and stepped to one side.

She bumped into a stack of shovels leaning against one wall, and Micah surged forward to keep her from being pummeled by the falling tools. He only managed to catch one shovel. The rest clanged and bounced against the hardwood floor. One took out a whole shelf of soaps which cascaded across the floor in all directions.

"Oh my, I'm such a mush-head." She pressed her hands to her cheeks, eyeing the mess. Then she flapped a hand at it. "I'll get this cleaned up momentarily. As for your wagons, if you pull them around back, Pa will open the barn for you, and you can park them in there."

Mercy sank to her knees and started gathering soaps.

Micah bent to gather the bars that would be out of her reach as Gid went to work picking up shovels and leaning them against the wall again.

"Please, you don't have to—"

But with the three of them working, the task was already almost complete. Except, as he went to stand the fallen shelf upright, he saw that one leg of it had been broken. There wouldn't be any saving it. He turned his hat upside down and placed the bars of soap he'd collected inside.

Miss Chancellor must have changed her mind, for she fell to her knees beside Mercy. "Thank you so much. I appreciate it."

Mercy smiled, balancing bars of soap in the cradle of one arm. "We don't mind helping. Perhaps the first thing I can do to help tomorrow is to lay out a plan to make this room less . . . crowded?"

Miss Chancellor chuckled. "If you can accomplish that, I'll know for certain God sent you straight to my door yesterday."

Mercy only smiled. "We'll see what we can do." She started to rise, but with one arm filled with bars of soap, she lost her balance and nearly sprawled flat.

Micah's free hand shot out to grip her elbow.

She gasped and reeled away from his touch, almost causing herself to lose her balance in the other direction. She shot him a wide-eyed look that lasted for only a fleeting moment. But he didn't miss the terror that had filled her at his touch.

"Sorry." Her tongue darted over her lips. "It's just . . ." She shook her head as though unable to finish the thought.

She didn't have to finish it. He knew well what had caused her reaction. And it churned up all sorts of emotions better left buried.

Mercy was once again struggling to stand.

"Just helping you up," he offered, reaching for her arm more slowly this time.

She didn't react other than to keep her focus on the bars of soap as she gained her feet.

Still balancing the hat full of soap in one hand, he released her as soon as she attained her balance.

He stepped back. Rubbed his palm down his breeches, wishing that he could as easily eradicate the delicate floral scent she wore as he could the feel of her bony elbow in his clasp. It was different than the scent Georgia had worn. Still floral, but more like . . . the smell of spring in a peach orchard with subtle undertones of warm shortbread.

He huffed at his ponderings and strode across the room to deposit the contents of his hat on the counter. And when he turned to find Gid watching him with eyes narrowed in assessment, he clamped his teeth together.

Between his hearing voices and the pressure to make sure those in his charge were taken care of, he might just go crazy before all this was over.

"I'll be back at the camp," he said and strode toward the door. He was almost to the boardwalk when he realized he ought to collect Joel and say something to Mr. Chancellor, so he reversed course, ignoring Mercy, who was now depositing her soaps in neat little stacks next to the ones he'd dumped from his hat.

"Son. Time to go. We need to get some things packed up at our camp." He thrust his hand toward Mr. Chancellor. "Sir, thank you for the opportunity to work for you. What time should we arrive in the morning?"

Micah liked Mr. Chancellor's firm grip. He never could abide a handshake that felt like he was squeezing a dead fish.

"Felicity's opens at five. So you can eat whenever you are hungry. But we won't start work until seven. I usually throw down my hammer come evening, around six. My old body can't work the long hours it used to anymore."

Micah nodded. "Seven it is." With that, he nudged Joel to lead the way. Only an eleven-hour shift. Wouldn't that be nice? He used to work fifteen hours, six days a week, back at the factory. And with their recent long days on the trail, he wasn't sure what he would do now to occupy all his free time.

He brushed past Mercy again, and hang if that scent wasn't still lingering in the air.

Guilt slashed through him.

His wife had only been in the grave for a few months.

He had no business noticing the scent of another woman.

He yanked open the door, sending the bell above jangling like a runaway sleigh.

Maybe it would have been better if she had gotten herself hired on to one of those caravans. However, they had both pulled out this morning, only a few hours apart from each other. So he was just going to have to put up with her and the feelings of remorse, agony, and guilt that she kept layering on him. There was also the frustration over the loss of Oregon acreage. If only they'd arrived a couple of weeks earlier . . . But there was no undoing the past now. Like Gid had said, they would simply have to save up and buy their land. It would take longer to build their spread, but it could still be accomplished.

His boots scuffed to a stop at the edge of the boardwalk, and he hung his hands from his beltloops.

"Pa? You okay?" Joel spoke around the piece of candy he was still sucking on.

Micah settled a hand against his head. "Yeah, son. Just a lot on my mind. What do you say we hunt down that school they mentioned here in a few minutes and get you scheduled to start tomorrow?"

Joel did a little tap dance of excitement. "Ma would be happy for me to go to school, wouldn't she, Pa?"

Micah prodded a toe at some dust on the boardwalk, even as he nodded. "She would indeed."

She would also want Joel to have a mother and for Micah not to ignore God's voice nor all that the minister had told him the evening before, but he wasn't ready to face any of that. He was still wallowing in too much grief to even contemplate the one and filled with too much anger at God to delve into the other.

He slammed his teeth together and marched off the porch. "Come on, son."

Chapter Sixteen

Mercy arrived at work the next morning with a list in hand of ways she had envisioned to organize the floor of the mercantile. But now, as she stood in the center of the chaos holding Avram's hand, she wasn't certain she knew the best place to start.

She'd been disappointed not to get her bath the evening before. However, today was Saturday, so she would relish the luxury this evening.

For now . . . she surveyed the room.

There was a set of harmonicas on a small table in the back corner and a violin on the opposite side of the store. Here stood the stack of shovels that had fallen yesterday, and across the room, a barrel filled with picks and axes, and in the far corner, she could see what she felt certain from this distance was a crosscut saw. It seemed to her that it would make much more sense to put similar things next to each other.

Since she hadn't yet found time to visit the schoolhouse and check on the availability of classes for a boy Avram's age, she nudged him behind the counter and pulled the paper that had been beneath their breakfast sandwich from the pocket of her apron—or she should more accurately say Georgia's apron. She spread the paper before him and tore off the greasiest corner. Then she provided him with a stub of a pencil from the jar beside the cash drawer.

"Mama is going to get to work. You sit here and draw for a bit, yes?"

Avram, still sleepy from his short night, nodded solemnly. He'd been too excited with their new circumstances and to be sleeping in a real bed to fall asleep right away last evening. It had taken several stories from *McGuffey's Primer*—the book Gid had purchased for the boys when she'd fallen so sick—to get him to relax enough to even lie still. And another before he'd finally fallen asleep.

As Mercy began gathering like items together, her mind drifted to yesterday afternoon. After they had spoken with Willow and her father, Micah stalked from the premises like a man with a bear on his back. She, Gideon, and Avram followed at a more leisurely pace, and by the time they reached the wagons, Micah and Joel were nowhere to be seen.

Mercy had felt a bit flummoxed as to what she ought to do. After all, none of the supplies at the wagon belonged to her. And she did not want to make choices that the men might not agree with. So she mostly stood back and waited for Gideon to instruct her. She made herself busy drawing water for the horses and hauling the wood they had gathered for their campfire to the stack that she had seen near the door at the back of the mercantile.

Her ribs still pained her some with the exertion, and when she was about half finished with the task, she paused near the stack of firewood at their camp to give herself a moment to breathe.

Micah reappeared and demanded to know what she was doing. When she explained, he snapped his fingers at Joel and instructed him to finish carrying the wood. After that, she struggled to feel helpful, so she had taken Avram to their room and set about to create the list that Willow had approved enthusiastically just a few minutes ago for the organization of the floor.

The bell above the door jangled, and Mercy glanced up. It was Gideon.

She greeted him with a smile. "Good morning."

He turned his hat through his fingers. "Morning. We didn't see you over at the diner and wanted to make sure that you ate."

Mercy nodded as she hefted a crate of ice picks and carted them into the corner where she was setting all the tools. "Oh, yes." she tipped a nod to where Avram entertained himself with the paper and pencil. "Someone woke with the first rooster. We had probably been and gone."

She wouldn't add that she was just fine with that since she would rather avoid Micah. Something had changed with him since they arrived in town. Perhaps it was just the loss of his wife settling in. Or perhaps it was the fact that they had not arrived in time to head west this year. Whatever it was, she felt a tension building between them and was fine with keeping her distance from the man for a while.

Gid tipped her a nod. Settled his hat on his head and tugged the brim. "All right. Glad to hear it. You have a good day." He scanned the interior of the room. "You sure you're making it better in here?" There was a twinkle in his eyes.

She chuckled. "Things always look worse when you're trying to get organized until you, at some point, get everything in its place."

Gid looked dubious. "I guess I'll just have to check this evening to see your progress." There was a hint of something intimate in the humor that tugged at one corner of his mouth.

Mercy searched the room for some way of escape. She had no desire to invite any man into her life this soon—in fact, maybe never again.

She hurried toward the large spool of rope by the window. "Have a good day." She hefted the spool. Now where should this go? With the tools? Or with the equestrian and farming equipment? She decided it would be better cataloged with the farming supplies, and deposited it in that pile. When the bell above the door jangled, indicating Gideon's departure, she breathed a little sigh of relief.

Willow spent the morning greeting customers and collecting their payments. And thankfully none of them complained about the small chaos Mercy was creating in order to organize to the room.

By noon, when Willow insisted that it was time for Mercy to take a break for lunch, she had the back quarter of the room set up to her satisfaction. She had pushed a table against the corner and arranged

all the bolts of fabric on it, side by side so that they were easily visible.
Next to that, she'd placed the small rack of thread and sewing notions.
It made sense to her to bring the women all the way to the rear of the
store, since Willow had said they were usually the ones who did the
most buying. She figured the more things the women had to see on the
way to the sewing notions, the more chance there was of them putting
something into their basket.

It took her more than a bit of work to repair the leg on the soap
shelf. The leg itself had been shattered beyond repair, but she'd found
a block of wood in the back room that had been about the right height.
She had taken off one of the back legs and brought it to the front, then
put the block of wood at the back and nailed it into place. It wasn't
perfect, but it was functional. Once she had that done, she placed it
near the folded sheets of toweling and the small stack of galvanized
tubs, then filled it with the soaps once more.

"Mercy!" Willow shook her finger. "You have been saying you are
going to lunch for the past half hour." She tipped her head toward Avram.
"Someone's little stomach has been grumbling louder than a steam
engine." She winked and ruffled Av's hair. "Come and feed your son."

Mercy smiled and stretched a hand to Avram. He didn't miss a beat
before he leaped to the ground and trotted to her side. Mercy bent to
look him in the eye. "Shall we go for a walk?"

He nodded in that quiet way of his.

Mercy took her apron off and tossed it to Willow, who placed it
in a cubby beneath the counter. "Right then. But first, let's go up to
our room for a moment."

Mercy had not wanted to say anything to Willow, but she didn't
have money to buy Avram lunch until she received her first paycheck.
She had saved back half the fried potatoes from her breakfast at
Felicity's. It wasn't much to tide him over to their evening meal, which
would be paid for. But tomorrow, she would try to save more. It didn't
take any time at all for Avram to scarf down the cold, greasy potatoes
that she had kept in a paper in their room. She helped him wash his

hands, and then they headed for the street. Despite the fact that she had been running to and fro all morning, it felt good to stroll and stretch her legs.

When they reached the end of the boardwalk, the sound of happy children at play drifted to them from the schoolyard.

Mercy eyed her son. "Shall we go up to the school and talk to the schoolmaster about getting you enrolled?" Her heart panged her at the thought.

Av frowned and shook his head. "I be good. I pwomise."

Mercy squatted to his level, her heart squeezing even harder. "It's not about me thinking you are not being good, Av. Schooling is beneficial. Wouldn't you like to learn to read like Mama does so that one day you can read books all by yourself?"

If possible, his brow scrunched even tighter. He darted a look toward the school and then back to her. "I like you wead me."

"I know you do." Mercy felt weary and didn't have more words to convince him at this moment. She wasn't even certain that she was ready for him to hie off to school each day just yet. But neither could he continue to entertain himself with only a pencil and a greasy piece of paper every day. Nor would she be able to buy him any toys or a slate until she got her first pay. Even then, she needed to save her money because she would need something to survive on when they reached the Oregon Territory.

She thought of the wood that she'd hauled to the pile behind the mercantile just yesterday and felt of the four nails that remained in her apron pocket, left over from fixing the soap shelf. "Tell you what, I don't have time right now because I need to get back to work, but this evening, we'll make something fun. How does that sound?"

His eyes sparkled. "What?"

"You'll see. You've been a very good boy today, and I'm proud of you."

He sucked on his lower lip, and there was something about the way his little face turned so serious that made Mercy realize she needed to pay attention. "What is it?"

He took a step toward her and spoke quietly as though to keep his words confidential. "I not want you to die."

Mercy's heart took a dive and then raced in horror. Had this been weighing on him for all these months? "I'm not going to die, sweety." Her mouth turned dry. Had she just lied to her son? Because, of course, she had no way of knowing whether something might happen to her.

Av's little brow scrunched into a series of furrows. "Okay."

Mercy felt all sorts of hopeless in that moment. She wanted to take all the pain her little boy was feeling and swallow it down deep inside her, where he would never be able to access it again. But she knew that was impossible. And she didn't have the strength to speak of this right now. If she started crying, she might not be able to finish the workday.

She rose and reached her hand down to him. "For now, let's enjoy the sunshine. We don't have long before we need to go back to the mercantile."

Av's warm fingers settled into her own, but he hung his head, and she knew she hadn't been very convincing in her reassurance of his fears.

But how did she go about erasing his memory of a father who had stood over her and tried to stomp the life from her? How did she erase the memories he must have of sitting beside her and listening to her breaths slowly give out before Gid noticed something was wrong with her? How did she erase his memories of Micah thrusting a quill into her chest?

She obviously didn't have the power to do any of that.

Her heart was heavy all afternoon as she continued to organize the floor of the mercantile. Her attention kept drifting to her son, who continued to sit quietly and draw with the pencil. At one point, when she looked over, she realized that Willow had snuck him a piece of the penny candy. Despite her concern for her son, gratefulness to have found a position with such kind people filled her heart. Maybe she had finally settled in a place where the horrors that seemed to have stalked her for the past several years would eventually be banished.

Before she realized the time, Willow stepped out from where she'd been tallying the books in the little office when she wasn't needed at the cash drawer. She gave a small gasp. "Oh my! I can't believe the transformation!"

Mercy stepped back and eyed her handiwork. She had to admit that even she was quite pleased with her work. There were actual rows of shelves now instead of a haphazard scattering of piles. With judicial use of the outer walls for shelving units, there now was ample room for patrons to browse without feeling like they were crowded against one another.

She dusted her hands. "The floors still need a good mopping, but I can tackle that first thing tomorrow."

Willow darted her a surprised look. "Tomorrow is the Lord's Day."

Mercy frowned. "Right." So . . . did that mean there would be no work tomorrow? A whole day to lie around and do nothing but be with her son? Had she ever experienced such a day? Why, even when she lived with Pa, he treated Sundays like any other day. He'd said it was only a fool who took time to lounge around when he could be getting ahead.

"You do plan to come to services with us, don't you?" Willow searched her face.

Mercy opened her mouth to decline but snapped it shut before she spoke. Was attendance at services a requirement of this job? Even if it wasn't, she didn't want to get off on the wrong foot with these kind employers who had done so much for them.

"You're right, of course. We'd be happy to attend services with you. What time?"

"We don't meet until eleven. So there will be plenty of time for lying in and taking it easy in the morning." Willow beamed her approval. "Now, why don't you take your boy on to dinner, and I'll get the water heating for your baths. By the time you get back, it should be good and hot."

Mercy hummed in pleasure at the thought. "I have to tell you that I've been looking forward to that all day."

Willow looked momentarily taken aback. "I should have thought that you might have appreciated one last night! I didn't even—"

"No. No." Mercy rushed to reassure her. "I wasn't trying to say that anything should have been done differently." Before Willow could continue lambasting herself, she reached into the pocket of her apron and withdrew the four nails. "I did want to ask if it would be all right if I used these to make Av a toy? I will, of course, pay for them as soon as I get my first payment."

Willow took her hand and folded her fingers over the nails resting in her palm. "After the transformation you wrought on this room today? The nails are yours! In fact, you take absolutely anything you need from the storeroom to make the toy."

Mercy once again felt overwhelmed with gratitude. So overwhelmed that she found herself blinking back tears. Perhaps it was only the sharp contrast with the way she'd been treated for so many years. Whatever it was, she felt blessed beyond measure as she thanked Willow and then made her way with Av across the street to the diner.

Micah left Gid soaping his hands in the basin outside the diner's door and stepped inside with Joel. Mercy and Avram were seated at a table pushed against the back wall of the room, and before he could stop Joel, he dashed to their table and blurted a greeting.

Chagrined, Micah sauntered after him. The poor woman might not want to endure the boys' chatter after a long day of work. But more than that, he didn't want her to feel encroached upon.

He paused by the table. "Evening."

She scarcely met his gaze as she returned his greeting, then promptly instructed Joel to fetch one more chair from a nearby table to round theirs out to five seats.

"Hope it's not a bother if we join you?"

Again, she offered only a flicker of cognizance, but he saw surprise written on her face. "Of course not. Here, Av, change chairs with me, then you can be at this end next to Joel." She moved so that she sat in one of the seats next to the wall. Joel took the extra seat he'd dragged to the end of the table from nearby, and Avram settled on his knees on his new seat.

Okay, he would take her at face value. He tugged out the chair across from her, leaving the one closest to Joel on the end for Gid.

Mercy turned her spoon in circles, intently studying the play of light on its surface. "Micah, can I ask you something?" When she lifted her face, concern furrowed her brow.

"Sure."

"If something were to ever happen to me . . ." She smashed her lips together, searching his face. "Would you . . . Could you . . ." Her focus shot to her son, and a fathomless pain filled her brown eyes.

Instant understanding filled him. "Yes."

Gid arrived and sank into his seat just as Felicity breezed up with water glasses for all of them.

Mercy mouthed her thanks as Felicity thumped the cups before each of them. He could read her relief in the way all the muscles of her face seemed to relax. Had she worried that he might say no? Come to think of it, maybe he should make provisions for Joel should anything ever happen to him. Of course, Gid would take care of him, but shouldn't the boy have a woman in his life too? He swallowed that thought away, not ready to contemplate that yet.

Felicity stepped back and tucked her tray beneath one arm. "Dinner tonight is fresh caught trout or fried chicken. Both come with mashed potatoes and buttered carrots. What'll it be?" She plunked one fist on a broad hip as though impatient to be off and moving again.

"Trout for me," Joel piped up.

Micah let it slide but made note that he ought to talk to the boy about his manners. Both he and Gid looked to Mercy, letting her speak next.

She swung a finger between herself and her son. "We'll share the fried chicken."

Felicity gave a sharp nod and turned her inspection on Micah.

Both he and Gideon ordered the fish, but something about the quiet way that Mercy had ordered a meal to share with her son gave him pause. He waited until Felicity scurried away before asking, "You certain that one meal is going to be enough?"

She was too quick to nod and reassure. "Yes. We'll be fine. How was your day?"

She bounced a glance between them, but Micah wasn't fooled. Her question seemed more about changing the subject than actual interest in how their day had gone. He let Gid answer and carefully watched her face instead. She looked so much like Georgia. The same prominent cheekbones—Mercy's were clear and smooth where Georgia's had been freckled. The same dark brows—though Mercy's left one had a distinct white scar cutting through it. He felt an ache in his jaw. Likely from that crowbait husband of hers. The pink lips were also similar, though Mercy's were slightly wider. The same short nose, but Mercy's was less turned up at the end. Georgia's hair had been straight when she let it down. Mercy's had plenty of curl to it—he knew that from the night he'd tended her when she'd collapsed from fever back in Blacksburg.

So similar and yet so different.

Mercy squirmed and brushed at her face, and he realized he'd been staring.

He shifted and glanced down at the table.

Beside him, Gid gave him a hard glance but then transitioned the conversation smoothly and carried it while both he and Mercy gave short, succinct answers only when Gid asked direct questions.

Their meals arrived, and Felicity thoughtfully provided an extra plate for Avram and a bowl of rolls for the table.

Micah watched carefully as Mercy studied the two pieces of chicken—a leg and a half breast—on her plate. He could almost see her shoulders sag, except her posture didn't change. She seemed to be trying to decide what to do. After a moment, she scooted the chicken leg, half the potatoes, and half the carrots onto Avram's plate. Micah ate quietly, watching her do the same, except she only ate half of what remained. Then she took the paper from beneath the bread rolls in the basket and carefully wrapped two rolls and the remainder of her food into a neat little parcel.

Micah sat back with a frown. No wonder she was as slender as a reed. She'd hardly eaten enough to sustain a kitten, much less a full-grown woman. Surely she couldn't be satisfied? He opened his mouth to ask her about it but then snapped it shut again. She was none of his concern. A full-grown woman could eat in whatever way she liked.

It irritated him—the way his thoughts seemed constantly drawn to her, this woman who had cost him so much.

But the scene nagged at him. It nagged as he paid for Joel's meal, which wasn't part of their pay agreement. It nagged as he tossed and turned in the pretense of sleep. It nagged through his morning ablutions and the breakfast that Mercy and Avram didn't arrive for. And now, as he sat in the back row of the church, it nagged him still.

Mercy had arrived a few minutes ago and scurried with Avram onto the bench beside Willow and her father near the middle of the sanctuary. When he and Gid had entered, as if by mutual agreement, they'd both turned immediately for the bench farthest from the front. Mr. Chancellor had made it clear yesterday that he expected to see them at services today. He hadn't said it like their jobs depended on it, but neither of them wanted to disappoint him—or to risk his ire.

Adam Houston stepped up behind the pulpit, drawing Micah's attention away from Mercy. Adam grinned broadly and gave him a subtle nod. Or had that been for the family on the pew in front of him?

Micah returned the nod, more as an example to his son than because he felt a need to be polite to the preacher.

Adam's gaze swept over the congregants then, and he began to speak. His sermon was simple.

Micah halfway expected the man to preach right at him after their talk the other day. But Adam's sermon didn't seem to have anything to do with him.

He spoke from the book of Isaiah, chapter fifty-three, and how the prophecy given over seven hundred years prior to the birth and life of Jesus fit Him perfectly. Micah was mostly thinking of other things—memories of Georgia, wondering how Joel would get along in the school, thinking through the things he'd learned in the one day he'd been working with the wainwright—until one verse from Isaiah seemed to reach out and grab him by the front of his shirt and give him a shake.

"The chastisement for our peace was upon Him . . ."

His palms turned clammy, and his heart thumped erratically. *Peace.* Wouldn't that be a wonder? When was the last time he'd felt at peace? Even before the kids took sick, he'd felt a yearning for change. A dissatisfaction with life in Virginia. If he were honest, with life with Georgia and the kids. Something always felt like it was missing.

Peace.

After Jess passed, he had thrown himself into finishing plans for their trip. Loading the wagons just so. Trying not to worry that Georgia had refused to take the steamer to Independence. Buying a good team. Wondering if they were young enough, strong enough, to make the trip. Once they'd commenced their travel, he'd fretted over the balance between days short enough to keep Georgia happy and long enough so they might reach Independence on time.

Then they'd met Mercy and been attacked . . .

He shook the thoughts away.

He must be strong. Peace was just an illusion that kept men in line. Kept them hoping for something better. Kept them productive. It was an ethereal dream that no one ever achieved, but everyone spoke of as if they had.

And yet . . . He swallowed. Thought of Adam's face as he'd shared his story. Despite the pain of it—the heart-pulverizing pain of losing a child—he'd seemed . . . still. Quiet. Accepting. Peaceful.

Ask of me.

Micah snatched his hat off the bench beside him and set to crimping the crown.

He'd gone cracked, hearing voices.

Next week on Saturday, if Mr. Chancellor said he'd see them in services the next day, Micah needed to put his foot down.

Everyone rose suddenly, and Micah realized he'd missed the closing of the sermon. He fidgeted through the closing hymn and then nudged Joel out the back door as soon as the last "Amen" was spoken. Gideon's footsteps shuffled behind them.

Micah took a big breath of fresh air. The church lawn lay vibrant green beneath the golden warmth of the sun. It was going to be a hot summer in Independence. He brushed away the irritation that rose up with the thought. There was no sense in being upset by circumstances he could not change.

"What we need is a good long afternoon swim in the creek behind the Chancellors' place. What do you say, men?" He ruffled Joel's hair to include him in the question.

"Yes!" Joel leaped into the air and kicked up his heels.

Gideon waved a hand. "Bought me a copy of *Pilgrim's Progress.* I think I'll laze the afternoon away by the window in our room."

Micah nodded his acknowledgement, then settled one hand on Joel's shoulder as they passed through the churchyard gate. "Guess it's just you and me, son."

But Joel didn't dash ahead as he'd half expected him to. Instead, he dragged to a stop. "Can Avram come?" He looked up, hands clasped beneath his chin, eyes pleading, lower lip protruding.

Micah paused beside him and plunked his hands on his hips. "Sure. Run fetch him."

Mercy again.

And the familiar anger that lingered so close to the surface these days.

Strong. Sure. Familiar. Attainable.

Definitely not illusive.

Far from peaceable.

Chapter Seventeen

Adam stood on the church porch, his attention only half on the people whose hands he was shaking, for his focus kept wandering to the lone statue of a man who had rushed out of the church with the Holy Ghost on his tail as soon as the last note of the closing hymn ended.

Micah shuffled his feet, focus fixed on the ground, hands plunked on his hips. He was likely waiting for his son, who had dashed into the sanctuary against the current of the crowd a moment ago.

Joel reappeared now, with the hand of little Avram Adler clasped tightly in his. "Here we are, Pa!" he hollered as they hurried down the steps. "Avram's ma said she'd come to fetch him at the creek after a little while."

The three headed off down the street, Micah's shoulders sagging, his boots scuffing up dust.

Chase him to the creek, Lord. Chase him through all the attempts to push You away. Hound him to the gates of heaven.

He returned his attention to the remaining parishioners, but the burden for Micah's soul would linger with him, he knew, until the Lord either released him from it or answered his prayers.

Just as he was shaking the hand of the last person leaving, he heard a man's voice from the foot of the church stairs.

"Excuse me? Parson Adam Houston?"

Adam blinked, brought up short by the presence of the man with his hat clasped to his chest.

"Yes?" His heart thumped. So this was it. He wasn't ready.

The man waited until the last of the churchgoers descended the steps before climbing to stand before him. He thrust out his hand. "I'm Parson Miles. Your replacement."

Adam swallowed. His hand automatically stretched toward the man, but even as he did so, he scanned the horizon as though, by magic, Eden would appear. Of course, she wasn't there.

He swallowed again, mouth as dry as a sunbaked biscuit.

Parson Miles shifted. "I do have the right church?"

Adam cleared his throat. Released his hand. "Yes, yes. You're in the right place. I've been expecting you."

Just not hoping for his arrival until Eden changed her mind.

He motioned through the open sanctuary doors. "Let me show you around."

His heart felt like a ball of molten lead in his chest.

So much for that peace he'd been preaching about this morning. *Lord, if ever I've needed You, it's now. Flood me with Your peace that passes understanding.*

The molten ball of lead squirmed around and spread to his lungs.

Adam fought for breath.

He was a faithless creature, full of weakness.

Mercy was thankful for the distraction an afternoon of swimming would provide for Avram—and also for herself. Because something Parson Houston had said in his sermon had practically snatched her breath away this morning, and she wanted time to ponder.

After services, when she'd reached the mercantile, she worked up her courage and knocked on the door of the Chancellor's rooms behind the store. When Willow peered out, Mercy clasped her hands tight and asked if she might borrow one of the Bibles from the bookcase in the storefront, promising that she would be very careful with the pages to insure they did not get bent.

Willow's smile bloomed full and bright. She looked over her shoulder to her father, who Mercy could see seated at a little table in the kitchen nook. His smile matched Willow's and he boomed his agreement.

Now, back in her own room, as she set the book on her bed and smoothed it open, Mercy tried to remember if she'd even offered her thanks.

Her hands trembled as she turned the pages. It was a big book with an overwhelming number of words. It had been chapter fifty-three. She remembered that much. But what was the name of the book the parson had read from? It was a man's name . . . Not Isaac . . .

Disappointment slipped through her. Would she even be able to find the passage?

One of the first pages of the Bible contained a list divided into two sections. At the top, the first list read, "The Books of the Old Testament." The lower list was the same but for "the New Testament."

Mercy stroked a finger over the names of the books.

There! Isaiah. That had to be it.

She noted the page number and found the place, then flipped the thin onionskin until she came to chapter fifty-three.

It only took her a few moments to find the two verses she was looking for. Her pulse quickened as she read them.

He is despised and rejected by men,
A Man of sorrows and acquainted with grief.
And we hid, as it were, *our* faces from Him;
He was despised, and we did not esteem Him.

Surely He has borne our griefs
And carried our sorrows;

Yet we esteemed Him stricken,
Smitten by God, and afflicted.

The words had the same impact they'd had earlier in the service. Her legs lost their strength and she fell to her knees, elbows planted on the quilt, staring at the words.

Despised and rejected by men.

She knew what that felt like.

Acquainted with grief.

That too. How she had railed and writhed with agony at the rejection. Women who called her friend before her attack, had crossed the street to avoid her after. Anger with her father for propelling her into a marriage of abuse had ruled her for years—not to mention her anger with Herst.

But the next verses . . . She held her breath as she read them again.

But He was wounded for our transgressions,
He was bruised for our iniquities;
The chastisement for our peace was upon Him,
And by His stripes we are healed.

All we like sheep have gone astray;
We have turned, every one, to his own way;
And the Lord has laid on Him the iniquity of us all.

Wounded for our transgressions. Bruised for our iniquities. The chastisement for our peace was upon Him. The Lord laid on Him the iniquity of us all.

Parson Houston had said that no one could be saved unless they believed on the Lord Jesus Christ and the gift of salvation offered by the reconciliation of His death.

She wasn't sure she understood just what it all meant, but one thing she did know.

"Lord, I want this peace." She hadn't meant to speak out loud, but she could no more have stopped the outcry of her heart than she could have stopped her labor with Avram once it had started. "I want to be healed. I don't want to be a straying sheep, always turning to my own way." She pulled in a tremulous breath. "I don't want to constantly carry this anger." Her fist thumped against her breastbone.

And then she was sobbing. Not because of sadness or terror or horror but purely from relief. For it was as though a huge burden had just been lifted off her. For the first time in years, she felt unshackled.

She cried so hard that she struggled to breathe, and then, just as suddenly, she was laughing uncontrollably with the same effect. Not sure what to do with this crazy jumble of emotions, she collapsed onto the rag rug and simply let the tears of freedom continue to fall.

She slept for what must have been at least two hours because when she woke, the sun was hanging midway down the sky. Scrambling to her feet, she scooped her curls into a knot at the back of her head, gathered up the Bible, and returned it to the mercantile. After she pushed it onto the shelf, she let her finger trace the gold lettering of the spine. She didn't want to part with the book. She wanted to delve deep into all the passages. To drink long from the words that filled the pages.

But it cost a whole dollar. She didn't have enough. Maybe when she got her first paycheck, she would be able to justify the purchase.

For now, Micah had played nursemaid long enough. She needed to fetch Avram.

Yesterday after work, she had borrowed both a hammer and a saw from the Chancellors and cut four rounds of wood from the end of a small log about the thickness of Avram's upper arm. These she had nailed onto the remainder of the log to form a wagon of sorts. They had laughed about how all the items loaded into that particular wagon would fall right off the top, but Avram hadn't seemed to mind that defect in the design of his toy. He had played with it until she'd finally made him put it away so he could go to sleep the evening before.

This morning, she'd allowed him to eat one of the rolls and some of the carrots for breakfast. And now, he could finish the rest and maybe play with his wagon again. With the sun just dipping behind the trees along the horizon, she made her way down the path to the hearty creek behind the Chancellors' barn.

Her stomach grumbled. But with her current feeling of contentment, instead of raising a frown of frustration, it brought a smile. She had gone many days before without eating and would likely do so again. Tomorrow's breakfast would be all the sweeter.

She heard the boys' giggles underscored by the burble of the creek before she rounded the last bend in the path. When she topped out on the berm above the water, Joel and Avram were tiptoeing as quickly as they could through the shallow part of the sandy creek bed. They seemed to be hurrying away from something, but by their expressions of delight, there was no danger. The only other movement she could see came from Mattox, who paddled in circles near the deeper middle.

"Aaaaarrrghhh!" Micah gave her a start as he surged from under the water near the dog, coppery arms arched above his head and hands formed into large claws. "This grizzly smells meat!"

Mattox barked happily as, with a great splash, Micah dove toward the boys, who squealed like scared rabbits and scattered in opposite directions. Muscles rippled along his shoulders as, with two swift strokes, he reached the midpoint between the fleeing boys.

"Got you! And you!" Micah stood with a squalling, squirming boy in each arm, the creek flowing at his waist. He pretended to eat Avram's shoulder.

Avram laughed so hard that he hardly seemed able to breathe.

Mercy pressed one hand to her chest, tears blurring her vision. When was the last time she'd heard such carefree laughter from her son? Had she *ever* heard it?

"Pa! Don't eat him!" Joel whacked helplessly at Micah's bare shoulder while fruitlessly wriggling to gain his freedom.

"Don't worry. I'm coming for you next!" Micah growled again, effortlessly lifting Joel with one arm to gnaw at the skin on the back of his ribs.

Joel shrieked at the tickling, floundering, flopping, and clawing at Micah's hand.

Mattox barked and lunged against Micah's back in an attempt to come to the boys' rescue.

Micah stilled and darted his blue gaze to where she stood on the berm.

Mercy felt the impact of his scrutiny as though a steam locomotive had just crashed into her. She wasn't sure she'd ever realized just how handsome he was, but standing there with two giggling boys in his arms, it struck her that he was handsome indeed. She'd come to think of him as safe. She could speak her mind and rely on him without worry that he would want or expect more from her. But with the way he looked at her now . . . She swallowed. Her heart just might be in danger—and she couldn't find any anxiety at the realization.

She lowered her eyes to catch her breath—and to search out her footing. It wouldn't do for her to go tumbling down the path with him watching.

Noting his sudden stillness, both boys and the dog also stopped cavorting.

"Hi, Mama!" Avram called. "Joel's pa is a gwizzly beaw." A huge grin bunched his cheeks.

"Is he, indeed?" Mercy drew a calming breath and took the shortest route from the top of the berm to the shore of the creek, trying to ignore the way Micah's scrutiny followed her. He lowered Avram carefully into the water and then tossed Joel into the deepest part of the pool.

Joel came up sputtering and giggled when Mattox pounced on him and almost gave him another dunk.

Avram paddled an escape route toward Joel. "Be careful, or he will eat you!"

Mercy almost huffed at that. From the intent way Micah watched her, she had no doubts on that score.

Avram squealed, looking back with obvious hope that Micah would once again commence the chase.

Instead, Micah waded toward her, coming out of the water like a honey-colored warrior ready to take on the world. He didn't seem bothered by his half-state of undress as he paused on the small beach before her and raised one work-hardened arm to scoop back his tangle of dripping curls. Water droplets caught the sunlight where they clung to the bristly plains of his face.

Heart thudding disobediently, Mercy forced her focus to the boys and searched for something to say. "I d-didn't know Avram could swim."

Micah propped his hands on his hips. She felt more than saw him turn his attention on the boys as well. "Only took two pieces of penny candy to get him to warm up to me."

She gasped, snapping her attention back to him. "Two pieces?!"

He winked. "After that, he was a quick study. Inside ten minutes, he was paddling around on his own."

She smiled, watching her son and Joel splash each other with Mattox paddling circles around them. It was such a contrast to his concerned little face when he'd told her he didn't want her to die.

"What is it?" Micah's words were soft.

She bent and picked up a pebble from the beach to roll through her fingers. "Just the other day he told me he didn't want me to die, so it's wonderful to see him enjoying himself, and for that, I thank you."

Micah nodded. "That's why you asked me to take care of him if something happened to you?"

"Yes."

He watched the boys cavort for a few moments before a smile curved his lips. "Playing grizzly is good for boys to get their minds off things too serious."

She eyed the way Micah's face seemed to have relaxed since she'd left him at the diner the evening before. "And for grown men, too, perhaps?"

His grin turned devilish. "Maybe even grown women. I wager I'd enjoy playing grizzly a sight more with you in the water. Care to join us?"

Surprise crashed through her.

Despite the awareness his look had raised in her earlier, the last thing on earth she'd expected from him was flirtation. He was staid and solemn. Stoney. Stolid.

Still grieving his wife.

And yet there he stood, looking at her with those piercing blue eyes of his, all soft and inviting, the corners crinkled with decided charm.

Mercy worked her teeth over her lower lip.

This was, without doubt, a different Micah than the one she was used to. He seemed . . . relaxed and at ease for the first time since she'd known him. She liked this version of him too much for her own good.

She couldn't withhold a smile. "I think I'd best pass. I'd hate to become a grizzly's next meal." She arched a brow.

Micah chuckled, and the sound warmed her clear through. He ought to laugh more. If she'd thought him handsome before, he was breathtaking with that twinkle softening his eyes.

With a jut of her chin, she indicated the boys paddling circles in the creek. "Thank you for taking time for him." She swallowed hard, choking back unexpected emotion. "It means more than you can know."

Humor seeped out of his expression until only a perceptive understanding remained. "I know more than you realize."

What did that mean? She wanted to press for details but was reluctant to dispel this softened version of him and felt certain if she did press, he would secure himself behind his stony façade. Still, she couldn't stop herself from saying, "If you ever need to talk about it, I'd be a listening ear."

Just as she'd expected, a frown slumped his brow, and his jaw hardened. But instead of turning away as she'd thought he would, he remained still. He seemed surprised by her words. Hesitant for the first time since she'd met him.

After a long moment, he offered softly, "It's not a story for a day like today."

So much pain laced the softly spoken words that her heart ached. She gave a short nod. "I have a few of those stories myself."

"I'm sure you do." His expression turned soft again as his focus rose to her eyebrow. Slowly he reached out to touch it. She barely felt the brush of his fingertip. "Is this such a story?"

She closed her eyes, wishing she had the freedom to lean into the gentle caress. Instead, she remained steadfast. Willed her legs to hold her upright.

She didn't want to recall the night Herst had come home drunk and angry. He'd lost at cards. When he'd sunk onto the edge of their bed to remove his boots, she'd made the foolish mistake of reminding him they needed food in the cupboards. He'd grabbed the nearest item to hand, which happened to be the clay candle holder. It had smashed into her face before she'd even realized it was coming. She felt the warmth of tears slipping down her cheeks.

"Mercy . . ." The understanding in Micah's tone could easily be her undoing.

She lifted her chin. Forced her eyes open. Brushed away the tears with the flats of her fingers.

Things were different now. Especially after today. Somehow, despite her tears, the memory didn't hold the terror it once had. "What's past is past. But Micah . . ." She searched his face, hoping he could read her sincerity. "I need you to know how sorry—"

"Don't." He shook his head. "What happened . . . It wasn't your fault." A flicker of something tightened the skin at the corners of his mouth as though he might be surprised to hear himself say the words. "I don't hold you responsible."

His soft scrutiny held her captive. His gaze swept down to pause on her lips. He inched a step nearer.

Mercy's thoughts stuttered. Her mind screamed for her to flee, but her foolish heart overruled the order, and her feet refused to budge.

Easing closer, he transferred his focus to her shoulder and reached slowly toward her. He lifted an escaped curl of her hair and swept his fingers the length of it. He wrapped the strand over his first finger and stroked it with his thumb, lifting his eyes to hers once again.

Emotion intensified the blue of them this time, making her mouth dry and her breaths waft shallow and fast. Darting her tongue over her dry lips, she lowered her eyes, willing herself to find her footing in this sea of uncertain emotions.

But instead of obediently turning to the boys as she'd intended, her attention snagged on a drop of water that seeped from the hair at his shoulders and cascaded along the firm curve of his bronzed chest. Her fingers reached to catch the droplet before she thought better of it. Despite only recently coming out of the creek, his skin was a warm contrast to the water.

Face blazing with the sudden realization of what she'd done, she spun to present him with her back. Only she forgot that he still had her curl entwined around one finger. She yelped at the sharp tug and stumbled a step back, coming up against the solid, damp wall of his chest.

"Easy, Merc." His voice rumbled in her ear. "Just let me . . ." With her back still to him, he worked his finger free of her hair, cupped his hands over her shoulders, and for a moment, he held her close, his thumbs rubbing gentle strokes into her tense muscles. She felt the press of his cheek against her hair above her ear and heard him breathe in, long and slow. Only when she trembled did he set her from him gently.

Eyes closed, she kept her back to him and measured an inhale. Willed her heart to calm its pounding. Willed away the feel of his warm words on her cheek and the gentleness of his thumbs stroking her shoulders. Willed away the warmth of his skin contrasted with the cascading droplet beneath her fingertips.

Heavens! Had she even known that the presence of a man could make her so discombobulated?

She certainly had never been attracted to any man in such a way. Not even, she'd dare say, to Carl Johansen. At least not with this wild force!

The strength of it filled her with terror. And the danger of it made her palms sweat.

For any man who could make her feel with this untamed, feral intensity wielded a power that could break her.

Herst's cruelty had marred her body, but he'd never been able to wound her heart.

It would not be so with a man like Micah, who had the ability to reach her very core. He was a bright flame, tempting and alluring. She must never again be a moth.

She had to be smart. Think of Avram's future as well as her own. Never again.

She should call Avram and take her leave. If only she could find her voice!

Behind her, she heard shuffling. And after a moment, Micah said, "You can look now."

She cast a hesitant peek over one shoulder, and only when she saw that he'd donned his shirt did she turn to face him.

He set to rolling up the cuff of one sleeve, a decided twinkle sparkling in his eyes as he studied her quietly.

She swallowed.

Moth. Flame. Moth. Flame.

If only her heart would quit flopping erratically.

"I—I'm..." Her voice squeaked worse than an adolescent boy's. She swung her attention to where Joel and Av continued to swim. Gulped a breath, hoping to calm her jitters. "I'm just here to fetch Avram." The high pitch was still irritatingly present.

From the corner of her eye, she could see that Micah's attention remained on her. He watched her for so long that she gave up her pretense of indifference and narrowed a glower at him.

With both sleeves now rolled, arms folded, and one broad hand cupping his chin, humor gleamed in his eyes. The creek water made his shirt cling to him in several places. His bare feet were planted wide to maintain his balance in the soft sand.

Mercy yanked her attention back to the trio in the water and pressed her sweaty palms together, wishing she'd thought to ask Gideon to come fetch Avram.

"You look different," he finally said. "The rest seems to have done you good."

Her mind flashed to the moment she'd felt her burden lift, and she was suddenly overcome with the need to tell someone about it. Especially to tell Micah because of their shared pain. "The most amazing thing happened." Her voice emerged miraculously normal. "Something the parson said in church this morning seemed to grab hold of me. I borrowed a Bible from the mercantile and reread the passage where it said, 'the chastisement for our peace was upon Him.' And I think we were wrong in our assessment about God not caring, Micah. I prayed. I told God I wanted that peace." She studied the sunlight sparkling on the surface of the water. "I didn't really . . . expect anything, I suppose. But it was as if a blanket of despair lifted at that precise moment! And then I slept . . . such a deep sleep. I'm honestly quite surprised that—"

She stopped speaking abruptly, realizing that Micah was slapping sand from his feet and yanking on his socks and boots.

Something had hardened in his expression.

"Boys," he snapped. "Time to go!"

The Micah she knew was back.

And while there was some relief at again being on familiar footing with him, there was disappointment too. If only he could feel a tiny measure of the joy surging through her, she felt certain he would want more of it.

Chapter Eighteen

Micah finished tying his boots and stood just as the boys clambered from the water. He was a fool to have contemplated kissing her the way he had.

Their similar histories had cracked open his resolve. She'd taken him off guard, arriving unexpectedly like that, and then . . . the way she'd looked at him when she'd offered that she'd love to hear his story . . . Not even Georgia had ever done that. She'd always cut him off with the excuse that it was too painful for her to dwell on. But despite what Mercy had endured and the fact that she likely didn't want to ponder something she'd so recently escaped, she'd offered a listening ear.

And then there was that blamed hair of hers. He'd wondered if it would feel as soft as it looked and before he'd realized what he was doing, he'd reached to touch it. And then her fingers caressed his chest.

He swallowed to work some moisture back into his mouth.

This wouldn't do. Not at all.

And what was with that particular passage this morning? It seemed that he wasn't the only one who had been punched in the heart. Only Mercy had gone and done something about it, and now . . . blazes and tarnation . . . that contented look in her eyes raised a longing in a man.

A longing that he had no hope would ever be fulfilled. God seemed always available to those around him and ever just beyond his reach.

He shot out a hand to keep Joel, who had scrambled into his boots, from dashing onto the trail before Mercy. "Ladies first."

Joel sighed. "Yes, Pa."

Mattox padded from the creek, distracting Joel as he shook a spray of water in every direction.

"Mattox!" Joel laughed. "You'll soak Mrs. Adler. Come here." He took the dog by his collar and led him off a ways, giving him the instruction to shake.

Micah turned his focus back to the woman who had his thoughts in turmoil.

Squatting before Avram, she finished tying his last boot and made to stand, but the soft ground slid beneath her feet. "Ah!" She propped her fingertips into the sand to regain her balance. She glanced up at him with a small self-deprecating smile touching her lips.

He shouldn't touch her again if he wanted to stay out of danger, but a gentleman wouldn't leave her to fend for herself. He reached down. "Here."

Her eyes widened as they settled on his hand. "No, that's all right, I'll just—Oh!" She was thrown off balance once again by the shifting beach. "Fine."

Micah braced himself, but he wasn't prepared for the warmth of her fingers skimming over his palm. His heart flitted like a blamed butterfly in a spring garden.

He slammed his teeth together and clasped her wrist instead. That somehow seemed like it would be less intimate. Only her wrist was so slender that his fingers overlapped where they met on the other side, and when he hauled her to her feet, he realized he hadn't calculated that it would leave her standing even closer once she was upright.

He held onto her for a moment—only to ensure she had her balance. "You good?"

Her lips rolled in and pressed together before she nodded. "Yes. Fine. Thank you." The words were more air than sound.

He ought to release her, but standing this close, he could see her eyes were a near match to the water-darkened sand at the edge of the bubbling creek—browns and greens and gold all melded together and encircled by a ring that brought to mind the burnt-sugar candy his mother used to make when he was a boy. Eyes that flitted over his features, wide with caution.

Small breaths flared her nostrils, and he could feel her rising emotions in the hammering pulse beneath the stroke of his thumb. He wanted to reassure her. "Mercy, I—"

Avram shoved between them, pushing Micah back with a ferocity he hadn't known the boy possessed. The kid planted himself in front of Mercy, folded his chubby arms, and glowered up at him.

Micah's first instinct was to laugh, but then the import of the action hit him like a mule kick straight to his lungs. No four-year-old ought to know anything about protecting his mother, but Avram obviously did. It was like seeing a ghost of himself at the same age.

Mercy settled one hand on Av's shoulder, but she cautiously kept her attention on him. She darted her tongue over her lips, and he could read the tension in the line of her shoulders. She wasn't sure how he might respond to the boy's impertinence.

He lowered himself to Avram's level and raised his palms. "I'd never hurt your ma, Av."

A hank of damp curls slid down nearly to Av's eyebrow. He shook it back, his frown easing first, followed by his stance. After a long moment, he turned to look up at his mother as though to assess whether she was indeed all right.

Mercy tried to smile at him, but anyone paying attention could see that it was forced.

Micah regained his feet, roughed a hand through his still-wet hair, and gripped the muscle at the top of one shoulder. He was a blasted fool. He'd scared her with his forwardness. Scared himself a little, too, if he were honest. And condemned himself to pushing away thoughts of her for the rest of the day.

"I'm fine," she reassured Av, her words still barely audible. She cleared her throat. "Mr. Morran was just helping me to stand." Her eyes darted his way as though she wished to drive home the point.

Micah wished he didn't feel such unaccountable anticipation at the challenge.

Avram tossed him one more glower before returning his focus to his mother. "I'm hungry."

That comment seemed to unshackle her. She ruffled a hand through Av's curly mop. "Yes, I'm sure you are. Come on." She nudged him to lead the way up the trail.

Joel and Mattox fell into step behind her, and Micah brought up the rear, still kicking himself for this whole blamed few minutes but hardly able to dredge up any sorrow for his part in it all.

Once they reached town, he expected her to head toward the diner, but instead, she stepped onto the mercantile porch like she was headed inside. He frowned and spoke over the rattle of a passing wagon. "Aren't you coming to dinner?"

She pressed a hand to Avram's back and didn't even miss a step as she offered over her shoulder, "We have some food in our room. Good evening, Mr. Morran."

Dismissed.

He was once again calling himself every sort of fool. He'd discomfited her so much that she was practically running from him.

But . . . Food in their rooms? Surely not the half-eaten meal that she'd tucked away at dinner the evening before? Especially not when he'd not seen her at breakfast and doubted that she'd eaten anything at noon either since Avram had been with him.

"Mercy, wait." In two swift strides, he caught up to her and took her elbow.

She gasped and jerked away from him, scooping Av behind herself in a gesture that was pure instinct. Fright widened her eyes for the briefest of seconds until truth caught up to reflex. "Micah, please. I'm asking you n-not to touch me again."

At least they were back to a first-name basis. But anger churned through him on such a swift current that it was a good thing for Mr. Adler that he'd already passed out of the realm of his reach. He raised his palms. "Sorry. I keep doing that. I'll do better from here forward. Please, can you just stop for a moment?"

A puff of frustration left her lips. "What is it, Mr. Morran?"

He narrowed his eyes. She was deliberately putting distance between them with the use of such formality. Yet . . . Maybe that was good. He'd been so relaxed earlier by the creek that he'd let reality slip from his grasp. He needed to get hold of it again and hang on tight because this attraction between them was not something he could nurture. There were too many obstacles.

"Well?" A touch of impatience draped the question.

Despite his resolve, he wasn't callous enough to see her go hungry. "Join me—us—" he swung his hat to indicate Joel "—at the diner?" His gaze involuntarily swept the length of her. "You're nothing but skin and bones and need to eat."

Crimson swept a path across her cheeks. Her mouth gaped, but she couldn't seem to summon any retort.

He clenched one fist. He'd called Gid sapheaded not long ago, and now he'd wallowed right into his brother-in-law's swamp. She'd taken the words as an insult. Of course, she had. "I didn't mean that you were ugly. Just . . . underweight." He checked the flow of his words. Had he just added insult to injury? His brow furrowed. What was a better way to say it? "Like Georgia, you are a very comely woman, I only wanted—"

She held up a hand. "Yes, I know that I resemble your wife . . ." Resignation drooped her shoulders, and for one moment, he thought he'd won her over. Then she continued. "But we . . . can't join you. I wish you a good evening." She took Avram by the shoulders and turned once more toward their rooms.

Stubborn, mule-headed, willful woman! Why couldn't she—

A sudden memory flashed into his mind. The first day they'd arrived in town when the young lad with the accent had offered rides on his contraption, she had seemed to fret over the cost.

It was the money! How much more of a fool could he be? She'd come to them with nothing but the clothes on her back.

"I'll pay," he blurted.

She froze, but her ramrod-straight back remained toward him.

"Please, Ma?" Av looked up at her with pleading eyes.

Good. Let the kid weigh in on his side.

"Fine." Mercy turned to face him.

He smiled. "See, that wasn't so hard—"

Mercy thrust the boy toward him. "Av may join you, and I'll eat the food in our room."

Before the smile could hardly fall from his lips, she disappeared inside the mercantile.

Micah sighed and motioned for the boys to follow him.

Stubborn. Mule-headed. Willful woman!

Gideon put down his book, realizing just how hungry he was. Surprise lifted his brows when he noted how low the sun hung in the sky. He arrived down at the mercantile floor to find Willow standing back from the lace-curtained window but intently studying something outside.

He frowned. Canted his head to see past her.

Ah.

On the front porch of the mercantile, Micah and Mercy seemed to be in a bit of a heated discussion. What else was new? Mercy didn't take well to Micah's bossing. Not that Georgia ever had either, but Micah had been . . . softer back then. Less stressed and intense.

"Spying, are we?" He whispered as he stopped by Willow's side.

With a breathy squeak, Willow clutched at her chest and spun to face him.

He couldn't withhold a grin as he looked down at her. "My pa used to say that if you were living right, you never needed to fear what might sneak up on you."

"Oh, do go on with you," Willow whispered fiercely. "I'm not living *wrong*. I simply didn't hear you approaching, is all." She smacked at him.

He dodged away from her swing with a chuckle. "So spying is...?"

"I'm *not* spying! I was heading out and saw that they were in a ... discussion." She flung a gesture toward the porch. "I didn't want to interrupt them, is all."

Gideon pulled a face. "They always seem to be in a discussion of some sort. You might have been doing them a favor."

Willow leaned closer, lowering her voice even more. "I think they have ... feelings for one another."

Consternation tightened his brow. "You do know that Micah's wife— Never mind." He peered through the window to see Mercy thrust Avram toward Micah and then reverse course and burst through the door.

When she saw them, she hesitated, fingers on the handle.

Gideon gestured. "I—we were just going out."

She released the knob and brushed past, head lowered.

He watched thoughtfully as she disappeared up the stairs and then caught the sympathetic expression in Willow's gentle watchfulness. He pressed his lips tight, looking back toward the empty front porch once more.

Surely Willow was just living in some fanciful world where women liked to linger? A world where they imagined love always in the air? Micah would never—

He choked off the thought. Couldn't even contemplate it.

But why was that?

Georgia deserved better? It had been several months now. It wasn't like he figured Micah would remain single forever. He had Joel to consider too.

Mercy was a comely woman. Hard-working. A good mother. Had proven that she was as tough as hide leather. She would be a good match for Micah.

But it was more than that. His palms were suddenly clammy. He worked his tongue over his teeth. Surely it was only that he didn't want to see Mercy hurt? There couldn't be anything more to it, could there?

Willow smoothed her hands over the front of her skirt. "I'm going to Felicity's. You?"

Careful.

He studied her, wishing she didn't have such a hopeful, soft look in her blue eyes. The last thing he wanted to do was to give the young girl hope for anything other than friendship. "How old are you, anyway?" He winced, regretting the question the moment it left his lips.

Her chin notched upward a degree. "A lady does not answer such questions, Mr. Riley. But I dare say I'm older than you think I am."

One of his brows quirked. He may have regretted the question, but he now wanted to know the answer more than he ought. Yet, didn't her irritation prove his point? She was old enough to be offended but young enough to refuse to answer. "Where's your pa?"

She huffed and turned for the door. "My father knows that I'm old enough to walk across the street all by myself, Mr. Riley." She calmly opened the door and stepped onto the boardwalk.

"I didn't mean—"

The door shut firmly in his face.

He couldn't stop a bark of laughter. Maybe he deserved that. Verona would have shined him up good for the prying questions. It seemed like she ought to have an escort to dinner, was all—whether she was of age or not.

He reached for the doorknob with the intent of catching up to her, but a glance through the lace revealed that another man had already usurped his place. They were halfway across the street. He lingered for a moment—only to ensure her safety. Their conversation seemed friendly enough, but when they reached the other side of the street, Willow tossed a glance back toward the mercantile, and there was something underlying her expression that filled Gideon with a protective instinct.

He was turning the handle when a voice spoke from beside him. "Flynn is her cousin."

Gideon's hand dropped of its own volition toward his holster as he spun toward the sound. Seeing his new boss, he released a breath.

Wayne Chancellor's focus lowered to the hand now propped at his hip and then raised to settle against his own. "My daughter is very important to me." A nearly imperceptible squint tightened the skin around his eyes.

Gid nodded. "Yes, sir. I'm sure she is." He swallowed, and for some reason, he had the urge to fidget.

"Are you a trustworthy man, Mr. Riley?"

Gid frowned. "I'd like to think so."

Wayne leaned his head to one side as though pondering whether it were true. "I thought about confiding in Mr. Morran, but he seems to have much weighing on him."

Caution rose inside Gideon even as he dipped a nod. "That's true enough, what with the death of my sister and the burden of raising a son alone." Or maybe not alone, depending on what was transpiring between Micah and Mercy. The thought grated, and his next words came out more harshly than he intended. "What is it you wish to confide?"

"I'm not sure I wish to confide at all, but I saw a connection between you and my daughter just now and—"

Gid thrust one hand into the air. "No, sir. I'm certain whatever you think you saw was misconstrued."

Mr. Chancellor pushed on as if he hadn't spoken. "And should any danger befall me, I want to know that she'll be taken care of. Can I count on you to be that man, Mr. Riley?"

Gideon's brows shot into his hairline. "Me? I hardly know her, you" —he waved a hand— "your family." He thought of Mercy and

Avram. Joel and Micah. All of them living above the mercantile. "What danger?" It would behoove them to know.

All the fortitude seemed to leave Wayne at once. "It has to do with my sister's husband." He nodded toward the street. "That was her son, Flynn, you just saw speaking with Willow."

"And?"

Wayne pegged him with a look. "I need to know that what I'm about to say will be held in the strictest confidence."

Gideon folded his arms. Leaned into his heels. "Does the law need to be involved?"

Wayne's attention fell once more toward his tied-down holster. "Were you a lawman?"

Gid shook his head. "No." He didn't add that he'd once fancied that he'd like to be a gunman.

"Could you defend my daughter if the need arose?"

The image of Herst Adler falling, cut down by his bullets, swept in, along with the guilt that plagued him each time he remembered. Mercy would be dead if he hadn't been there to defend her that day. Yet . . . He wondered what God thought about what he'd done. Ought he to have given the man more warning? More time to back away? Would Herst have stepped away from her if Gideon had announced himself? Even a few more moments might have finished crushing the life from her. He had no answers. He'd acted quickly to save a life. In doing so, he'd taken another. That of a man who would have taken both Mercy's and his without hesitation. He always came back to the same conclusion. He would choose to save an innocent every time—even if that meant taking the life of another.

Mr. Chancellor continued to watch him.

He shrugged one shoulder. "I've done so for others in the past, sir." He felt a knot forming in his gullet. What might he be getting himself into?

Wayne searched his face, arms folded and seemingly wearing the weight of the world. Finally, he relaxed his arms and spoke. "This store used to belong to my parents. My sister married Grant Moore." He hesitated as though waiting to see if Gid knew the name.

Gid raised a hand. "Never heard of the man."

That seemed to ease a measure of Wayne's tension. "He owns Moore Brewing." He hesitated again.

Gid shook his head.

"Moore Brewing supplies bottled spirits to saloons all over this region and beyond. Grant has *more* money," he gave a quick wink, "than he knows what to do with. But not long ago, there was a fire at his main plant. And it cost him exorbitantly." Wayne sighed. "For some reason he has gotten it into his head that his wife was cheated out of her half of this store. The truth is that my father spoke to both of us near the end of his life and because my sister had married a man who seemed set, he proposed—and my sister agreed—that the store be given solely to me." A breath puffed from his lungs. "I would gladly support my sister. But not her husband nor her son, I'm sorry to say. With the sale of only one of their homes—they have five—they could make more than my store profits during the course of a year. Grant believes that we're making a much greater profit than we are. It keeps us, Willow and me, living comfortably. But it would by no means give Grant the financial boost he's looking for to save his company."

Gideon frowned. "Does your sister not back up your story?"

Wayne mashed his lips together and shook his head, sadness filling his eyes. "I'm afraid she's become rather attached to her worldly goods. She's pressing me to split the store proceeds with them, but they don't want to provide any of the labor to keep the place running." His shoulders drooped. "I should have had Father put it in writing. Unfortunately, I did not."

"I see. And this Moore . . . he's not the kind to let something like this drop?"

Wayne shook his head wearily. "I'm afraid not." He lifted his gaze to Gideon. "I've quite honestly been afraid for my life since this started.

When I told him how much profit the store made last year, he flew into a rage and called me a liar."

Gideon's fists tightened into hard knots by his sides. If there was one thing he couldn't abide, it was a bully. "You have my word that I'll do my best to protect Willow if anything happens to you."

Relief eased the tension in the line of Wayne's shoulders.

"In the meantime, do you have need of protection for yourself?"

Wayne brushed that concern away. "He values his reputation too much to try something openly. And I don't think he would ever hurt Willow. He loves that girl as if she were his own."

"It would be hard not to love someone as guileless as she is."

Wayne cut him a sharp look.

Gid shot out a hand. Shook his head. Wayne had obviously taken his words wrong.

Thankfully, the man didn't push for more of an explanation.

"I've been staying close to home at night, and I don't think I have to worry during the day."

Gideon swung him a look. "That's still no way to live."

Wayne shrugged, and one corner of his mouth lifted. "I've been thinking about Oregon, if I'm honest. It's why I started this wagon business, though I've not said anything to Willow yet. If things settle before spring, we'll stay here. We have a good life and good friends here. But if not . . ." He shrugged. "I think we'll join a train and head west."

Gideon scowled, somehow not liking the picture that formed of Willow toiling away to skin and bones on a trail he'd heard one old-timer refer to as the Trail of Death.

But that, he reminded himself, was no concern of his.

Chapter Nineteen

Mercy paced in her room. The short space between the bed and the wall didn't offer a long enough path to remove even a measure of her frustration.

Overbearing, bossy, mule-headed man! She was not his wife, and he well ought to remember that! So what if she looked like the woman?!

Tears welled in her eyes. *Lord, forgive me for that offense.*

She would change that reality without hesitation if she could. But the infirmity of living bound by time was that it only flowed in one direction.

Guilt swept in fast on the heels of that thought. She could never let herself fall for that man, no matter how her heart tempted her with yearning. Such a relationship would be nothing but a loathsome reminder to them both of the grief staked in their shared history. That was why she'd asked him not to touch her again. She knew her longings would lead her to places she couldn't go.

A soft knock sounded on the door. She spun to face it and froze. Her heart hammered out hope. Had he returned to—

She huffed. Such a traitor her heart was.

"Who is it?" she called cautiously.

"'Tis Gid."

She shook out her shoulders and her hands as she crossed to the door. When she cracked it open, he stood in the hallway, leaning into his heels, thumbs hooked in his belt loops. His blue eyes were soft and gentle, so opposite of Micah's intensity.

He tilted his head. "Just wanted to make sure you were all right?" This. This was the kind of man she ought to yearn for. He had protected her, yet didn't hover as though she were a child who needed his monitoring. And she had never felt powerless over her emotions in his presence.

She gripped the doorpost and leaned against it. "I'm fine."

A barely perceptible quirk nudged up one of his brows. "And that down there with Micah? What was that?"

Irritation surging once more, she straightened and folded her hands. "It was nothing. Just . . . Micah being . . . Micah, is all." She turned her face to the wall and swallowed away the memory of his broad hands resting tenderly on her shoulders down at the beach.

Gid shifted and nudged his chin toward the stairs. "I was just heading to the diner. Care to join me?"

Wouldn't that set Micah in his place? Just imagining the irritation in his countenance if she entered by Gideon's side almost convinced her to do it. Instead, she shook her head. "I have some food here in my room. I'll be fine for tonight. Thank you."

"All right. Suit yourself." He lifted a wave. "See you in the morning."

Mercy bade him farewell and closed the door.

She strode to the small table that sat by the bed and unwrapped the paper that encased the remaining food from last evening's meal. A wasp buzzed into her face before settling right back down on the chicken. Ugh!

She hurried to the window that she'd propped open earlier to allow in a bit of a breeze. She tossed the chicken and the wasp down onto the rubbish burn pile that lay between the back door of the mercantile and the barn and then eyed what remained. There was only a little mound of cold hard potatoes left, and one nibble convinced her the food would only awaken her appetite without quenching it. She crumpled the paper around the potatoes and then hurtled it after the chicken before slamming the window into place and throwing the latch.

Earlier, she'd happily acknowledged her hunger and been content. Now, it seemed all she could think about was the ache in her belly.

With a sigh, she flopped onto the bed.

Her newfound peace and contentment had been dispelled by only a few minutes in Micah's presence.

The chastisement for our peace . . .

Mercy angled a glance at the ceiling. *Lord, I don't suppose there's anything You could do about that overbearing, bossy, mule-headed man?*

Still puzzling over his earlier interaction with Mercy by the creek, Micah watched Joel and Avram giggle as they slid a flat pebble back and forth to each other across the table. Their game involved seeing how close they could get the stone to the edge without it falling off. One of them must have brought it into Felicity's in their pocket. He probably shouldn't let them continue with the game. He'd hate to see Felicity's table scratched, but right now, he was too weary to come up with something else for them to do as they waited for their food.

Ever since he'd entered with the boys, two women seated at a nearby table had been glancing at him and then speaking to each other behind their hands with soft giggles.

Now, one of them leaned toward him. "Your boys are both very handsome."

He murmured an automatic thanks even as his brow puckered. It was uncanny how much Avram looked like Joel, he realized. No wonder the woman mistook the boys for brothers. Both had curly hair and large brown eyes. Even their laughs were similar.

"How many years separate them?"

"Ah. Three, I believe."

The women looked at one another, laughing.

"So much like a man not to know the ages of his own boys," one said.

"Is there a missus?" the other pried, brows arching.

Micah was thankful for the interruption provided by the arrival of Felicity with their dinner.

And then Gideon tromped in and plunked into his chair. He stopped Felicity before she could bustle away. "I'll have one of the same, please." He nodded toward Micah's plate of roast.

"And one for me to take across to the mercantile when we leave," Micah quickly added. He nudged Joel's plate closer to him and went to work cutting Avram's meat and potatoes.

"Coming right up." Felicity pegged him with a look, propping one fist against her hip. "I know you know that I know where to find you if you don't bring my plate back."

Micah smiled. "Yes, ma'am."

With a quick nod, she bustled off.

He was turning back to Avram's plate when he encountered Gideon glaring at him as though he'd happily remove his head if it wouldn't land him in the hoosegow.

"What?" Micah finished cutting Avram's food as he searched his memory. He hadn't had any contrary interactions with Gid for days.

Tapping the table irritably with one finger, Gid continued to glower.

Micah gave Av a fork and then set to his own food.

"Who's your friend?" one of the women from the next table prodded. Her chin rested on the back of one hand, and she coquettishly batted her eyelashes at Gideon.

Gideon appeared ready to explode. Lips pinched, his gaze bounded between the two women and Micah. He leaned forward and kept his voice low in an obvious attempt to keep their conversation private. "Really? You just left Mercy on the porch of the mercantile, and you are already—" His hand flailed irritably toward the two women. "—conversing with two others?"

Micah tossed his fork onto his plate with a loud clatter. "First of all . . ." He realized his volume had risen too high and forced himself to take a breath. "I tried to get Mercy to join me, but she was stubbornly insistent. Second—" He flung a matching gesture at the nearby table. "—*I* was not conversing with anyone." Irritated that Gid's anger had caused him to be rude, he side-eyed the two women. "Sorry."

Neither seemed to want to look at him any longer. They both rose, leaving their money on the table. "We'll just be on our way."

It was Micah's turn to glare at Gideon. "What is this all about?" He folded his arms, irritated that Gid was ruining a perfectly good meal.

Felicity arrived with Gid's plate and filled both their coffee cups. To Micah, she said, "Just let me know when you are ready to depart, and I'll dish up a plate, fresh and hot." She bustled off, leaving his thanks hanging in the air.

Gid snatched up his fork and poked it in Micah's direction. "Do not hurt her. She's had enough hurt to last a lifetime."

Micah had no doubt which "her" Gid referred to, but . . . He forced himself to relax casually against his chair, reaching to curl one hand around the warmth of his cup. As realization dawned, the bites he'd already eaten turned sour in his stomach.

So it was like that, was it?

Gid had feelings for Mercy?

Sharp jealousy shot through him.

Jealousy? Until earlier today, out at the creek, the emotion would have shocked him. However, now he wasn't surprised by the feeling at all.

He dropped his attention to his rapidly cooling meat and potatoes. It was good that this had come up now before anything too . . . lasting passed between him and Mercy. He wouldn't do anything to hurt Gideon. But . . .

No. No. No.

No "but." He wouldn't do anything to hurt Gideon. Period.

And Mercy *had* asked him not to touch her again. Maybe she'd been trying to send him a message.

He wasn't sure what he'd been thinking out by the creek anyhow. What kind of man harbored feelings for a woman who had been the cause of his wife's death—even if it hadn't exactly been her fault? He bit back a grunt. Apparently, a man like him. But he wasn't some animal in rut. He could control his feelings. Gid was a good man. It would be better this way.

He opened his mouth to say as much, but instead of speaking, he hunched over his plate, snatched up his fork, and shoveled in a large bite. He needed a moment to figure out what to say. That was all.

He and Gid devoured their food in complete silence, and the boys seemed to have caught on to the tension at the table because they weren't their usual rambunctious selves.

Micah finished and shoved his plate closer to the outer edge of the table, where Felicity could more easily take it. He took a gulp of coffee but could barely swallow it because of the way his muscles seemed to be frozen.

He pried his lips apart in order to speak. "I'll not get between you, Gid. If she's who you want, then . . . I wish you all the best." The words were bitter on his tongue. He pegged his brother-in-law with a look. "But don't take too long, because . . . Well, just don't dally over making your feelings known." He gulped more coffee and let it burn the whole way down. Now why had he gone and added that?

Gid shook his head. "She's not ready."

Micah spun the coffee cup in circles on the table, weariness heavy in his heart. He thought of the way Mercy had reacted when he'd touched her hair. Gid was right. She needed time. "Yeah. You're right." His resignation hung heavy in the words.

Avoiding Gid's sharply prying scrutiny, he looked at the boys, wishing they were finished, but both were still working on their last few bites.

He ought to be happy to see Mercy cared for by a good man such as Gideon.

But happiness was the furthest emotion from him right about now.

He needed a distraction. "Hey Avram, what do you think about joining Joel at the schoolhouse tomorrow?"

Mercy had spent the last half hour darning one of Avram's socks. How long before Micah and the boys were done eating? She needed to get Av to sleep soon, for she hoped to try again tomorrow to convince him to go to the schoolhouse.

She tied off the thread on the sock and was once again pacing when another knock came at the door. This one more firm than the last.

Her stomach tangled into a web of knots.

This time when she opened the door, Micah stood before her with his hand on one of Avram's shoulders. Behind him, Gideon was escorting Joel into their room across the hall. He tipped her a nod.

She returned it.

Micah swung a glance from her to Gideon behind him and back again.

It was only then that she noticed he held a plate in one hand. He nudged it toward her. "Brought you some pot roast."

Her stomach betrayed her and rumbled loudly.

The soft smile that curved his lips didn't quite reach his eyes, but it grated on her, nonetheless. However, it would be very rude to decline his kindness. She reached for the plate, and Avram ducked beneath her arms as she did so.

"Whoa there!" Micah lifted the plate to keep it from getting knocked from his hands.

"Avram. Slow down, please." Mercy sighed.

"Sowwy." Her son landed on the bed with a hearty bounce.

Now, with just the two of them standing at her doorway, Micah wasn't so quick to offer her the plate a second time. With one of his forearms propped against the lintel above, he held the plate off to one side as he looked down at her. She would practically have to step into the circle of his arms to take it and escape him, and she wasn't about to do that.

He rubbed at his forehead with his thumbnail. "I talked to Av, and he said he'd like to join Joel at school tomorrow."

Mercy pressed her lips together. It irritated her how quickly her son had gravitated to this man.

He searched her face. "This frustrates you?"

She lowered her voice. "I'm not sure why he's listening to you when he wouldn't listen to me when I tried to encourage him to do the same."

He matched his level to her own. "'Tis the way with parenting sometimes. Where one parent fails, the other is sometimes able to connect. Not that I'm . . ." He frowned. "Trying to be a parent to him. I only meant—"

She lifted one hand. "I understand what you meant." Recognition of her son's parental poverty drooped her shoulders. Av had never had that privilege in his entire life. It had always only been her watching out for his needs. The temptation to give in to the powerful force that was Micah Morran once again loomed before her.

Her focus blurred on the floorboards between them as she did her best to picture a candle flame consuming a moth.

Now was assuredly not the time for Av to start experiencing a proper two-parent relationship. At least not with this man who she knew could hurt her so fully. Softly, so as to keep Avram from hearing her words, she said, "Please be careful with my son, Mr. Morran. I don't want him growing too attached to you, is all." She lifted her gaze to his, willing herself to be as strong as he was. "Not when we are sure to part at the end of the trail."

Micah straightened. She was surprised to see the blue of his eyes dim with hurt as he searched her face for a long moment before he held the plate out to her. "Understood. Enjoy your supper, Mrs. Adler." A muscle pulsed near the hinge of his jaw.

Willing her hands not to tremble, she accepted the plate, dipping a little curtsy of thanks.

He pivoted toward his own door.

It seemed she had successfully put him at arm's length, and now she ought to soften their parting. After all, they still had months before they reached the Oregon Territory. "This was very thoughtful of you. Thank you. I'll pay you back when I can."

He spun back toward her so quickly that she snatched a breath. He stilled.

Why did she keep doing that? She had no fear of him—well, other than the fear of what her own heart might convince her to do. But she'd lived so long on the edge of a blade. Always one moment of inattention away from being sliced in two.

His countenance softened as he gripped the back of his neck and studied her. "I did not buy the meal with the expectation of repayment. Please put that out of your head."

She ought to press the issue, but she was weary today of battling. So instead, she conceded with a nod. "Then I thank you even more. Good evening."

With that, she withdrew into the safety of her room and closed the door. She sank onto her bed, set the plate on the table beside her, and shook out the trembling of her limbs.

Overbearing, bossy, mule-headed man!

But he was thoughtful too. Despite the prickly way she'd treated him earlier, he'd brought her dinner.

She glanced at Av. He had flopped onto his stomach on the floor and was looking at the illustrations in the primer.

She sighed. Took up the knife and fork and cut into one of the potatoes. Her stomach rumbled happily, and she closed her eyes in contentment as she slipped it and a sliver of the meat between her lips.

Heavenly.

She murmured a little sound of appreciation.

Doomed. She was doomed to a battle she wasn't sure she wanted to win.

Her eyes flew open. A battle she wasn't even sure Micah was engaged in! Maybe that hadn't been hurt in Micah's eyes a moment ago, but a measure of surprise at her words.

Other than his touching her hair earlier today, what had he ever done to indicate any interest in her? Nothing. He'd bossed and hovered. But that was simply part of his personality. It was how he took care of people. He'd been treating her the same way from the moment he'd saved her life on the night Georgia died.

And with her looking so much like his wife, of course, he'd probably touched her hair out of some nostalgic emotion directed at Georgia, not her.

Her face flamed.

No wonder he'd seemed confused. He probably wasn't even harboring feelings for her but was only missing his wife! And she'd overreacted and had narrowly avoided tugging a handful of her hair out in the process. And then had the audacity to tell him not to get too close to her son!

Daft, Mercy. So daft!

But at least she didn't need to worry about giving in to a man who would hold so much power over her.

Distress swept through her.

This realization ought to fill her with relief, so why did she feel just the opposite?

Chapter Twenty

On Monday morning, Mercy could tell that Avram was a bit tense when they headed across the street for breakfast. He was grumpy and didn't want to carry the pail she'd procured for his lunch. She took his hand, and thankfully, he did walk beside her to Felicity's.

The men and Joel were already seated at their usual table with a platter of pancakes in the middle. Mercy helped Av into a seat and then took her own. "Morning."

Both men gave her nods, but other than that, neither spoke. Both seemed intent on their plates.

"Is something amiss?" She served a pancake onto Avram's plate.

Both shook their heads.

"We're fine." Micah pegged Gideon with a look that seemed to hold more than a little animosity.

With a pancake drooping over the sides of the server suspended above her plate, Mercy divided a glance between them. What was this about?

The remainder of the meal passed in sullen silence. Micah and Gideon both scarfed down two heaping stacks of pancakes without one word of shared conversation. Mercy thanked God for the need to help Avram cut his breakfast into bites because the tension between Gid and Micah stretched as taut as a drumskin, and she felt it the better part of valor to let their business be their own.

Micah downed the last of his coffee and stood. "Would you mind walking Joel over to the school when you take Avram?"

"Of course."

"Thanks. See you this evening." With that, he stalked out the door.

Gideon shifted in his seat, dawdling over the last of his coffee.

Mercy wanted to pry. Oh, how she wanted to pry, but she took a bite of pancake instead.

Only moments later, Gideon stood, offered his farewells, and followed Micah to work.

Mercy frowned at the door closing in his wake. Why had they both awoken on the back side of the sun?

Felicity paused with one hand plunked on her plump hip and a steaming coffee pot in her other hand. "Wondered how long it would take."

"Pardon?"

Felicity opened her mouth as though to reply but then seemed to change her mind and lifted the coffee pot instead. "More coffee?"

Laying one hand over her cup, Mercy shook her head. "I'm fine, but I wondered if I could buy a piece of fruit and maybe a slice of bread with cheese for Avram's lunch?"

Felicity bobbed a nod toward Joel. "Micah already bought the boys a lunch and instructed Joel to share with your son."

Joel nodded. "We got oranges and sausages rolled in pancakes!"

"And . . ." Felicity winked. "Perhaps there *might* be two small pieces of apple pie."

Joel grinned so big that Mercy would have sworn he was showing every one of his molars. "Thanks!"

Felicity gave his hair a friendly ruffle and then, with a parting farewell, hustled to the next table.

Mercy sank against her seat, sucking the inside of her lower lip in irritation. First, Micah had purchased her dinner yesterday, and now lunch for Av. She was racking up quite a debt with the man. She would have to take it up with him later.

She and the boys lingered for several more minutes over coffee and cold glasses of milk.

Joel brought a smile to her face with his chatter about all he was excited to be learning in school, and Av seemed to relax a little throughout the conversation.

After breakfast, Mercy walked with the boys from the diner to the schoolhouse. There were still twenty minutes before school started, but that would give them a few minutes to play with other children and get settled in. However, at the door, Avram held back, tugging on her hand and refusing to budge another step.

Holding their lunch pail, Joel waited to one side of the door.

Mercy squatted to her son's level. "What is it?"

"I not want go." Avram fidgeted, focused on his chubby fingers.

Several children thundered past them, rushing into the school.

Mercy reached to tuck part of his shirt back into his knickers. "I think you'll have fun."

Av shook his head.

"Joel will be right here with you all day. Won't that be better than sitting and drawing pictures at the counter in the store?"

Another shake of his head.

"We've got pie for lunch," Joel tried. When Mercy gave him a grateful nod, he grinned at her slyly.

The reminder about pie made Avram hesitate. Face scrunched into a delightful frown of thoughtfulness, he seemed to be weighing the pros and cons.

Mercy held her silence, not wanting to tip the scale of his deliberations to the wrong account. What had Micah told him the evening before to get him to agree?

When he still hadn't made a decision after a few stretched moments, Mercy decided that she'd better speak up if only to let Joel get to class. And, since the pie seemed to be a weighty factor . . .

"Tell you what . . . If you go to school with Joel all week, we'll go on a picnic on Sunday afternoon. And I'll make you a pie of your very own to celebrate your first week of lessons." She cringed inwardly at her bribery but wanted to whoop in victory when he snapped his gaze to hers.

"Can Joel come?"

Mercy nodded. "Of course, he can come."

"And Joel's pa? And can we pway gwizzly in the cweek?"

Mercy's heart lurched at just the thought. Heavens. "Ah . . . I think we'll have to ask Mr. Micah. I can't make promises for him. But . . . I'll ask him." She gulped.

Avram shrugged one shoulder. "Okay." He marched past Joel and into the schoolhouse without so much as a backward glance.

Fluttering a breath of relief through her lips, Mercy gave Joel a wave of thanks. She wondered if she oughtn't follow the boys inside to make sure Avram got to the proper seat, but when she poked her head through the doors, the young schoolmarm was already bent in front of Avram, all smiles and introductions. She gave Mercy a subtle gesture to let her know all was well, and Mercy retreated to the schoolhouse steps.

She ran her attention over the town that was just beginning to come to life and blew another frazzled breath.

She'd gotten Avram to go to school, but now she had to work up the courage to invite Micah on a picnic! Wonderful.

On Friday morning, Mercy woke with the reminder that she hadn't found the courage to invite Micah to Avram's picnic all week. She'd had several opportunities over the meal table, but neither Micah's nor Gideon's mood had seemed to improve over the last few days, and each time, she had talked herself out of it.

She decided to ask him when they got to breakfast, but then Avram had needed a second trip to the necessary, and Micah was just leaving when she and Avram hurried in a bit late.

He touched his forehead in greeting as they passed but didn't pause.

Mercy craned her neck to watch him leave, almost bumping into Felicity, who carried a tray filled with plates. "Oh! Sorry!" Only Mercy's quick reflex of angling sideways and shooting up on her tiptoes kept them from an outright disaster.

Felicity breezed past with a brush of her hand that indicated well-practiced ease at avoiding such disasters.

Mercy blew out a huff. Maybe Micah was upset with her? Though she hadn't had a chance to speak to him alone all week, she'd thought she handled the end of their last conversation rather well, but perhaps she'd said something that upset him?

The thought elevated her nervousness about speaking to him.

Nevertheless, she determined to find a moment to pass along Avram's request. She didn't want to be the kind of parent to let her child down.

After breakfast, she took the boys to school and then spent the morning dusting every shelf and item in the store and washing the front windows.

Now she hauled the dirty wash water out back to dump it on Willow's potted herbs.

Micah was just lowering the dipper back into the crock of water that the Chancellors kept cool for the men in the shade of the porch. He froze and since he stood between her and the raised herb planter, she did too. The heavy bucket of wash water hung awkwardly by her side.

"Hi," he offered, swiping one broad brown hand over his mouth to dispel any lingering droplets.

So he *was* still speaking to her? That was at least promising. "Hi, yourself." She wouldn't get a more perfect opportunity than this to ask.

Across the yard, in the entry of the barn where the sun streamed in, she could see Gideon planing a board. Long golden curls of wood rolled up and then spilled off to the side. But he stood far enough away and likely had enough noise in his ears from the scraping of the planer to keep their conversation private.

Micah stretched a hand toward the handle of the bucket. "Here, let me get that for you." His shirtsleeves were rolled almost to his elbows, exposing the corded muscles of bronzed forearms. The shirt itself stretched to its limits around his broad shoulders. And moisture from the effort of whatever work he'd been doing this morning glistened in droplets on his forehead.

He shifted, and Mercy realized that she'd been staring, and his hand was still outstretched.

"Uh, thank you." She willed down the warmth in her face as she handed over the bucket. His hand brushed hers when they made the transfer, sending a lightning bolt of awareness straight to her heart. She massaged her fingers over the place to dispel the feel of him.

This was all such a heap of tangled yarn. Why had she gone and gotten soft on the very last man on earth who would want her?

His feet shuffled again, and seeing his arched brows, she realized that she'd once more kept him waiting.

"Just on the soil at the base of the herbs there, if you don't mind." She swept a gesture behind him and was gratified to see him carefully pour the water so as not to splash it on the leaves of the herbs.

When he finished, he sluiced some water from the rain barrel into the bucket, gave it a swirl, and poured that onto the herbs also. After that, he held the bucket toward her.

Working her lower lip, she thanked him, then hung it on its hook by the back door.

With a nod, he pointed toward the barn. "I'd better get back to work."

Mercy took a quick step forward. "Micah, may I have a moment? There's something I need to ask you."

He cut her a surprised look, hands falling to rest on his hips. "I'm listening."

She curled her fingers into a tight knot to avoid their fidgeting. "On Monday, when I took Avram and Joel to school, Av didn't want to stay."

A tick of confusion puckered the skin above his pinched brows. "Okay?"

Mercy hurried on before she lost her nerve. "I promised that if he would attend classes all week, I would take him on a Sunday picnic."

Humor softened the blue of his eyes till they were a near match to the gray-blue of the sky beyond the barn. "Ah, the tried-and-true bribery technique."

"Yes, but..." Mercy's fingers squirmed despite the tight clench she held them in. "He then asked if Joel could come."

Micah's brow smoothed, and his shoulders seemed to relax. "Of course. Yes. He can join you." He pivoted toward the barn.

"And then he asked if you could come too!"

He froze with this back still to her.

Mercy scrunched her face as she waited for her request to register.

One of those broad brown hands rose to rake through his hair. He didn't want to join her, and how could she blame him? Especially not after the way she'd asked him not to let Av get attached to him.

In the distance, Gideon straightened from his task and looked at them as he used a bandana to wipe his brow.

"I know I asked you to be considerate of my son's feelings, but I thought... Just this once... couldn't hurt." Mercy waited.

Slowly Micah turned, searching her face like he hadn't quite heard her right.

She felt her shoulders hunch around her ears as she splayed her hands. "He wants to play grizzly in the creek."

That made his lips twitch, and his soft gaze lazily slipped the length of her before it rebounded to sweep the perimeter of her hair.

A curl of awareness swept through her. She could almost feel the gentle tug of his fingers on her lock of hair. The way his hands had held her shoulders so gently.

With a blink, he hung his head and once again worked his fingers through his curls.

He was going to say no, but she surprisingly wanted to convince him more than anything. "I know you've been upset at me about something all week, but . . ."

His head snapped up. "I haven't been upset with you."

"Oh." It was her turn to frown in puzzlement even as unaccountable relief eased the tension in her shoulders. "Both you and Gid have seemed . . . I mean . . . It would be understandable if . . ."

He huffed a breath and tossed a glance toward the barn.

Gid had returned to work, but though the planer moved again, his steely attention remained fixed on them.

Prodding a toe at a pebble in the dust at his feet, Micah spoke quietly. "Neither of us are upset with you. We had some words. We'll get past it."

She bit her lip to keep from demanding what kind of words. Instead, she prodded, "So? The picnic?"

He massaged the lower half of his face, working fingers and thumb along his jaw. Finally, he shrugged one shoulder and turned to her. The first real smile she'd seen all week parted his lips even if there was still a hint of melancholy in his expression. "I'd love to join you." The seriousness in the blue of his eyes was like a siren song, holding her trapped in a current she couldn't seem to escape.

She clutched for the support pillar of the porch and rested her weight against it, hanging on for dear life. "Wonderful. Avram will be so happy."

Micah poked his toe at the pebble again, and she was relieved for the release from the intensity of his scrutiny. He thumbed a gesture over his shoulder toward the barn. "I should get back to work."

"Yes. Me too."

Neither of them moved.

After a long moment, Micah spun toward the barn without looking at her again.

Mercy took herself in hand and returned to her duties in the store. But somehow, her heart felt ten times lighter.

Micah stalked back into the barn. Hang, but he was in trouble. How had he come to feel so much for any woman this soon, much less . . . her?

Gid tossed his bandana onto the bench next to the one where he worked on smoothing the boards they would use to construct the beds of their wagons. He immediately snatched it up again and scrubbed his face with it.

Micah strode to the wheel he'd been working on all morning and was pleased to see how tightly all the spokes fit into the hub.

He could feel Gid's scrutiny drilling into his back. His questions wouldn't be long in coming.

He went to work smoothing the round curve of the first felloe he would need to attach to two of the spokes.

Gideon thumped around, putting a rough board on his sawhorses, and then he quietly asked. "What'd she want?"

Just as he'd suspected—not long in getting to his questions at all. Micah pressed his lips together, wishing Gid hadn't been witness to the conversation. "I'm not going back on my word, if that's what you're worried about."

"I know you mean what you say. Just curious, is all."

Micah adjusted the holes in the felloe over the pegs at the end of two of the spokes and banged it flush with the short-handled sledgehammer. "She promised Avram a picnic. He wanted to go swimming and included Joel and me in the invitation because of a game I played with him last week."

"Which you declined, of course?"

Micah shot him a look. "No. He's just a kid, Gid."

Gid plunked his hands on his hips and worked his tongue over his teeth. It was a long moment before he snatched up the planer and went back to work.

Micah winced, wondering how thin that board was going to be by the time he was done with it.

Taking up the next felloe, Micah worked until he finished the wheel. That task completed, he set it aside. Wayne would eventually need to take all the wheels to the blacksmith, who would band them with the rims. With Gid still maintaining a stubborn silence, Micah took up his drawknife and went to work on the spokes for the next wheel.

He tossed a glance out the door at the angle of the sun. About noon on Friday. He sighed.

It was going to be a long day and a half locked up with Gid in this barn.

As far as he was concerned, Sunday couldn't get here soon enough.

After she'd worked up the nerve to invite Micah, Mercy's next worry had been the expense of the meal. While she had enough in her savings jar to afford to buy a picnic meal from Felicity's, she remained mindful that she had no idea what she might need once she reached Oregon, and loathed to spend it.

Instead, she laid snares by the creek and then bought a dime's worth of flour, salt, lard, and spices from Willow and secured her permission to use her kitchen. Willow also mentioned a wild peach tree, and they'd gone together after work and spent an hour picking a basketful. Even though it was early June, the fruit was so ripe that the peaches practically fell off the tree into their hands. Willow traded extra flour, cinnamon, and sugar on the promise that Mercy would make extra hand pies for her and her father.

A check of her snares had revealed two plump hares and she'd been so thankful when Mr. Chancellor had offered to dispatch and butcher them for her.

Mercy spent Saturday evening making handheld meat and fruit pies, and now, on Sunday, as the service was concluding, she felt her nervousness begin to rise. Both Avram and Joel were practically dancing in anticipation as she met Micah in the churchyard. She had planned to invite Gid too, but he was already striding away, motioning for Mattox to stay. The dog sank to his haunches but kept his golden gaze fixed on their party through the slats of the gate.

Micah ruffled one hand over each boy's head. "You two ready to be grizzly meat?"

"Yes!" Joel shouted.

"I'm a gwizzly too!" Avram roared so loudly that Parson Houston looked over from where he stood on the porch introducing the parishioners to the new parson.

Mercy offered him an apologetic wince. To Av, she said, "Come on, bear. We have to wash up and gather our picnic basket." She nudged him out of the churchyard gate, patting Mattox's head on her way by. The dog fell into step beside them, tongue lolling.

She looked past the dog to Micah. "Give us fifteen minutes?"

He nodded but then gave Joel an exaggerated sigh. "I guess the grizzly will have to wait fifteen minutes to eat."

Joel chortled.

But when Micah angled a sly wink at her, recognition blasted her cheeks with fire.

"You know," she offered casually as though speaking to Avram. "I think it might be better to keep the grizzly weak with hunger. What do you think? Maybe no rabbit or peach pies for the mean old bear? He likely won't be as dangerous that way."

Both boys giggled and glanced up at Micah, who tracked along the street beside her. Humor intensified the blue of his eyes as he met her teasing look with one of his own.

"You know, boys, you have to be careful keeping an animal too hungry. It might just come back to bite you!"

On the word "bite," he bent and pretended to snap at both boys. This sent them scurrying ahead with shrieks of laughter and Mattox barking on their heels. And when he returned to an upright position, he arched both brows at her. His next words were spoken for her ears alone as he leaned a little closer.

"Be warned, Ms. Adler."

With a tightening in her chest threatening her oxygen supply, Mercy retorted, "Don't worry, Mr. Morran, I made plenty of food."

He made a click of disappointment with his tongue. "More's the pity."

Chapter Twenty-One

Micah knew he had stumbled onto thin ice. He chastised himself for flirting with her as he opened the door to the mercantile and held it for her. The boys had long since disappeared through the store. He kept his focus obediently on a group of riders trotting down the street instead of on her where it wanted to be. He'd promised Gid that he would step out of the dance. And well he better remember it.

Mercy tilted her face up as she passed. "Meet you here on the porch?"

"Yeah." Though the word wasn't much more than air, she didn't seem to notice.

"I planned to invite Gideon along but didn't catch him after church. Would you please pass along my invitation? I don't think he went into Felicity's, so I assume he's in your room."

Her words ought to be a relief. Instead, he found himself tamping down irritation and disappointment. Had she been thinking of Gideon through this whole conversation? Maybe his chances wouldn't even get off the ground. She might already be harboring feelings for his hopeful brother-in-law.

He swallowed an exhale of frustration and only replied, "Sure. I'll let him know."

Mercy headed for the kitchen, and he, upstairs.

Joel barreled out of their room in his knickers and with a scrap of toweling over his shoulder. "I'll get Avram." He dashed across the hall to Mercy's room.

Gideon was lounging morosely on his bed with one hand tucked behind his head when Micah entered their room. His brother-in-law didn't move. Simply continued to stare at the ceiling.

Micah shrugged out of his go-to-meeting coat. "She looked for you. Asked me to invite you to join us."

Gid's brow puckered, but he didn't move.

Micah undid his cuffs and removed his good shirt. "She specifically instructed me to pass along her invitation."

That did garner him a glance. But then Gid returned his scrutiny to the ceiling. "If she really had wanted me to come, she would have asked me at the same time she asked you."

Micah pondered for a moment. He didn't want to give false hope. Yet . . . "Sometimes it's harder to speak to those we care about the most." Ouch. It hurt to say those words aloud.

But they brought Gid to a sitting position on the edge of his bed. He propped his hands beside himself, and this time, his attention fixed on a spot on the wall. "You think so?"

Micah only swallowed and lifted one shoulder as he shrugged into a clean shirt. What did he know when it came to women? Nothing. Being married to Georgia had certainly taught him that.

Gid breathed out a growl and hung his head. "Please give her my thanks and tell her I'd be happy to come next time, but today, I can't."

Micah frowned at him. "Why not?"

"Because I already accepted an invitation from Wayne to join him and Willow for lunch." He sighed so loudly it sounded like a stiff wind.

One corner of Micah's mouth tipped up, and if it had more to do with him getting to have Mercy all to himself this afternoon than it did over his humor at Gid's predicament, well . . . Gid didn't need to know that. "You realize that invitation didn't initiate with Wayne, right?"

Gid roughed a hand through his hair, looking uptight. "Probably. But since he's our boss, I couldn't very well say no."

"Since he's our boss, it's probably not wise to get involved with his daughter, either."

"I'm not involved with his daughter!" Gid shot him a razor-sharp scowl.

Micah raised his palms. "I'd better check on the boys." With that, he made his escape from the room.

Mercy sat on a quilt in the shade of a large oak that grew along the banks of the creek with the leftovers from the picnic in a borrowed basket beside her. Propped against her hands with her legs stretched out before her, she smiled at the boys' antics as they chased Micah through the water. He'd mercifully kept his shirt on today, most likely for the sake of her sensibilities. Mattox paddled in circles behind them as usual.

The game of grizzly had long since collapsed into minimally controlled chaos. Mercy didn't envy Micah the task of keeping both boys from dunking each other. He would toss the first one into the deeper part of the watering hole, only to have the boy he was protecting swim after the one who had just been tossed to get revenge.

There was no animosity in the game, simply much fun and boyish foolishness.

Much more patient than her, Micah endured the silliness far longer than she would have. Finally, he clapped his hands sternly. "All right. Enough. You two have worn me out. No more dunking each other. I'm going to take a nap on the quilt." With that, he padded out of the water, streaming rivulets from trousers and shirt.

Mercy found sudden interest in a broken bit of grass on the quilt beside her, willing herself to unsee how his shirt plastered to every ridge and contour.

Gracious! Had her patch of shade moved? It was currently hotter out here than it had been standing over Willow's stove all last evening. She glanced right and left. No. The shade was still broadly covering her. She needed to stop this foolishness at once. Where was a fan when she needed one?

In her periphery, she saw him pause on the bank to dry off with a scrap of toweling they'd draped over a bush in the sun, and then he pivoted and padded toward her.

He flopped onto his back beside her, tucking both hands behind his head, eyes closed. "Got to love a lazy Sunday afternoon."

"Yes." She broke the blade of grass into bits with one thumbnail.

He squinted one eye at her. "You too hot?"

She felt her discomfiture blaze through her cheeks again. She didn't meet his scrutiny. "No. Why do you ask?"

"You seem a little flushed, is all. That water will cool you right down." A slow, taunting smile spread across his lips.

She refused to give in to his teasing. "That will not be happening. I'm perfectly happy right here, thank you very much."

He grunted and sat up suddenly, resting his forearms against his knees and clasping one wrist with the opposite hand. For a long moment, they both watched the boys and Mattox. But then Micah looked over at her. "I didn't think . . . That is . . . do you have a fear of the water?"

Not unless he was in the water with her, setting her every nerve ablaze. "No."

"I just wondered if Herst—" He angled his head sharply away from her and raked one hand through his damp curls.

Horror washed through her, erasing every thought except the ones that wanted to comfort him. "Is that what happened to your . . . mother?" Her first blade of grass was completely shredded, so she reached for another.

"No." He cleared his throat. "I just know what . . . men like that can be like."

Mercy looked over at him then. She searched the side of his face, the muscle ticking in and out at the hinge of his jaw, the defeat that she could read in his posture. "Tell me about her."

His features softened, if only imperceptibly. His attention remained fixed on the boys. "She was beautiful. Full of life and laughter when Pa wasn't around." He tipped a nod toward the trio in the creek. "Joel's laugh reminds me a lot of hers sometimes." His hand fidgeted for a better grip on his wrist. "She had these prize-winning banty roosters. Meanest little cusses you ever could meet." He chuckled. "Got myself pecked and clawed by both those cocks more times than I care to remember, but she was *proud* of those critters. Used to keep the ribbons she won at the fair all in a row just under the roofline of their coops."

Only when he'd stopped speaking for several moments did Mercy let herself pry. "Do you have siblings?"

He shook his head. "No, it was just me and Ma."

She hated the ache in his voice and the way he'd left out any mention of his father.

"And your mother? Where is she now?"

He cut her a sharp look. "Not sure why I thought you knew. My father . . . He uh . . . He killed her when I was thirteen. I left home right after. And haven't seen him since. I lived off of scraps and soup kitchens for a couple of years until I procured my first job."

"Oh, Micah." Mercy's hand shot out to rest on his arm before she thought better of it. She let it remain for just a moment before pulling it back into her lap. "That's why you decided to help me back in Chamblissburg and then . . . Herst . . ." She couldn't finish the thought.

"Yeah." His voice was only a notch above a whisper as he stared off across the creek. "Savage men have taken a lot from me. Maybe God just finds fault with me for some reason."

Tears blurred her vision. She knew just how he felt, and yet . . . "Would you say the same of me?"

His brow furrowed, and he angled his body toward her but made no reply.

"Would you?" she pressed. "I was ravished, had my father turn his back on me, and then force me to marry a man I had absolutely no desire to even be in the same room with. Were those things God did? Or things men did?"

"Men, of course. But God could have stopped it—all your pain, all my pain—so why didn't He?"

"I asked Parson Houston the same thing because of what you said that time about God maybe creating you—us—for His wrath. And the parson said that God so values a relationship with us that free will has to be given. A relationship is not a relationship unless both parties choose each other. If one forces himself on another, that's not a relationship. That's abuse. God already chose us. Now, He longs for us to choose Him in return, but the bad side is that people—most people, according to Parson Houston—don't choose Him. They choose sin and selfishness instead."

He nipped at the inside of one lip. Seemed to be considering her words.

Mercy once again found her hand resting on his arm. "But sometimes there are amazingly good men who do choose to help another, and it costs them dearly. If I could take it back—"

His hand pressed over hers. He shook his head. "I keep telling you not to do that."

"I can't help it. I'm so grateful for . . ." She gestured toward the boys, whose laughter floated to them on the breeze. "And yet so horrified all at the same time. And I just need you to know that I know you paid such a high price for our safety." She hesitated as a thought struck her. "Jesus paid a high price for our safety too. Only in that case, it cost Him His own life."

He made a sound in the back of his throat. "You think that I might be able to find some of that . . . peace that verse talks about?"

Mercy's heart thumped hope in her chest. "I do, Micah. I really do. He has paid the price already. All we have to do is choose to accept it."

He glanced over at her. "And you've honestly felt different since . . . that incident you told me about last week?"

Mercy felt inadequate to answer his questions. "I'm so new to all this that I'm probably not the best one to ask. But yes. I mean, I don't want to give the impression that I no longer feel worry or distress at times, but there's just . . . something underlying it all now. A knowing that no matter what happens, Jesus will be with me through it all."

He nodded, pondering again.

After a long moment, he glanced down and seemed to realize for the first time that Mercy's hand lay on his arm, and his own hand covered it. He cleared his throat and eased back. "Sorry. I didn't mean to . . ."

She remembered her request that he not touch her again and realized that he hadn't. Not once, all week. She drew her hand into her lap, but she felt no embarrassment because she'd made the gesture out of simple concern and friendship with no ulterior motives. "It's fine."

They sat beside each other quietly after that.

Mercy tried not to savor his companionship too much because, just like she'd feared about Avram, she didn't want to grow too attached.

Mattox had long since given up on the boys and climbed from the creek to shake himself off and then snooze in a patch of sunlight nearby. The boys had been doing more playing on the sandy beach than in the water for at least thirty minutes and the sun was dipping below the treetops on the horizon. It would be time for them to leave soon.

Beside her, Micah shifted. "Mercy?"

"Yes?"

"Thanks for listening. And thanks for asking about my ma. She was a good woman. Strong. But maybe not as strong as you. You did the right thing getting your son to safety."

Mercy let that comment sink deep into her soul. After pondering, however, she shook her head. "I don't know if I'm so strong, Micah. It's you and Gideon who have helped me through these past months.

And I fear raising Avram alone, but I might be too broken to—" She cut off, unable to finish the sentence.

She felt the sharp drill of his scrutiny. "You're not too broken, Merc. Don't doubt your strength."

She shook her head. "It's just that after . . . Herst . . ." A shudder coursed through her, even as embarrassment made her hang her head. Why was she baring this fear to Micah, of all people? Maybe because she knew, with his history, he might understand.

Micah shifted. "Remember that what you had wasn't love, Mercy. Love is . . . gentle and kind and puts other's needs first." He shifted again and scraped one hand through his hair in agitation. He was as uncomfortable with this topic as she was.

She clamped her tongue between her teeth to keep from blathering more of her fears.

Searching the horizon, he offered, "You'll find a man who will love you." His voice broke, and he clasped his wrist tighter as though to keep his arm from slipping from his grip. "Someday soon."

She frowned, once more studying the side of his face. Maybe there was a man out there somewhere who would love her, truly love her with tender care. But . . . apparently, she'd been right about the fact that Micah had simply been missing his wife that day at the creek last week. Because this had been a blatant opening for him to declare his feelings if they existed.

What she had seen as teasing and flirting must not mean to him what it had meant to her.

And yet, she was the one who had asked him not to touch her. It was better all-around for both of them and their boys this way.

Despite that knowledge . . . She snatched another blade of grass. Would she ever be able to feel for another man the things she suddenly realized she felt so strongly for this one beside her?

She wanted the joy of toiling with him in the Oregon Territory. Of greeting him at the door each evening when he arrived home, weary and work worn. Of throwing her arms around his neck and teasing him about a swim in the creek to wash off his workday.

She wanted to feel his lips pressed to hers and—

No. She leaped to her feet, snatched up the basket that she'd packed with the leftovers earlier, and then paused with her focus on the boys and her back to him. She wasn't sure she wanted intimate moments with any man ever again.

Behind her, she could hear him standing and folding the quilt.

She closed her eyes and spoke before she could lose her nerve. "You're a good man, Micah Morran. And God has good plans for you. Please don't doubt it."

With that, she hurried forward, calling to the boys that it was time to head back into town. The boys joined her, chattering and showing her pretty rocks they had found, and as she oohed and aahed over their discoveries and led them toward the Chancellors', she wasn't sure whether to be grateful or heartbroken that Micah dragged behind.

When Micah barged into their room, Gideon lay on his bed reading a book. He jolted a little and laid the open book on his chest, searching Micah's features. "What is it?"

Micah paced, unable to relax enough to sit. "Nothing."

Gid huffed his disbelief at that. "My lunch with the Chancellors was high ace, thanks for asking."

The boys clattered into the room, bounding over to Joel's bed, where they laid out a circle of string for a game of marbles.

Micah scooped both hands back through his hair. "Sorry. I'm not much company right now."

"I never would have guessed," Gid retorted dryly.

Micah flopped onto his bed and then immediately sat up again. "You've got to stake your claim, Gid. Make a move or get out of the way."

Gid slammed his book shut and tossed it onto the table between their beds. "And just what brought this on?"

Micah released a sharp breath, not willing to delve that deeply into his feelings with his brother-in-law. "Just quit dawdling and jump into the race."

Folding his hands over his chest, Gid shook his head. "I keep telling you. She's not ready. Not sure she'll ever be ready, after what she went through, to be honest."

"She needs love, Gid. And she needs it sooner than later."

Gid continued to shake his head. "I can appreciate that you want an end date to this little agreement of ours, but you have to give me at least until Christmas."

"Christmas!? That's months away."

"That's my deal. Take it or leave it. You always barrel ahead without giving others time to adjust to their feelings. I don't want to be that man, Micah. I think she needs more time."

Micah yanked his boots off and flopped onto his back. Maybe a nap would free him from this boxed canyon he'd accidentally wandered into. The problem was, his body was zinging with so much energy that he doubted he'd be able to sleep for at least a week.

Chapter Twenty-Two

Adam was with Parson Miles in the tiny office that passed as his study at the back of the sanctuary. He'd been incrementally handing things over to Parson Miles, upon which they had agreed since Adam would remain in town until the spring caravans began heading west. His heart panged him at the mere thought.

This Sunday would be Parson Mile's first behind the pulpit, and after that, they would trade off Sunday by Sunday until Adam preached his farewell sermon sometime in the spring.

Now, he thrust the ledger he'd just pulled from a drawer across the desk toward the other minister. "This tells you the funds the church has and what is dedicated to each ministry. Be aware that Mrs. Candle has a mind like a steel trap when it comes to numbers, and woe to you if the Women's Aid for Orphans account is off by even a penny at the annual church meeting." He offered the man a grin. "She will most righteously let you know where you stand before the Almighty."

Parson Miles grinned. "Noted."

Adam glanced around the room. Shelves lined with his study books filled the back wall. He wouldn't be able to take but one or two west with him. It would be a hard decision to make. "The books will mostly remain. I hope you'll get good use from them. I'll want to take a few, but—"

A knock on the door interrupted.

"Come in," he called.

Young Declan Boyle poked his head through the doorway. "Begging yer pardon, parson, but the postman asked me tae deliver ye this." He held out an envelope, and Adam's heart lurched when he caught sight of the handwriting on the front.

Eden's sloping scrawl—so efficient, so feminine.

He stood frozen, unsure whether he wanted to read the letter or not. Declan remained in the doorway with the envelope stretched toward him. "Don't ye want it? The postman thought you'd wantae read it right away, which is how come he sent me ower wi' it rather than putting it in yer box."

Adam forced his feet and hands to move. "Ah, yes, thank you so much, Declan." He took the envelope and dug in his pocket for a penny.

But Declan raised his palms. "Na need. 'Twas ainlie a short jaunt from the post office."

Adam nudged the coin closer. "Use it to get yourself a meal, lad. Fair payment for only a short jaunt."

Sheepishly, Declan accepted the coin and then disappeared back the way he'd come, calling over his shoulder. "I thank ye fer yer kindness, Parson."

Adam leaned against the desk, looking down at the envelope. In the back of his mind, he registered Parson Miles collecting his coat and hat. Words penetrated the fog of his mind but were too ethereal to take hold of.

He raised his head with a snap. "Sorry. I missed what you said."

Parson Miles's focus lowered to the unopened envelope still in Adam's hands. "I asked if it were bad news. From your expression, it seems that it might be."

Adam tapped the envelope against the fingers of one hand. "It might, indeed."

Parson Miles nodded his understanding. "I'll leave you to it then. And you'll be in my prayers as I go about my day."

Adam thanked him and fell into his chair behind the desk as Parson Miles left him in the office alone. He took up his letter opener but only fiddled it through his fingers, staring down at the envelope in dread.

Finally, he took a short, sharp breath, then released it. "Father, I need your strength."

With that, he took up the envelope, sliced open the top, and then tugged the thin pages from within. He was immediately struck by the faint scent that was distinctly Eden. Gardenia. An exotic oil that her wealthy parents had brought back to her from one of their trips to India. The heady scent, soft, floral, intoxicating, filled his senses as he drew the pages closer and inhaled. The ache inside him threatened to cripple him.

With another breath for strength, he focused on the words.

Dearest Adam,

He swallowed. A hopeful start.

I have received your many communications and have thus taken it upon myself to respond. First, I thank you for the money, but as you know, it is unnecessary since Father and Mother support me well. It is with deepest regret . . .

His eyes fell closed mid-sentence. Not hopeful, then. Not hopeful at all. Like one returning to a torturer, he focused again on the writing.

. . . that I must decline your entreaties to join you in the West. It is not that I hold ought against the Snohomish, as you well know, but the thought of perhaps never seeing my parents again and even, dare I admit, dread of leaving the civility of city life that sways me thus. I hope you will continue to write because I will ever hold you close to my heart. Mother and Father . . .

He read the rest of the frivolous details about garden parties and charity balls, his dread and anger mounting with each word.

Until the loss of their child, she had been full of excitement to go with him into the wilds of the West. It had been after sitting through a talk about the Whitmans that they had both felt called by the Lord to this mission. Separately, they had each been impressed by the Lord, and trepidatiously, they had greeted one another at the breakfast table the next morning. Eden had been the first to speak of what she felt the Lord calling them to, and Adam remembered the relief that had coursed through him to have her already so willing to submit herself to what would no doubt be a difficult undertaking.

They had joyously hugged, him swinging her in great circles, and had gone to the mission board that very day to begin the process.

Then grief had become their daily companion, and Eden had pulled in on herself. Still, he hadn't known that she would refuse to travel with him on the first step of their journey—ministering for at least a year in the far west town of Independence as prescribed by the mission board—until the very morning they were to leave.

Admittedly, he'd known something was wrong, but he'd attributed her reclusiveness to grief and stress.

Now, he eased back in his chair, rested his head, and studied the ceiling. *Okay, Lord. She is bone of my bone and flesh of my flesh. I thought she but needed some time to adjust after our deep loss. But . . . now what do I do?*

No answer, save one.

Verses from near the end of the gospel of Matthew, chapter ten.

He who loves father or mother more than Me is not worthy of Me. And he who loves son or daughter more than Me is not worthy of Me. And he who does not take his cross and follow after Me is not worthy of Me. He who finds his life will lose it, and he who loses his life for My sake will find it.

Adam crumpled the letter in his fist and held tight until his trembling ceased.

Finally, he forced himself to speak aloud. "Yes, Lord. Where you lead me, I will follow."

Grief crashed over him.

Great sobs shook him as he dropped the crumpled letter onto his desk and pressed the heels of his hands into his eyes. He was thankful to be alone. Thankful for the release of the pent-up emotions that had been jailed in his chest for these many months. Thankful to know the One who would walk with him through another sea of loss.

But he was angry, too—angry at a woman who had promised to stand with him through all life's ups and downs and who had reneged on her word at the first valley of darkness.

After a few moments, despite his anger, he took a bracing breath, wiped his hands on his trousers, and took up his nibbed pen. He withdrew his sheaf of paper and wrote the date in the top corner. If it were letters that would maintain their connection, then he would do his best not to be the reason that line was severed.

The days turned one into another, all melding into a blur of sameness for Mercy—and yet it was good to feel a measure of boredom after her years of living on pins and needles around Herst.

School had let out for the hottest parts of the summer but had started up again in early September. Avram settled into school well, and even though he was in the youngest level, he could already form some letters and pronounce their sounds. The other day he'd even counted all ten of the geese that flew overhead as they migrated south.

Frost often glistened on the blades of grass of a morning when she escorted the boys to school from Felicity's. They played at blowing streams of air and imagining fanciful creatures in the ensuing clouds.

She had purchased herself the Bible with her first pay, and the expenditure continued to bless her many times over. Each morning, she read one chapter. And each morning, it raised a new question inside her. Parson Houston was the epitome of patience and answered all her queries to the best of his ability. He'd fallen into a pattern of joining them at Felicity's for dinner each evening, and Mercy looked forward to the time each day, pushing off her inquiries until she could ask them over their meal.

Micah hadn't approached her for a conversation even once in all these months. Though he still bossed her occasionally and still included Avram in his adventures with Joel, he'd mostly kept his distance and had even quit badgering her to eat more.

The distance hurt her more than she cared to contemplate.

Their plans for next spring were beginning to feel like a reality. Mr. Chancellor sold Micah and Gideon each a good strong wagon. She'd never seen two men more like little boys than the day they'd celebrated the completion of the second wagon bed.

"That there is a Prairie Schooner if ever I saw one!" Gideon whooped as he slapped the end of the box.

Mercy smiled, but her heart felt heavy. She had no worldly goods to her name, which made traveling easy. But what would she do when she got to Oregon? She would arrive with nothing. Micah and Gideon would settle into their new routines, and she would have to learn to provide for herself and her son.

Her concern for Micah's salvation was growing, too. Sometimes when the parson wasn't near, she asked Gideon questions about a Bible passage or a spiritual concept she felt she didn't understand. Gideon was always patient to answer her questions, but Micah inevitably found an excuse to go elsewhere.

Her worries knotted her stomach and cost her sleep.

But then Parson Houston pointed out a verse about how she should not worry about tomorrow. So she'd tried to concentrate on the good. She knew that she and Avram would be taken care of until they reached Oregon. Gideon had assured her just the other day that they still wanted her to accompany them.

Now that Parson Houston's replacement had arrived in town, he even planned to join the caravan, though his shoulders had sagged terribly when he'd made the announcement at dinner the evening before. It seemed that Micah had already known that was the minister's plan, because he had not seemed surprised at all.

None of them ever pried about the parson's wife, but Mercy had a feeling he'd been holding out some sort of hope with regard to the woman. He'd looked weary and dejected at the table last night.

To get his mind on things that would set him more at ease, she'd asked him about a passage she read that had left her puzzled. In the passage, Jesus hung on the cross with two thieves on either side of Him. One thief reviled Jesus. The other begged for His forgiveness. "What made one of them believe, do you think?"

Joel and Avram were busy drawing figures on Joel's slate. And she and the three men lingered over their coffee.

Parson Houston twirled his fork on the table while Felicity bustled in the background. "What makes any of us believe? One man lives a life of sin and then, in his last hour, chooses Life. Another lives a life of sin and, in his last hour, scorns Life. Free will. It is a mystery. Yet each of us is afforded every opportunity to choose Life right up to our last hour. God does not force us as some are fond of teaching. Nor does He choose some for salvation and others for destruction. Jesus gave His life for all. Both thieves could have chosen Life. One scorned our Lord. One humbled himself. First John 1:9 tells us, 'If we confess our sins, He is faithful and just to forgive us our sins, and to cleanse us from all unrighteousness.' 'Confess' . . . this is the pivot point laid before us all. Christ's death makes cleansing possible for all people. But confession is what allows us to enter into salvation. What makes one man scorn, and another confess?"

For a brief moment, the parson leveled his gaze on Micah, who shifted and concentrated on his coffee with a furrow in his brow, but then Adam turned his soft eyes back on her. "If I had the key to make everyone believe, I would use it with abandon. However, that's not the heart of our Father. He longs for true relationship where we have chosen Him, just as He has chosen us."

"Amen," Gid said softly.

Mercy looked at Micah, wondering if he was remembering their conversation from the picnic all those months ago, as she was.

He didn't meet her scrutiny. Instead, he rose from his chair and clamped a hand on Joel's shoulder. "Time to head in, son. Morning comes early."

Joel obediently rose from his seat, and the parson excused himself to trail them outside.

Mercy's heart ached as she tugged Avram close and watched them go. If only Micah could feel just a measure of the peace she now experienced. *Lord, set him free from the burden of his anger. Forgive me for bringing my problems into his life and adding to his pain.*

When they'd disappeared into the cold night, she turned to find Gid watching her. Gentleness softened his blue eyes as he twisted his mug absently. "I wondered . . ." He cleared his throat, looked into his coffee for a moment, then lifted his gaze to hers once more. "Well, I wondered if you and Av might like to join me on a trek to fetch a Christmas tree. Just a small one. There's a spot in the corner of our room where I thought . . ." He shrugged. "For the boys."

Mercy frowned. Counted the days in her mind. "Oh my. It is almost Christmas already, isn't it." She pressed Av's too-long curls back and peered into his face. "What do you think? Does that sound fun?"

Avram's eyes sparkled, and he gave a little hop. "Can I chop it down?" he asked, hopefulness filling his expression.

Gid choked down a laugh. "Well now, I'm not so sure about that. But I'll let you take a couple of swings."

Mercy gasped.

"Careful swings," Gid quickly amended. "Very careful swings." Humor ticked up one corner of his mouth. He arched a brow to remind her she hadn't answered yet.

Mercy nudged Avram out of her way and rose, taking his hand. His request made her uneasy, but not from fear of being with him. So what was it then?

She took in his soft eyes, still resting hopefully on her, and knew at that moment that he thought himself in love with her. The thought made her mouth dry and her palms damp. Why did it agitate her so?

He was the kind of man she would be blessed to have love her. The kind of man she ought to choose—sweet, gentle, considerate. If she couldn't have Micah, why not let this good man love her?

She forced the words past her tight throat. "A Christmas tree expedition sounds like just the thing. We'd love to join you."

Gid's grin bloomed full and joyous. "All right." He bobbed his head. "Okay. Tomorrow's Saturday. How about then? I'll confirm with Mr. Chancellor, but I don't think he'll object."

"That sounds fine. For now, we bid you good evening." Mercy hurried Avram across the diner, wondering why she felt as though she'd been cinched into a too-small corset.

Chapter Twenty-Three

Micah lurched upright in his bed, chest heaving. He gulped for air, scowling at the puddle of moonlight on the floor of their room. Pushing back the covers, he swung his feet to the floor. He pressed both hands into the mattress, gathering his bearings, then padded quietly past Gid's bed and scooped a little water from the pitcher by the door into his cupped hand. He dashed it over his face and propped his hands on either side of the table, letting the liquid fall back into the basin.

Scrunching his eyes tight only made his dream all the more vivid.

Three crosses with an eerie darkness cloaking them. A darkness that was thick and black, and yet he could see the crosses clearly. Three men, broken, bleeding, dying. One of the faces filled with so much love that it raised an ache inside him. One face filled with awe and wonder. And the third man—one with his own face—spewing curses.

He hung his head, feeling such shame to be so filled with hate in the presence of such love. The emotions inside him stood in stark contrast to the expression he'd seen on the face of love, and he suddenly knew without a doubt that the anger that filled every part of him each day was sheer hatred.

Hatred at the sickness and evil that had taken his baby girl from him.

Hatred at Georgia for not being stronger.

Hatred at himself for even daring to feel such a thing when Georgia had been so broken with grief.

Hatred toward Mercy for bringing her problems to them.

Certainly hatred of Herst, first for all he'd done to Mercy and then for the part he'd played in Georgia's death.

Hatred toward his own father, who had built the foundation that compelled Micah to help Mercy that day back in Chamblissburg.

Hatred of God, who could have prevented it all but hadn't.

His mind stilled. He focused in on that last thought. Hatred of God? Who was he, a mere man, to hate the very one who had created him? To hate the one with the face of such love from his dream.

But did he really create you? Die for you?

The undulating whisper sent a shaft of ice down his spine. He spun from the table, half expecting to see someone behind him.

Empty except for the sonorous breathing of Joel and Gideon.

He shook his head. Still half asleep was all. Dropping onto the edge of his bed, he propped his elbows on his knees and cupped his head in his hands.

If God truly loved you, wouldn't He have saved you from a life of so much pain?

The thought stabbed through him even as his fingers swept over the knot at the back of his head that had never fully dissipated after his father had thrown him into the corner of a doorway and split his skin open.

He clenched his teeth, feeling the familiar bile rise in his throat. So much blood cascading over his shoulders. Ringing in his ears. Ma screaming, trying to get to him while Father stood over him and pushed her back, yelling that it was time he became a man. He never had known what infraction he'd committed that day. One moment he'd been sitting at the table doing sums, and the next, he'd been flying through the air.

God could have spared you.

Micah frowned. Touched the bump beneath his hair again.

Adam opened his eyes and stared into the darkness above.

His heart ached with the burden for a soul. Ached like it had when he'd been in the birthing room and could do nothing for Eden.

Pain-filled blue eyes swam into his vision.

Micah.

There was something he could do. Something that lately, Lord forgive him, had felt futile where that man was concerned.

In obedience, he rolled out of bed and fell to his knees beside the mattress.

Lord, I pray that You would overwhelm Micah with Your love . . .

Micah rose and strode to the window. There was nothing to see but the dark façade of the building next door.

Mercy and the parson had spoken of free will. Father had assuredly made hay in that sunlight. So much anger rose inside Micah that he could almost feel it filling his throat, blocking his airway.

The face of love from the dream swam into his vision.

He inhaled long and slow.

Confess. Faithful and just to forgive.

Confess? What did he have to confess? He'd done his best to be a good man. To treat people with kindness. To always take care of and provide protection for those he could.

Yet hate consumed him. And he knew without a doubt that such love as he'd seen could not co-exist with the hatred in his heart.

He fell to his knees by the window, peering past the frost on the windowpane to the stars that twinkled in the inky black sky. *God, I want to believe. But how do I know You are real?*

He's not real.

Even as the dark words were whispered, however, he remembered the verse that Parson Houston had first shared with him.

Most assuredly, I say to you, whatever you ask the Father in My name He will give you. Until now you have asked nothing in My name. Ask, and you will receive, that your joy may be full.

He wanted joy. Oh, how he wanted it. Peace, too. He was weary of this constant burden of hatred in his heart.

Lord God . . . Father . . .

That word stopped him. Was God a Father like his own had been?

Yes.

Micah grunted. Laced his fingers behind his head. He closed his eyes and focused on the face of love that he'd seen in his dream. He suddenly recognized that lie for what it was. His father never would have gone to a cross for anyone.

Father, help me believe . . . I ask in Your name.

The darkness faded till he once again saw his dream. Jesus, arms stretched wide, looked directly at him, and Micah was no longer the man spewing curses. He was on the other cross, tears streaming down his face.

Remember me!

The cry emanated from the depths of his soul.

Jesus smiled gently. Nodded.

The vision faded, but the overwhelming love remained.

And then Micah was sobbing silently into his hands. These sobs were different from the ones that had nearly broken him several months before. This was relief. The unshackling of a burden.

The tightness in his chest dissipated. The dark voice spoke no more.

Hatred, flat and lifeless, fled in the face of love, full and consuming!

Micah gulped a breath. Another. And another.

He crawled back to his bed, slipped beneath the coverlet, and took his first-ever breath that felt like freedom. He fell asleep with tears in his eyes and a smile on his face.

Snow began to fall, fat and languid, as Mercy arrived at Felicity's with Avram the next morning. Gideon, already at their usual table, faced the room with Joel in the chair by the wall at his side.

"Morning. What did Mr. Chancellor say?" She hoped they wouldn't be leaving till the day had a chance to warm a little.

He eased back in his chair. "Because of our . . . outing, Wayne told us to take the day off. We can leave as soon as we want and have the whole day." His smile could have lit the room.

"I see." She was a callous woman, indeed, to be dreading the day ahead when he so obviously looked forward to it.

She helped Avram remove his wraps, scanning the patrons. If the men had the day off, would Micah be joining them on this outing? Her traitorous heart gave a double beat at the thought. They could leave right now if it meant she got to spend the day with Micah.

She mentally chastised herself . . . again. She ought to be content to spend the day with a kind man such as Gideon. She ought to be flattered that he wanted to spend the day with her and her son. Her heart ought to thrill at the prospect.

Yet all it could do was yearn for another. Another who was not here. Another who did not want her.

Brow puckering, she returned her focus to Gideon, and found him watching her. Aiming for a casual tone, she asked, "Where's Micah?"

His lips pressed together as he lowered his attention to his mug and gave it a couple of turns. "Left him pacing the room like an old bull trying to decide what to attack first. Not sure what's gotten into him, but . . ." Something shifted through his eyes when he raised them to her as he sipped his coffee.

Something that left an ache in her heart because she desperately didn't want to break his.

"I'm looking forward to our trip today." His eyes crinkled at the corners, but there was uncertainty in their depths.

Avram sat across from Joel, and she dropped into the seat next to Avram. Maybe she could get out of it. "I was too, but with the snow falling, do you think we should go?"

He chopped a hand through the air, dismissing her concern. "I already put the runners on the wagon. And the trees I wanted to show you aren't far from town. We'll be back inside two hours, I'd guess."

"Okay." She looked into her empty cup. Her stomach tightened, but it didn't have anything to do with the storm. It was that same tight dread from the evening before. She couldn't quite pin down why she felt so agitated at his attentions. They had been friends for months now.

She simply wasn't ready for another relationship right now.

At that moment, Micah appeared by their table with the parson, who wore a smile wider than the Mississippi. Adam took the chair next to Gideon, and Micah sank into the one next to Mercy.

And her traitorous heart suddenly made things very clear to her. She wasn't ready for another relationship *with Gideon*. How unfair of her heart to fall for the one man she could never have.

The parson continued to smile broadly. What was that all about? Beside her, Micah shifted, and when she glanced over, there was a softened aspect to his features that made him seem . . . more at ease, somehow. He had his fingers clasped on the table and hadn't spoken or looked at any of them.

"What's happened?"

"What's happened," Adam boomed, "is that Micah has surrendered his life to our Lord!"

Mercy held her breath, hope soaring.

A slow smile stretched Micah's lips, and he glanced across at Adam, who immediately started apologizing.

"I'm sorry. You're right. It was your news to tell, but I just can't help myself! God is so good!"

Mercy felt like her heart might burst with joy. "Micah, that's wonderful!" She contained her joy just enough to keep herself from resting a hand on his arm.

"Go on, man. Share your news!" Parson Houston thumped the table enthusiastically.

Micah's hands remained folded before him. He swept his thumbs one over the other. That joy-inducing smile still played on his lips. "Don't rightly know what to tell other than what you just said." He nodded, then frowned. "Not sure I have all the answers yet, but I hope that will come in time."

Parson Houston guffawed so loudly that several from other tables glanced their way. "All the answers, he says."

Happiness bloomed, full and overflowing. A wide-stretched smile bunched Mercy's cheeks even as her vision blurred with moisture.

"Well, I'll be." Gideon grinned, his head bobbing. He reached across the table and thumped Micah's hands with his fist. "Right happy to hear it."

Micah thanked him and then pinned that inscrutable blue gaze on her.

Still smiling, she blinked away her happy tears. "I've been praying for you."

She felt his soft assessment to her very core. "Thank you."

Felicity arrived with the coffee pot and Micah leaned back to give her room to fill their mugs. His shoulder brushed Mercy's.

She felt the connection as surely as she would have felt a glowing red firebrand burning into her skin. She was thankful for the distraction of a warm cup to curl her hands around.

Micah nodded toward the windows. "Looks like it's set to fall fast and heavy today."

Gideon grinned at the boys. "A good day for a lovely surprise!"

"A surprise?" Joel squeaked, leaning forward to better see his uncle.

Avram looked up at Mercy, a sparkle in his eyes and a question on his face.

She nodded. "Remember?"

"Chwis'mas twee!" Av clapped his hands.

"A tree? For true?" Joel's eyes widened in excitement.

Gideon ruffled a hand through his nephew's hair. "For true. And you are welcome to join us if your pa says it's okay."

All eyes turned expectantly to Micah.

He gave his son a wink and a nod.

"Yes!" Joel shot one fist into the air.

"And you?" Mercy wanted to bite her tongue. She hadn't meant to blurt the words, but now that they were out, there was no going back. "Gid says you both have the day off. Will you be joining us?"

Micah didn't move except to angle a look across the table toward Gideon. The men scrutinized one another for a long moment. Mercy didn't see anything change in either of their expressions, but Micah finally straightened. He set to flipping the knife by his empty plate front to back, back to front. "If you'll forgive me, I think I'll take the chance to do a little bit of nothing today."

So there it was. Even when he had the opportunity to spend time with her, he chose not to. For Gideon's sake, Mercy tried not to let her disappointment show. "Just don't let Wayne talk you into that workroom. You deserve some time off." She clamped her lower lip firmly between her teeth and held it there. Now she was the one bossing him.

Av bounded up to his knees in his chair and clapped his hands. "Let's go wight now!"

Everyone chuckled, and Mercy, thankful for the distraction, nudged him to sit properly at the table. "Breakfast first. Then we'll go." She swallowed down a lump of uncertainty.

If Micah didn't want her, who was she to turn down a good man like Gideon? That was . . . if her suspicions of why he'd asked her on this outing were right. Her heart ached with the tension of worry. She didn't have to decide right now. Maybe he just wanted to spend time with her as friends. She gladly put off the decision. She might be fretting over nothing.

It wasn't long before Felicity placed steaming bowls of porridge before each of them and a large platter of bacon and eggs in the middle of the table. As she did so, she spoke to the parson. "I'm sorry to be the bearer of such news, but the doc sent round a message asking for you to come to his office. Apparently, there's a soul lingering at the gates of heaven."

The parson didn't seem perturbed to have his meal interrupted. He pushed back, bade them farewell, and then hurried from the premises.

The boys ate so fast that Mercy was only half finished when they both popped to their feet and declared that they were ready.

Micah's brow slumped. He shot a look through the window at the falling snow. But surprisingly said nothing.

The chair across the table squeaked as Gideon rose. He pulled some money from his shirt pocket. "Wayne asked me to settle our tab with Felicity. I'll be ready to go as soon as I'm done."

With the boys busying themselves making patterns in the frost on the window next to their table, Mercy filled her mouth with porridge. Then promptly wished that she'd set the remainder aside because Micah angled his chair in her direction, and she wasn't sure she'd be able to swallow.

"Christmas tree, huh?" he offered. "I dare say the boys will enjoy that."

Mercy nodded and hid behind one hand as she worked to swallow. "I'm sure they will," she was at last able to say.

He searched her face, bounced a glance off Gideon's empty chair, and finally focused on the falling snow again. He flipped his knife a couple more times. "Take care to stay warm enough out there."

There was a distant note of detachment in the words that sent a wave of disappointment through Mercy. They'd hardly exchanged two words since the picnic by the creek all those months ago, so she wasn't sure why she had hoped for more today.

"We shouldn't be too long," Mercy replied. Though now she felt certain the day would stretch interminably until she found out why Gideon was acting so strange.

Abruptly, Micah rose, grabbed his hat from the newel, and nodded a goodbye in her direction.

She pushed her porridge bowl toward the middle of the table and was thankful for the distraction when Avram asked, "Now twee?"

Mercy nodded. "Almost." She bussed him on the cheek, but her perusal drifted above her son's head to Micah's retreating back. And as she watched him leave, she realized he hadn't lectured or bossed or interfered.

She felt a tug at her brow, unsure why she felt so let down by that.

Chapter Twenty-Four

Mercy folded her arms against the cold as she and the boys crossed the street with Gideon toward the mercantile.

Gideon paused on the mercantile porch. "Why don't you fetch your caps and mittens and maybe a blanket or two while the boys and I bring the wagon around?" He strode off before she could remind him that she didn't own a cap or mittens for her or her son.

With a sigh, she slipped inside and wandered to the shelf of knit goods. There was a cap-and-mittens set made from a soft blue carded wool—one in her size and another in a darker shade in Avram's size. The price was dear at a whole two bits each, but the set would likely last her a lifetime. And she would need some once they reached the Oregon Territory anyhow. She'd read a report in the newspaper about how bitterly cold it was in the foothills of the Rocky Mountains this winter. Avram would likely outgrow his, however . . . She put aside the one that was his size, in favor of one the next size up. Maybe she could stretch that for a couple of years. She placed them on the counter by the register, giving Willow a smile she hoped didn't look too annoyed. "I'll be right down with the money for these."

Willow nudged them back toward her. "Take them as a Christmas bonus."

What a dear friend Willow had become. Mercy wanted to reach across the counter and hug her neck. But she shook her head instead. "No. I couldn't. Thanks just the same."

Willow leaned her elbows on the counter and narrowed her eyes. "Did anyone ever tell you how stubborn you are?"

Mercy laughed. "I could retort the same to you."

Willow tossed a quick glance toward the door before she leaned farther across the counter to whisper. "So tell me, what is this trip that Gideon has been so excited about?"

Stomach twisting, Mercy's laughter faded. "He's been excited?"

Willow's brows nudged upward as she nodded. "It's practically all he's talked about." She gave Mercy a searching look. "You two aren't running off to get married or anything like that, are you?"

The outlandish question drew a gasp from Mercy. "Of course not. We're going to fetch a Christmas tree with the boys, is all."

Willow straightened. "Oh! I see. Well . . . That will be a lovely outing for the boys! They'll love it."

Mercy nodded and started for the stairs. She couldn't withhold a small smile as she considered Willow's tense tone. The girl was quite smitten with Gideon. Maybe she could avoid any of Gid's potential intentions by doing a little matchmaking on this Christmas tree expedition.

"I'll be down in two shakes." Behind her, she heard the store's front bell ring and Willow's greeting, but she didn't look back to see who it might be.

It only took her a few moments to extract two quarters from the savings jar under her bed and then strip and fold the quilts from her mattress. She stepped out of her room and closed the door, only to find Micah blocking the stairs since he had just reached the landing. In one hand, he held a loop of braided harness. He lifted it. "Figured with all of you off on your jaunt, I'd spend the day mending harness."

Despite saying that, he didn't move to let her pass. He studied her face instead, with an indecipherable softness in his eyes. Almost like he was lost in a memory.

She held her breath. Was he seeing all the ways she was similar to Georgia and wishing she were here instead? She fisted one hand so tight that her fingernails dug into her palm, which was good because it might tether her to reality. No matter that her crazy heart seemed to have a mind of its own, there were simply too many obstacles stacked between her and Micah.

He perused her armful of quilts, but still, he didn't move. Instead, he leaned into his heels, looking like he planned to stay a while. Did he have something to say? Or were they to stand here frozen in the hallway? She ought to ask to pass but was held captive by steely blue magnetism.

He started to speak but then snapped his mouth shut and hung his head. He slapped something repeatedly against his leg. It sounded too soft to be the harness, but she couldn't see it for the barrier of her armful of quilts.

She darted her tongue over dry lips, holding her silence in the hope that he would speak whatever was on his mind.

But it was not to be. Without raising his head, he lifted his hand. "Brought these up to you." He stepped to one side, so he no longer blocked her path. And placed the items atop her load.

The blue hats and mittens. Along with a green set in Joel's size.

Mercy pinched her lips together. "I told her I would pay."

"It's taken care of."

"You didn't have to do that! Here . . ." She worked to balance the quilts, not drop the knit sets, and hold out the quarters in her hand. "I was bringing the payment down."

He held up his palms and side-stepped past her, a twinkle leaping to life in his eyes. "Could you make sure Joel puts his on? That boy is forever forgetting his hat."

"Of course." She nudged the coins closer to him.

He ignored them. "Better not keep Gid waiting." He reached behind himself and turned the handle of his door across the hall, then disappeared inside, shutting it with a soft click.

Mercy frowned at the quarters held between her fingers. With narrowed eyes, she clutched her bundle tight, bent, and slid the coins beneath the gap at the bottom of his door, then made a dash for the stairs. He would have to run to catch her, and she couldn't envision the staid Micah Morran doing anything of the sort.

Hopefully, by the time she returned, he would have forgotten all about it.

Micah stepped into his room, leaned his back against the door, snatched off his hat, and forked his fingers into his hair. He'd been doing his best for months now to put Mercy from his mind. Out of faithfulness to Georgia, his word to Gideon, and the realization that Mercy herself wasn't ready to move on, he'd tucked those yearnings away and buried them deep.

There was also the taunting reality that he would have nothing when he got to Oregon. No land. No way to provide for a family—at least not in the way a woman would expect.

Yet watching Mercy and Gideon jaunt off on an intimate outing had his emotions clambering from the hole where he'd buried them.

Micah laced his fingers behind his head just as he heard a clatter and looked down to see two quarters scoot to a stop between his boots.

He grinned and bent to retrieve them. He ran his thumb over the time-smoothed etching of the metal.

Stubborn woman!

It had taken every bit of willpower he possessed not to tell her how he felt just now.

But he'd given Gideon his word, and he would not break that. Not even if it required cutting his own heart out.

Besides, for her to fall for Gid was the more sensible choice. He had been alone longer. Didn't have a child. Had been the one to rescue her from the lout of a husband who'd been trying to kill her.

None of that reasoning made Micah's heart hurt any less. And it certainly didn't soften the shock of realizing that despite his best efforts to maintain emotional distance over the past few months, his feelings for her had only increased since that first time at the creek.

In fact, from the way his heart begged him to yank open the door and holler after her to ask if he might tag along, he was in a whole passel of trouble.

He pictured Gid's frown at seeing him approaching beside Mercy. A grin tugged at his lips. Maybe he wasn't so magnanimous toward his brother-in-law after all.

But something held him in check.

Besides the conditions that made Gid a good choice for her, his brother-in-law and Mercy were also well-suited in disposition. Both were quiet, contemplative souls who would make a good match.

There was also Joel to consider. He didn't know what his son might think of having another woman in his life someday, but he didn't want to add to Joel's turmoil by having that woman be Mercy, of all people.

And yet . . . Joel no longer seemed to resent her. In fact, quite the opposite. He often ran to talk to her first when he wanted help with some sums or the spelling of a word.

His jaw ached. Why had he given Gid his word all those months ago?

Micah paced to the window and tugged the curtain aside. Of course, all he could see was a bit of snowy sky and the haze of the building next door through the thickly falling snow.

Hang it, but this wasn't a good day for an outing.

They needed to call the whole thing off. He pivoted and reversed his course.

They could all lounge here in the room. Maybe Gid could read to them from the paper while—

Hand on the doorknob, he froze. No.

They were grown adults who could make their own decisions and didn't need him controlling them.

He spun and dashed the quarters into the corner of the room. One bounced off the floor, ricocheted off the wall, and rolled to a taunting stop once more in front of his boots. The other clattered to a stop beneath Joel's bed.

With a guttural grunt, he snatched the near one up and, in two swift strides, snapped it down on the table between his and Gideon's beds.

His focus fell on Gid's Bible.

With a sigh, he sank onto his own bed and drew the book onto his lap.

Well, Lord, I guess it's just You and me today.

The prayer made him smile.

Hope You don't mind me yammering at You a bit after all these months of silence. I think I've got a few emotions to work through.

Since Pa was taking a day away from the wagons, Willow asked him to cover the store. The excuse she gave was that she needed to go to the women's sewing circle, because that was easier than the truth. With Gideon off on an outing with Mercy, she felt jumpier than a frog with a fly to chase.

Of course, he was in love with Mercy. How could he help but love her with her porcelain skin and big brown eyes? More than that, her heart of gold.

She didn't cry until she was almost to the church where the women held their quilting bee on the third Saturday of every month. And then she ducked into the side yard of the church and hid beneath the overhang on the backside of the gardener's shed.

She sobbed into her palms, feeling irritated to be so emotional over a man who obviously didn't give her a second thought. Feeling even worse for wanting a man that Mercy must be interested in—especially when Mercy had a son who needed a father much more than she needed a husband!

Mercy said it was only a trip to get a Christmas tree with the boys, but Gid wouldn't have asked Mercy to join him if he wasn't feeling something for her, Willow knew that much about him.

"You are such a fool, Willow Chancellor!" She swiped at her face and stamped one foot. "I'll not give him another thought!"

"Beggin' yer pardon, Miss Willow?"

Willow screeched and spun to face the voice.

It was Declan Boyle, shivering in the cold as he peered at her from around the corner of the shed.

"Declan? What are you doing here?" Willow dashed at her tears, wishing for a hanky to deal with her nose. She sniffed instead. Declan carved small toys that they sold in their store, but no one had purchased one for several weeks now. She'd felt terrible when he'd come by the other day asking if she owed him any money, and she'd had to say no.

Declan folded his arms and leaned a shoulder against the wall of the shed, trying to look casual. But he was only one shade away from blue. "Who is it ye'll nae give anither thought, mam?"

Willow was already shrugging out of her coat. He backed away, but she rounded the corner after him. "Look at you. You're nearly as blue as a spring creek. What are you doing out here?"

He held up a hand. "I will nae take yer coat."

Willow wanted to force the issue but decided to give him that bit of dignity. After all, he'd come out of his shelter to see if she was okay. She shrugged back into the warm leather.

The door of the garden shed squeaked and swung on its hinges behind him. Inside, she could see a mound of dried grass with a boy-shaped indent in the middle.

Willow's eyes widened. "Have you been staying here? Declan! It can't be but a few degrees above freezing."

He hung his head, arms folded tight.

Willow reached past him and put her hand on the handle. "I'm taking you to our place, and I won't take no for an answer. Do you need anything from here?"

He shook his head.

A quick scan of the little building revealed there wasn't much other than the grass, some clippers, and Declan's speed walker leaning against the far wall. Willow tugged the door tight and nudged Declan toward the mercantile, wrapping one arm around his shoulders to lend him some warmth. "When's the last time you had a hot meal?"

As if spurred by the question, the boy's stomach gave a loud rumble. Willow did him the courtesy of pretending not to hear.

"I've some leftover soup from last night. It's been keeping cold on our back porch. Won't take but a few moments to heat it up."

She felt a shiver slip through the boy. "I cannae take yer charity, mam."

"Charity? Nonsense! I've a good number of chores that need doing, and I'll expect them to be done well, too. So don't think you can go shirking."

She hurried him into the store and right on through to their quarters at the back. Thankfully, Pa was busy helping a customer and only had time to lift one eyebrow. Behind Declan's back, Willow flapped away his questions but also tipped a nod to indicate that he should join them as soon as he could.

He nodded.

Once in their kitchen, Willow nudged Declan toward the black stove in the corner. "Right, the first chore is for you to build up the fire good and strong so that we can heat your soup." The room was rather chilly, and she lamented having let the fire die down so far.

"Aye." Declan's hands trembled as he fumbled to add some of the smaller pieces of wood and adjust the damper.

Willow set a pot on the stove. "Ah, an old hand with a stove, I see."

"Aye, mam."

Willow hesitated when she took note of the moisture glistening in his eyes.

But as soon as he saw her watching him, he scrunched them closed, blinking hard and rubbing one with the back of his hand. "Got smoke i' ma e'es."

Willow settled one hand on his shoulder as she poured the stone-cold soup from the crock into the pot. "That's what happened to me out at the shed too. Had smoke in my eyes."

He huffed a little and glanced up at her. She was glad to see at least a little humor in his gaze this time.

"Yer a corker, Miss Willow. A real corker."

"Oh, dear." Willow pretended to look offended. "I hope that's not as bad as it sounds. A what?"

Declan grinned. "Means a verra guid person."

Her heart melted a little. "Oh, well, in that case, you may call me one any time you like." She gave him a quick wink. "Got the fire going? Good. Now . . ." She patted a spot at the table closest to the stove. "How about you sit down and tell me what brings you to be sleeping in the church's garden shed?"

Chapter Twenty-Five

Mercy was ever so thankful for the hat and mittens. With her shoulders up near her ears, she snuggled under her quilt on the bench beside Gideon, with the boys between them. He had his blanket draped over his head and shoulders, but more to keep the snow off than for the warmth of it, it seemed. The two boys seemed of the same mind as they haphazardly shared the other half of Gideon's quilt.

She shuddered, thankful that she'd gotten a quilt to herself. She'd worried about one or the other of the boys getting too cold, but neither of them were even shivering!

For miles in each direction, the landscape glistened white. Tree-covered hillsides looked like freshly washed down ticks laid out on bushes to dry. The layer of snow buffered sound and even the runners gliding over the road only made soft squeaking noises.

"Whoa!" Gid reined the horses to the side of the road and jumped down. The boys scrambled after him, leaving the quilt in a heap on the boards near her feet. Rubbing his gloved hands like a little boy on Christmas morning, Gideon grinned and swung a proud gesture to a small stand of evergreens about shoulder height. "Here we are."

"Yay!" The boys dashed through the drifts.

Reluctant to leave the warmth of her quilt cocoon, Mercy waited to move until Gideon reached her side of the wagon and reached up a hand. She tucked both blankets under the bench, where they would avoid as much of the damp snow as possible, then braced herself on Gideon's shoulders and allowed him to help her down.

Before she could even turn toward the trees, his hands tightened around her waist ever-so-slightly. "You've got—" He brushed her brow with the back of one gloved finger. "Snowflakes in your eyebrows." He grinned and gently cleared the other one.

Mercy felt a tightness in her middle as she looked up at him. Why could she not feel more for this man?

In the distance, she could hear the boys frolicking with each other.

Gideon's blond hair curled from beneath his gray hat, and his blue eyes twinkled with merriment. A tall man, he towered over her, yet, even standing this near to him, she had no fear whatsoever. He had been a God-sent friend exactly when she needed one.

Looking down at her, his smile softened, turned serious. The backs of his fingers stroked her cheek now. "I have a confession."

Dread and awareness prickled through her. This was the moment she'd sensed was coming. But no matter how she wished he would keep his thoughts to himself and not add tension to their relationship, she didn't suppose she could stop him from saying his piece.

And then she would have a decision to make.

"You do?"

He leaned closer. "I asked you on this tree hunt more to get some time with you than because I wanted to surprise the boys."

Mercy felt the beginnings of a headache squeeze the base of her skull. But she didn't step back. Wasn't sure if she should. After all, this man never made her jumpy or angry. He never bossed her. He certainly had never compared her to his first wife or told her she was a homely pile of bones. She nipped the side of her tongue between her teeth, realizing she wasn't quite being fair to Micah with that last thought, yet irritated that even here with Gideon so close, it was still Micah occupying her thoughts.

But . . . Maybe a place to start in building a marriage was friendship?

Yes! Friendship.

Surely, that was a solid foundation?

Gideon dipped his head closer, searching her eyes. "No reply to that?" His knuckle stroked her cheek again.

Mercy wished she could find her voice, but it had been stolen by a sudden realization. If she went into this with Gideon, she would be bound to proximity with Micah for the rest of her life. For though these men weren't blood-related, she knew they would never be far from each other. They had passed through too many fires together.

That nearness would force her to watch Micah someday grow in a relationship with someone else. And she wasn't sure she wanted to endure that. But if she held her ground and remained single, then at the end of the trail, she could part from them. At least then, she wouldn't have to endure the pain of watching Micah court and marry someone else.

Nor would it be fair to Gideon not to give him her full heart.

And she knew with sudden clarity that despite his being a wonderful man, her heart remained too divided—maybe still too damaged—for him to capture it fully.

A tattoo of dread thumped in her chest because of the words she must now speak. She inspected her mittens and brushed at the snow clinging there. "Gid, you have been the best of friends to me over the last months."

He straightened. Took half a step back.

Her heart nearly broke at the discouragement swimming in his eyes. "I'm simply not looking for more right now." She rolled her lips in and pressed them into a tight line, willing him to believe her.

He rubbed two fingers at a spot over his heart before his hands settled against his hips and his shoulders sagged. "At least not with me." Seeming defeated, he shifted his scrutiny to the blanketed trees and the boys throwing packed snow at each other in the distance.

Mercy shook her head, wishing she could take some of the sting out of her rejection. "Not with *anyone* . . ."

Lies. None of her valiant efforts could banish the memory of a different pair of blue eyes—one's with darker lashes and more intensity. She tugged her mittens on more firmly, holding back a sigh. "At least . . . I don't think with anyone. I only recently escaped a war zone, Gid. I'm not ready to leap into a new one." And that was the blatant truth.

Without turning his head, his gaze drifted back to her. "It's not a war zone when two people love each other, Mercy."

"I-I know that in my head. But my heart . . ." The blue of her mittens had been made almost white with a coating of snow. She dusted her hands together. "I guess I'm just not certain what love is anymore. What it feels like. What I should even be looking for."

"Love is self-sacrifice." He lifted one shoulder. "Knowing so surely that you can't live without someone that you'd be willing to give up every dream of your own—even your life—to ensure theirs."

Mercy raised her chin. "The only person I feel that way about is Avram."

And Lord forgive her, for her love had cost Micah his wife. And Gideon, his sister.

Reality slammed into her then. It was patently foolish to reject Gideon's offer when no other waited in the wings. But she could tell from his posture that she'd already hurt him deeply. It was too late to retract her words now.

Slowly, Gideon dipped his chin. "Maybe you do only love your son, for now. But don't discount love, Mercy. It will find you someday." He swung a nod toward the trees. "Now—" He reached into the wagon to extract an axe. "—how about we find the prettiest little tree this side of Virginia?" His voice had lost all the excitement that had filled it only a few minutes ago.

She moved to follow in his footsteps—literally jumping from one indent to the next. "I could say the same to you, Gid. You won't be a bachelor forever."

His head wagged uncertainly. "I may have had my one and only chance."

She remembered her thoughts about Willow. "I don't know about that. There's a certain pretty redheaded shop mistress who wouldn't be opposed to some attention from you, in my estimation."

Gid huffed. "She wouldn't have even started school by the time I was done. I'm not interested in robbing a cradle."

"Posh. I happen to know that she'll be twenty-four come the twelfth of March."

Gid cut her a sharp glance. "She's twenty-three?"

Mercy nodded, holding her breath. Willow would lambaste her up one side and down the other if she knew what she was doing.

He grunted. "Never would have thought her that age. Still, that's seven years between us."

"Is that so many when—"

"I'm not interested, Mercy."

She clamped her lips together and let the matter drop. But she could hope and pray that they would find happiness together with time.

When he paused before the trees, Mercy stepped out of his footprints to stand beside him. The snow was deep enough that it spilled into the tops of her ankle boots, and she bit back a gasp at the frigidity. Looping her arm through his, she looked up at him, hoping he could read all her appreciation in her eyes. "Then let us at least be friends, yes? The two of us, loveless but battling onward."

He slid her a half smile and chucked her under her chin. "All right. Friends, it is. But don't expect me to be happy when some man swoops in and snatches your affections." He said the words too quickly, and she could hear the hurt lingering beneath them, but at least he was willing to concede to her request.

Mercy squeezed his arm, grateful for his kindness. "I promise to let you be as grumpy as you want to be if that ever happens."

With a bark of laughter, Gid rolled his eyes. "You're hopeless. All right, which tree? Boys!" he called, motioning them over. "We need to pick one of these trees. Nothing taller than I am." He didn't give any of them time to reply before he pointed. "How about that one over there?"

The boys concurred with happy dances and gyrating arms.

Gid met her gaze above their heads.

She nodded. "That one looks lovely."

More snow tumbled into her boots as she moved to follow him to the tree. This time she didn't bother masking her shiver. "This tree better be worth it, Gideon Riley!"

Chapter Twenty-Six

Willow could hardly believe the story she'd just heard from Declan. "So your ma passed away in Scotland, and then you and your da immigrated here, but then your da went west with a wagon train and left you here in Independence?"

Declan's chin notched another degree into the air. "He'll return."

Willow closed her lips around the retort that wanted to spew forth at his faithfulness to a father who'd abandoned him. "How old were you when he left?"

"Thirteen, mam. Weel able tae care for maself."

Right. "How long have you been living in the church shed?"

Declan hung his head and rubbed a finger against the grain of the table. "Don't want ye tae think I've been stealing anythin'. Ah ainlie gaed in thare on accoont o' the uncommon cauld these bygone few weeks. Mostly, ah bin paying Saul Smith tae sleep in a bed on his enclosed porch. But when the waither turned, I wasn't able tae make enough tae keep payin' him."

"So he turned you out in the cold!?"

"Yes'm." He nodded. "But he's a guid sort. Don't want ye tae think poorly o' him. Our understandin' was clear. The kip—ah, bed—was mine, but soon as I couldnae pay mah dollar for the night, he had tae give the bed tae anither."

A dollar a night! Why that was thirty dollars or more per month. That was highway robbery for only a cold bed on a screened-in porch! Willow thinned her lips. Whether Declan wanted her to think poorly of the man or not made no never mind to her. "And what about Parson Houston? Does he know you've been living in the shed?"

Declan's eyes widened. "Och nae, mam! Naeone goes near that shed in the wintertime…" One corner of his mouth ticked up. "Except folk wi' smoke in thair e'es."

Cheeky little scamp! Willow gave him a teasing squint.

He grinned and hung his head.

"So how about we come to an agreement of our own over rent for a bed?"

When he lifted his head, she could tell he was trying to disguise the hope in his expression.

"In exchange for a bed each night, and three meals each day, you will complete a list of chores that I will give you at the beginning of each week."

His brows shot up. "That's it?"

Willow nodded. "Yes. And you may have what parts you need to fix your speed walker, but you have to agree to set by at least half of the money you make because one never knows when they might need a rainy-day fund."

"Dae ye think I cuid find my da if I gaed tae Oregon in the spring??"

Thinking of him wandering the wilds of the Oregon Territory searching for a father who'd abandoned him, Willow wanted to pull him into a fierce hug. Her own heart threatened to break at the thought of losing him—and he'd only been sitting at her table for less than an hour. She pressed her fingers over the grain of the wood. "Do you have a last known address?"

He frowned. Shook his head. "Da cannae write none."

"I see. I'm not sure how you would find him in that case. But I can ask at the expansion office."

There was a light of weariness in his expression, though he did straighten his posture. "I'd best plan tae bide 'ere, then. Wouldn't want Da tae turn up an' find me gaen."

Willow's first instinct was to point out that his father could be dead—or worse, not coming back for him—but she pressed her lips tight and only gave a nod of relief instead.

Between now and pushing-off day, she would do a whole lot of praying that the Lord would keep young Declan Boyle right here in Independence with her and Pa.

Micah paced the confines of his room, tamping down his irritation with Gideon for keeping Mercy and the boys out in this cold for so long. He hated days like today with nothing to do. Give him work over lounging any day of the week. He had read Gideon's Bible for the better part of an hour—finally setting it aside to ponder on the things he'd already read.

He'd gone for lunch, hoping they would return while he was out, but now the day had crested into mid-afternoon, and worry tightened his chest.

Thinking he might need to mount up and go look for them, he was just opening the door to the hallway when the four of them arrived, all laughing and bright-eyed.

"Pa!" Joel exclaimed with a hop of excitement. "Uncle Gid found the best tree! Look!" He pointed to Gideon, who was the last in line and hauling a tree up the stairs.

Micah smiled, more relieved to have them back safely than he was excited about the tree. "Did he now?"

He split a glance between Mercy and Gideon. Mercy's gaze flicked off of his before she lowered her face to scrutinize her armful of blankets and lost a bit of her smile. She seemed tense somehow.

Gideon was focused on the tree and not looking at him.

His heart panged him. So . . . Gid *had* staked his claim then? He ought to be happy for them. However, he couldn't seem to dredge up an emotion even close to that.

He stepped forward and took the armful of damp quilts from her. "Oh, I can deal with these," she protested, but he'd already secured them. She opened the door to her room. "Thank you." She gestured to the door. "Let's hang one here and maybe one over your door too? That way, they'll hopefully dry before we need them tonight."

He complied, draping the first quilt over her door and the second over his own, with Mercy helping to spread the material smoothly. When they finished, they were both standing near each other in the doorway of his and Gideon's room. The boys stood in the middle of the room, watching Gideon prop the tree in the far corner.

Micah's attention drifted of its own volition to the woman by his side.

Her cheeks were rosy-red from the cold, and she was just tugging off the mittens, reminding him that he owed her two quarters and that he needed to fetch the one from beneath Joel's bed. When she tugged her cap free, several strands of her hair stood on end. He shoved his hands into his pockets before he could be tempted to do something like reach out to smooth them.

"Ma says we can put co'ncobs on the twee!" Av turned to face him with a huge smile but then frowned immediately after. "Do you think they will stay? O' fall off?"

Micah bit off a laugh, shooting a wink in Mercy's direction. "I suppose your ma will have a solution for getting them to stay."

Had her cheeks turned redder? Or was he imagining things?

"Popped corn," she corrected her son, resting one hand on Av's head. "In fact, if you stay here with the men, I'll run down and make it and buy a spool of thread. Then I'll show you just how we keep it from falling off."

"Can we play and read books?"

"Tell you what," Micah offered. "While your ma pops the corn, how about we sweep up all these pine needles that your unc—ah . . ." Calling Gid the boy's uncle probably wasn't best when the man might soon be Av's father. "That Gid has tracked up the stairs. Then when the work is done, you boys can read and play all you want."

"I like to sweep." Av nodded.

At the same time, Joel moaned, "Do we have to, Pa?"

Humor crinkled the corners of Mercy's eyes, and she gave him a little wave as she mouthed, "Thank you," and made her escape.

Micah rubbed a thumb at the pulse pounding beneath his pocket. He tossed a glance at Gid, who remained busy helping Joel get the tree balanced in a bucket.

These feelings wouldn't do. Not at all. Not if Gideon and Mercy had an understanding between them. He needed to take himself in hand and promptly.

He sighed. Rather loudly, apparently, because Gideon turned to face him. He dusted damp, clinging pine needles from his hands. "She turned me down."

Micah blinked. Oh, the blessed hope springing to life in his chest!

Gid nodded. "Just thought you should know." He patted Joel's shoulder. "Come on. Let's go get a few more rocks from outside while your dad and Avram sweep up."

Before Joel could move, Micah shot out one hand to grab his arm. "Beneath your bed there, you'll find a quarter. Fetch it for me, will you, son?"

"Sure, Pa." It only took him a moment to shimmy under the low frame and retrieve the coin. When he handed it to Micah, he seemed puzzled. "How'd you know that was under there, Pa?"

"I, ah, let loose of it earlier, and it rolled under there."

Joel scampered out the door, seeming satisfied with his answer, but Gid snorted over his explanation and clapped one hand to his shoulder. "I wish you all the best. I mean that. But be warned that she told me she doesn't love anyone but her son."

Micah deflated as he searched his brother-in-law's face. His happiness over Gid's rejection wilted like summer grass. That didn't bode so well for him, now did it?

He wanted to pry for more details but resisted the schoolboy urge to ask if she'd said anything about him.

"You know," Gid continued. "That day we stopped in Chamblissburg, I asked myself why we stopped in that no-bit town. Lord forgive me, I didn't want to help Mercy and bring her trouble on us."

Gut twisting, Micah dipped his chin. If anyone needed forgiveness, it was him because, despite his history, he'd felt the same.

"But I had this feeling clear deep inside." Gideon pressed his fingertips together and tapped his chest. "My gran used to call it a 'knowing in her knower.'" A barely perceptible smile touched his lips. "When I was there on the street in Chamblissburg, and I thought that question in my mind, it was like . . . Well, I couldn't seem to put my finger on it that day, but looking back, I knew Mercy would be important to all of us someday. Like we were meant to be there right at that exact moment in time. Our lives were *supposed* to intersect." Gid's gaze sharpened on him. "It was the craziest thing. I'd been working myself all into a dither over these last months, wanting to give her the right amount of time but worried that you might decide I was taking too long and beat me to it. But when she turned me down, I had this sense of relief that . . . well, it surprised me, I'll not lie about it." He shook his head. "Maybe there will never be another woman for me after Verona, but . . . If that intersection wasn't for me, maybe it was for you."

Micah's thoughts flashed to the conversation he'd had with Adam on that first day. Adam had told him the Lord hadn't answered his prayers about his child because God had something better in mind. That true joy came only from God.

Micah had experienced that last night when he'd finally surrendered. Would he ever have recognized his need for a Savior if Jess and Georgia hadn't been taken from him?

Gideon continued to watch him. He tipped a nod toward the hallway.

Micah turned to see Joel playing with a marble right outside the door as he waited for Gideon.

Gideon dropped a hand on Micah's shoulder. "Georgia would want him to have a mother, Micah. And there's another who could use you, I'm thinking." He angled his eyes toward the boy beside Micah.

Avram stood looking up at them with curiosity furrowing his brow as though he were trying to decipher Gid's words.

Giving his shoulder one more squeeze, Gid brushed past, and he and Joel tramped down the stairs.

Micah gave a little shake of his head. He'd thought himself past this stage of life forever, and yet suddenly, his mind was spinning with all the possibilities that could become reality if he allowed himself to court Mercy.

One thing held him back. They'd missed the deadline for getting land. He had no security in his future. He couldn't offer her that. He wasn't the green-behind-the-ears boy who had courted and won Georgia. The stars had been, one by one, knocked from his eyes. Marriage was hard. Even marriage to a woman you loved.

He frowned. Was he in love with Mercy?

His and Georgia's relationship had started out on such a different footing. They had started as friends—okay, maybe flirtatious friends. Nevertheless, friendship had been the foundation of their bond.

With Mercy, he felt like they'd been skirting tentatively around one another for months now. First, because of his anger over what her presence in their lives had cost them.

Then, slowly, he'd found himself thinking of her more and more.

He admired her beauty. Appreciated her work ethic. Had done his best to take care of her.

But no. He hadn't given himself over to love for her yet. He still had a choice. Didn't he?

The memory of how he'd longed to kiss her by the creek all those months ago came to mind, making his mouth dry at just the remembrance. He remembered her hand resting on his arm to comfort him after he'd told her of his ma.

Blazes.

It didn't matter how he felt. He didn't have to act on his feelings.

Besides, he had no reason to believe that she felt anything for him. That day at the creek, she'd practically run from him. Now he wondered if he oughtn't take Mercy's rejection of Gideon as a warning that he should expect the same response.

He released a breath that was half growl. Keeping all of this to himself would be best for her. Once in Oregon, a beautiful woman like her would easily find a more affluent man who would be better able to care for her and her son.

Speaking of whom . . .

Avram continued to peer up at him curiously. He roughed a hand through the boy's hair. "These butterflies are annoying, kid."

"Buttewflies? I want to see."

Micah chuckled. He squatted to Avram's level. "To say you have butterflies means you feel all . . . jittery inside. It happens when one is uncertain about what comes next."

Av's lips twisted to one side. "Like on the fiwst day of school when you don't know if the teachew will like you?"

Micah grinned. Nodded. "Exactly like that. Now, what do you say we go find the broom?"

Av took his hand. "All wight. But, my teachew liked me. So don't wohwy. You jus' havta be nice and not fwown so much." The boy tugged him toward the door.

Micah chuckled. "I frown a lot, do I?"

Av wobbled his head back and forth. "Sometimes. Except when you look at Ma. Then you don't fwown."

Micah feared his smile had contorted into something closer to a wince.

Hang, but he was standing on a trap door with his neck in a noose.

As he let Avram lead him in search of a broom, Micah found his thoughts turning to prayer. *Lord, You know I'm pretty new at this talking to You and truly meaning it. All those months ago, the parson shared that verse where You said, 'Ask of me.' And so, on faith, I'm here asking for strength. You know I've got nothing to offer that woman on the other end of this journey but some hard-scrabble living. So I'm asking for two things. First, that You help me do the unselfish thing and keep my mouth shut, and second, that You give me the courage to let her go when the time comes.*

His stomach turned sour.

This was no good. No good at all.

His first day of praying and he was already hoping the Lord didn't answer his requests.

Mercy headed toward their room carrying a tray laden with a bowl of popped corn, a spool of thread, bread and cheese, and an apple for each of them. It would be a light dinner, but it would keep them from having to go back out into the cold. When she pushed open the door, she found the boys sitting on the corner of Joel's bed while Joel read Avram stories from the *McGuffey's Reader*.

Both Micah and Gideon rose to their feet when she paused.

Mercy didn't meet the eyes of either man as she hurried to the small table that one of them had dragged to the middle of the room. She must keep her mind fixed on what she had realized earlier today. This journey she had set herself upon—fleeing Herst and now heading for Oregon—was all for Av. There was no happiness she wanted other than for her son to have a safe home to grow up in. One where he would know without doubt that he was loved. She must fix her mind on that instead of pining for a man who would never return her affections.

Pining? Surely not. No, not pining.

And yet, from the moment Micah had flirted with her that day by the creek, he seemed to occupy every waking moment of her thoughts. What was that, if not pining?

"Here, boys. Come and get a sandwich." Micah motioned the boys over, and Gideon spoke a quick prayer over the meal.

Despite her mental lectures, she was even now aware of Micah's exact position—even though he stood beside her, and she wasn't looking at him. And that continued throughout the evening.

When they all sat around the little table, and Mercy showed the boys how to string the popcorn, she felt his probing examination from across the table as surely as she would have if he'd reached out and touched her.

When Joel pricked his finger and howled first in pain, and then with laughter about the dangers of Christmas trimmings, Mercy couldn't help but laugh along with him, but it was the impact of Micah's smile as he angled a glance between her and his son that whisked her focus to her own string of popcorn.

When they looped the strands around the tree, and Avram wanted to place his at the very top, Micah stepped to her side and hefted her son high so that he might have his wish. Even though Av had shot up several inches over the last few months and put on a good many pounds now that he was eating regularly, the effort didn't seem to bother Micah in the least. Avram squirmed to be released as soon as he was finished and, when Micah set him down, dashed toward the bed in the corner calling for Joel to come read to him again.

Micah propped his hands on his hips. His perusal shifted to her.

Embarrassed, she realized she'd been watching the man and not the boy. She quickly offered excuses about taking the pot and tray back to the kitchen and made her escape. She felt the sharpness of his scrutiny drilling into her back the whole way across the room.

Chapter Twenty-Seven

Willow and her pa were in the kitchen when Mercy entered, which, of course, was not a surprise. Willow was just setting a plate of fried chicken on the little kitchen table. What was a surprise was that the table had been laid for three.

"Oh, good evening. I hope I'm not interrupting." She lifted her dishes. "I was just going to wash these."

"Not at all." Willow motioned her toward the sink. "Please make yourself at home."

As she crossed to the sink, movement drew her eye to young Declan Boyle, who stepped into the kitchen from the Chancellors' quarters.

"Hello." Mercy offered him a smile.

"You know Declan, right?" Willow asked. "And Declan, this is Ms. Adler."

Declan gave a deferential bob of his head, but tonight his posture seemed weighted with burdens.

"We've met." Mercy nodded. "How is your speed walker running these days?"

Declan's head hung. "Needs a few repairs an' naebody be wanting tae pay tae ride in the cauld o' winter."

That explained the likely reasons why he stood here in the Chancellors' kitchen. She wondered about his parents but didn't feel it her place to pry. She washed her dishes quickly and left them on the drainboard to dry so that she could leave them to enjoy their supper in private.

By the time she returned to the room, both Joel and Avram had fallen fast asleep on Joel's bed. Gid sat on his bed with his back to the wall, reading a newspaper. And Micah sat in a chair at the little table which had been returned to its place between the two windows, reading a book in the light from the lamp.

He lifted his head when she entered and pushed the book back. He nodded toward the boys and spoke softly. "He's welcome to stay here for the night. I'll knock on your door if he wakes and fusses."

"That's fine." She crossed to make sure both boys were covered with the blanket and then offered her thanks. She felt the quilt hanging over the men's door and found it still damp.

Drat. It would be a cold evening in her room without any coverings. But she would make do. She could layer on an extra skirt and wrap another shawl around her shoulders.

Micah shifted in his chair, glancing from her to the blanket and back again.

Feeling a sudden need to escape his scrutiny, she dipped a parting curtsy. "Good evening to you both."

"Night." Gideon's reply sounded normal, and he tipped down one corner of the paper to offer her a parting smile.

Mercy felt relief sweep through her. He couldn't be smarting too painfully from her refusal.

Micah shifted again, and this time when she looked at him, he tilted his head and arched one brow. A searching light glinted in the soft blue of his eyes, as though he were silently asking if she were all right.

She gave him a subtle nod.

He cut a look toward his brother-in-law, who had returned to hiding behind his paper, and then back to her. His lips notched up at the sides, but his eyes didn't fill with humor. He seemed to be telling her not to worry about Gid.

Had Gid told Micah everything then?

Micah jutted his chin toward the hallway and rose to his feet. He slid something from the table into his hand, but she couldn't see what it was.

Mercy retreated and waited for him near her room. He paused by his door, scooped the damp quilt onto one arm, and then dumped it in a heap to one side of the entry. When he stepped into the hall, he pulled the bedroom door closed behind him, allowing them some privacy.

"He told you?" she whispered as she tucked both hands behind herself and leaned against the wall across from him.

Micah remained in the middle of the hall. Folding his arms over his chest, he leaned into his heels. "He did."

If only she could read that inscrutable expression. "I didn't want to hurt him."

"He knows that."

She couldn't remain still a moment longer. She paced to the wall at the far end of the hall and then back to her door. "Do you think I've cost us our friendship?"

Micah pressed one broad hand to his chest. "Our friendship? I think we'll be fine. I bear no hard feelings toward you."

Her gaze flew to his. He was teasing her! She narrowed her eyes. "Do be serious." She paced away from him again. "I feel quite awful about the whole ordeal. The last thing I wanted was to hurt him." Attention focused on her feet, she pivoted and started back to her door.

"Mercy." Micah's voice held a gentle warning.

She looked up just in time to avoid crashing into him. "Oh! So sorry." She had wandered closer to the middle of the hallway than she'd realized. She froze, clasped her hands tight, and willed herself not to fidget.

His attention slipped down to her intertwined fingers. "I'm going to touch your hands now." His words were spoken so softly that she might not have heard them if she hadn't been so near.

She felt every muscle tighten.

But after a moment, they eased again because he'd said the words, but he hadn't moved. And since when did Micah ask for permission to do anything? He simply acted and apologized for the consequences later. So, to have him give her warning filled her with a warmth that brought to life the hope she'd been quashing for months now.

Head lowered, he peered at her through his brows. "If you don't want me to touch you, you've only to say so."

Her heart threatened to fail and then tumbled into a riotous tumult. "O-okay."

Still, he didn't move. He watched her carefully, brows nudged up slightly as though waiting for her to speak.

But she couldn't—didn't want to—find her voice.

Ever so gradually, he slid closer, and then slowly, his hand reached toward her own.

She watched as though he'd cast some sort of spell over her, terrified of what allowing him to touch her might reveal to him and yet powerless to ask him to stop. His fingers skimmed her wrist and then slid between her clasped palms to separate one of her hands into the warmth of his own.

For one heartbeat, she envisioned him tugging her closer, sliding his hand behind her neck, and settling his lips against hers.

Her mouth went dry.

But he didn't.

Of course, he didn't. She was a fool for even thinking that he might. Yet . . .

He studied her palm as though trying to memorize every line. His thumb grazed over the heel of her hand.

Trembling, Mercy retreated a step.

Their hands remained linked, stretching between them.

He didn't advance, only lifted his eyes to hers. Slowly, he held up his other hand. He rolled the edges of two quarters between his first finger and thumb and then gently pressed them into the palm of her hand that he held.

His grin started as a minuscule tick upward at the corners of his mouth but gradually spread until he was smiling down at her as he softly folded her fingers over the coins. "When I say something is covered, I mean it's covered." He released her and stepped back.

She was thankful for the space, but more than that, for a return to their normal stubborn banter. Playfully, she narrowed her eyes and sing-songed, "You're just forcing me to find a different way to pay you back."

His brows arched, and his lips twitched. Deliberately, he clasped his hands behind his back as his focus slid to her mouth. "Oh, I can think of at least one way I'd approve of."

Heat flared into her cheeks. The coins in her hand suddenly seemed quite fascinating. She hardly dared to believe that the impassive Micah Morran stood here flirting with her.

From the corner of her eye, she saw him point toward the stairs. "I'm going down to fetch you some quilts. As cold as it is outside tonight, you can't sleep without them. I'll return momentarily. Maybe you'll have thought of a satisfactory way to repay me by the time I return?"

Mercy hung her head farther, hoping to hide her grin. If only she had an easy retort, but all thoughts seemed to have fled.

His footsteps retreated, and she made an escape into her room, leaving the door with the quilt on it propped open. Tossing and catching the two quarters in one hand, she paced the short space between the bed and the wall until his knock sounded on the wall by her door.

He still wore that annoying yet oh-so-attractive crooked smile as he handed her a stack of two folded quilts. "Willow says to bring the damp ones down tomorrow, and she'll help you wash them and hang them by the fire."

"Thank you. I will." She set the new stack of quilts on her bed and dropped the quarters on top.

She needed to remove the damp quilt from her own door to be able to close it. She motioned to it. "I just need to—"

Seeing what she intended, he nodded and stepped out of her way.

But when she tried to scoop the quilt off the door as he'd just done a moment earlier, hers snagged on a rough spot along the top. The door creaked farther open until it stopped against the wall of her room. She stood on tiptoe to try to unhook it.

"Here, let me help you with that." Micah stepped up right behind her.

The warmth of his body along the length of her own as he reached above her to help with the snag froze her in place. She hung her head and willed herself simply to breathe with him trapping her between himself and the door. Desire had her trembling, but fear of intimacy made her mouth dry and her heart thunder in her ears. Funny how she hadn't really considered intimacy with Gideon, but with Micah, it was at the forefront of her mind. She wanted it, but . . .

She clenched her eyes shut.

Herst had demeaned. Belittled. Destroyed.

Micah's chest grazed against her back as he freed the quilt. He swept it off with one hand and tossed it into the hallway, but she could feel him lingering just behind her, hear his ragged breathing, feel the soft waft of each breath brushing against her neck.

Maybe he would just go.

As though reading her mind, he whispered, "Mercy, do you want me to leave?"

She should say yes. It would be better for him. Easier for her. And yet . . . With her hair still pressed against her door, she shook her head. "No."

"Then, will you look at me, please?" His voice sounded husky and tight.

Slowly, she eased around to face him. But fear of what she might read in his expression kept her focus glued to the middle button on his shirt.

He leaned closer until one of his arms propped onto the door beside her head. Gently, softly, slowly, he stroked a wayward strand of her hair behind her ear. His hand lingered. His thumb caressed her cheek. "Mercy . . ." His voice broke. "I prayed and asked God to help me be unselfish, but I don't think I want Him to answer that prayer."

Confusion furrowed her forehead. "Unselfish?" She reached one finger to touch the button.

"Unselfish." He captured her hand and cradled it against his chest.

Eyes falling closed, she worked moisture into her mouth. "Why are you feeling selfish?"

"I've got nothing to give, you, Mercy." His thumb swept over her knuckles. "I've enough set by to maybe buy some land, but living will be rough. At least at first."

Nothing to give her . . . Wild hope flared to life at those words. Her heart thumped as though begging for release. But she must proceed with caution.

She raised his hand and pressed it to her cheek, then turned her face into his palm, still unable to meet his gaze. The warmth of his skin grazed her lips as she forced herself to ask the question she was terrified to know the answer to. "Micah . . . Are you sure you're not just missing Georgia?" She finally found the strength to search his face, needing to read his response.

He eased back just enough to give her a searching look. His hand cupped her cheek. His thumb tantalized her with sweeping caresses.

At his continued silence, she felt she might need to explain. "You know, because . . . I look like her? I mean, it's not that I want you to forget her. It's just that I don't want to—" She tucked her lower lip between her teeth before she blurted something that would reveal more of her feelings than she was ready for.

"Ah, Mercy." The pad of his thumb slid across her chin. "Forgive me for saying so, but if this ache that drives me mad with needing you was just me missing Georgia, you would be the last person I'd want to be with."

For one moment, humor tucked around the edges of his eyes, but then he was shaking his head. "There will always be a corner of my heart

where Georgia lives. She was my first love. But ..." His focus drifted to
her scarred brow, and he ran a finger over it. "Not my last love."

"L-love?"

"Mmmm." He slid his hand into her hair, curved his fingers around
the back of her head, and nudged her into his embrace. With her cheek
resting against his chest, he dipped his head and spoke his next words
into her hair. "Despite my best efforts, you have captured my heart,
Mercy Adler."

"How long have you known?"

"Months."

Months? "Why didn't you say something sooner?"

He grunted. "I gave my word to Gid that he could speak to you first."

She leaned against the door and shot him a look. "That's what you
two have been so tense about?"

With a chuckle, he nodded. Stroked his hands over her shoulders.
"Then this morning, I was terrified and almost broke my word."

She swallowed. "I almost accepted Gid's proposal because
I thought I had no hope with you. But I knew that wouldn't be fair
to him. Nor would I have the strength to, eventually, watch you fall
for someone else."

His knuckle traced along her jawline. "No chance of that."

Mercy felt a sudden terror clawing at her chest. Not a terror born
of fear of what Micah might do to her, but a terror born of the fear
that she might be too broken to be what he needed.

Intending to pull away, she shifted but only found the strength to
break eye contact. She rested her forehead on his chest and pressed her
palms there too, ready to push off once she found the will. Instead, she
found herself clutching handfuls of his shirt. "Micah ..." She shook her
head, tears spilling to drip off her nose. "I'm naught but ashes. I might
be too burnt up to-to be any good as a wife." Embarrassment swept
through her. She shook her head. "Sorry, that's presumptive. I know
you didn't say anything about ... marriage, but if this is going anywhere,
you deserve to know upfront. A man has needs and after—after— Well,

like I said at the picnic, I simply don't know if... if I can ... meet your needs. Herst used me and then tossed me aside like refuse for the burn pile, time and again and again."

She kept her forehead pressed against the solidity of him. Held her breath, waiting for his response.

Micah's hands moved over her back, gently soothing, stroke after stroke. After a long while, he slid his hands to her shoulders and used his thumbs to lift her face to his. He swiped her tears, and she was surprised to see moisture glimmering in his own eyes. "First, you weren't being presumptive. I'm the one who first mentioned having nothing to offer you, which implied the direction of my thoughts. Second, it seems to me that wanting to *be* happy is no good reason to get married."

Mercy frowned. She didn't make him happy?

He cupped her face and lowered his head so she could look nowhere but into his eyes. "But wanting to *make* someone happy, now that's a good reason to get married. I want to make you happy, Mercy. To wake up each day with the joy of spending it with you, if only to show you that you deserve so much better than what you had." The pad of his thumb grazed over the moisture on her cheeks. "While you were out earlier, I was reading Gid's Bible. I was reading a book called Job. You know that story?"

She nodded.

"Just like Job, you and I have experienced dust and ashes, Merc. But God used those trials in our lives to bring us both to Him—to help us see Him."

His thumbs trailed gently over her cheeks once more. "So if that's all I get—the knowledge that God used our sufferings to bring us to Him—then I'll be fine. But ... I want more."

Mercy closed her eyes and turned her face into his caress. She relished the gentle sweep of his thumb over her lower lip. Trembled with a hunger for him, yet at the same time with the dread of anything more. She didn't want her first moments with Micah to be marred with memories of Herst. And she knew she didn't have enough distance from her past to put Herst and his . . . assaults from her mind.

She despaired, fearing she never would.

"If anyone could tempt me to marry again, it would be you, Micah." She closed her eyes so she wouldn't have to see the pain her next words would cause him. "But I need more time."

"Take as much time as you need."

His quick response surprised her, and she searched his face. No pressure? "Truly?"

He nodded. "I'll wait as long as you need me to."

"And if I'm never ready?"

A pinch of consternation ticked his brow, but then it was gone. "Then I'll have to be content to be your friend. But fair warning, God's been trying to teach me to ask for what I want, so you can be sure I'll be beseeching heaven. However, I'm also not very good at waiting, so . . ." He grinned. "You should expect me to try to persuade you otherwise." He dropped a quick wink.

Relieved by his attitude, Mercy felt her trembling ease. She tilted him a coy look, unwilling to let their conversation end here. "And what form might this persuasion take?"

His face softened to seriousness again. His gaze lifted to her forehead. "Something like this . . ." He stroked his fingers across her brow, tucking a curl behind her ear. "And like this . . ." His fingertips tantalized her jawline, dancing all the way to her chin, where he crooked his first finger and coaxed her face upward. "And like this . . ." He eased forward to plant his arm against the door behind her again but didn't lower his lips to hers. Instead, he simply lingered near, breathing with her, letting her look at him as he looked at her in return. After a long moment, one side of his mouth nudged upward. "And then I wait to see if my fifty cents was well spent."

Mercy couldn't help a shy giggle. He was waiting for her to kiss him! And oh, how she wanted to. It was so out of character for Micah not to take charge.

Maybe he would meet her halfway? She raised her lips another notch, breath hitching in expectation laced with panic. Still, he didn't move.

Surprisingly relieved, she searched his eyes, and he only shook his head slightly. "Doesn't have to be tonight or any night. The choice will always be yours."

"Micah . . ." Tears once more spilled from her eyes, but this time they were tears of happiness. Because she believed him when he said he would wait as long as she needed.

With a frown, he started to lean back. "I'm sorry I didn't mean to—"

"No. No." She clasped his sides and held him near. "These are happy tears, Micah Morran." Easing forward, she pressed her ear to the thumping of his heart and slid her arms behind his back. "Hold me?"

He complied, wrapping her firmly in his arms and cradling her head to his chest with one hand.

She closed her eyes and relished a deep-drawn breath of his scent of cedar and soap. "I thought I'd never find happiness again, Micah. But you're right. I want to make you happy more than find happiness of my own. So . . ." She shored up her fortitude and lifted her face to his. "Please kiss me."

Micah's focus drifted to her lips. She saw his pupils flare with desire, but then one of his brows knit in consternation. He slid his gaze to hers once more. Easing into his heels, he cupped her face in both his hands, and pressed his forehead to hers.

He was too close to focus on, so she simply closed her eyes and steeled herself for his kiss.

A kiss that never came. After the silence stretched long, Micah's soft-spoken words wafted warmth over her face. "You are beautiful, Mercy and you make me happy, just because. No other reason. You don't have to perform, or be, or do anything. Hear me? You take all the time you need to heal. And when you are ready to kiss me because it's what *you* want to do and not simply because you want to make me happy, then you let me know and I'll be right there with you, trust me, I will. Until then, Mercy . . ."

She felt him shake his head.

"Don't tempt me to use you for my own pleasure." He eased back and pierced her with those serious, blue eyes. "Promise me."

A breath eased from her and with it the last of her anxiety. She blinked hard to hold her tears at bay, hardly able to believe this man that God had gifted to her. "Okay, Micah. I promise."

She rested her cheek against the beat of his heart once more, and simply relished the warmth of him enveloping her. And as she did, she breathed out a prayer of thanks to God, who had carried her through dust and ashes and given her the gift of Micah Morran.

Dear Reader,

Please note: this letter discusses domestic violence. If that's not something you want filling your mind, please stop reading.

Sadly, the concept for this story came to my attention through a real-life incident that took place only one street over from my house. A man and his wife were separated, and she had a restraining order against him. He hired his cousin to kill her—with his own children in the house! At around two in the morning, the cousin had his girlfriend knock on her door while he stood off to one side, and when a woman opened the door, he shot her multiple times through the side of the door. He and his girlfriend then fled. Thankfully, another adult was in the house—the children's nanny. Only the next day was it discovered that he'd shot the wrong woman. The wife had been on a business trip, and it was her sister who was at the house that night to spend some time with her nieces and nephew. She was only twenty-four and had only recently married her husband. Heartbreaking! Thankfully, the law did finally catch up to the three criminals involved.

If you are interested, you can watch a documentary about this situation in episode one of season twenty-five of *On the Case with Paula Zahn*. You can find the season here: https://www.amazon.com/gp/product/B0B8TQX1PB.

If you or someone you know is, or has been, a victim of domestic violence, please get help. At the risk of sounding trite over situations that are very complex, Jesus loves you and did not create you to be a vessel for someone else to abuse. There is a national hotline you can call to get you started: 1-800-799-7233.

On a happier note, I promise you that Micah and Mercy's story is not over. I hope you will come along on the ride to the Oregon Territory and experience the rest of their journey along the way.

With all sincerity,
Lynnette Bonner

Please Review!

If you enjoyed this story, would you take a few minutes to leave your thoughts in a review on your favorite retailer's website? It would mean so much to me, and helps spread the word about the series.

You can quickly link through from my website here: https://www.pacificlightsbookstore.com/collections/the-oregon-promise-series/

Now Available...

BENEATH
Brazen Skies

OREGON PROMISE - BOOK 2

You may read an excerpt on the next page...

Excerpt

Willow Chancellor stood at the mercantile register, trying to ignore Gideon Riley, who was greasing one of the hinges for the portion of the counter that could be raised. If only she could get the numbers in her ledger to come into focus, she could maybe forget about how she had made such a fool of herself last year when he'd first come to town—okay, and for a few months after.

But once the man had made it clear he had no interest in her other than as a friend, she'd determined to set him from her mind. She'd put her head down and concentrated on her work. Or, at least, she had tried to.

For months, she'd hardly spoken to the man other than a polite greeting when necessary, and he'd seemed just fine with that, treating her in kind.

She pinched her lips into a tight line and returned her gaze to the top of the column. Some of her addition must be off.

In her defense, much of today's anxiety had nothing to do with Gideon Riley—none whatsoever. For just this morning at breakfast, Papa had informed her that he was selling the store, and they would be traveling west with the first of the spring wagon trains to leave Independence! He'd known for months, he'd said, but he hadn't wanted to burden her with the knowledge until he was absolutely certain of the undertaking.

She lifted her head and tapped her pencil against her lips. Tears blurred her vision as she swept a look across the store. The corner window where her earliest memory was of her and Mama arranging a new selection of china all the way from England. The basket of eggs nearer to the counter that she had knocked to the floor one day in a twirl of excitement over some accomplishment at school and received a hug from Papa instead of the expected punishment.

And now Papa was using words like "certain of the undertaking." So certain, in fact, that the buyer was due to arrive this morning.

The only home she'd ever known!

Hadn't Papa realized that it would be better for her to have time to reconcile with their departure rather than finding out only hours before the sale of the store—and that ripping of her heart, only a couple of weeks before they were to have a wagon packed with all the essentials they might need for the next six months?

And on top of all, she had to make sure the books were properly reconciled, which she'd been putting off for two months without knowing she would dread that particular bit of procrastination to the utmost.

Now, she had an hour or less to reconcile the books before she needed to present the store to one Hoyt Harrington.

"Your problem is here." Gideon made her jolt as he reached past her on the opposite side from where she'd last seen him to stab a broad blunt finger at a set of numbers. "Seven and nine is sixteen, not fifteen."

Of course it was. Defensiveness rose inside her. She'd been so concentrated on her feelings of loss that she hadn't heard him approach. Nor felt him reading over her shoulder. "You're right, of course. I do know that." Allowing her pique to reflect in her features, she tossed him a glance.

He was wiping grease from his fingers onto a rag, which would explain why he was on the wrong side of her—the rag bin sat under the counter on the far end.

Gideon lifted his blue eyes to hers. "I know you do for all the arithmetic help you've given the boys."

His reference to his nephew and the son of Mercy Adler, who was now courting his former brother-in-law, eased some of her irritation. A reminder of some of the good that would come about because she wouldn't need to say farewell to those—and especially this one—who had become friends over the past few months, for they would travel to Oregon together now.

She slid her books farther down the counter and moved to join them, creating more room between herself and Gideon without comment. Putting her eraser to good use, she bent over the book and, once the column was tabulated correctly, stood to arch out the ache in her back.

Gideon remained where she had left him—still watching her. When the silence between them had stretched to near its limits, he said, "Your father informs me that he plans to start another store once we reach Oregon. In a few years, you'll have another place that's just as near and dear to your heart as this one."

Not "just as," but perhaps he was right that a new place would also become dear.

Realization dawning, she narrowed her eyes, plunked fists to hips, and pivoted to face him. "And just when did he have time to share this information with you?" After Papa had told her the news over breakfast, he'd promptly left to meet their buyer as soon as he arrived in town.

A furrow ticked Gideon's brow.

She stabbed a finger in his direction. "Caught out! How long have you known?"

He seemed solely concentrated on cleaning his fingers again. His teeth worried one side of his lower lip.

Willow sniffed, unexpectedly hurt by the sudden realization that she might just be the hindmost to know of her father's plans. "Am I the last he told?"

He shook his head. "If it's any consolation, neither Micah nor Mercy were aware of your father's plans until I told them this morning—as Wayne asked me to do. Further . . ." His lips pressed into a tight line for a moment before he continued. "I felt he should have told you sooner. You are strong Willow. Could have handled the knowing. But just as you could have handled it then, that strength will see you through now."

Her chin shot higher, more as a precaution against allowing her tears to fall than from any of the other plentiful emotions surging through her. She could not acknowledge his encouragement of her strength, or she would prove him very wrong by collapsing into his arms to bawl out her lament. Instead, she clarified, "Father asked you to tell them—Micah and Mercy?"

A single nod. "He did."

She gave a sharp sniff and resumed her focus on the accounting book. "I have to finish this. I don't have more time to talk now. If you'll excuse me."

Despite her words and her vision blurring against numbers that refused to make themselves clear, all her attention was attuned to the man who didn't move for the longest of moments.

Finally, from the corner of her eye, she saw him lower his hands and stride toward her, which he would need to do to get out from behind the counter, provided he'd even finished his work on the hinge. He paused behind her. "Wayne knew that you'd be some upset and didn't want Mercy and Micah worrying over what troubled you. That was all."

Despite herself, she spun toward him. "And yet, you've known for months!"

She blinked as she realized just how close her spin had brought her to the man. From here she could see the light glinting in the stubble he hadn't shaved for the past few days. See that today, the blue of his eyes seemed nearer the color of a storm-tormented lake than the vibrant blue of placid waters under cerulean skies.

He didn't seem perturbed. He only inclined his head. "Yes, I've known for months. Because last fall, your father extracted a promise from me that I'd keep you safe if ever anything happened to him."

"If ever—" A frown tightened her brow. "Why would something happen to him?"

A look of consternation touched Gideon's face. He raised one hand to scrub his jaw with the back of one thumbnail. "Didn't he tell you why he's selling in the first place?"

Willow's heart began to hammer, and she felt a bit of dampness touch her palms. "Not a word. Only that we are selling and leaving for Oregon."

Gideon lowered his gaze. "I think it's best you ask him his reasoning then." He started past her.

Her hand shot out and clamped on his forearm before she thought better of it. "Gideon Riley, if you know of some danger my father is in, you had better tell me right this instant."

Gideon looked at her fingers that held his arm firmly and then raised his gaze to her face. Sincerity shone in his eyes when he said, "Willow, this really isn't my story to tell. But you can rest easy in knowing that neither your father nor I believe him to be in any immediate danger." He eased his arm from beneath her hand. "I need to go help Micah begin the transfer of his crates from his old wagon to the new. Try to ease your mind so you can finish the books."

He took a step, hesitated, turned back to her, and raised one hand to skim the point of her chin with the knuckle of his first finger. As though the gesture had surprised him, he snatched his hand back to his side and left her.

It was such a light graze that if it wasn't for his reaction, she might have thought she had imagined it. She remained still and watched him walk to the hinged portion of the counter, step out, and then lower it back into place.

He raised and lowered it a couple of times, smiling slightly in satisfaction at the lack of squeak. Then, with one more flick of a glance in her direction, he took Papa's wooden toolbox and disappeared out the back door of the mercantile, which would take him across to the barn.

With a sigh of resignation and more questions than she'd started the conversation with, Willow returned to her calculations. But not before she rubbed her palm several times on her skirt in hopes of removing the feel of Gideon's strong forearm beneath her hand.

"Is it done?"

The meeting of two was taking place in the dim interior of a small brick room at the back of Moore Brewing's Independence offices. A room with access from a back alley that would prevent most from seeing who came and who went.

The shorter of the men, one with handsome features and a charming smile, offered that smile now. "I am hired by men such as yourself on the basis of my reputation, Mr. Moore. If I don't complete a job, word begins to travel, and then I have trouble securing the next." There was a moment of pause where his smile fell away, leaving only a cold stare in its place. "I always get the job done."

Grant Moore hated that the lifeless eyes suddenly had him adjusting his collar. "And he won't be found?" He cleared his throat and forced his fidgeting hands to his knees beneath the desk.

The man sighed as though Grant's questions taxed his patience. "He won't be found."

Grant nodded, opened a drawer, and slid a stack of bills across the table. A very thick stack. "Payment for the first part of the job being done. And of course, as agreed, you will receive the remainder, once you complete the next. You are supposed to arrive in less than an hour. Don't be late."

The man snatched the money and fanned one end as he leveled all the animosity of his icy stare at Grant. "I won't be late. You just be sure that my payment is ready in full."

Grant narrowed his eyes and met the man look for look. In a game of machismo, there was one hard and fast rule. Never let them see your fear. He didn't bother forming a response. They both knew he would have the man's money when the time came. Not to have it would mean certain death.

Finally, with a nod, the hired one sauntered through the outer door into the alley. In one last act of defiance, he left the door swinging open.

Grant waited until he was certain the man could not hear him before releasing a sigh of relief and rising to shut the door. After closing it tight, he slid the bolt lock into place and turned the deadbolt too.

A shiver worked down his spine.

Business was cutthroat, especially here on the edge of beyond. It was good that he had the courage to be the kind of businessman who could make it in this new era. Too bad his brother-in-law had gone behind his back and tried to sell the store out from under him. But no matter. All would soon be his despite Wayne Chancellor's best efforts.

His brother-in-law was barely making a living off the store. But Grant had better plans. This was the last stop before immigrants headed across the barren midlands. Once he put Independence's other mercantile out of business, he would own the only store the wagoneers could access near the pushing-off point. He would be able to ask any price he wanted.

A thin smile touched his lips.

Soon. Very soon.

ABOUT THE AUTHOR

Born and raised in Malawi, Africa. Lynnette Bonner spent the first years of her life reveling in warm equatorial sunshine and the late evening duets of cicadas and hyenas. The year she turned eight she was off to Rift Valley Academy, a boarding school in Kenya where she spent many joy-filled years, and graduated in 1990.

That fall, she traded to a new duet—one of traffic and rain—when she moved to Kirkland, Washington to attend Northwest University. It was there that she met her husband and a few years later they moved to the small town of Pierce, Idaho.

During the time they lived in Idaho, while studying the history of their little town, Lynnette was inspired to begin the Shepherd's Heart Series with Rocky Mountain Oasis.

Marty and Lynnette have four children, and currently live in Washington where Marty pastors a church.

Printed in Great Britain
by Amazon

42827699R00182